by nancy thayer

Surfside Sisters

A Nantucket Wedding

Secrets in Summer

The Island House

A Very Nantucket Christmas

The Guest Cottage

An Island Christmas

Nantucket Sisters

A Nantucket Christmas

Island Girls

Summer Breeze

Heat Wave

Beachcombers

Summer House

Moon Shell Beach

The Hot Flash Club Chills Out

Hot Flash Holidays

The Hot Flash Club Strikes Again

The Hot Flash Club

Custody

Between Husbands and Friends

An Act of Love

Belonging

Family Secrets

Everlasting

My Dearest Friend

Spirit Lost

Morning

Nell

Bodies and Souls

Three Women at the Water's Edge

Stepping

surfside
sisters

nancy thayer

surfside
sisters

a novel

ballantine books
new york

Published in the United States by Ballantine Books, an imprint of Random House, a division of Penguin Random House LLC, New York.

BALLANTINE and the HOUSE colophon are registered trademarks of Penguin Random House LLC.

Hardback ISBN 9781524798727
Ebook ISBN 9781524798741

Printed in the United States of America on acid-free paper

randomhousebooks.com

2 4 6 8 9 7 5 3 1

First Edition

Book design by Elizabeth A. D. Eno

For
Merry Anderson
&
Jill Hunter Burrill
&
Robb Forman Dew
&
Dinah Fulton

Can you believe it's been 40 years?
Do you know how much I love you?
I love you four—arms spread wide like we did
with our children—*this much!*

acknowledgments

This book is dedicated to the four women who were my best friends when I was writing my first novel so many years ago. They were all beautiful, glamorous, generous, and funny. Someone said that a good friend will help you when you're down, but a best friend will help you celebrate. Believe me, they knew how to celebrate! I decorated the top of a long bookcase with empty champagne bottles.

Strangely, all my dearest friends are people I envy. I even envy my husband. It's a selective envy—I wish I had Charley's eyes, or Jill's quick mind, or Merry's thick hair, or Dinah's laugh, or Robb's soft, seductive Southern voice.

Or maybe by envy I mean admire. Admire to the sun and back.

I'm grateful to all my friends, old and new, young and old, on and off island, who inspire me with their wisdom and their humor and their kindness.

I'm enormously grateful to all the people who work in the glamorous and turbulent world of publishing. My editor, Shauna Summers, is like a book jeweler, finding the flaws and the sparks and patiently guiding me as we polish my novel. I send thanks to the wonderful Ballantine team: Gina Centrello, Kara Welsh, Lexi Batsides, Allison Schuster, and Karen Fink. I am enormously grateful to Jennifer Rodriguez. Kim Hovey, I know you know I love you.

I'm full of gratitude for my literary agent Meg Ruley and her associate Christina Hogrebe at the Jane Rotrosen Company.

Sara Mallion and Chris Mason, techies extraordinaire, thank you for your help!

Charley, Josh, David, Sam, Tommy, Ellias, Adeline, Emmett, Annie—you fill my heart with joy.

I'm grateful to all the bookstores, libraries, and Facebook, where I meet my brilliant (of course!) readers.

Someone once said, "How do I know what I think unless I've heard what I have to say?" Writing a novel somehow brings thoughts to the surface that I didn't know I had. In *Surfside Sisters*, I write that a certain man didn't have a lot of money, but his life was his fortune.

That's how I am. My life is my fortune, and I'm thankful every day.

surfside
sisters

prologue

The JetBlue Airbus A320 hummed as it approached LaGuardia Airport. Keely Green checked that her seatbelt was fastened (it was), closed her eyes, and let her mind roam back to the moments she'd loved best on her latest book tour. She didn't know how it could be—it had to be through the magic of books—that the women she met at her talks in libraries and halls and homes were women whom she'd met for the first time and yet seemed already to be her dear and closest friends. She could tell them everything.

Well, almost everything.

She didn't tell them that she spent most of her life in isolation, joined only to her computer as she wrote and revised her books. She didn't tell them she woke up, made a big cup of coffee, and sat at her desk for four hours every morning, never dressing or even brushing her teeth until she'd finished writing.

She didn't tell them that the man she loved didn't love her.

She didn't tell them that she was lonely.

She would never tell them that.

The plane landed with a roar and a thud. Everyone in the cabin sighed in relief and began gathering their possessions. Keely was in no hurry. She'd flown first-class, because, damn it, after all her years of riding the gasoline-smelling, lurching, coughing dinosaur of a bus from Hyannis to Boston, she could afford to travel in comfort. She had only her purse and her computer with her. Making so many stops, she'd had to pack a wardrobe for various climates, so she'd checked her luggage. In a kind of fugue state, she strode down the wide corridors toward the baggage claim, waited while the conveyor belt began to roll, lifted off her suitcase, and headed for the taxi stand.

Outside, the October weather was surprisingly mild. She stood in line, waiting for a taxi, and scrolled through her messages on her cellphone. Her agent's assistant, Fiona, wanted Keely to attend an art opening tonight. Keely hesitated before answering. It had been a busy month, and she was dreaming of a hot bath, her soft bed, and Jamie Brenner's new novel. But she knew it was important to be seen, both professionally and personally. She'd moved to New York last summer, when she sold her first novel. In so many ways, her life had changed completely. She'd made friends in the city, she'd even dated, but she hadn't experienced the slightest blip of electricity with any of the men she'd met, and she was longing for one small shock, a charge that reminded her she was not just a fortunate writer, but also a real and sensual woman.

Tonight she was too tired for any kind of shock. Tomorrow night she was going to a concert at Lincoln Center with Erica Reynaud, another transplant from Nantucket. Saturday she was having lunch with her British agent who was here for only a few days, and Saturday night she had plans to join Fiona at a party in Brooklyn.

The area she was renting in was lovely, old brick and brownstone buildings with small gardens facing the street. She felt safe here, and she needed that, because even though Nantucket and Manhattan were more or less the same size, Nantucket had no buildings higher than three stories and no alleys or back streets she couldn't walk through safely in the middle of the night. Manhattan was different. The pace, the lights, the voices, the horns, the sheer enormity of it all—it was a lot to take in. Did she feel at home here? Some people, like her friend Erica, knew they were at home the moment they set foot in this electric city. Keely didn't feel that way yet.

She sighed as she unlocked her thousand locks and let herself into her apartment. Its bland, impersonal furnishings were a relief. Everything was exactly as she'd left it . . . piles of pages for her new novel rising from what could serve as a dining table but worked perfectly as a desk in this two-room apartment. Breton crackers and peanut butter for dinner or breakfast and apples in the refrigerator crisper. She'd lived for days on less when she was in the heat of writing. Tomorrow she'd do a proper shopping.

Tonight she dropped her laptop on the table, wheeled her suitcase into her room, opened it, and groaned. The weight of the last month when she'd flown from city to city settled on her. She collapsed on her bed, removed her high heels, and rubbed her aching feet. Some women had Botox shot into the soles of their feet to numb them so there would be less pain.

Keely's cure was a long, soaking, very hot bath. She felt her muscles melt and her mind empty. Wrapped in her silk kimono, she took a glass of sparkling Perrier water and settled on the sofa. She turned on the television. CNN's Erin Burnett was on, so it was only the beginning of the evening. Keely spent a while thinking that if all the female anchors didn't have each hair so exquisitely in place, they'd have more gravitas, and then she chided herself for criticizing Erin or any female reporter, and then she wondered when Anderson Cooper would come on because she had a massive crush on him even if he was gay, and then she fell asleep.

She woke at five in the morning with the television still on, displaying an ad for Cialis. She clicked the remote control off, turned over, and went back to sleep.

She woke again at nine, and she was starving. She made coffee, which helped, although she didn't have any fresh milk. She fixed herself two whole wheat crackers with peanut butter and smiled, because that had been one of her favorite breakfasts when she was a kid. When she was a kid, she'd dreamed of becoming a writer. And so had her best friend, Isabelle.

Keely missed Isabelle.

She missed walking in sandals. She missed walking in sand.

She missed her island, her friends, her home. She missed her mom.

Pathetic.

And yes, she disliked the sniveling bore living in her mind. How dare she be unhappy! She was fortunate, she knew that, almost freakishly fortunate. Her first novel, *Rich Girl*, had been published to an astonishing reception. She'd toured the country and everyone told her how much they loved her book. She loved *her readers!* She loved writing. She was wealthy beyond her wildest dreams, and she was only twenty-eight years old. Her second novel, *Poor Girl*, was ready for proofreading and would come out next summer. She was working on her new novel, *Sun Music*.

And she was all alone in the world.

part
one

chapter
one

Two different kinds of people exist: Those who wade cautiously into the shallows and those who throw themselves headlong into the roaring surf.

At least, that was what Keely and Isabelle thought.

As girls, Keely and Isabelle preferred Surfside to Jetties or Steps Beach, even though that meant a longer bike ride to the water. Jetties Beach was mild and shallow, perfect for children, but Surfside had, well—*surf!*—often dramatically breathtaking surf leaping up and smashing down with a roar and an explosion of spray that caught the sunlight and blinded their eyes with rainbows. Their parents worried when they went to Surfside. People could get caught up by the power of the water and slammed mercilessly down onto the sand. People had their ankles broken, their arms. Once, a classmate of Keely's had broken his neck, but they'd medevaced him to Boston and eventually he was good as new. He never returned to Surfside, though.

Keely couldn't remember a time when Isabelle wasn't her best friend. They met in preschool, linked up the first day, and went on like that for years. They were equally spirited and silly. They played childish pranks, using the landline to punch in a random number; if a woman answered, they whispered in what they considered sultry, sexy voices, "Tell your husband I miss him." Usually they couldn't keep from giggling before they disconnected. At ten, they smoked cigarettes at night in the backyard—until they realized the nicotine only made them nauseous. Once, when they were eleven, they stole lipsticks from the pharmacy, which was really stupid, since they didn't wear lipstick.

Isabelle lived in a huge marvelous old Victorian house in the middle of Nantucket. It had a wraparound porch and a small turret. Odd alcoves and crannies were tucked in beneath the stairs, both the formal, carpeted stairs from the front hall and the narrow, twisting back stairs from the kitchen. It was the perfect place for hide-and-seek, and on rainy days, they were allowed to rummage through old trunks and boxes in the attic, pulling on ancient dresses as soft as spiderwebs and floppy hats heavy with cloth flowers.

The Maxwell house was rambling and mysterious, a home out of storybooks, and for Keely, the amazing Maxwell family belonged there.

Isabelle's father, Al Maxwell—his full first name was Aloysius, which his children used when he reprimanded them—"Yes, sir, Aloysius!"—was a lawyer, a partner with the Nantucket firm Maxwell and Dunstan. Mr. Maxwell was larger than life, tall, broad, ruddy-cheeked, and energetic. He didn't talk, he bellowed. He didn't drink, he gulped. He didn't laugh, he roared. His wife, Donna, said the vertebrae of his spine spelled out EXTROVERT. When he arrived home after a day at the office, he threw off his jacket, loosened his tie, and strode out to the spacious backyard. He'd join a game of baseball or pick up Izzy or Keely, settle them on his shoulders, and chase the other children, bellowing that he was a wild and angry bull, all the time keeping tight hold on the legs of the child he carried.

Mrs. Maxwell was movie star beautiful. Tall, blond, and buxom, she was the careful parent, the watchful one. She seldom joined in their games, probably because she was busy cooking enormous meals for her family and baking cakes and pies that sold out at church and school fundraisers. She was the mother who volunteered as chaperone on all the school trips, who helped decorate the gym for special occasions, and when her son stomped into the house with most of the high school basketball team, she was ready with hearty snacks like taco bakes and pizzas. She did everything the perfect mom would do, and still remained, somehow, cool, restrained. At least it seemed she was that way toward Keely.

There were the two remarkable Maxwell children. The oldest was Sebastian, tall, lanky, blue-eyed Sebastian. How he managed to be so handsome and so modest at the same time was always a curiosity to Keely. She thought that it must be because he grew up in a house where everyone was gorgeous, so it seemed as normal to him as breathing. He played most of the school sports—baseball, basketball, soccer—and he was on the swim team.

After Sebastian, two years younger, came Isabelle. Mr. Maxwell often bragged, "I hit it out of the park with her!" At which Mrs. Maxwell would respond, "Not by yourself, you didn't." Such casual remarks alluding to sex made the Maxwell parents urbane and superior in Keely's eyes.

Isabelle was a beauty like her mother, only willowy instead of voluptuous. Unlike Sebastian, she was aware of the power of her looks, and she was a friendly girl, but deep down inside not really a team player. She liked secrets, liked sharing them with Keely and no one else. She liked plotting and disobeying and sneaking and hiding. She liked mischief. She was often in trouble with the school or her parents, but she was also almost genius smart, so she got good grades and she knew when to rein in her wild side.

The Maxwell house was always crowded with kids of all ages, playing Ping-Pong in the basement, doing crafts at the dining room table while Donna baked cookies, or giggling in Isabelle's room while trying on clothes. Fido, their slightly dense yellow Lab, roamed the house looking for dropped food. He always found something. Salt and Pepper, their long-haired cats, gave the evil eye to any humans that tried to remove them from whatever soft nest they'd made, but if they were in the right mood, they'd accept gentle stroking and reward the human with a tranquilizing purr.

Keely was fiercely, but secretly, jealous of the entire family. It wasn't that her parents weren't rich like the Maxwells—well, it wasn't only that. It wasn't that the Green house was a small ranch outside town. It wasn't that Keely had longed for a brother or sister and had remained an only-lonely. It wasn't even that her parents were allergic to animals, so she never had a kitten or puppy. She never even had a damn hamster!

But she wouldn't have traded her parents for anyone. Her father was a car mechanic who taught her how to change a tire and make window washer fluid. Her mother was a nurse who taught her how to use a butterfly bandage and stop a nosebleed. Mr. and Mrs. Green were well-liked in the community, and they loved Keely with all their hearts. Her father taught her to surf cast and bodyboard. He showed her where the prickly pear cactus grew on Coatue and where the sweetest wild blueberries grew on the moors. He told her why the Red Sox and the Patriots were the best teams anywhere, ever. He gave her books by Jack London and Jules Verne so she wouldn't read only what he called "girly books." Her mother adored him. She made delicious jams and jellies from the fruits they picked. She dressed and grilled the fish they caught and brought home. When she could, she went with them in late autumn, during islander scalloping time. The three of them drove to Great Point in the winter to see all the seals, and the first "book" Keely wrote was about an orphaned seal adopted by a family just like hers.

Isabelle loved hanging out at Keely's house because she could escape her noisy family, and Keely loved being at Isabelle's house because she loved being around that noisy family. Plus, secretly, Keely had a crush on Sebastian.

Sebastian was two years older than Keely. She was ten, he was twelve. The end.

She hid her hopeless childish love from Isabelle, who had sharp edges when it came to her brother. Isabelle was constantly confiding to Keely about how Sebastian was so perfect she felt she could never measure up. She carried a massive inferiority complex on her slender shoulders. It didn't help that half the girls in town, older and younger, sucked up to Isabelle, acting all sweetie pie—best friends only because they wanted to get into the Maxwell house and flirt with Sebastian.

That wasn't the case with Keely. She had chosen Isabelle first, and knew they would always be best friends. She couldn't even *imagine* life without Isabelle. And often, she felt as if she were a small but real part of the Maxwell family. When they went to the fair in the summer or a Theatre Workshop play in the winter or out in the Maxwells' Rhodes 19 sailboat for a day at Tuckernuck, Keely was often invited along. They even kept a life jacket just for Keely hanging on the hook in their back hall. The fifth chair at the dining room table was called "Keely's chair," no matter who sat in it. Mr. Maxwell made Keely feel bigger, better, more worthy of simply being on the planet. Keely adored him, but she kept this to herself as much as she hid her infatuation with Sebastian. She was an only child, good at keeping her own confidences.

"My parents are boring," Keely confessed one day when she and Isabelle were idly dangling on the complicated swing set in the Maxwells' backyard. They were ten, too old to play on the swings, young enough to enjoy their joke: "hanging out."

"You're nuts!" Isabelle said. "I'd give anything to live your life. No big brother flicking my ear and forcing me to play catch. I could lie in my quiet room reading and reading."

"Or writing and writing," Keely said.

In fifth grade, they confessed to each other they wanted to become writers. They were already best friends, but this shared, slightly eccentric hope bonded the two girls like superglue. They spent long summer hours writing scenes and stories, reading and discussing them with each other. They'd phone constantly to suggest new plot ideas, to mention a cool new word (*quixotic, ethereal*) they'd learned. They planned their glamorous new lives. They'd have their novels published at the same time. They'd have apartments across from each other in New York. On the island, Isabelle would drive a Porsche convertible. Keely decided on a Mercedes SUV so she'd have room for all her children.

But they weren't snobs or freaks. They did stuff with the other girls. They went to all the home football games, to slumber parties, and even the occasional day trip to the Cape with friends to shop and eat at the mall.

Still, they treasured their secret ambition. They felt like superheroes, masquerading as silly girls secretly aiming for the stars.

The summer the girls were ten, the Maxwells went off on their European "jaunt"—as Mrs. Maxwell called it. One afternoon in the middle of August, they returned. As always, even before she unpacked, Isabelle phoned Keely. "I'm home!" Then she biked to Keely's house as fast as her legs would pedal.

Keely was out on the lawn, waiting, jumping up and down with excitement. The girls screamed with joy when they saw each other. Keely and Isabelle hugged and whirled around and fell down on the soft green grass, laughing like hyenas.

"I missed you *so* much," Isabelle cried.

"I missed you more," Keely insisted. "You have to tell me everything."

Keely's mother came out of the house. "Isabelle. Let me look at you. Oh, honey, I think you're two inches taller."

Isabelle jumped up and hugged Mrs. Green. "I know. I'm a giraffe," Isabelle said, fake mournfully.

Keely's mother laughed. "You're a beauty. Now tell me if I'm correct. You girls like a large pizza with onions and pepperoni and a Pepperidge Farm chocolate cake."

"Yay, Mom, you remember!" Keely stood up, brushing grass off her shorts. Every time Isabelle returned from the Maxwells' European summers, Isabelle and Keely celebrated by eating on the back patio, just the two of them, stuffing themselves with pizza and cake and laughing and whispering and eating more cake until two or three in the morning when Isabelle, groggy with jet lag, said she had to sleep. They'd bring the mostly empty boxes of food into the kitchen and quietly tiptoe to Keely's bedroom. Without even brushing their teeth, they collapsed on the twin beds and slept until noon the next day.

This summer, when Keely woke, Isabelle was gone. Keely wandered into the kitchen. Both her parents were at work, but her mother had left a note for her.

Isabelle has an appointment with the orthodontist. I drove her to her house at nine this morning. She said she'll call you.

Poor Isabelle, Keely thought. To have to spend the morning getting fitted for braces—*tragic*.

Also, Sebastian wants you to call him.

Well, that took her breath away. Sebastian wanted Keely to call him?

Keely stared at the penciled note on the scrap of paper, willing it to reveal the true meaning. She was certain Sebastian had no idea how she felt about him. She had never told Isabelle because, face it, no matter how many multi-syllabic words Keely knew, no matter what fabulous grades Keely received, she was still too young, too *childish* to be in love. If she did tell Isabelle, Izzy would fall over laughing till she wet her pants. Keely would die of a thousand sharp stabs of embarrassment if she ever told Isabelle.

Plus, Isabelle might think Keely was being her best friend just to have access to Sebastian. Keely never wanted Isabelle to think that.

She was so confused! She was such a loser! She wished she could talk this over with Isabelle, but that was the last thing she could do.

But she had to do something. She had to do something definite, memorable.

For once she was glad her parents weren't home. On a shelf with the olive oil and balsamic vinegar was a bottle of cooking sherry. Keely poured herself a small sip of the amber liquid. She went into the dining room where her mother had two candlesticks on the table on either side of a woven basket of shells. Keely lit both candles. She took out two scallop shells and placed them side by side.

She said aloud, in a somber voice, "I, Keely Green, vow that I will never tell Isabelle Maxwell that I am in love with her brother, Sebastian."

She tossed back the sherry (it tasted terrible). She put her hands on the shells and blew out the candles.

There. It was done. She had made a vow. She felt more mature, as if she had consciously created an important part of who she was.

She returned to the kitchen, ran a glass of cool water and drank it down. She took a quick shower and pulled on one of her bathing suits with a Kylie Minogue T-shirt over it. The day was hers. Isabelle would probably take a nap after the orthodontist visit. Keely would see her this evening. Until then, she could read the latest novel from the library, or—

Someone was pounding on the door. Keely opened it and found Isabelle's brother standing there with steam coming out his ears.

"Sebastian!" Her heart nearly exploded.

"Didn't your mom tell you to call me?"

"Um, yes."

"The sand castle contest is today. I need your help."

Good, this was something ordinary, normal. Something she, Isabelle, and Sebastian had done for several summers. Isabelle might join them after she got her braces fitted. All Keely had to do was act natural, like her own childish self.

"Okay, sure. Do you know what you're going to do? Do you need, I don't know, bowls for molds or something?"

"I've brought buckets and stuff. I'm not sure what to do. That's why I want to talk to you. Get your bike and let's go."

"I've got to leave a note for my mom and dad."

She scurried into the kitchen and scribbled a note. She shoved her feet into flip-flops, and checked the beach bag she always had waiting, filled with a thermos of water, towels, and sunblock. She pulled the front door shut, stuck her beach bag in her basket, and wheeled her bike next to Sebastian's.

"So what are your ideas?" she asked as they biked toward Jetties Beach.

"Maybe Iron Man and Hulk and—"

"We did action heroes last year."

"Well, what then?"

"What about a whale? A great big whale . . . smiling. The judges always go for what's islandy and cute."

"You're right. We'll do it," Sebastian said.

Keely grinned.

They were late to the contest. All up and down the beach, people were on their knees, shaping and patting the sand. Keely and Sebastian locked their bikes to the stand and raced down the beach to an open space at the far end.

First they carried buckets of sand to their spot. The sand had to be just right, damp enough to hold its shape but not so sodden it crumbled. Sebastian drew an outline in the sand and they began molding the gigantic body of the whale. The tail was the most difficult, so Sebastian had it raised and slanted to show the entire fluke.

Keely's eyes kept straying from the sand to Sebastian's tanned hands and body. It was so intimate, working next to him like this. She could hear him breathe. She had to get him out of her sight.

She had to distract herself. "I'll build a baby whale here, below the mother."

"Fine," Sebastian said, bent over his whale.

He probably thought a baby whale was a girly idea. Good, Keely told herself. Because she was young and girly and hopelessly not in his league.

The sun rose high in the sky. They took quick dips in the water to cool off before getting back to work. At the end of the day, they were exhausted. Their structure didn't win—a group of college guys had built a miniature Main Street—but their whales did get photographed for the newspaper. Their theme was so Nantucket and if she said so herself, and she did, the baby whale, with its smile, was adorable.

In the late afternoon, they biked to the Maxwell house. They took turns using the outdoor shower. Keely went around to the back deck to dry off. She collapsed in one of the Maxwells' fancy cushioned chairs.

"You guys!" Isabelle stomped out on the porch, arms folded over her chest, pouting. "Why didn't you call me? I wanted to help."

"You were with Mom at Dr. Robert's," Sebastian yelled.

"Show me your braces!" Keely demanded.

"Don't have them yet. It's such a major *project*." Isabelle flopped into a chair next to Keely.

Sebastian came up the back steps, dripping from his shower, his towel wrapped around his waist, the sun gilding his hair. He'd acquired muscles over the summer. His shoulders were broader, his thighs thicker. The sight did something funny to her stomach. She looked away.

"You are SO going to have a sunburn all over your back," Isabelle told her brother.

Sebastian shrugged. "Call me when you start the movie."

It had become a custom for the three of them to spend the Maxwells' second night back with fish dinners from Sayle's and a movie. Keely and Isabelle said it couldn't be too scary and Sebastian said it couldn't be too romantic and it really couldn't be a musical. They agreed on *Dude, Where's My Car?* The girls both had mad crushes on Ashton Kutcher. Keely made sure Isabelle was in the middle of the sofa, between her and Sebastian. If she sat next to Sebastian, her leg might touch his. It frightened her even to think about that.

As always, Keely phoned her parents and got permission to spend the night at Isabelle's. The Maxwell house had central air.

What a lush luxury it was to slide into the silky sheets beneath a light down comforter in the twin bed in Isabelle's room.

Life was back to normal, Keely thought, and she was smiling as she fell asleep.

When Keely was eleven, Sebastian did something extraordinary.

The Maxwell family had spent February vacation in Eleuthera, and Isabelle had brought Keely a cute T-shirt, like that could compensate for the difference between their two lives. Yet Keely didn't want to be all pitiful. First of all, that would be lame and icky. She'd keep her self-pity to herself, thank you very much. No one liked a whiner. But second, and really more important, Keely had loved this past week when most of her friends were gone and there was no school and she checked out a big fat pile of novels from the library and she'd spent her days and much of her nights lost in worlds that required as a passport only the ability to read.

And she came up with a totally cool project.

Keely and Isabelle were in the Maxwells' dining room on a frigid, gray Sunday morning. Sebastian had taken over the den to play the videogames he'd missed on vacation. Mrs. Maxwell was shopping for groceries, and Mr. Maxwell was, as always, at work.

"So, Isabelle, now that you're all tanned and fabulous, let me tell you what *I* did all week."

"What?"

"I've started a newspaper!"

"We have a newspaper."

"No, the town has a newspaper. The adults have a newspaper. Kids don't."

"How are you going to make a newspaper? You're *eleven*."

"I'll show you." Keely unzipped her backpack and pulled out a sheaf of papers she'd stapled together. "Look."

The first page said simply: THE BUZZ.

The second page headline read: AUDITIONS FOR THE SPRING

PRODUCTION OF *ANNIE*. The column told where and when the auditions were being held, and continued with a short summary of the musical, followed by a brief recap of past productions.

The third page was headlined LETTERS TO THE EDITOR. There was one letter, which read, *Dear Editor, I'm not that fussy about what I eat, but I wish the cafeteria would put real cheese in the macaroni and cheese instead of the orange superglue they use. I'm writing this because I can't talk because my teeth are stuck together. Hopefully, Glenda.*

"Wow, Keely. This is amazing!" Isabelle said. "But we don't have a Glenda on the island. Isn't that the name of the good witch in the *Wizard of Oz?*"

"Silly, this is only a prototype." Keely nearly fainted with pleasure at using the word *prototype.* "I wrote the letter. I made everything up. So I get to be the editor and you can be the assistant editor and since you have your cool camera, you can be the photographer."

"But how can we make copies?"

Keely flicked Isabelle's leg. "We'll talk to the school about making hard copies on their printer."

Isabelle squinted her eyes, conveying deep thought. "If the school makes the copies, they'll know what we're writing and they'll be able to edit it."

"Well, Isabelle, it's not like we'll have a lot of scurrilous material."

Isabelle's eyes widened. *"Scurrilous."*

"It means scandalous. Outrageous." Keely grinned. Isabelle might have gone far away in physical space, but Keely had traveled far in her mind, and brought back souvenirs.

Isabelle tapped her index finger on her lower lip. "Okay. I see the potential. But it needs something else. Maybe a logo? A cartoon? I don't know, something graphic."

"Good idea, but you know I can't draw."

"Maybe we could use a sticker?"

Keely shrugged. "I guess."

The girls felt a gust of icy air as Mrs. Maxwell entered the house.

"Kids! Come help with the groceries!"

Keely jumped up and followed Isabelle. The number of bags Mrs. Maxwell filled at the Stop & Shop always astonished Keely. She made three trips to the SUV and back, lugging a bag in each hand.

"Mom," Isabelle complained, "I don't see Sebastian helping. He and his friends eat most of the fruit."

"He shovels the walk and the drive," Mrs. Maxwell reminded her daughter.

In the kitchen, they made a kind of game of putting away the zillion items. Huge bundles of toilet paper, paper towels, tissues. Mountains of fruit. Gallons of milk, pounds of butter, acres of bread.

"Take that toilet paper upstairs, Isabelle," Mrs. Maxwell said. "Then you're done. Thanks, girls."

Keely returned to the dining room table while Isabelle stomped up the stairs.

At her spot, next to the first page of *The Buzz*, was a piece of paper with a loosely but cleverly drawn bee. It was very fat. It had a huge face with a mischievous smile.

"*Sebastian.*" Keely scanned the room, as if he could be hiding behind the mahogany sideboard.

She studied the bee more closely. Under one of its wings were the initials KG. Keely's letters. So he wanted people to think Keely had drawn this.

Okay. She could do that. Quickly she picked up a pencil and drew her own versions of the bee on fresh sheets of paper. They weren't as good as Sebastian's bee, but they weren't that different, especially because Sebastian's bee had a slightly wavy outline.

So. Sebastian had been aware of her. Okay, of her and Isabelle. Still. It made her fingers tingle to think that he had overheard and tried to help. As if Sebastian even knew she existed. That thought was overwhelming.

She wondered how she could thank him.

"Done!" Isabelle rushed into the room and pulled her chair close to Keely. "Hey, what's that? It's so cute!"

"Do you think so?" Keely cocked her head, giving the smiling bee a serious evaluation. She waited for Isabelle to say that the drawing looked like something Sebastian would do. "I don't know."

"Well, I do! It's adorable, Keely. Definitely it has to be on our masthead. You are so talented! Now. We need reporters. Then we'll have more news."

They leaned shoulder to shoulder, scribbling lists, chattering away, thrilled with their plans. For a moment, Keely felt— *something*—so she looked up. Sebastian was standing in the doorway watching her. Keely smiled at him. He smiled at her.

Sebastian smiled at her.

One afternoon when they were twelve, Keely and Isabelle sat on the rug of the screened porch, designing and cutting out the figures and the clothes for their Women in History paper doll project.

Keely had labored over an extremely fancy ball gown and was cutting it when it tore.

"Rats!" Keely cried. "It took me forever to make that dress!"

"Silly, just tape it together. On the back. No one will notice."

"Where's the tape?"

"You know, in the kitchen by Mom's address book."

Keely jumped up and went into the living room and through to the kitchen.

"Can't find it!"

"Sebastian probably took it."

Keely headed up the stairs to Sebastian's room. She assumed he wasn't home—he was seldom home, except for dinner—so she hurried down the carpeted hall, threw open the door of Sebastian's bedroom, and stepped inside.

Sebastian was at his desk, a big fourteen-year-old boy with long hairy legs sticking out of his soccer shorts.

"Oh." She scrunched up her shoulders. "Sorry. I need the tape."

"Fine." Sebastian found it on the far side of his desk. "Here."

Keely approached him to take the tape in its black dispenser. She couldn't help noticing the pad on his desk with the intricate pencil drawing of the Nantucket harbor.

"Did you do that?"

Sebastian shrugged. "Yeah."

Without asking permission, she stepped closer, studying the sketch. "This is cool. And I love the whales you put near Great Point." She was so astonished she forgot to be in awe of him. "I didn't know you could draw this well."

"No one needs to know." Sebastian pulled a blank sheet of paper over his drawing.

"Oh. Okay." Keely carried the tape dispenser in both hands as she left the room.

"Close the door," Sebastian said. "And don't come in here again without knocking."

As Keely took hold of the brass doorknob and pulled it shut, Sebastian said, "And don't tell my parents. Especially don't tell Izzy. She can't keep a secret."

"Okay." Keely shut the door. Then, on an insane whim, powered by courage she didn't know she had, she pushed the door open again and went into the room. "But, Sebastian, why is that a secret? Is it a present for someone?"

"Ha. Right." Sebastian gave Keely a look that seemed almost friendly. "My parents want me to play team sports. Not sit alone in my room doodling."

"But that's not doodling! That's art!" Keely protested. "And Izzy and I sit in our own rooms all the time. We're writing a book."

Sebastian's mouth crooked up in a half-smile. "Cool. So just keep it a secret for me, okay, Keely?"

He said her name.

Keely went hot all over, pleased and surprised and funny feeling. Of course he knew her name! She was such a total freak!

Too embarrassed to speak, she nodded and left the room—pulling the door shut tight. She returned to her paper doll dress with the tape and also with an odd happiness in her stomach. She shared a secret with Sebastian, one that not even Isabelle knew.

chapter
two

Keely and Isabelle started high school. *Big change*, Keely thought. Like a bucket of water thrown at her face. The door to her grown-up life was opening.

Her classes fascinated and terrified her. She was torn between wanting to be smart and wanting to be cool. Girls who'd been boring in first grade were suddenly super cool. Cool was hard to achieve. Everything was so new, so weird, so *funny*! Keely and Isabelle always got stern looks from teachers when they giggled behind their hands in class.

She still had a powerful crush on Sebastian. Worse, as she grew older, her infatuation grew into an obsession. When she was at Isabelle's house, she locked the bathroom door and picked up his toothbrush. It was like a holy icon. *Sebastian* had touched it. Sometimes she saw his boxer shorts in the bathroom laundry basket. Seeing something so intimate made her heart pound.

It helped keep her steady and sane that they had to concentrate on their homework in order to make good grades—and Keely especially needed good grades so she could eventually get scholarships for college.

The homework was hard, the social stuff was harder. Just walking from class to class was like taking some kind of bizarre test. More kids, more teachers, more staff crowded the halls. Everyone was so much older.

"I feel like a gazelle caught in a stampede of elephants," Keely told Isabelle.

"I know, right? The seniors are so big."

"Hi, Isabelle!" A junior, Diane, one of the cheerleaders, all glossy and cool, came right up to Isabelle. "How do you like it here so far?"

"It's great, I guess." Isabelle flashed an SOS at Keely.

Another cheerleader, Daisy, with such perfect makeup Keely couldn't help staring, elbowed her way between Isabelle and Keely. "Hey, Isabelle, listen, if you ever need help with your homework or anything . . ."

"Plus we could give you the scoop on which teachers are cool." It was another junior, Kyra.

Isabelle faked a smile. "Um, well . . ."

Diane pounced. "You could come to our houses, or we'd be glad to come to yours."

So that's their strategy, Keely realized. They were fawning over Isabelle so they could get access to Sebastian. She wanted to share her thoughts with Isabelle, but by now Keely had been nudged too far away even to see Isabelle.

What would Isabelle do? Keely knew these unctuous juniors with their long, silky hair were powerful. She would understand if Isabelle joined them. She'd be miserable, but she would understand.

"Thanks," Isabelle said. "But I do my homework with Keely. We've got a perfect system set up."

"Oooh." The juniors made disappointed little chirping noises.

"Plus, I help them," Sebastian said.

The hair on Keely's arms stood up. She hadn't heard him coming.

Before she could turn to speak to him, Sebastian put his arm around Keely's waist and pulled her close to him.

"I help you learn a lot of things, don't I, Keys?" Sebastian's eyes danced with mischief as he looked down at her.

Keely was breathless. Sebastian had gotten so tall. His shoulders were so broad. The heat of his body ran all up and down her torso.

She was surprised she didn't melt into a puddle right there and then.

The three cheerleaders did about-faces, flipping their short pleated skirts.

"Oh, Sebastian, *hi!*"

"Hi," Sebastian said.

He leaned down, put his mouth next to Keely's ear, and whispered, "Just go with this, right?"

Keely nodded.

Diane, the leader of the pack, cooed at Isabelle. "If you ever think you'd like to try out for cheerleader next year, we'd love to teach you the basics. And you, too, Keely."

"Thanks," Isabelle said. She was turning burgundy, and Keely knew Isabelle was holding her breath to keep from laughing.

Sebastian said, "Keely won't have any free time."

He bent down, getting his face right in front of Keely's, and kissed her sweetly, but firmly, on her mouth.

On her mouth!

His lips were soft and warm. He smelled like the Ivory soap all the Maxwells used, mixed with a very enticing aroma of warm male.

When he pulled away, Keely kept her eyes on the ground, knowing she didn't dare look at Isabelle. Sebastian pulled her tighter against him, so her cheek nestled against his chest. She knew her face was red.

She could hear his heart beat.

"Okay, then," Diane said pertly. "Isabelle, give us a call. Byeeee."

The three cheerleaders sauntered away, chattering.

"OMG, you guys!" Isabelle whispered. "Sebastian, you are the most fabulous brother in the world!"

"Those girls are witches," Sebastian said. "Don't let them get to you."

"You can let go of Keely now," Isabelle said. Reaching over, she put her hand on Keely's arm and yanked her away.

Isabelle's expression jolted Keely from her state of shock.

"Yeah, thanks, Sebastian," she croaked.

"Anytime," Sebastian said with a sideways quirk of his mouth. He loped away.

Keely did a few yoga breaths and gathered her thoughts. "You could be a cheerleader!"

"I don't want to be a cheerleader," Isabelle said stormily. "I don't want to be a cutesy snob."

"I don't, either," Keely said, still so stunned she could scarcely speak. She opened her locker and took out her backpack, organizing what books she had to take home. She couldn't begin to think what to say to Isabelle about Sebastian kissing her. If Isabelle weren't Sebastian's sister, if Isabelle didn't kind of *own* Sebastian, Keely might have been honest. *Sebastian kissed me*, she might have said.

Isabelle stood with her hands on her hips, like a mad mom or a soccer coach. "And I hope you're not going to get all stupid because my brother kissed you. You know he was only pretending so those girls wouldn't dis you. He only did it because you're my friend and he knows how much you mean to me."

"I know that!" Keely couldn't say his name without blushing. She rolled her eyes. "Those girls. What brats."

They shouldered their backpacks, slammed and locked their lockers, and strolled to Keely's house. Her mother had the day off and always made chocolate chip cookies.

In December, along with their friends, Keely and Isabelle were allowed to go to the Cape on the Iyanough ferry by themselves, without parents. During the trip over, they snickered like excited five-year-olds. They took a cab to the mall and shopped for Christmas presents and had fattening French fries and enormous Cokes at the food court. As they ate, they watched the other shoppers, especially the terrifyingly cool Cape girls, walk by. These teens wore jeans with high heels. They wore shirts that stopped at their midriffs even though it was winter. They tossed their long hair carelessly and bent toward each other, whispering. Tall, cool boys in down jackets and hoodies came along and they clustered together, sometimes breaking off in pairs, a boy running his hand up beneath a girl's shirt.

Keely had never felt so immature. During the ferry ride back to the island, Keely and Isabelle were quiet, absorbed in their own thoughts. They'd always thought they were so cool, and they were, but they were only fake cool. They yearned to be cooler.

And dreaded it.

Over the winter and spring, they spent more time with their other friends, Janine and Theresa and Ceci. They became a clique, which they proudly designated as the Smart Girls. The ones who wanted to go to college, who did not want to get pregnant in high school, who cared more about books and volunteering and cleaning the beaches than flirting with guys or getting drunk or choosing the color of their nail polish. Of course they were hiding their interest in boys, or at least pretending to. The girls were dealing with changing bodies, zits and menstrual periods, mood swings that came upon them without warning, like a gale force wind. They cried a lot, and didn't really know why. They ate a disgusting amount of junk food, sometimes the five of them devouring Cheetos and Ben & Jerry's and a Pepperidge Farm cake in the same evening.

Suddenly summer arrived. Windows and doors all over town opened. They were freed from school! Everyone but Isabelle took a job to save money for college. Isabelle went off with her family to Scotland.

"She's so lucky," Ceci complained one hot afternoon when she

and Keely had finished their work for Clean Sweep house cleaning. They were gathered in Ceci's air-conditioned family room.
"She always gets to go someplace amazing. Paris last year. Scotland this year. It's hard to like her sometimes."

"Don't be mad at *her*," Keely replied. "It's her parents who
make her go away for the summer. They always have a big family
trip. Izzy never comes home bragging about it or being all la-
de-da. Plus there are worse places to be in the summer than Nantucket!"

"Maybe we all want what we can't have," Ceci said.

"Well, listen to you, Ms. Philosopher!" Theresa laughed.

"What do you want that you can't have?" Keely asked.

Ceci grinned. "Tommy Fitzgerald."

"Damn, girl, you dream big," Theresa said.

"It doesn't hurt to dream."

Tommy Fitzgerald came from a gigantic family, one that had
been on the island for decades, even centuries. Part Cape Verdean,
part Wampanoag, part Irish, his black hair and black eyes in his
craggy face were compelling. He was tall and lean and quiet. In
school, Tommy seldom smiled, always walked hunched with his
hands in his jeans, staring at the ground as if expecting it to fall
away from him at any moment. But he was a great athlete, and
quarterback for the junior varsity football team. All bets were on
Tommy making varsity his sophomore year.

"Could we talk about something other than boys?" Keely asked.

"Do you mean there *is* something other than boys?" Theresa
laughed.

For Keely, there was definitely something other than boys.
Books. She had always cherished the dream of being a writer, and
all the books she'd read about writing advised her to read, read,
read. That was exactly what she did whenever she had any free
time that summer. She kept a record of what she'd read and what
she thought of each book in a plain three-ring binder. As the summer passed, the pages filled with titles. *Wuthering Heights. To Kill*

a Mockingbird. Peyton Place. The Good Mother. The Giver. Bleak House. Lives of Girls and Women.

Sunday was her favorite summer day. She didn't have to work, so she got to lie in bed reading, only venturing out occasionally to fetch a bag of potato chips or an apple. Many summer days her father took her out to Great Point to surf cast, but on this Sunday in late August, her father was out deep-water fishing with a friend. Her mother was at work. Keely was lazing around in boxer shorts and a tank top with a novel in her hand. She heard someone knock on the front door, and her first thought when she opened the door was that she hadn't brushed her hair yet.

"Sebastian!"

"Hey."

For a moment, she could only stare. He was tall, big-boned, his hair white-blond, his skin tanned, his nose sunburned. He wore board shorts and an old rugby shirt, so many times washed it had faded from red to pink.

She gathered herself enough to speak. "Are you back from Scotland?"

He held his hands out to his sides in a *duh* gesture. "Probably."

"Oh, well—is Isabelle home?"

"She is. I'm sure she'll be phoning you any minute now. But I wanted to give you something before she hogs all your time."

"You want to give me something?" Keely echoed.

Sebastian held out a book.

The Mysterious Benedict Society.

"Oh!" Keely's heart sparked when their fingers touched as she took the book.

"Have you read it?"

"No. No, I don't know about it. Why—" Keely was so moved she was about to cry.

"Because you and Izzy like to read and write." He leaned on the door jamb, his face close to hers.

"Um . . . do you want to come in? Have . . . a Coke?"

"No thanks. I've got to get back."

"Oh. Well . . . thank you for the book." She ran her hand over the cover. "It's really . . . nice."

Sebastian leaned forward and kissed her forehead quickly, lightly, and moved away, smiling. "See you."

She watched him walk away. After a moment, he broke into a jog and disappeared down the street.

She shut the door and sank right down onto the floor, cradling the book to her rapidly beating heart. What did it mean? It was only a book, but it was a *present*.

Had Sebastian really thought about her when he was in Scotland?

Did Isabelle know he'd brought Keely the book? Oh, she wished she'd asked him, because either Isabelle would tease Keely unmercifully or she'd be furious that her brother had given her a gift.

She wouldn't tell Isabelle. She'd let Isabelle bring it up, and if she didn't, she wouldn't say anything. She wouldn't put the book, in its distinctive British paperback version, on her desk or shelves. She'd hide it under her mattress and bring it out to sleep with her at night. And what dreams she'd have.

Isabelle never mentioned Sebastian and the book. She gave Keely a green tartan headband that looked great with Keely's brown hair. This year they were sophomores, higher up the coolness ladder. They went with a group of friends to shop for clothes on the Cape, and school started, and everything was easier than the year before. They knew their way around the school, which teachers were super strict or boring. School was easier, yes, but Keely's nerves were tuned up to super sensitive. She knew from her mother, the nurse, that adolescents were crazy from hormones, but knowing that didn't soothe her.

It helped to keep a diary. Almost every night, Keely wrote in her journal, pouring out on the lined paper of the red leather

Daily Diary with its brass lock and key—she had bought it herself, needing the privacy, not that she thought her parents would ever pry. The actual facts of the day, the grade she'd gotten on a test, the after class pep rally for the high school football team, the Whalers, all that she mentioned only briefly. It was her emotions that came spilling out of her onto the page. The embarrassment she'd felt when the math teacher called on her and she didn't know the answer. The odd force field of physical sensations that shivered around her when a senior on the basketball team said, "Hi, Keely," as he passed her in the hallway. The jealousy she felt when she saw Isabelle and Paige, who was kind of slutty, whispering to each other at lunch. The pages of her diary were not long enough to contain all she needed to write. She also used a three-ring binder, where, for privacy's sake, she wrote about her life in the third person, as if she were writing a novel about a tenth grade girl. The tenth grade girl, who Keely named Trudy, endured all manner of humiliations. Huge red zits on the end of her nose. A senior she had worked with on a community Clean Beach project striding past her in the hallway, giving "Trudy" a blank-eyed stare, as if she'd never seen her before. Her growing awareness that her clothes, even her shoes, were not what the best of the cool seniors wore.

And, shamed to put it in black and white, she wrote about her envy of Isabelle, who was popular with all the girls in every grade, even though Isabelle said it was only because Sebastian was her brother.

Keely and Isabelle and the Smart Girls sometimes went places with a bunch of guys—to the movies at the Dreamland, to beach parties on autumn nights, to talks at the library. Out for pizza. Up to Boston to visit the MFA and see a play, with adult supervision, of course. Sledding at Dead Horse Valley at night, with a full moon.

Keely waited every day for a phone call from Sebastian, maybe asking if she liked the book. It never came. She even, hopelessly, *ridiculously*, checked the snail mail every day—nothing. She lingered in the school halls, hoping to run into him, but no such luck. She spent more time than ever at the Maxwell house, but Sebastian was always out—soccer practice, swim team, basketball practice. When she did catch a glimpse of him in his house, he quickly said, "Hey," before running down the stairs and out the door. She didn't know what to think. Why would Sebastian bring her a present and then ignore her?

Maybe he had liked her, just a little, but now he was a senior, dating popular senior girls.

During the long Christmas break, Mr. Maxwell took his family to New York to see all the new plays. The old familiar jealousy stung Keely. She didn't care about Europe that much, but how she longed to see New York, the city packed skyscraper to skyscraper with writers, editors, and publishing houses!

She shoved away the jealousy and allowed herself to enjoy the familiar traditions in her own home. Her parents rarely had free time, but the Christmas season was one they cherished. Two weeks before Christmas, the Greens had a tree-decorating party, with friends of all ages enjoying eggnog—spiked and natural— and bacon-wrapped scallops and pumpkin spice cookies. Christmas Eve they watched *Home Alone*, which never got old. They raced off to church for the "midnight service," which started at ten-thirty and made Keely cry (quietly) at the laurel-decked sanctuary and the soaring hymns. Christmas morning they opened presents, nothing surprising now that Keely could no longer be thrilled by the sight of a doll or a bike, but a fun tradition all the same. Of course Keely received books. She helped her mother stuff the turkey and set it in the oven. For the rest of the day, the three of them did exactly what they wanted, where they wanted. Her father watched football on the living room television. Her mother luxuriated in bed, watching the Hallmark Channel. Keely curled up in her own bed, reading. She thought they were like a kind of bee family, each with its own cozy spot in the same honeycomb. The family sat formally at the table to eat the extravagant turkey dinner, but her father ate his pumpkin pie in front of the TV. It was a lazy, cozy, luxurious time, when Keely felt as safe as a little bear cuddled by her parents in a warm cave.

Real life resumed December 26. Friends called, came to her house, took her to their house for marathon games of Monopoly or poker. Or they all went to the Dreamland to see a new movie. If a winter blizzard roared over the island—and everyone wanted one to come—they piled on their warmest coats and boots and went out to the beach to scream with the howling wind.

"Sebastian is *disgusting*!" Isabelle snarled as she and Keely walked home from school. It was spring of their sophomore year, when they needed coats in the early morning but not in the afternoon.

"Why, because he's dating Sherry?" Keely suspected what Isabelle would say, but she knew Izzy needed to vent.

Also, she needed to know that it was true. If it was really happening.

"Because he's *having sex* with Sherry!"

Her breath caught in her throat, but she forced herself to act nonchalant. "Give the guy a break. He's *seventeen*."

"I don't care. I don't like her. I hate it when he brings her to eat dinner with us! I can't believe my parents allow it. They've got to know what's going on!"

Keely wanted to weep. Ever since last summer when Sebastian gave her the book, she'd expected something else to happen between them. Something *romantic*. And he *had* kissed her. Twice! Once on the forehead and once—it made her shiver to remember—on the mouth.

"He's just a normal guy," Keely said dismissively. "What can you expect?"

"At the least, I'd expect him to date someone smart."

Keely laughed. "Yes, because that's what guys like in a girl. Come on, Isabelle, you've seen Sherry in the girls' locker room. She's got enormous breasts!"

"Oh, you're disgusting, too!" Isabelle fumed. "*I'm* not going to get all hung up on some guy. I'm going to concentrate on my writing."

"Me, too." Keely noticed the Andersons' yard, strewn with daffodils. She nudged Isabelle. "Pretty."

Isabelle couldn't be bothered about someone's yard. "It's the way Sherry *twinkles* her fingers at me in the hall. As if she thinks I like her. SO not true!"

"Don't get your knickers in a twist," Keely said, rolling her eyes at herself for using an expression her parents used, although in this case it was kind of pertinent. "School will be out soon. You and your family and your precious Sebastian"—she blushed just speaking his name—"will be traveling off in France somewhere."

"Italy this year."

"Whatever. Out of the wicked Sherry's clutches."

"I know. It's the first time I've actually wanted to go on the stupid trip."

Maybe, Keely thought, just maybe, Sebastian would bring her a present from Italy.

More likely, he'd bring Sherry one.

Ciao, cara! Come va?

Keely stood in the front hall of her home, grateful for the air-conditioning as she read the postcard in her hand. Her parents weren't home yet, so she sank to the floor right there and then, allowing all her emotions to crowd in together. Happiness because Isabelle sent the card. Jealousy, as always, because Isabelle was piling up such exotic experiences for her novels while Keely worked at Clean Sweep and babysat in her free time.

Longing for Sebastian.

Disgust because she was so lame, allowing herself to daydream about him.

Also, for the first time, maybe a little spark of smugness. Keely was writing. Really writing. Any free time she had, Keely spent working on short stories and reading how-to books by famous writers. She couldn't wait to share her fiction with Isabelle.

"What do you think?" Mrs. Maxwell asked Keely.

"Delicious!" Keely lied. The pasta Bolognese on her plate reeked of garlic, and the sausage Mrs. Maxwell had used had an unfamiliar, gristly texture.

Plus, Sebastian wasn't here for their first family dinner back home on the island. He'd gone to "visit" Sherry. This year, the childhood traditions changed, because the children had changed. Mr. and Mrs. Maxwell insisted Isabelle stay home. Keely was allowed to join them.

"In Italy," Isabelle said, "I was allowed to drink wine." She shot an evil eye at her father.

"We're not in Italy anymore, darling," Mr. Maxwell reminded her.

After dinner, the girls secluded themselves in Isabelle's room. They sat on the floor between the twin beds so no one could overhear them. It was too hot to be outside, so luxurious to be in the cool air.

"So tell me everything," Isabelle urged.

"Wait, you tell me about Italy."

"I don't care about Italy! What did you do? What did anyone on the island do?"

Keely grinned. "Bliss got pregnant! She had to marry Gavin!"

"Is she going to finish senior year?"

"I doubt it. Her baby's due in December."

"Poor Bliss. Where are they living?"

"With Gavin's parents."

"I would *die*."

"I'm not having sex until I'm in college," Keely announced. "I've decided."

"But what if you, like, fall in love before then?"

"That's so not going to happen."

"Good. Because I'm going to wait, too. I want to get really good grades. I think I might join the girls' basketball team, too." Isabelle made a funny face. "I'm tall, plus I'll exhaust all my adolescent hormones that way."

"I'm not going to do a sport. Nothing interests me. Besides, I want to keep writing. I have so many short stories I want you to read!"

"You got to write all summer," Isabelle said mournfully. "I'm so jealous."

Keely scoffed. "Yeah, right. While you were in Italy, you were jealous."

"It's true!" Isabelle stood up and stretched. "I'm so *antsy* these days! Are you?"

"I don't have time to be," Keely answered. "I'm either working or writing."

"You don't have to be so pleased with yourself. Come on, let's go to your house so you can show me some of your fabulous *writing*."

Keely was babysitting for the Cronins' kids when someone knocked on the front door. She hesitated. Both children, Katrina and Kit, were already tucked away, asleep. But she was wary about opening the door even though it was late August and still light. She pulled back a pinch of curtain and peeked out.

Sebastian!

All at once she was so nervous she wasn't sure she could force herself to move. But she opened the door.

"Hey, Sebastian." She was good, so calm, so blasé.

"Hey yourself, Keely. Can I come in?"

"No. Sorry. The Cronins don't want me having friends in the house. How did you know I was here?"

"It was really hard. I called your parents to ask where you were."

Sebastian had called her parents? What would they think? Keely didn't even know what she thought!

"I just wanted to see you before I take off for Amherst."

Keely couldn't get her breath. "Um . . ."

"I didn't bring you anything from Italy."

Her gift for sarcasm surfaced just in time. "Yeah, because Sherry would love it if you gave me a present."

"I'm not seeing Sherry anymore."

"Because you're going off to college?"

"Yeah. She's going to Tufts, not so far away. But we both want to take a break."

"Um . . . okay." *What did this mean?* Keely's hopes spiraled upward.

"Look. I'd like to talk with you. Just the two of us. I really like you, Keely."

Her heart stopped beating. Her breath caught in her throat. Her eyes met his and for a moment they were the only people in the world.

A car passed by. The spell broke.

"I'd like to talk to you, too," Keely admitted, her voice faint.

"I have to leave tomorrow. But I'll come back to the island a lot. Can I text you?"

"Um, I've got an old phone . . ." She almost burst into tears.

"I'll email you then, okay?"

Had she entered an alternate universe? Her heart galloped like a racehorse. "Sure."

"I'll get your address from Izzy."

"No, don't. She'd kill me. I'll tell you. It's easy. Keely90 at gmail."

"So I'll see you at Thanksgiving."

"What about Christmas break?" The question popped out before she could stop herself.

"We're going to New York again. You know the drill."

"Right. Yeah, okay."

"Okay." Sebastian smiled down at her.

"You've gotten even taller," Keely said.

"Older and wiser, too," Sebastian quipped.

Without warning, he leaned forward and kissed her gently, quickly, on her lips.

"See ya," he said, and ran down the Cronins' walk and onto the street and around the corner.

Keely stood in the doorway, paralyzed with happiness and wonder until Sebastian was out of sight.

"I'm going to lose my virginity this year," Isabelle announced.

"Why? Because we're juniors?" Keely and Isabelle walked side by side, laden with heavy new textbooks after their first full day of school. It was as hot and humid as an August day. Who could take school seriously?

"Yeah, maybe. I just want to get it over with. With some guy I like, but don't love."

"You are so weird."

"No, Keely. I'm logical. Thinking ahead. I want to make top grades. I want to get into a good college. I don't want to be ambushed by 'love' and get obsessive over some guy."

"I know. Look at Bliss. I saw her at Island Variety yesterday. She's so matronly. She was desperate to know about school. We invited her to some beach parties this summer. She didn't come."

"Would *you*?"

"We were all in bikinis and she looks like a beach ball."

Isabelle laughed, shoving Keely's arm. "You're terrible."

"But I'm right."

"I know. That's what I mean. I really don't want to lose my mind—my *life!*—over some guy."

"Like that's something you can control." Keely bit her lip, thinking of Sebastian. She secretly congratulated herself on keeping her feelings for him private, because she didn't get why he had stopped by at the Cronins'. It had to be more than friendship.

Keely wanted to talk it over with someone, but Isabelle was her best friend, and Isabelle would flip if she knew Keely liked Sebastian.

They went to Isabelle's house today because the badminton set was still up in the backyard. They played a few games—it was therapeutic to run around on the soft grass slamming the birdie with the racket. They ate apples while they worked on their math homework in the kitchen. When Mrs. Maxwell came in to start cooking dinner, Keely gathered up her things and went home.

Her parents were both working late, so Keely chopped vegetables for a quick stir-fry when they got home. She went to her room, woke up her computer, and checked her emails.

Sebastian.

She had an email from Sebastian. She screamed—no one was around to hear her.

She opened the email.

Hey, Keely,

So sometimes it's easier to say things this way. I've been wanting to tell you some stuff, but I feel like you belong to Isabelle and I know your first allegiance is to her, so I haven't told you everything. Because, you know, she would kill me. Or you. Or both of us. But now, off the island, in my dorm, I guess I feel free to say some stuff. I just don't want Isabelle to know. I hope you understand.

So . . . it's pretty obvious how I feel about you, right? I mean giving you the book, and then seeing you this summer. I grabbed at the chance to talk to you when you were babysitting because none of my family would be hanging around eavesdropping. But that wasn't the best time or place, was it?

I wish I could spend more time with you. You and me, alone. I think you get me in ways no one else does. Because of your writing and my art, I mean. My pretensions to art. But more than that.

I think you're beautiful.

I've written and deleted that line about ten times. I'm kind of hanging off a roof here, emotionally speaking, and I don't know if you'll grab my wrists and pull me up or step on my fingers. (You can tell I've been watching too many thrillers.)

So, can you do this? Email me and well, let's have a conversation. And please don't tell anyone about this, especially Isabelle.

XO Sebastian

does Because of
pretension to an
"I think you'd l
I've written an
I'm kind of hangin
ing, and I don't b
can do it, can you?
So, can you do
conversation. And I'd
especially Isabelle

chapter
three

K eely didn't scream. She didn't burst into tears. This moment
was too profound for that. She sat there, reading the email
over and over, stunned with joy.

She hit "Reply." She wrote:

I think you're beautiful, too.

She deleted that. *Act like an adult,* she told herself. *Act like Sebastian's email isn't as miraculous as the creation of the universe.*

She wrote sentence after sentence, deleting them all. Her parents came home. She shut down the computer and went out to
help make dinner. She moved as if she were an imaginary Keely, a
dream Keely—a *beautiful* Keely.

Later, she emailed Sebastian.

> Wow, Sebastian. Thanks for the compliment. I'd love
> to have a conversation with you. I'm definitely ready
> to grab your wrists and pull you up onto the roof.
>   I think you're beautiful, too.
>
>   XO Keely

She pressed "Send."

Keely waited until midnight for a reply from Sebastian, but
nothing came. Nothing the next day, either. Paranoia crept over

her. Had Sebastian been fooling around, playing with her, and now making fun of her? She couldn't concentrate on her homework. She couldn't even eat.

Two days later, his email came.

> Sorry not to answer sooner. College is tougher than high school. I don't have time to do much but study.
>
> But thanks for your compliment. Glad you want to have a conversation. Afraid it will be short now that I've been loaded down with course work.
>
> Let me know how you are.
>
> XO Sebastian

What? Keely thought. The emotional temperature of his two emails was totally different. Was it only college courses that made him shortchange his email? She burned to talk with Isabelle about this, but of course she never would. She never could.

She didn't send a reply to Sebastian. She needed to figure this puzzle out. Days passed and her grades were sinking. She wrenched her mind out of its obsessive daze and forced herself to concentrate on her homework.

Isabelle was busy with homework and girls' basketball. She and Keely talked and emailed, but Keely noticed a distance growing between them. Of course they didn't have as much time because of school, but Isabelle was absentminded, even cold toward Keely.

Keely decided the entire Maxwell family was insane.

She wept into her pillow every night, when not even her parents could hear her.

The first Friday night in October, a gale force wind and a full moon slammed the island, exploding into the air with crazy ions.

Isabelle phoned. "Keely, come to Surfside with me. I've got to be there!"

"Pick me up now," Keely said.

On the way to the beach, Keely and Isabelle talked about school stuff. Keely's ruffled emotional fur smoothed out. Isabelle was still her best friend, just so busy.

At the beach, waves reared up and plunged down, whipping their tips into frenzies. The sea pounded, the wind wailed. The moonlight transformed the girls and the entire world into silver. As they had done so many times before, Isabelle and Keely danced on the sand, screaming and laughing and running along the jagged shoreline until they were breathless. They fell down at the edge of the waves.

Isabelle burst into tears. She reached out toward the white froth, as if to pull it up over her, and sobbed.

Keely knelt next to her. "Isabelle! What's wrong?"

"I hate myself! I hate my life! I want to die!"

"What? How can you say that? You have everything! You're beautiful and smart and popular—"

"I'm in love with someone and he doesn't even know I exist."

Keely was stunned. "In *love*? Who's the guy?"

"I can't tell you. It's too stupid. He's way out of my league."

"How old is he?" Keely asked. Her heart swelled with sympathy for Isabelle. She could understand. She was in love with Sebastian, who seemed to be playing a kind of game.

"It doesn't matter. He hasn't even looked my way."

"Stop it. All the guys look your way and you know it." She took Isabelle's shoulders and pulled her away from the water, farther up onto the sand.

"You're so cool about guys," Isabelle said. "I wish I could be like you."

Keely shrugged. "I think I've turned off my love switch. I want to concentrate on getting good grades so I can get a scholarship to college. I want to write a book before I even think of going nuts over some man."

"It's too late for me," Isabelle said.

"Who is it?" Keely pleaded. "Come on. I'll keep it secret."

"Oh, God, I'm such a loser!" Isabelle turned toward Keely with fury. "It's Tommy Fitzgerald! The guy who can have any girl he wants."

"Wow." Tommy Fitzgerald, with his black hair and ebony eyes, looked like a pirate who knew he could steal anything he wanted and get away with it. "I don't know what to say, Isabelle. You're as gorgeous as Tommy. And probably way smarter."

"Yeah, because I'm so *smart* all I can think about is him."

"Have you tried, I don't know, catching his attention? Maybe, um, flirting?"

"Why no, Keely, that didn't even occur to me," Isabelle answered sarcastically.

"Okay, let's think. Who does he hang out with?"

"Anyone he wants."

"You're beautiful," Keely stressed. "You're popular. You're—"

"Stop it, Keely. Just stop it. You have no idea how it feels to be in love with a guy. Seriously, truly, painfully in love. *Hopelessly* in love."

If only you knew, Keely thought. She flashed on the foolish vow she'd made with cooking sherry and seashells, her vow never to tell Isabelle that she loved Sebastian. "Let's go to my house and eat everything in the kitchen."

Isabelle snorted. "Food as therapy. I've got a better idea. Let's go to my house, sneak some of my parents' booze, and get drunk."

"Not my favorite thing to do," Keely said.

Isabelle sighed theatrically. "Fine. Let's go stuff our faces." Linking her arm through Keely's, she said, "I don't know what I would ever do without you, Keys."

Hey, Keely, how's it going? I'm buried under home-work. I'm taking an introduction to art class that's great. Wait till you get to college. It's like another uni-verse here.

More later, Sebastian

Keely wanted to throw her computer across the room. What was his *problem*? What was he doing? Had she been too eager to respond to his first email?

Furious with herself and with him, she didn't reply for several days.

> Hey, Sebastian, I'm snowed under, too. Everyone's going nuts because the homecoming game between the Vineyard and the Whalers is in three weeks. Even the teachers are giving us a break.
>
> More later, Keely

There, Keely thought. She could be as cool as he was.

She reread his first email, searching each word for hidden meanings. Why would he want to "start a conversation" only to drop out of sight?

She prided herself on her self-control. Isabelle was mooning around, losing weight, dropping grades, turning into a tragic heroine. All she could talk about was Tommy Fitzgerald. His eyes as black as night. His thick black crow hair. He smiled at her one day. She was trying to learn his class schedule so she could plan to be in the hall at the right time with the other girls who clustered around him.

"Get over yourself," Keely said to Isabelle as they walked home from school one day. Leaves fluttered down around them, scarlet and orange and brown. "Really, he's not worth it."

"I know that," Isabelle said. "I know with my mind. Smart doesn't change the heart."

"Hey." Keely knocked Isabelle's shoulder with hers. "Kind of a great mantra there. Smart doesn't change the heart."

"It's infantile and meaningless," Isabelle groused.

"Come to my house," Keely said. "It's chocolate chip cookie day."

• • •

Two weeks before the homecoming game, at the end of the school day, Keely arrived at her locker to find Tommy Fitzgerald standing there. In front of her locker. So she couldn't open it without asking Tommy to move.

Her mouth went dry. "Hi."

"Hi." His black eyes shot through her like lasers.

He was so *real*.

"Um, you're standing in front of my locker."

"I know." He seemed amused.

Keely felt a blush break out over her face and neck. She summoned up all her cool. "Well . . . I need to get into my locker."

"Sure. But I want to talk to you first."

Keely blinked. "Do you even know who I am?"

"Of course I know who you are. You're Keely Green. I want to take you to the homecoming dance."

Keely clutched her textbooks as if they were the only things that could keep her from falling through the floor. "You want to take me to the homecoming dance."

Tommy nodded. He almost smiled.

Keely hesitated. Was this some kind of sick joke? She looked around. Other students were taking things out of their lockers, slamming them, walking away. But Tommy Fitzgerald asking her to the homecoming dance? Nope. Not a real thing.

She fastened her gaze on his, lifted her chin, and bravely said, "Are you kidding me?" Her voice squeaked on "kidding," which took away some of the cool.

That made Tommy break into a full-on smile. "Not kidding. Why would I kid?"

"I . . . I . . . I need to think about it," Keely stuttered.

His smile dazzled her. "You need to think about it?"

"My parents—they have something planned . . ."

"Want me to call you tonight after you talk to them? Or come by your house?"

"Come by my house?" She had brain freeze.

"Or I'll call. Or text."

"Good. That's good."

Tommy moved. Keely froze. What was he going to do?

He put his hand on her shoulder. "If you'll step back, I'll get out of your way."

It took a few moments for her to make sense of his words. "Oh. Oh, my locker."

She stepped back, thrilled that she didn't trip on her own feet.

"See you." Tommy walked away.

Keely hid in the girls' restroom when school let out. She didn't want to talk to Isabelle. She had to think about it first. About him. She wasn't in love with him like Isabelle, but she couldn't *not* be attracted to him, that would be like preventing herself from breathing oxygen.

If she thought Sebastian was interested in her, she wouldn't think twice about Tommy. But—no. Whatever Sebastian meant by that first email, he'd changed his mind.

It would be fun to date Tommy. It would make her the absolute coolest girl in school, even if only for a while.

It would be interesting to have sex with Tommy. Having her first time with him would certainly make the event memorable.

But why was she thinking this way? Isabelle was in love with Tommy, and Isabelle was Keely's best friend.

Keely stuck her books in her locker, grabbed her fleece, slammed the locker door, and sauntered down the hall. She was *not* going to act like a groupie who'd just talked to Justin Timberlake. She was a junior in high school. She was cool. Still, it was hard not to grin.

When she was outside and two blocks away from the high school, she broke into a run toward Isabelle's house. The Maxwell house was on Fair Street, near the Episcopal church. Over the years, it had become Keely's second home, and she ran up the steps and across the porch and rapped quickly on the front door and opened it and ran inside.

She crashed right into Sebastian. He was tall and blond and gorgeous in khakis and a blue button-down shirt with the sleeves rolled up.

"What are you doing here?" Keely asked, panting.

"I live here," Sebastian said.

"Well, I *know* that. But why aren't you at Amherst?"

"Maybe I came home to see someone." Sebastian looked amused.

Keely's temper flared. "Good. You're going to stand there and make fun of me. Great big *busy* college man. After sending me that email . . ." Keely knew her face was red. She felt as if her hair was on fire.

Sebastian's expression changed. "I'm sorry, Keely. Let me ex—"

"Oh, forget it," she said, trying to squeeze past him. It took all her willpower not to burst into tears. "I need to see Isabelle."

Sebastian took hold of her arm and gently moved her out to the porch. He pulled the door shut behind him.

"Please, Keely. Listen to me a moment."

Keely's mouth tightened. She stared down at her feet. No way she could look him in the eyes.

"I know I behaved like a jackass. Writing that email that was so . . . extreme, and then cooling off so fast without explanation was just stupid. I want to apologize. I think you'll understand when you're in college. It's so different from living at home and being in high school. The world opens up so wide it could swallow a person. It spins you. I was spinning. What is your major going to be, what are you going to do with your life, where are you going to live, who's going to be your friend, and the *women*. I mean, kid in candy store, right? I got drunk like I never have before, and I heard some professors talk about stuff that made me want to change my life, *be myself* and not just do what my parents want me to do. It was exciting. It was like being strapped into a roller coaster and the end is nowhere in sight. That's how you're going to feel when you get off this island and start college, I promise."

Keely raised her head and faced him defiantly. "So what you're saying is I shouldn't let some poor gullible chump think I like him because once I'm off this island, I won't find him interesting anymore."

"Right!" Sebastian said, then immediately corrected himself. "I mean, no. Not exactly that. You've never been any kind of gullible chump to me, Keely."

"Well, that's a relief," Keely said dryly. She was proud that her voice was so sarcastic.

Sebastian smiled. Keely didn't. She was angry with him and intoxicated by him. It was all she could do to hold on to her anger like a person clutching a plank in the middle of the ocean.

"Keely, listen. I . . . have feelings for you. I always have. But one thing I've learned is that I'm young. I want to take some chances while I can. I want to find out about myself. I don't want to be some kind of idiot when I talk to you."

"I'm afraid you've already done that," Keely said. She pulled away from him, proud of her quick response. She shoved open the door, and went into the house, longing to think of another cool thing to say, but she was too emotional, so close to tears.

Maybe she hoped Sebastian would pull her back to him. He said he had feelings for her.

But he didn't come after her. Without another word, Keely ran up the stairs to the second floor. She stood for a moment in the doorway to Isabelle's room, replaying the moment with Sebastian. What had just happened? What had Sebastian said? What had he *meant?*

She was glad she hadn't remained in front of Sebastian, like a dog begging for some treats. She was proud of herself.

Isabelle was on the floor of her room, bent over her geometry homework. "What are you doing?" she asked.

Keely's knees went wobbly so she sat right down in the doorway. *Your brother talked to me,* she wanted to say. Instead, she said, "Tommy Fitzgerald asked me to the homecoming dance."

Isabelle went pale. "Oh no, he did not."

Keely smiled. "Oh yes, he did. I had no idea he even knew I existed!"

Isabelle burst into tears.

"Isabelle, wait. Listen. I didn't accept."

"You didn't accept? What did you say?" Isabelle's lovely creamy face was blotchy with emotion.

"I said I had to think about it."

"*You* told Tommy Fitzgerald you have to think about it?"

"Yes, Isabelle, because I know how you feel about him. I didn't want to hurt your feelings."

"Oh, thank you very much for your amazing kindness!"

Keely rocked backward. She hadn't expected *anger* from Isabelle. "Isabelle, come on. It doesn't mean anything."

"To *you*, it doesn't! It means *everything* to me! You've so totally won!"

"Izzy, we're not in a contest. And if we are, look at all you have that I don't. You've got a brother. You've got this ginormous house! You're beautiful and smart!"

"Obviously not beautiful enough for Tommy. What did you do, flirt with him?"

"No! Don't be an ass! I would never flirt with Tommy!"

"He probably asked you to the dance because he knows he can get in your pants."

Keely recoiled. "Well, that's a mean thing to say. Plus, not true and you know it."

"I'm sorry, I'm sorry," Isabelle wailed. "But why would he choose you?"

"Are you girls okay?"

Keely and Isabelle turned. Mr. Maxwell was standing in the doorway.

"We're fine, Dad," Isabelle said. "Just having a fight."

"Don't worry, there will be no broken limbs," Keely joked, but it fell flat.

"I would hope not," Mr. Maxwell said, tight-lipped, obviously angry.

"I'd better go home," Keely said quietly.

"I think that's a good idea," Mr. Maxwell said.

Keely waited a moment for Isabelle to say something, to ask her to stay. But the room was quiet. Keely left, hurrying down the stairs and out the door. Sebastian was nowhere in sight.

Keely was almost dizzy. She and Isabelle had never had such a fight before. As she trotted down the street and around the corner on the way to her house, she realized that Sebastian could have heard them. She *hoped* he heard them. She hoped the truth dawned on him: Keely was a girl the most popular guy in school wanted to date. She hoped that might make Sebastian wish he'd kept up their *conversation*.

After dinner with both parents at home for once, someone knocked on the door.

"I'll get it!" Keely raced to the door, opened it, and stepped outside, pulling it closed behind her.

Tommy stood there, all six foot four inches of pure hunk. His hands were in his pockets. He slouched almost lazily, a knowing smile on his face. *And now*, Keely thought, *I know what the word* charisma *means*.

He was so sure of himself. "Hey."

"Hi. Listen, Tommy, I'm sorry, really, but I can't go to the dance. I've made other plans."

"Are you going with someone else?"

"No, it's my parents, but maybe, I have to see how their schedule . . ." She was blithering and blushing. "I'm sorry."

Tommy shrugged. "You're being mysterious. But I get it. You don't want to go with me."

"It's not that. Well, it *is* that. I can't explain, I don't want—"

"No worries. I'll probably be able to find someone else."

Without another word, he turned, walked back to his truck, and drove away.

"Crap. What did I just do?" Keely stood on the front porch for a long time, trying to untangle her emotions.

Later that evening, Keely called Isabelle. "Isabelle, listen. Tommy came by—"

"Your house? Tommy came to your house?"

"I stood outside to talk to him. It took about two seconds. I told him I can't go with him, that I had to do something with my parents."

"So virtuous of you. So now he'll ask *me* to go?"

"What else can I do? I hate this . . . this spat. I want to make it right somehow. You tell me."

"This *spat*?" Isabelle hissed. "You think this is a *spat*? I'm in love with Tommy and he wants to date *you*? Keely, this is serious. You and I are done. There's no coming back."

"Isabelle, that's just silly! You are the person I love most in the world. I can't be happy without you. So I'm not going to the dance with him."

Isabelle's voice was formal and prissy. "Thank you very much. It's generous of you to be so charitable."

"Izzy!"

"You know I hate that nickname. Call me Isabelle."

"Call me Ishmael," Keely joked, and she thought that was actually pretty funny, because they were reading *Moby Dick* for school.

Isabelle's line went dead.

Keely walked a wandering route to school the next day. She didn't want to run into Isabelle. During classes, she ignored Isabelle when they passed in the hall or sat in the same room. She walked home along unusual streets, wishing she could stop thinking about Sebastian, wishing she could talk to Isabelle about Sebastian.

She thought he was being honest with her about how being at

college opened up the world. Nantucket was small and isolated and at the same time endlessly fascinating. It was a natural lab for science geeks. The ocean, the sheltered harbor, the growing population of sharks, the increase of snowy owls, anything connected with nature brought experts from all over the world to study and photograph and write about. You could live here all your life and never be bored.

Keely never felt detached from the rest of the world, although she did often feel provincial. The seniors she knew were exhilarated and terrified at the prospect of living off-island, and she could understand that. She wanted the beauty of the island but she also wanted the excitement of the city—she wanted it all. At least she thought she did.

So as much as she knew her heart had been well and thoroughly broken by Sebastian, she also understood with the tiny rational part of her brain that what he had said was true.

And then there was Tommy. And Isabelle. Keely's heart was heavy. In one day, it seemed, she'd lost them both. She'd lost the chance to talk to Isabelle about Sebastian. She couldn't talk to Isabelle, period.

She took her homework out to the back patio and sat at the table, taking comfort from the bright low sunlight, the crisp air, the changing colors of autumn, the birds too busy with their own lives to notice her. She shoved her homework to the side, folded her arms on the table, put down her head, and cried.

Why was life so difficult? What had she done, turning down *Tommy Fitzgerald*? Isabelle was angry with her simply because he'd asked Keely to the dance, so she should have gone with him, Isabelle couldn't get angrier! Should she phone Tommy and say her plans had changed? Did she even *want* to go to the dance with Tommy? Could she just give herself a minute to appreciate the reality that Tommy Fitzgerald had asked her to the homecoming dance? Really, it was remarkable. If it didn't exactly mean he liked her, at least it meant he noticed her. If she had accepted his invitation and gone to the dance, Isabelle would have told Sebastian, and then Sebastian would know he wasn't the only guy who liked Keely. And what did "like" mean, anyway?

No wonder women became nuns!

"Keely."

Keely lifted her head.

Isabelle stood at the edge of the patio, wringing her hands together like someone from *Macbeth*.

"Keely, can we talk? I want to apologize. You're such a good friend to refuse Tommy. I'm sorry I was so mean. It does break my heart, and I do feel *hideously* jealous that he asked you instead of me. But I know it's not your fault." Isabelle was crying now, tears running down her face and her mouth quivering as she spoke. "You were a good friend, and I behaved like a bad friend. I'm sorry."

Keely sat up straight. She wiped her eyes and gave a quavering smile. "I guess I understand. Anyway, I don't want to fight over any stupid male. Our friendship should mean more than that."

Isabelle came up on the patio. She slid into a chair. "It does mean more than that, Keely. It does. I can't believe how nice it was of you to refuse him because of me. I guess I lost that fact in the total misery that he had asked *anyone* but me." She stretched her hand across the table. "Sorry, okay?"

Keely took her hand. "Okay."

Isabelle said, "I am *so* over men."

Keely said, "Me, too."

The autumn afternoon grew chilly as the sun sank in the sky. They went into the kitchen to search for a snack, something comforting more than nutritious. Keely made hot chocolate from scratch and topped their cups with fat marshmallows. They went back outside, the better to enjoy the warm sweet treat in the cold air.

Keely turned her marshmallows over and over, melting them slightly. Isabelle was doing the same thing, gazing down into her cup. "So what was Sebastian doing at home?" Keely asked casually.

"He had to get some of his warmer clothes. Winter coat and stuff. It gets cold on the mainland earlier than it does here. He's already left."

"Ah. Good. I was afraid he'd gotten kicked out of college."

Isabelle laughed. "Sebastian? Sebastian the Good kicked out of college? Never!"

Sebastian emailed me, Keely wanted to say. *He told me I'm beautiful. Then he forgot I exist.*

"So Jeff Morton asked me to the homecoming dance," Isabelle said. "I bet Jasper Childs will ask you. He's Jeff's buddy and he's always staring at you."

"I don't think I can go to the dance," Keely reminded Isabelle. "I told Tommy I had to do something with my parents."

"So you don't want to hurt Tommy's feelings?" Isabelle rolled her eyes. "You think he *has* feelings? Tommy's after sex like a shark after meat."

"You're gross."

"I'm right."

"Why are you in love with him, then?"

"Because love is so irrational," Isabelle moaned. "Come on, let's find a way to go together. Pleeeeeeze?"

"Sure," Keely agreed. "If Jasper asks me."

The Whalers won the homecoming game. Tommy Fitzgerald, the quarterback, drilled the ball right to the running back three times in a row. People in the bleachers screamed themselves hoarse. Tommy was mobbed at the end of the game, and the school was wild with victory. The dance at the school gym was insane. When it slowed down, half the crowd congregated at Surfside Beach. Someone built a bonfire. Someone else blasted Queen's *"We Are the Champions,"* from his iPod. Lots of people brought coolers of beer or flasks of something stronger. Up on the cliff, authorities were watching, the kids knew that, and they knew that most of those police had been students here just like they were now.

They knew that if there was a problem, the police would rush in. They knew the police watching them understood what it was to be young, and silently shared in their celebration.

Jasper Childs was a good guy, low-key, undemanding. Keely felt comfortable with him. Isabelle and Jeff and Keely and Jasper hung around in a clump, and when people started dancing at the edge of the water, the four of them took off their shoes and danced, too, slipping and tilting in the cold sand, singing with the music, laughing for no reason. Some couples wandered away from the bonfire, into the darkness. Isabelle and Keely spun away from the guys and danced with each other, waving their arms, screaming and laughing. While other students slid into the shadows to smoke pot or get drunk, Keely and Isabelle existed in their own personal high, as if they were moving within the eye of a hurricane, as if they were *causing* the hurricane, they were so happy, so *alive*, it was their own spirits that whirled around them and into the night, filling the air with jubilation.

The day before Thanksgiving, school let out at noon. Half the families were traveling off island, the other half of the island families were preparing to meet friends and relatives at the ferries.

The ocean had turned a dark, forbidding navy blue. The wind seemed to need to push harder to swell the surly water. Keely and Isabelle walked home, kicking at the last scarlet leaves scattered like tapestries on the ground.

"So," Keely said casually, "when does Sebastian get here?"

"He doesn't," Isabelle answered. "He's going to his girlfriend's uncle's house in the Berkshires."

"His girlfriend."

"Yeah, Ebba. They've been a couple since the beginning of October. He's going to bring her into New York when we go down for Christmas."

"Oooh, sounds serious." Keely made her voice light, jokey. She wanted to fall to her knees and howl.

"He's a freshman. It's probably *intense* but I doubt if it's *serious*."

Keely dug her fingernails into her palms. She felt like a wounded wolf. She needed to growl, to bite. "Sort of like how you feel about Tommy."

Isabelle rounded on Keely. "No. Not like that at all, and you know it. I'm in love with Tommy."

"He hasn't even asked you out, Isabelle."

"He will. He's *mine*. I know it. I can wait."

Keely kicked at a pile of leaves, making them flutter up and drift back in place. "You're a little bit crazy."

"Hey," Isabelle joked, "it's part of the job description of adolescence, right?"

At Fair Street, they parted ways, heading home to do homework. Keely managed a bright smile as she walked away from Isabelle, but inside, her emotions raged like little kids did when they sat in shopping carts and their poor beleaguered moms didn't let them have candy.

So Sebastian was dating Ebba.

It would have been nice if he'd emailed her to tell her so she could let go of her hope.

She'd been a fool, anyway, to believe Sebastian had romantic feelings for her.

No, she hadn't been a fool! Sebastian had started it. He'd been—he *was* a total *rat*.

She hated him. No, she wouldn't waste her time hating him. She would forget about him.

Keely's mother worked all holidays so that nurses with small children could have the time off. Keely's father didn't mind. Friends invited him and Keely to their house for Thanksgiving dinner. Keely was happy to sleep late, loll in bed, reading something that had nothing to do with school.

That was what her father thought she was doing.

Keely was on the floor, weeping. She stuffed her old teddy bear's arm in her mouth to stifle the sounds of her sobs. Hope about Sebastian was a ship on the horizon, sailing out of sight. Without it, Keely was alone, on the empty island that was her life. She felt about Sebastian the way Isabelle felt about Tommy—he *belonged* to her. But the truth was, her feelings, her silly adolescent infatuation, didn't matter at all.

She increased the volume on her music—Enya, whose songs were mystical and full of courage. Keely let the music pour through her, wash her clean, surround her with light. She played the same CD over and over again. She wept for hours, until she was afraid she would vomit, until her eyes burned, until her head ached, until her heart was empty.

She stood up. She was exhausted. She clicked off the music and fell on her bed. Sleep bathed her in a pool of calm.

That evening, she showered and dressed and went with her father to the O'Reillys'. They had a twelve-year-old girl who adored Keely, which was both cute and irritating. Keely forced herself to be "normal," pleasant, polite.

When Keely and her father went home, Keely went straight to her room and shut the door.

Later, her father tapped lightly on her bedroom door.

"Are you okay?"

"I'm fine, Dad. Just tired."

A moment of silence. "Call me if you need anything. I'm just watching football."

"I will. Thanks, Dad."

Keely heard him walk away and thought what a good father he was. He was present for her, and he was sensitive, not intruding on her when she hid in her room. He was a good man, her father. He was solid, sound, strong. Someday perhaps Keely would meet her own good man. Until then, she would channel every drop of pain and sadness into her writing. She would make good grades, great grades, she would focus on getting a scholarship, she would get off this island and go to college and out into the real world.

• • •

The summer before their senior year, Isabelle went with her parents to Australia, and so—Keely learned from Isabelle's emails—did Sebastian. Isabelle texted that Sebastian hadn't brought a girlfriend along.

For Keely, it was just another summer. She cleaned houses and babysat and read and wrote. She wasn't unhappy—okay, she was. She was still sick at heart about Sebastian, about what they could have had. But the knowledge that she had only one more year of high school was like an open door in a flooded room. Soon, in one quick whoosh, she would be out in the world. She would meet many men more interesting than Sebastian.

When she had free time, she went out fishing with her father or picnicking on the beach with her friends. Toward the end of the summer, she went with her parents to look at the University of Massachusetts at Amherst. It was a sprawling campus that seemed as big as a town to Keely. But it had an excellent creative writing program, and this was her first choice. Maybe her only choice, because she would have to get a scholarship.

The Maxwells returned home at the end of August. Keely and Isabelle talked on the phone, but before they had a chance to see each other, Isabelle's parents whisked her off to tour colleges. Keely had no idea where Sebastian was. To her own private shame, she drove by the Maxwell house one evening when she knew Isabelle and her parents were off-island. Keely wanted to see if there were lights on in the house. There weren't.

Their senior year was intense and emotional. Keely focused on getting good grades in all her classes, but she was aware of a new tension in the senior class, a sense of importance and anticipation shadowed by the looming knowledge that this was their last year in this particular building with these particular people.

While everyone else was partying, Keely was studying. She

wanted to get all A's. She *needed* that scholarship. In early December, when she had dozens of job offers to babysit and even more invitations to parties, her father had what her mother insisted on calling a *minor* heart attack. Keely spent much of the Christmas season traveling with her father and mother to Massachusetts General Hospital in Boston. Her father was tested and diagnosed and given three different types of medications to bring down his blood pressure and slow his hardworking heart. After only one night in the hospital, George Green and his wife and daughter began the trip home, this time hiring a driver instead of taking the bus to Hyannis, spending two nights at the Hyannis Holiday Inn because a blizzard kept the ferries from running, and finally bumping home on the fast ferry. Keely's father had pills and orders to slow down, to stop working so hard. It was a scare, Keely's mother said, but it was not the end of the world.

No, it was not the end of the world, but it was pretty much the end of any social life Keely wanted. On New Year's Eve, she babysat instead of going to the fabulous dance party the seniors held in the school gym. She needed the money, especially since her father wasn't working full-time. She didn't want her father worrying about money for her. When she wasn't at school or babysitting, she spent as much time as possible watching sports on television with him.

"You don't have to check on me, Keely," her father told her. "I'm fine."

"I know that. But I want to watch the Patriots, too."

When her mother returned from work, Keely talked with her in the kitchen, giving her mother a report on how her father had seemed during those few hours. Her mother promised her that if he followed his doctor's orders, George Green would be fine. Keely wanted a written guarantee.

By February, they knew where they were going to college. Miraculously, Keely was given a full scholarship to the University of Massachusetts at Amherst. Isabelle was attending Smith, where

Gloria Steinem, Julia Child, and the poet Sylvia Plath had gone. Tommy also chose UMass. The two institutions of higher learning—of course people joked about the "high"—were within a few miles of each other. Buses could take you to Northampton, the hub.

Sebastian would be nearby, too, at Amherst College. Keely didn't expect to see him. She knew he was still involved with Ebba.

At last, it was May. The students lined up in the room next to the auditorium. Twenty-six graduating seniors. Most of them had known each other since preschool. They were about to be set free from the captivity of law-mandated classes. Some were leaving immediately for the military or for jobs or for trips. One girl, Brioni, would be leaving to have a baby; her gown covered her swollen belly. Keely and Isabelle grumbled that this rite of passage was juvenile, almost embarrassing, but they shook with nerves and kept blinking back tears.

From the front of the room Mr. Carpenter, the vice principal, gave the order to fall in line. He opened the door. The class of 2008 processed onto the stage. Cameras flashed. The audience murmured. Jenny Perry, the valedictorian, spoke. Keely had never liked Jenny, but she couldn't keep from silently weeping. The other girls around her were crying, too. Tim Madden, the Cape and island state representative, gave a brief, inspiring speech. The principal stood to hand out the diplomas. The class rose.

Keely walked to the front of the stage to accept her diploma, and from then on, time blurred. How long did she spend hugging and kissing her classmates? Jimmy Jordan, a year younger and the most handsome guy in school, walked up to Keely, said, "If I don't do it now, I never will," and kissed Keely so thoroughly her knees went weak.

Isabelle and Janine and the other girls hugged each other and with much emotion and crying promised they'd never forget them, as if they wouldn't see each other tomorrow and every day of their lives that they remained on this fifty-square-mile island.

Gradually the drama relaxed. Kids left to find their parents. Keely met her mother and father in the school parking lot, where they'd agreed to meet.

"Congratulations," Keely's father said.

"We're so proud of you," Keely's mother added, starting to weep again.

"We got a little present for you," her father said. Stepping to one side, he gestured to a used but very clean Honda Civic.

"Oh, Dad, Mom, thank you!" Keely hugged them both.

"Why don't you drive it," her father said, handing her the keys. "Follow us to the Seagrille. We're taking you out to lunch."

"Thanks, Dad, I will!"

Keely opened the door and sank into the shining interior of the old car. The engine kicked over at once. Keely put her hands on the wheel. "And this, my friends," Keely said aloud, "this is the sensation of freedom."

On the way out of the parking lot, Keely passed the Maxwells and Isabelle. Isabelle waved, then gestured like a game show babe at her new cherry-red convertible Jeep. Behind her, Sebastian stood, very close to a gorgeous blond woman. He waved at Keely. She pretended she didn't see him.

The first day of summer vacation, Keely began the schedule she'd made for herself. She rose at six, two hours before she started cleaning houses. She sat at the kitchen table and drank coffee and wrote. Was what she wrote any good? Was she wasting her time? Cleaning houses was hard work, but having no one to share her writing with was harder.

The Maxwells were in Scandinavia. Sometimes Keely hung out with girlfriends, going to the beach on Sunday, a movie on

Saturday night. She loved them all, but she couldn't share her fiction with them. It was intimate, private.

Occasionally over the summer, Keely saw Tommy in the distance. He worked for his father's accounting office and went out on the family's boat when he found time. Keely knew this, as if by osmosis, just as everyone who lived on the island or at least went to school there knew what everyone else was doing.

She never heard from Sebastian. It was as if he'd never sent her that first romantic email. But she couldn't bring herself to delete it.

chapter
four

Keely sat looking out the café window, tapping her fingers against her coffee cup. She'd taken off work at the UMass shop to meet Isabelle. She wasn't amused that Isabelle wasn't here yet. Keely had been afraid of this, that college life would cause a breach between them.

Then Isabelle raced in, out of breath. "Sorry I'm late!"

"It's fine," Keely replied. "I got you an iced mocha cappuccino."

"Great. Thanks." Isabelle slid onto the bench across from Keely. "So. Tell me. How do you like it so far?"

Keely leaned back in her chair, squinting at Isabelle. "You look much too happy. What's going on?"

"I'll tell you in a minute. First, tell me how you like UMass."

"It's great. Why are you glowing? You can't like Smith that much."

"I love Smith! I *adore* it here. I love being a college girl, excuse me, woman. I love being away from my parents. I love being off the island, driving anywhere I want whenever I want. I love my teachers, my courses, I even love my homework!"

Keely studied Isabelle. Izzy had chopped off her beautiful blond hair in a kind of ersatz crew cut. It had been only two months since they'd started their college classes, but Isabelle looked so *different*. She was absolutely radiant.

Only one thing could make Isabelle look so happy.

"You're seeing Tommy," Keely said.

Isabelle flushed scarlet. "How did you know?"

"Oh. My. God. You're *sleeping* with Tommy!"

"I wouldn't say 'sleeping' exactly," Isabelle joked and looked very pleased with herself.

"Tell me everything."

"Okay. You know he's at UMass, too."

"Yeah, but I never see him. There are, what, twenty thousand students."

"I friended him on Facebook, and he IM'd me, wanting to see me. That was three weeks ago. We've been with each other every minute except when we're in class."

"At last! I'm so happy for you, Isabelle."

"Thanks! Keely, he says the sweetest things. And his kisses—"

I'm going to be a spinster, Keely thought as she listened to Isabelle recount every moment of her time with Tommy. *I'm going to get a cat and live alone in someone's attic and spend my life reading and writing novels.*

Actually, she thought, *that didn't sound like a bad life at all.*

". . . he told his parents about us and they've invited me and my entire family to Thanksgiving dinner at their house, and Sebastian is invited with his girlfriend, but Sebastian's going to Sweden for Christmas . . ."

Great, Keely thought. Sebastian would spend Christmas with his gorgeous artistic Swedish girlfriend, eating lutefisk and drinking aquavit.

". . . and I told my parents, and they're so happy for me. I mean, I know Tommy and I are only eighteen, and we've got four years of college to slog through, but we're so much in love I know we'll stay together even after college."

"Lucky for you Smith and UMass are about three inches apart," Keely joked. "You'll have to spend sooo much time traveling to see each other."

"Listen, Keely. I *still* want to write novels, and I am *serious* about getting a good education, and I've told Tommy this and he *totally* understands. But he's not into studying as much as I am. He's an action guy. He's really all about getting out on the ocean, having a deep-water fishing business, but his father's pressuring him to get a college degree, so he is."

Keely nodded, listening. Isabelle couldn't talk fast enough. Keely had never seen her quite like this. She wouldn't be surprised to see Isabelle spin right up to the ceiling.

"Sorry sorry," Isabelle said after a while. "I'm hogging the conversation. Tell me about you. Do you like your classes? Do you like your dorm? Have you met any cool guys? Gone to any insane parties?"

Keely held her hands up in a "stop" sign. "Whoa, Isabelle, slow down. You act like you're on speed."

"I *feel* like I'm on speed. And look, I haven't drunk a sip of coffee!" Isabelle held up her glass as evidence. "Sorry. Seriously, I want to know how you are."

"I'm good. I like all my classes except physics, which seems invented by a committee of asylum inmates."

"Ha!" Isabelle laughed. "Keely, you're so funny! I'll have to tell that to Tommy. He's good with physics, but I hate it, too."

And Isabelle was off again, confiding Tommy's every phobia or preference, why he didn't like sugar in his coffee, how he had seven shirts exactly alike because that saved him from thinking about what to wear, his favorite beer—of course Whale's Tale Pale Ale—his favorite food—Mexican.

"Who's his favorite superhero?" Keely teased.

"Oh, Superman, for sure."

Keely couldn't help it. She burst out laughing.

Isabelle went quiet. "You're making fun of me, aren't you? I don't even care! I *love* that I know Tommy chooses Superman. I love knowing everything about him! I love knowing what kind of toilet paper—"

"Stop right there. I refuse to listen to a Smith College student, a woman attending the same college Sylvia Plath attended, talk about her boyfriend's toilet paper."

"Sorry. I'm *sorry*. It's just that I've been dying to share this with you, Keely. I didn't want to email or text you about it. It's too important for that. It's too huge! And you're always working or in class, so it's hard to talk to you."

"It's fine. I'm truly happy for you, Isabelle. I hope this lasts."

"Why wouldn't it last? Don't you think Tommy can be faithful—"

"Whoa! I never said that. I meant I hope you can have everything you want without any problems. I mean, like, you can't write while you're spending all your free time with Tommy."

"I know. You're right. I know I'm on a high right now. I know this mad crazy rapture phase can't last, but I'm sure our love will last. And I'm not stressing about writing now. I mean, my classes are really challenging. I have to work hard to keep up. Everyone is so much smarter than I am. So my life is basically two parts: school and Tommy." Isabelle stopped to catch her breath.

"Very cool, Isabelle. Seriously."

"So what about you? Have you met anyone special?"

"Guys are everywhere." Keely shrugged. "I'm not in the mood for dating, really."

"Because you're in love with Sebastian?"

Keely dropped her eyes to her coffee cup. "I never told you I was in love with Sebastian."

"You never had to. I *am* your best friend."

"And Sebastian's sister."

"What, you think Sebastian and I sit around talking about love and *feelings*? I've never told him how you feel about him."

"*I've* never told *you* how I feel about him!" Keely snapped.

"I know. But I've got eyes. The way you stare at him says it all."

"Well, that's embarrassing."

"Stop it. I don't mean everyone understands you. I get it because I'm your best friend. And I wish you would talk to me about it, about Sebastian. I've seen the way he looks at you, too, you know."

Keely's heart ballooned with hope. "How does he look at me?"

"Not like you look at him. He's a guy. Plus, he's older. But his eyes go all soft when he sees you. When he sees you, he smiles."

Keely met Isabelle's eyes. "He sent me an email when he first started college. He told me I'm beautiful."

"Wow."

"I emailed him back. But his next emails were short, like duty messages."

"It was his first year in college. A lot of people get overwhelmed during their first year."

Keely shook her head. "It wasn't college. It was women. It was Ebba."

"I know. She's so gorgeous. Tall, blond, with those kind of *slivers* of ice blue eyes. And she's kind of mysterious."

Keely held her hand up like a "stop" sign again. "That's enough."

"I'm sorry, Keely. But for what it's worth, I don't think it will last."

"Isabelle! It's lasted two years. He's going to Sweden for Christmas. He's bringing Ebba home for Thanksgiving! I think it's pretty serious."

"Oh, who cares, it's only *Sebastian*. You're way too cool for Sebastian."

Keely allowed herself a sardonic grin. "It seems I'm way too cool for anyone."

"You were smart not to have sex with anyone in high school," Isabelle said. "Just think, if you hadn't been so obsessed with your grades, you couldn't have gotten the scholarship. If you'd been all dreamy about some guy, you might not have even applied to college."

"I know," Keely agreed. "You're right."

"You'll fall in love when you're here," Isabelle predicted. "Just wait and see."

Keely fell in love, but not with a guy.

During her sophomore year at UMass, Keely took creative writing classes from Uma Fairside, who looked like a pre-Raphaelite heroine with her long, wavy red hair and her floaty, loose dresses. Uma Fairside had had two novels published to fine literary acceptance. She was encouraging to Keely, but she was encouraging to all her students.

The day before the spring semester ended, Uma handed Keely a short story she'd carefully critiqued. Clipped to it was a brief note on her teacher's pale blush cards.

See me after class.

Keely's heart jumped a bit, but she reminded herself to stay cool. So many students at this college were writing brilliant books. Keely wouldn't allow herself to hope for anything.

But by the time class was over and Keely gathered her notebooks and approached the front of the classroom, her heart was racing.

Today Uma wore what looked like a light summer quilt with holes in it for her neck and arms. It rippled fluidly as Uma came around her desk and smiled at Keely.

"Keely. I like your fiction. I believe you are the real thing. A writer."

"Oh." Keely went numb all over with shock.

"I have an idea."

"Okay . . ."

"Have you heard of the Berkshire Writers' Colony?"

"Yes . . ."

"They have a three-year MFA program connected to UMass Amherst. Students receive intensive one-on-one tutorials on their writing—plays, poetry, novels, whatever. Of all my students, you show the most promise by far. I advise you to apply."

Keely felt her entire body flush with heat. "Oh. Well—thank

you." When Uma didn't say anything else, Keely took a deep breath and added, "The thing is, I don't have the money for grad school."

Uma shrugged. "That's not unusual. If you really want to go, you could get a full fellowship. I would give you a reference." She smiled. "And they like me there."

Keely flushed again. "That's—that's wonderful."

"Good. So here's what you should be doing now. Get *The Norton Anthology of Short Fiction*. You don't have to buy it, get it from the library. For the next two years, polish up some short stories. Send them out everywhere. I can give you a list of literary magazines. That should be your focus from now until senior year when you'll apply to the workshop. You need to get a couple of short stories published, something to prove other people have read your stuff and like it."

Keely nodded her head eagerly. "I'll do that."

"Sign up for this course for both semesters next year. I want to work with you."

"I will. I'll do it all. I'm so honored." Keely's voice trembled with emotion. "Thank you."

Was this when Keely broke her bond with Isabelle?

She knew Isabelle wanted to be a published writer, too, but Keely didn't tell her about the workshop.

Keely didn't allow herself to feel guilty. That summer, Isabelle went with her parents to British Columbia. If Isabelle wanted to write, she certainly had time to, Keely reasoned. The little gnat of envy that had irritated her for years whenever she compared her hardworking life to Isabelle's easy one began to hum in her heart. Keely mentally swatted it away. Keely had *this*, the chance to be a real writer.

Sebastian graduated from Amherst and went to live in Sweden with Ebba.

Keely cleaned houses. She sang while she cleaned. She awoke

at five in the morning, drank huge cups of coffee, and wrote for two hours before she started work.

Tommy was on the island, too. Sometimes she ran into him at beach parties on the weekends. They smiled, talked about the latest news from Isabelle, and politely wandered off to talk with someone else.

Keely wrote and wrote. She sent short stories off to magazines and every kind of fiction website. Often she received only a brief, polite refusal. One or two editors took the time to write a personal note, telling her to keep writing.

At the end of August, *storyshot* accepted one of her stories.

That October, Isabelle and Keely managed to steal an hour from classes to meet for coffee. Isabelle seemed more mature to Keely, which only made sense. They were juniors. Twenty-one years old. They had island friends who had two children by now.

As soon as they found a table in the corner, they sat, each of them with a coffee, and one plate between them with a gigantic cinnamon roll to split.

"How are you?" Keely asked.

"I'm mad at you."

"What have I done now?" Keely demanded.

"You had a story published in *storyshot* and you didn't tell me."

"I didn't think you'd care. You've been traveling everywhere."

"I *do* care! *Of course* I care. And P.S., I'm jealous!" Isabelle pouted.

Keely grinned. She knew Isabelle was only half-kidding. "You could have been writing last summer, too."

Isabelle sank her chin in her hand. "I know. I've got to stop taking these summer trips with my parents. It's not fun anymore."

"Poor you."

Isabelle shook it off. "We're juniors now!" Isabelle changed the subject. "So did Tommy cheat on me this summer?"

"How would I know? I scarcely saw him."

"But you would have heard rumors."

Keely put a hand on her textbook and her right hand in the air, shoulder height. "I swear I heard nothing about Tommy being unfaithful." She laughed. "Izzy, you know I would have killed him for you if I'd heard something like that."

Isabelle got a faraway look in her eye. "We're getting so old. I've been thinking I should break up with Tommy so he can date other women. That way when we graduate and move back to the island, he won't be bored with me and he'll want to marry me."

"Whoa. Twisted logic! Why would you even consider something like that?"

"Because I know Tommy. He likes to play around. He likes seducing women." Isabelle gave a frank, exasperated look at Keely. "I'm not stupid, Keely. I know what Tommy's like."

"And you want to marry him anyway?"

"Of course I do."

"You believe he'll be faithful when you're married?"

"Actually, yes. I think he'll have used up all his bad boy juju."

Keely sighed and leaned back in her chair. "What about you? What about your writing? Do you still even want to be a writer?"

"Of course I do! But I know it can't happen instantaneously. I know I've got work to do. I'm not looking for a limo and fame. Weren't we silly when we were little girls? We knew nothing. But I do want to write. I'm making notes for a novel."

"Gosh, when do you have time? You've got school and Tommy."

"I'm not saying I'm writing. I'm saying I'm keeping notes. And I truly am jealous that you're getting a short story published. But in just one minute, you'll be jealous of me."

Keely snorted. "Isabelle, I'm always jealous of you."

Isabelle ignored that. Leaning forward, she said, "I'm signed up for a class with Eleanor Shreves."

"Eleanor Shreves?" Keely forced a smile, but her heart was sinking into her shoes. Eleanor Shreves was an important writer. She'd published at least six novels, and one of them was being made into a movie. If Keely even *saw* Eleanor Shreves, she would fall to her knees in awe. "How . . . ?"

"She's agreed to teach a couple of writing classes this year. If we were interested, we had to submit a short story. She chose fifteen students—and I was one!"

"Oh, Isabelle, how wonderful! I am so jealous!"

"Good!," Isabelle said, laughing.

In March, right when the weather flirted with spring, Keely sat in her room at the dorm, hunched over her laptop, when her cell buzzed, interrupting her thoughts.

It was her mother. "Hi, Mom!"

"Keely, sweetheart, I need you to come home." Her voice broke. "Something's happened." Her mother sounded shaky, unlike her usual take-charge self.

"What's going on?"

"Keely, I hate to tell you this on the phone, but . . ." Her mother's voice choked. "Keely, your father died."

"What?"

"I'm sorry, Keely. Your father . . ." Eloise choked on the words. "Your father died."

For a moment Keely's mind couldn't decipher her mother's words, but Keely's heart thumped *hard*. Her hands went numb. She dropped the phone.

Her mother's voice floated up from the floor.

"Wait, Mom, wait!" She bent over, scrabbling with her hands to pick up the phone.

"Keely?"

"Mom? Did you say that Daddy *died*?" That couldn't be right. Her father couldn't be dead. He was young. Wasn't he? How old was he? She couldn't remember. Guilt fell over her like a gray veil, blanking out the world around her. She hadn't emailed him as much as she meant to—she was so busy, and he was always there, reliable, on the island. Maybe she could—

"He had a heart attack."

"But you're a nurse! Didn't you—"

"Of course I tried to save him. I gave him CPR, I did my best to revive him, and I called the ambulance and they came right away."

Her mother continued to speak. Keely crumpled onto her chair, shaking. She couldn't get her breath.

"Keely, honey, are you okay?"

"How can I be? I don't believe this. Oh, Mom. Are *you* all right?"

"I don't know . . . I can't think . . ." Her mother broke into wrenching sobs.

Her mother's anguish made it real. Keely's father had died. Keely wanted to throw back her head and howl with grief, with anger at the universe. But she knew her father would want her to be in control, to take care of her mother who had lost her husband, her companion, the love of her life. Keely couldn't turn back time, but she could pull herself together and be there for her mother.

"When did this happen?"

"This morning. I'm still at the hospital."

"Do you have someone with you?"

Keely's mother laughed weakly. "Keely, I'm a nurse here. I have all my colleagues here."

"But Brenda." Brenda, Eloise's best friend, lived on a small farm with her husband and their always-changing menagerie of rescued animals. "Can you call Brenda and have her help you?"

"Yes. I can do that. I will. But I need you to come home."

"Of course, Mom. I'll leave right now. I'll be able to catch the seven o'clock fast ferry. If not that, the slow boat at eight."

"Good. Let me know. I'll meet you there."

"Mom? Mom, I love you."

"I know, sweetheart."

Keely threw clothes in her duffel bag, grabbed her clutch and her backpack, and scribbled a note to her roommate. She didn't say when she was coming back. She didn't know.

As she drove, she knew she had to keep it together. She had to hold in her tears, she had to pay attention to the traffic, the exit signs, the stoplights. But her heart was swollen, almost bursting. She put on the radio, tuned in to heavy metal, and screamed along with the earsplitting, furious music. By the time she reached the ferry, her throat was sore.

Brenda was with Eloise to meet Keely's boat.

"Keely," Eloise cried, throwing her arms around Keely and hugging her close.

"It's okay, Mom," Keely said, knowing that nothing was okay right now.

They stood together, weeping, devastated, holding each other up. After a few moments, Keely gently pushed her mother away. "Let's go home." Keely tucked her arm into her mother's arm and steered her toward Brenda's car.

As soon as they were in the house, Brenda said, "I'll leave you two alone. Call me tomorrow if you need anything."

Brenda looked exhausted, Keely thought, and her mother seemed to have aged decades in a day.

"Sit down, Mom. I'm going to make us something to drink."

She found a bottle of pinot noir in the kitchen and poured them both a healthy serving.

"Take your shoes off, Mom. You look shattered. I'll sit here, put your feet on my lap. Now tell me. Tell me about Dad."

Needing to talk, her mother let it all spill out. "We were having breakfast. You know how George loves his bacon and eggs. He was eating, and he clutched his chest, and oh, Keely, he made an agonizing noise. I said, 'Oh, George, have you got indigestion again?' But I knew he didn't have indigestion. I knew he was having a heart attack. So I tried to get an aspirin down him, but everything happened too quickly. He couldn't swallow. He didn't say anything. He just made that horrible noise and then he slumped over." Eloise began to weep.

"Oh, poor Daddy." Sorrow wrenched Keely's heart.

"Keely, he fell out of his chair. Onto the floor. I tried to break his fall. I cushioned his head with my arms. And when he was on the floor, I called 911, and then I tried CPR. I talked to him. I told him I loved him over and over until the ambulance came."

"Oh, Mom, how terrible for you. How scary."

"It was. It *was* scary." Her mother put a handkerchief to her mouth to hold back sobs.

Keely waited for her mother to calm herself and listened as Eloise spoke about the rest of the day. The hospital room where her husband had a weak pulse, and then, in spite of the physician's efforts, no pulse. Dr. Lewis pronouncing George dead. The nurses hugging Eloise, the long minutes when they left Eloise alone in the room with her dead husband, how Eloise had talked to him and wept. Kind people bringing her tea. Someone giving her the phone, telling her to call Keely.

Eloise looked up at Keely, suddenly wide-eyed. "You'll stay with me awhile, won't you?"

"Of course, Mom. Of course." Keely looked around the room. "Daddy's chair!" she cried, catching sight of his slightly worn, beloved recliner. It had pockets on the side. His book of crossword puzzles and his notebook of game statistics were there, quietly waiting for him. It was like a relic from when the world was good.

"I know, Keely. He's everywhere." Her mother let out a wail like nothing Keely had ever heard before. "Everywhere and nowhere."

"Did the doctor give you anything to help you sleep?" Keely asked.

Her mother waved an arm toward the dining room table. "Yes. Ambien. You should take one, too." Eloise stared at Keely, a desperate look in her eye. "I want to sleep. I need to sleep. I need to be with my darling George."

A frisson of fear streaked through Keely's emotions. "Mom, you won't take too many pills, will you?"

Eloise swung her feet onto the floor. "No, darling. I'll take only two at the most."

They stumbled around the house like hunched, ancient crones, bent double with grief. Keely watched carefully as her mother took her pills. She tucked her mother in bed. She took two pills herself, knowing nothing could bring her the relief of sleep.

But she slept. When she woke in the morning, her grief was not shrill, not the urgent sorrow that felt like fear. It was slower. Heavier. It weighed her down.

Over the next few days, Keely helped her mother as they went through the necessary rituals of death. Rick Roberts still had his funeral home, and he was able to guide Eloise through the process of sending the body away to be cremated. Reverend Lisa from the Congregational Church held a brief service as Keely's father's ashes were interred in a handsome urn in a cemetery plot. Dr. Wayland had provided Eloise and Keely with a few low doses of Valium to help keep them calm during the funeral.

The day was dreary. The clouded sky was spitting snow and the wind was blustering. Keely kept her arm linked through her mother's during the service and at the cemetery.

"I've paid for the plot next to him," Eloise murmured to Keely as they stood by the open grave. "I bought an urn just like your father's, so when the time comes, you can put me next to him."

"Okay, but not for a long time," Keely assured her mother.

A black limo drove Keely and her mother to the reception at their home. Brenda was in the dining room, setting out the small sandwiches and finger foods. Brenda's daughter Sharon was in the corner, behind a table holding a choice of liquor and soft drinks. Keely dealt with her coat and her mother's, swiftly checked to see that their small house was as neat as it could be, then unlocked the front door for the friends.

Dozens of people—even their mailman, even the woman who

sold tickets at the ferry—came into the house, quietly at first, to
offer their condolences, and to tell Eloise how wonderful her husband had been. They hugged Eloise and Keely and went off to the
living room and dining room, replaced by other people. Some part
of Keely's heart took pleasure in the sight of so many people showing up. Nantucket families clustered near. So many doctors and
nurses arrived that Brenda leaned over to Eloise and whispered,
"Good grief, who's running the hospital?" Her words brought a
small smile to Eloise's face, and Keely was grateful.

The Maxwells were there, too. Mr. and Mrs. Maxwell, not Sebastian, of course. He was in Sweden. Isabelle and Tommy had
intended to come, but a blizzard hit that area of the state, making
driving impossible. Isabelle had called and cried with Keely. It was
fine, really, that she wasn't there. Keely was numb, dumb with
grief.

She was grateful that the Maxwells came, but secretly she resented how chic Donna Maxwell looked in her black silk dress,
her blond hair perfectly styled to show the tastefully small cluster
of diamonds in her earlobes. She seemed arrogant, malicious,
flaunting her beauty in front of Keely and Eloise, who were in
mourning.

"Call me if there's anything we can do," Al Maxwell told Eloise, his deep voice booming through the room.

"I will. Thank you." Eloise's voice was hoarse.

Donna Maxwell put her hands on Keely's shoulders and
brushed her cheek with an air kiss, leaving behind a cloud of Joy
perfume.

Keely said "thank you" for the seven hundredth time and closed
the front door on the back of the last person to leave.

"Well, that was exhausting," she said to her mother.

"So many people attended," Eloise said. "George would have
been so proud."

"Maybe he is proud, Mom. Maybe he's somewhere up there looking down at us."

"That's a lovely thought, dear."

Eloise had been restrained and gracious during the reception. Now she sagged with exhaustion.

"Here," Keely said, leading her mother to "her" recliner, which only a few days ago had been "his" recliner. "Did you get anything to eat? Anything substantial?"

"I'm not hungry, dear."

Keely turned the television to the Hallmark Channel. "I'm getting us both some of Brenda's casserole."

Keely joined her mother in front of the television with plates of comfort food. Until midnight, they watched beautiful people fall in love in beautiful places. Unreal, but soothing.

"Keely, are you ready?"

"In a minute."

Isabelle's father had been Keely's father's lawyer, although Keely had never known that until her mother told her they had an appointment with Mr. Maxwell for the reading of the will. Keely found herself stalling, panicking, searching for an earring that matched the pair she wanted to wear, an opal earring, the most expensive jewelry she possessed. Why it mattered to her so much she didn't know—but of course she did know.

All her life she had been privy to the secrets of Isabelle's life and house and family. And Isabelle had known about hers. Where the cookie sheet was stored, and the clean towels, and for that matter, the tampons. The mildly pornographic magazines Sebastian had hidden under his mattress on the side of his bed next to the wall. Donna Maxwell's birth control pills were in the drawer of her bedside table, beneath a box of allergy tablets.

And Isabelle knew the same things about Keely's house, although not as much, since Keely had no sibling. She knew the left back burner on the stove didn't work anymore. She knew what Keely's mother's bras looked like—formidably built for support, not seduction. Keely and Isabelle had actually tried them on when they were thirteen and Eloise was at the hospital, working— they'd nearly peed themselves laughing. And of course Isabelle knew that Keely's family didn't have as much money as hers. Keely was well aware that the Maxwells were, in her judgment, *rich*. The big house, the trips abroad, the nice cars.

But Keely never knew that Mr. Maxwell was *her father's* lawyer. When her mother told her, Keely cringed. This was embarrassing. Mr. Maxwell was so rich, and her father had been so, well, *not* rich. Besides, it was such an intrusion into Keely's family's personal life! Her father and Mr. Maxwell had never been friends. What had her father been thinking?

Well, of course, he certainly hadn't been thinking that he would die of a heart attack at sixty. He hadn't been thinking that having Aloysius Maxwell for a lawyer might embarrass Keely.

Keely dragged herself from the sanctuary of the bathroom. "I'm ready. Want me to drive?"

"Please," Eloise said, her voice still hoarse from crying.

Mr. Maxwell's office was on the second floor of a handsome white building on Centre Street. Keely found a parking spot on India Street and walked with her mother to the office. A heat wave had melted the March snow and brought sunshine to the island. People window-shopped, children laughed, dogs barked. The world seemed like a bright, happy, reasonable place.

Eloise and Keely went up the stairs and into the law office of Maxwell and Dunstan.

Courtney Paget, ten years older than Keely, sat behind the receptionist's desk. She smiled professionally and ushered them into Mr. Maxwell's private domain. Mr. Maxwell came around from behind his enormous mahogany partner's desk, and briefly embraced them both.

"Eloise, Keely. This is such a sad time for all of us."

Eloise nodded agreement.

"Please sit." He indicated the handsome leather chairs in front of his desk.

"Would you like coffee or tea?" Courtney asked.

Eloise shook her head.

"No, thanks, Courtney," Keely said, managing a polite smile.

Courtney left the room, gently pulling the door shut after her.

Mr. Maxwell wore a handsome pin-striped suit. A striped tie. He was older than her father had been, but looked ten years younger.

Mr. Maxwell leaned over the table to hand a folder to Eloise. "You both know how sorry I am that we've lost George. It's a tragedy. He was so young. Too young to go."

"Thank you," Eloise whispered.

Keely could tell her mother was gripping the folder with all her might, as if that was the only thing keeping her from wailing.

"But now we have to speak about estate matters. Are you ready to do this, Eloise?"

Her mother cleared her throat before saying, "Yes."

"Thank you. I won't waste time. Eloise, you asked me to review your financial statements, and I have. George has willed his entire estate to you. Unfortunately, when George died, his finances were not as healthy as one might have wished."

Eloise asked, "What does that mean?"

Mr. Maxwell sighed. "To be blunt, George had no savings. He wasn't able to leave you any money. He had no life insurance. You understand you had to borrow against the mortgage on the house to pay for the cremation expenses. You have a good job at the hospital, Eloise. You're senior staff. But after studying your finances, I have to advise you that alone, without George's income, you won't be able to make the mortgage payments. Or pay the homeowners' insurance or real estate taxes." He handed Eloise a sheet of numbers.

Eloise stared at the pages blindly. "Do I have to sell the house?"

Mr. Maxwell steepled his fingers. "If you sold it, you could only remain on the island if you bought a less expensive, which means much smaller, place. You know how real estate prices have changed in the past few years. Houses cost much more now than they used to."

Keely cut in. "So Mom would get a good amount of money if she sold."

Mr. Maxwell nodded. "True, Keely. You're absolutely right. But you need to think about where your mother could find another suitable home. Also, your father left a substantial debt to the mortgage. There wouldn't be much profit to put toward a down payment somewhere new."

Keely thought quickly. "We could leave the island. Mom, you could have a house as nice as ours for much less money. And you're a nurse, you can get a job anywhere."

Her mother spoke, her voice cracking. "I don't want to leave the island. I was born here. You were born here. My friends are here. My work is here."

Mr. Maxwell didn't speak, but he focused his attention on Keely, waiting for her to understand what she had to do. She looked at Mr. Maxwell, who had treated her as one of his own for so many years, or if not as one of his own, definitely the favorite of all his children's friends. He'd carried her on his shoulders. He'd pulled up a chair for her at their dining room table. He'd invited her out to dinner with the rest of the family for his daughter's birthday. They had a past between them, and wasn't that some kind of bridge?

"Maybe, a loan . . ." Keely began. She didn't know how exactly to say the words. "If we could have a loan, and of course we'd pay back the interest . . ."

Mr. Maxwell's mouth turned down, as if she'd disappointed him.

"Keely, no bank would consider giving you or your mother a loan. You have no collateral."

Keely straightened her shoulders and raised her chin. "I wasn't thinking of a bank. I was thinking of a personal loan."

His face was stone. "I suggest you forget that idea. Loaning money to friends only leads to trouble. I always advise against it."

How can you do this? Keely wanted to cry. *How can you be so cold?*

"Keely." Quietly, her mother reached over and held her hand.

"If you had an income," Mr. Maxwell continued, his tone neutral and formal, "you could help your mother keep the house."

Keely stared at Isabelle's father. More than anything, she wanted to help her mother. She also wanted to retain some semblance of dignity.

Keely turned toward her mother. "I'll move back here and work. I'm sure I can help with the finances."

Her mother gave Keely a heartbroken, heartbreaking look. Her sweet mother, so strong and caring for her patients, was broken now.

Mr. Maxwell spoke gently. "It is an option, Keely."

Desperately, Keely said, "But maybe you could change from a fifteen-year mortgage to a thirty-year mortgage and then the payments wouldn't be so high every month."

Eloise managed a weak smile. "What a smart girl you are, Keely. Your father and I used to wonder where on earth you got all your brains. Yes, you're right about that. But a few years ago we switched to a thirty-year mortgage."

So, Keely thought, there was no other way. She forced herself to sound confident. "I'll come just for a year. While you recover from losing Dad—not that you'll ever really recover, I don't mean that—I'll live with you and work two jobs and help pay the mortgage. Right, Mom?"

"Oh, Keely." Her mother's face was pinched with regret.

Mr. Maxwell spoke up. "Good for you, Keely. You're young, energetic. And of course, you could finish your last years of college later. Maybe take some courses online." A kind of satisfaction ran through his words.

Keely stared at Mr. Maxwell, searching his face for a gleam of malice. Had Keely ever believed that Mr. Maxwell really cared for her, about her, because she was Isabelle's best friend, because they did everything together? *You wouldn't ask Isabelle to leave college,* Keely wanted to hiss, but of course that was irrelevant. It was demeaning, humiliating, to sit here like this with a man she'd unintentionally thought of as, maybe not a father figure, but close to that, an adult who saw that Keely was *special,* set apart from the crowd, because Keely was his daughter's best friend.

But really, it didn't matter what Mr. Maxwell thought. What mattered was her mother, who had lost her husband and now had to face the world alone. She studied her mother, who had dropped at least five pounds in the past few days, and looked drawn and withered and frail. Eloise had never been frail. But these were exceptional circumstances, Keely realized. She had to help her mother.

Keely reached over and took her mother's hand. "Mom, let's do it. I mean, I'll do it. We can figure out our finances, and how much we need to meet the mortgage and living expenses. I always make a pile babysitting and house cleaning. We'll be very Swiss Family Robinson and live on twigs and snails and pay off some of that mortgage."

Eloise looked at Keely. "Oh, darling. You are such a wonderful daughter."

"You are, Keely," Mr. Maxwell agreed. "You should be very proud of yourself."

"Thank you," Keely said. But she didn't feel proud. She felt destroyed.

chapter
five

"But that can't be right!" Isabelle cried.

Cell phone against her ear, Keely lay on her bed in her UMass dorm—for the last time. She was taking a break from packing up, preparing to leave the university and return to the island.

"Lots of people drop out for lots of reasons," Keely replied. Her best friend's shock and indignation pleased her. It was how Keely felt, and good Lord, it helped to have someone on her side.

"I'll talk to Dad," Isabelle declared, righteousness strong in her voice. "He'll figure something out."

At that, Keely's heart sank. With those words, Keely knew she really was all alone, and her gratitude toward Isabelle for sharing her outrage vanished. What a *child* Isabelle was, thinking her father would fix everything. How fortunate Isabelle was, to have everything, always, and to be able to count on that.

"Your father knows. He agrees that I should drop out." Keely heard the bitter triumph in her voice, as if she, Keely, had somehow won a point. When really, she was losing everything.

For a long moment, Isabelle was silent. "Keely, listen. Wait. I'm too upset to think straight. We could loan you money. Let me ask Dad—"

"Absolutely not!"

"But—"

"I don't need his charity. He's already said there's nothing else to do."

"Keely, I can't wrap my head around this. I'm coming over to see you."

"Really, don't bother. I'm sure you have class, and I'm packing."

Another long silence. Now Isabelle's voice was meek. "I do have my seminar on the modern novel in fifteen minutes . . ."

"Go. Learn stuff. Be smart. Thanks for wanting to try, Isabelle. I'll be okay."

"Will you really?"

"Of course."

Keely held back tears as she tossed a duffel bag loaded with books into the backseat of her Honda Civic.

She had done it. She had signed the official documents, talked with the registrar, spoken to the professors she liked—some TAs wouldn't know her or care.

She had forfeited her chance for an education, for more classes on the modern novel or creative writing or even horrible trigonometry.

She had most likely forfeited her chance to achieve her most precious goal.

A couple of dorm friends had helped her carry her baggage to her car. They had hugged her and said they'd keep in touch—they wouldn't—and rushed off to class.

Now she was alone. Now she no longer belonged here. She'd left nothing of herself here, except her dreams.

"Enough!" she told herself, speaking out loud. Students on the sidewalk didn't bother to glance at her. People talked to themselves all the time here.

Or maybe she was already invisible.

She opened her car door and sank down into the driver's seat.

She reached into her bag for her keys and her fingers brushed paper. She discovered the envelope in her mail this morning, but couldn't find a moment alone to read the letter. And she needed to be alone to read this.

No one wrote real letters anymore, but this letter was real. It was on thin blue paper, with foreign stamps. Sweden. She knew it was from Sebastian, and she had restrained herself from opening it until this very minute. Even now, she only held it, touched her name written in his handwriting, brought it to her lips, inhaling any slight fragrance of Sebastian's hands.

Dear Keely,

I'm writing to say how sorry I am about your father. He was such a good guy. He didn't deserve to leave this planet so soon.

I'm also writing to say—and I know this is clumsy and probably inappropriate in a letter of condolence—I read your short story in the Amherst Review. *I thought it was clever and compelling. I liked the way you made the homeless man seem so real.*

I guess I'm writing this because I hope you know that even now when your father is not here on earth to cheer you on, I am. I believe in your writing, Keely.

With love,

Sebastian

Keely read it again. Folding it with great care, she slipped it inside her wallet, in a private zipper compartment. She would tell no one, it was her most important secret, her most valuable treasure. It was a raft in the dark ocean of her life . . . *Sebastian believed in her writing.*

She put the key in the ignition and started her trusty, rusty old car. She steered over the curving campus roads, diligently braking at every passenger crossing. She left the vast campus of the uni-

versity and drove along curving pastoral roads toward the Mass
Pike.

She cried while she drove. She howled. She missed her father.
She was like a little girl, wanting to see her daddy. She sobbed so
hard she frightened herself. She forced herself to stop at a Dunkin'
Donuts to buy juice and a glazed stick.

When she paid the clerk, she said, "I'm going to Nantucket. We
don't have any Dunkin' Donuts there."

The clerk's eyes widened in astonishment. "No Dunkin' Donuts? Well, that's just tragic."

"I know," Keely agreed. Tears ran down her cheeks and she
didn't care. She didn't care what anyone on the mainland thought
of her. She got into her car and headed off, drinking the juice and
eating the sugary stick. The sweetness soothed her.

It was all so familiar. She'd done it a hundred times before. Driving to Hyannis, getting in line for the car ferry, crossing Nantucket Sound, which on this spring day was choppy with waves.
This time, however, she didn't go up to the passenger decks to buy
a cup of chowder or a beer. She remained in her car down in the
hold with the other cars and trucks. She huddled in the driver's
seat, her legs stretching over the passenger seat. She didn't want
to run into anyone she knew. She didn't want her island acquain-
tances to hug her with false or even real sympathy. The car ferry
docked in Nantucket at ten-fifteen. Keely started her car and followed the line of Stop & Shop trucks, contractors' trucks, and
loaded-down Jeeps rumbling down the ramp and onto the land.
She knew the way to her house without thinking. For the first
time in her life, she felt no happiness at returning to the island.

The porch light gleamed brightly. Her mother opened the front
door the moment Keely pulled into the drive. During the few
days that Keely was away, withdrawing from classes and packing,
Eloise had lost even more weight. As her mother folded her in her

arms, telling Keely how glad she was to have her back, Keely knew she was doing the right thing.

Keely woke at five every morning. She made coffee, took it to her room, and sat down to write. She was determined not to give up her dream.

At seven, she left to join the Clean Sweep gang. It was almost spring, almost time for the earliest of the summer residents to return, and Jennifer Gonzalas needed help opening houses, freshening them for their owners. Because she'd written, Keely was happy during the days when she mopped floors and scrubbed sinks. Maybe writing was her elixir.

Gradually, she began to appreciate being on the island again. Many of the homes she cleaned had million-dollar views of the sweeping blue ocean or the rolling moors. Sometimes in the evening, she drove out to the beaches and sat cross-legged in the sand, watching the light fade and the ocean reflect the change. Blue to lavender to silver to slate. Sometimes there was a heavy fog and she would hear the haunting call of the foghorn.

After a while, she had the time and energy to get together with her high school friends. They met for dinner at the Brotherhood, luxuriating over their curly fries and red wine, their current hit of gossip. Janine, Theresa, the old gang, didn't mind if something made Keely cry, missing her father. They waited patiently. They patted her back. They hugged her. She was grateful. Sunday afternoons they went to the beach at Surfside, and although the water was still too cold for swimming, they waded in it, they kicked at the frothy waves curling up to meet them.

Isabelle emailed and texted often, usually going on in wild poetic paragraphs about how much she loved Tommy. He was so different from her boring family! He was teaching Isabelle how to roller-skate! On weekends, they went hiking up Mount Tom or Mount Greylock. He didn't live in his head, he lived in the present, he was like a yogi who never took yoga! It was no surprise, Isabelle said, that his grades were so abysmal. Some people weren't meant for the boredom of college classes.

June hit, and the summer deepened. Isabelle went with her parents to visit Sebastian, who was still living in Sweden with his girlfriend, Ebba. For most of the rest of the summer, the Maxwells toured Scandinavia and the countries bordering the Baltic.

By the Fourth of July, no one had any free time or energy for meeting for dinner or the beach. Keely took every babysitting job she could get. The summer people were glad to go out to the fabulously glamorous galas, and they showed it.

One night Keely returned home from babysitting with a wad of five hundred dollars in her hand. She entered her house to find Eloise in her robe, watching television and weeping.

"Oh, darling, give me five more minutes. This movie is almost over."

"Are you okay, Mom?"

"I am, darling. It's just so wonderful to watch a happy ending."

After the movie ended, Keely said, "I have something happy for you." She handed her mother a big fat check. "This should help with the mortgage."

Eloise's eyes went wide. "So much! Are you keeping anything for yourself?"

Enough to buy paper and toner for my printer, Keely thought. "I'm good."

"Oh, darling," Eloise said, rising to hug her daughter. "You certainly *are* good."

After Labor Day, many of the summer people returned home and the island population calmed down. September was always a bonus month for the islanders. The sun was bright, the water was warm, and they had free time to enjoy their island. Keely had just come from helping Jennifer close a house. In her white T-shirt and black shorts and sneakers—Clean Sweep's uniform—she raced into the grocery store to buy some supplies for dinner. She headed down the produce aisle, scrutinizing the berries.

"Keely, is that really you?"

Keely looked up to see Donna Maxwell standing with a small basket over her arm and a clearly smug expression on her face.

"Hello, Mrs. Maxwell," Keely said politely.

"I didn't believe it when Isabelle told me you dropped out of school in your *junior year*, such a brilliant girl like you, what a *shame*. And you're cleaning houses now?"

Keely could hardly deny it with the logo of Clean Sweep and a cartoon broom across the front of her T-shirt.

Keely would have bet her two front teeth that Mr. Maxwell had told his wife about Keely's mother's financial problems. Still, what else could she say?

"Well, you know my father died. I came home to help my mother."

Mrs. Maxwell looked satisfied, almost licking her lips like the cat who'd just eaten a canary. "What a wonderful daughter you are. Still, it's a shame you had to give up college and your dream of writing."

Offended by the patronizing tone in Mrs. Maxwell's voice, Keely said, "Don't worry, Mrs. Maxwell, I'll never give up my dream of writing. In fact, I have more time to write now than I had when I was in college." She picked up a tub of blueberries and put them in her cart.

"So nice to see you," Keely lied, and pushed her cart quickly down the aisle before she could blurt out what she really felt like saying.

Her day off dawned crystal clear. Not a breath of wind. It was early October, and the ocean called to her. She forced herself to write, and halfway through an hour, she shoved back her chair, ignored the blinking light of her cursor, and pulled on a bathing suit and sneakers.

She scribbled a note to her mother. *Going out. Back soon.* She yanked on a light long-sleeved T-shirt—that did *not* say *Clean Sweep*—stuck a scalloper's hat on her head and her sunglasses over her eyes, and rushed to her car.

Sometimes the island did this, beckoned her. No, *summoned* her. Ever since she was a child, she'd had these unexpected impulses to get outside, be near the water, be with the natural world. And she'd read that sometimes taking a break from your work made you work better the next day.

Keely drove to Washington Street, surprised the kid who was just starting to set up for the day, and rented a one-person kayak. She fastened her life vest, rubbed more sunblock over her face— the sun reflected from the water burned more than sunlight from the sky. She settled in, took up her double-bladed paddle, and set off, smoothly riding away from the beach and out into the harbor.

She found her rhythm immediately. The paddle made musical splashing sounds as she dipped and raised it. The water was still and mirror-clear. Many boats were moored in the inner harbor, although the giant yachts towering at the town piers had left for the season. She wove her way around the schooners and stinkpots, heading for Coatue.

Her breathing slowed, deepened. The island was working its magic, pulling her into this singular, irreplaceable, unrepeatable day. Gulls soared overhead, occasionally dropping a scallop shell on the hard bow of a boat to crack it open, soaring down to snatch out the sweet scallop, rocketing up and away with their treasure. On both sides of the harbor, people were starting their day. They were moving blots of color in the periphery of Keely's vision. With each dip of her paddle, Keely surged forward into the blue, the pristine blue of the air around her, the sea below her, the sky above her.

She moved along, finally arriving at the long strip of beach called Coatue. Her muscles ached nicely. She wished she'd thought to bring along a bottle of water. She walked up and down the beach looking for an oyster shell. She could crack it open on a rock and drink the juice.

"Keely?"

She heard her name called twice before she snapped out of her trance and into reality.

Anchoring near her in an old Boston Whaler was a guy in board shorts and sunglasses. His boat bobbed up and down as a ferry passed on its way into the harbor, its wake making waves.

Keely stared. "Tommy?"

Tommy jumped over the side of his boat and swam to shore, rising up out of the water, the sun sequinning his skin with the drops that dripped off his shoulders.

"Hey, babe!" Tommy walked right up to Keely and hugged her so hard he lifted her off the ground.

"Tommy, put me down. What are you doing here?"

"What does it look like I'm doing?"

"You should be in school."

"Really? You really think I should be in school?" He put his hands on his hips, threw back his head, and laughed.

"Stop it, Tommy. You're not making any sense!"

Tommy was slightly manic. She'd seen him this way before, in high school. He was a guy who did not like to be caged in.

"I dropped out!" He waved his arms victoriously. "I'm done with college. Done!"

"What are you talking about? You're a senior! You're going to graduate next spring."

"I couldn't take it anymore. I couldn't stand to be in one more class. The only reason I went to college in the first place was that my father insisted I go. He wants me to join him in his accounting firm. I knew it wouldn't be the place for me. I told him. He's a stubborn SOB."

Keely smiled. "You are, too."

Tommy nodded. "I told him I saved him a year's tuition, and I know enough about accounting and spreadsheets and all that crap.

When it comes to anything on the computer, I'm way ahead of
him. I told him I'd stay on the island and work for him during the
week, but the weekends are mine."

"Isabelle didn't email me about all this."

"Isabelle doesn't really know." Tommy hung his head with pretend guilt. "I told her I was starting school late. Because of flu."

"You lied to Isabelle."

"She would fight me tooth and nail on this, Keely, you know
she would. She's just as conventional as my father. College diploma, graduation, respect, blah blah . . ."

"When are you going to tell her?"

"Maybe tonight." Tommy brightened. "Or *you* could tell her!"

Keely snorted. "Yeah, I could tell her and take the first hit of
fury, right? You're a piece of work."

Tommy grinned wickedly. "I'm a bad, bad boy."

Keely rolled her eyes, but for a moment she was caught in his
bad boy spell. He was six feet four, broad shouldered, slim-hipped.
His wet black hair stuck out all over. He hadn't shaved today. His
chest was lightly furred with black hair that narrowed into a line
down into his board shorts. He grinned down at her, as if ac-
knowledging her interest.

He said, "If you tell Isabelle today, I'll treat you to dinner at the
Languedoc tonight."

Keely grinned back. "If *you* tell Isabelle today, I'll go to dinner
with you tonight."

It was a challenge, she knew. A dare. But for her, it was also a
test. Here Tommy was, handsome, sensual, physical, and flirting
with her. So how much did he really love Isabelle? If he was so
connected to Isabelle, what was he doing standing on this beach
with both of them practically half-naked, giving her a look that
stripped off the rest of her clothes and all of her inhibitions? What
did Keely owe Isabelle? Would Keely actually choose a little romantic escapade with Tommy over her friendship with Isabelle?
Of course not.

On the other hand . . . Tommy had asked Keely to the homecoming dance years ago. Because of her friendship with Isabelle, Keely had turned him down. How many times was Keely expected to sacrifice for Isabelle?

What would Mr. and Mrs. Maxwell think if Tommy broke up with Isabelle because of Keely?

But Keely wouldn't sleep with Tommy simply to get some kind of convoluted revenge on the Maxwells.

And why was she even thinking of sleeping with Tommy when all he was doing was asking her to dinner?

Tommy stopped smiling. He dropped his bad boy façade and stood quietly, seriously, looking solemnly into Keely's eyes. "I'll call Isabelle today. I'll tell her I dropped out. I'll pick you up at your house at seven."

He didn't touch her. He didn't have to. He waded back into the crystal-clear water and swam back to his boat. After he'd motored off, Keely shoved her kayak off the beach, jumped in, and paddled back to shore. She wanted to go home and sleep. She was hungry. She was thirsty. She was scared.

Deliciously scared.

chapter
six

By the time she returned the kayak, the sun was high in the sky. Keely drove home. Her mother was at work. Keely had no emails or messages from Isabelle. She drank two glasses of Nantucket's delicious water and ate an apple. She took a long soak in a hot bubble bath. As she dried off, she admired her tan. Nantucket stayed warm, even hot, into the fall, sunlight bronzing her skin.

She positioned herself at her computer, planning to work on a short story, but her mind, her senses, were full of Tommy. She'd had totally forgettable sex twice with a cute guy her freshman year in college. Neither of those experiences had seemed extraordinary, had made her, as Hemingway said, "feel the earth move." She'd bet Tommy could cause a tsunami.

It was late afternoon when the email came from Isabelle.

Keely! Tommy's dropped out! He's on the island now, working for his father and messing around with his damned boat and he's not coming back to college ever. We had such a fight! He is an idiot! Do you think you could talk sense to him? Because if he doesn't finish senior year, I'm done with him. I'm done.

Isabelle, take a breath. Why does it matter if Tommy finishes or not? Some of the best people don't finish their degrees. Like me, ha ha. You can't break up with Tommy over this. You should at least talk to him.

You're right. You're a genius. I'm driving down today. I'll catch the seven o'clock fast ferry. I've called Tommy. He'll meet me at the boat. I'm sure I can persuade him to change his mind. Thanks! I love you!

Her words hit Keely like a blow to her stomach. She wondered whether Tommy would bother to call her to cancel their date.

Rising from her desk, Keely looked around her bedroom. Her laundry basket was full, her desk was piled with printed drafts of short stories, her windowsill was lined with rocks and shells she'd brought home from the beach, and still, somehow, the world seemed empty. She'd lost her focus. She'd lost her energy. She should be writing now. It was her day off work. She had the time. But she felt—kicked. She felt that Isabelle still, as always, had everything. She needed to get herself back on track. She needed to write.

She lay on her bed, forcing herself to read the newest short story she'd written, and after a few minutes, her mind switched gears and she was thinking critically. This story wasn't bad. Maybe it was even good. Good enough to send off to some literary reviews.

Was it good enough to use as her writing sample when she sent in her application to the Berkshire Writers' Colony? The information didn't state that the applicant had to have a college diploma. She'd had *some* college. She'd had a few stories published in literary reviews. She knew her writing was more than proficient; it was pleasurable to read.

You'll never know unless you try. Her father had told her that so many times, when teaching her to surf cast or to pilot the boat through the rough waters between Madaket and Tuckernuck. When she tried out for the princess in the sixth-grade school play—and got the role of the angel, a smaller role but with wings. When she swore she would never be able to understand chess.

Keely proofread her sample short story for the thirtieth time. She put it and her application to the colony in a manila envelope, took it to the post office, and mailed it. She returned home with a smile on her face. She'd done it. She'd tried.

Her cell buzzed. Tommy. She didn't want to talk to him. She let it go to voicemail. Immediately after, she played it. "Keely, I can't see you tonight and you know why. I'll be with Isabelle. Sorry."

She'd done it again, Keely thought. She should be proud of herself. She'd stepped away from involvement with Tommy. She was a good friend. The best friend.

After that message, Keely couldn't return to her fiction. Her mind wouldn't settle. Restless, she headed into the kitchen and made a complicated casserole that would last herself and her mother for several nights to come.

Three evenings later, as she was driving home from work, her cell buzzed. Keely parked her car in the driveway before checking it.

A message from Isabelle:

I hate him. He's an imbecile. I did everything I could to change his mind. If he really loved me, he'd stay in school. And I suppose if I really loved him, I'd love him regardless. So it's good we broke up. Thanks for trying to help. I'm back at Smith now, and I'm going to concentrate on my courses and the hell with men.

As she was stripping off her dirty shorts and T-shirt, her phone buzzed.

"Keely."

"Tommy."

"I bet Isabelle has called you."

"No, but she messaged me. It sounds like she's not happy with you."

"She's not. She told me we're done. So I think I can take you to dinner, if you'll still go with me, and I won't feel guilty and neither will you."

Her heart did a somersault. She was just about to step off a cliff and she didn't know how far down she would fall. She didn't care.

"I'm free tonight," Keely said.

He took her to Le Languedoc, one of the best restaurants on the island. He parked on Broad Street and as they walked, he reached out and took her hand. Shops were still open in the evening. People—summer people and year-rounders—still strolled the streets. Keely knew Tommy was sending a message to anyone who knew them. She guessed she was sending a message, too.

They had a table in the corner, perfect for intimate conversation. Tommy ordered a good bottle of red wine to share.

"You'll never save up money for a boat spending that kind of money for wine," Keely teased.

"Some things are more important than boats," Tommy told her.

The way he gazed into her eyes made her shiver. Defensive, she asked, "What would Isabelle think of us right now?"

He didn't sound angry or even mildly concerned. But he didn't seem to take her question lightly. "I don't care what Isabelle thinks. Let's talk about something else."

He was so intense. She couldn't speak.

Tommy said, "Okay, ask me ten things you need to know about me."

"Um, favorite food?"

"Clam chowder. The way I make it."

Keely nodded. "Favorite music?"

"Everything."

Keely smiled. "Um, birth date?"

"June tenth." Tommy took her hand and rubbed his thumb lightly over her palm.

"I can't think when you're doing that to my hand," she told him.

"Do you want me to stop?"

Keely smiled, shaking her head. "You really are terrible."

Tommy did a lazy-sleepy-sexy thing with his eyes. "I can be really good."

The waiter arrived. Keely pulled her hand away.

"So did you like college at all?" She was serious.

"It depends on what criteria you're using to judge," Tommy said.

"Criteria. Get you with your big word."

Tommy laughed. "I managed to learn a few things."

"I'll bet you did."

With a shrug, he turned serious. "I admit it. I basically coasted. My grades were awful. My dad's furious. But I didn't end up drunk in a trunk or in jail for assault, so he can't really complain."

"And women?"

Tommy smiled, his white teeth flashing. "I was with Isabelle. Mostly." He shrugged. "I thought, if I can't have fun in college, I'll never be able to have it."

"Oh, Tommy, I think you'll always have fun," Keely told him, and as she spoke, she felt very affectionate toward him, and not jealous at all of the women he'd slept with, probably a number mounting into the dozens, and *mounting* was the appropriate word.

"What about you? You dropped out in your junior year."

"Because I wanted to help my mother."

"So do you miss college?"

"More than I can say," Keely answered truthfully.

"Why?"

"I loved my studies. I made all A's, not that I'm bragging. I loved it there, walking from the dorm to a class. I was high on the atmosphere, the smell of the textbooks, the sound of a pen on paper or someone tapping away on her computer . . ." She stopped talking, took a sip of wine, and lost herself for a moment in reverie. She had to change course now, or she'd get maudlin.

"You're weird," Tommy said.

Keely shrugged. "Probably." As she ate oysters and pan roasted lobster, she steered the conversation away from anything serious. She asked Tommy about his family, his friends. His new dog. Tommy was funny, charming, magnetic. She relaxed in his spell. The buzz of the wine, the pleasure of this gorgeous, attentive male was a tonic for her wounded spirit. Her entire body flushed every time Tommy looked at her or touched her knee with his beneath the table.

When they left the restaurant, light was fading from the sky.

"Let's walk down to Easy Street," Tommy said.

"Sure."

He took her hand. His hand was so much larger than hers. Easy Street was the short street between the harbor and the Dreamland Theater. Several benches were set along the brick sidewalk so people could watch the ferries come and go. Tonight as they rounded the corner from the theater building, Keely saw that the benches were empty, and Tommy must have, too, because he said her name in a husky voice and put both hands on her waist. He moved her so that her back was against the building. He pressed himself against her.

His kiss was sweet and rough with need. It was lovely to be kissed like this.

"I want to make love to you," Tommy said, his voice warm against her cheek.

She gently pushed him away. "Not yet. It's too soon for you— you should wait, be clear about Isabelle. I don't want to rush into something and then . . . lose it."

"Keely, you know I've always wanted you. I am clear about Isabelle. She's always been second best—"

Keely blocked his mouth with her hand. "Don't you dare say

that. If you even *hint* that what you felt for Isabelle wasn't true, I'll never talk to you again. Grow up, Tommy, for God's sake! You can't honestly believe I'll be *complimented* if you call Isabelle second best." She stepped away from him. "I shouldn't have come."

Tommy folded his arms and leaned against the wall, signaling retreat. "I apologize, Keely. I didn't mean to insult Isabelle. I loved her. I did love her. Maybe I still do, always will. But I am grown up. I know what I want. I know who I want. And I can be patient."

Keely relaxed. "Good. I think we have to be patient, Tommy. I don't want to be your rebound affair." She smiled. "And I don't want to have revenge sex with you."

Tommy grinned wryly. "I've heard that revenge sex can be mighty fine."

She smiled. He reached out and took her hand. "I'll take you home. I know you have to get up early for work tomorrow."

"Tommy . . . could we be friends for a while?"

"Of course, Keely. But remember, a guy can hope."

Her mother was in the living room, reading. When she saw Keely, she put down her book.

"Did you have a nice time with Tommy?"

Keely dropped into an armchair. "Too nice a time, actually." Quickly she clarified, "No, I don't mean what you're thinking, I only mean I feel guilty, going out with him so soon after he and Isabelle broke it off."

Her mother leaned her head back against the sofa, closed her eyes, and sighed. "I knew a Tommy in high school."

"Um . . . okay."

"His name was Fred, but he was every bit as sexy as Tommy."

"Mom."

"You're twenty-two. You can tolerate the fact that I once had sexual feelings."

"Not really."

Eloise ignored her. "Honey, there's a guy like Tommy in every school. It's like a life-coaching test—can you resist the irresist-ible?"

Keely thought about that. "So you think I shouldn't go out with Tommy?"

"No, I'm not saying anything. But you need to think of Isa-belle."

"I think of her. She's the one who broke it off with Tommy, because he dropped out of college. She texted me about it. Be-sides, Isabelle and I aren't as close anymore."

"That's natural, I suppose. You're both growing up. Still, I hope you'll take it slow with Tommy. For lots of reasons."

"Don't worry. I'm not going to get all crazy like a tween. For one thing, I'm too busy." Keely yawned. "And too tired."

Keely went to dinner or a movie with Tommy once or twice a week. October was the month a guy like him lived to the max every day. He worked for his father, and whenever he could, he got out on the water. He often presented Keely and her mother with a nice piece of striped bass ready for the grill. Eloise always invited Tommy to stay, to join them for dinner, and while Tommy was out on the deck grilling the fish, Keely set the kitchen table, lis-tening to her mother humming as she stirred butter into the rice.

It was good seeing Tommy this way. They both relaxed. The atmosphere in the house changed, as if Tommy's low male voice and muscular male presence soothed the very air, as it soothed and pleased Keely and her mother.

Keely emailed Isabelle to tell her she was hanging out with Tommy now and then—interesting, she thought, how choosing the right words could make whatever it was she was up to with Tommy sound so innocent.

"Hey, Isabelle!" Keely fell back on her pillows. "I haven't heard from you in forever."

"Sorry, and sorry to call so late. Did I wake you up?"

"Nope. Just trying to drag my weary body to bed. Will I see you next week?"

"No, but listen, Keely, I've met someone! Gordon Whitehead—could there be a more terrible name? But he's handsome and smart and kind and maybe a little bit wealthy. His family has a house in the Adirondacks. And I'm going there for Thanksgiving. But they live in Greenwich. Gordy's a history guy, all about the Middle Ages, I love him but he could put me to sleep talking about mace and mead. Good name for a pub, isn't it? The Mace and Mead."

Keely laughed at her friend's exuberance. Gordon Whitehead of the Mace and Mead pub sounded perfect for Isabelle.

"What does he look like?"

"Okay, he's not really tall, kind of on the short side, but he's got broad shoulders and a massive chest, and thick auburn hair and brown eyes and he wears tortoiseshell glasses. His father manages hedge funds. My father will adore him!"

Keely hadn't heard Isabelle sound so happy for a long time. Actually, she realized as she listened to her friend babble on and on, she hadn't heard Isabelle's voice for a long time. They were both so busy, Keely working and writing—although Isabelle didn't know she was writing. No one did except her mother, who muttered vaguely supportive clichés when Keely spoke about her novel.

"I only managed two pages today!" Keely would cry, and her mother would say, "Many a mickle makes a muckle," which was an actual Scottish proverb.

Isabelle was rambling on. "I met his younger sister, Giselle, when she came to tour Smith. I like her a lot. We had dinner together, Giselle and Gordon and I, and it was the best time! His family is so *cultured*. I mean, I've traveled a little bit, but the Whiteheads have been *everywhere*."

She's traveled a little bit, Keely thought sarcastically. Isabelle, who had gone abroad every single summer of her life, thought she'd *traveled a little bit.* Keely wanted to put the phone down and weep. Well, she was tired, tired from cleaning other people's toilets and kitchen floors.

Keely had intended for days to tell Isabelle she was seeing Tommy, *often,* as a friend, but after hearing Isabelle's chorus of rapture, she was too tired to mention him.

Oh, and how would Tommy feel when he learned about the cultured Gordon?

Keely's heart stung a little bit for Tommy, who was as sexy as hell but who never would be called sophisticated.

"Are you coming home for Christmas?" Keely asked when Isabelle had to stop talking to draw breath.

"No. The family's going to New York. Rockefeller Center, Christmas lights, a new play, the usual."

The usual? Did Isabelle know how smug she sounded, how heartlessly spoiled?

"Gordon's going to meet us there on Boxing Day. He's bringing his sister down for a few days in the city. They'll stay at their father's club, the Knickerbocker."

"Boxing Day? Wow, Isabelle, that all sounds terribly posh."

"Do you know where the word *posh* comes from?"

"So sorry, m'lady, I don't."

Isabelle didn't catch the sarcasm. "When England was an empire and India belonged to it, British people had to travel to India by ocean. And it was so hot down around India, people chose their cabins by which ones got less sun during the voyage. Port side out, starboard side home. *Posh*, get it?"

"Fabulously interesting," Keely said, exhausted by her day of work, irritated by all this posh talk.

"Oh, don't be so contemptuous, Keely. We've both always loved words."

"You're right. It's true. Forgive me." She took a deep yoga breath. "I'm happy for you, Isabelle."

"I can't wait for you to meet him, but I don't know how soon that can be, because we're talking about going skiing up in Vermont during January break."

Keely listened. Said the appropriate words. When their call ended, Keely knew that she and Isabelle were worlds apart. And drifting even farther from each other. It made her very sad.

Christmas at Keely's house was casual because her mother worked two shifts. Tommy was flying out to Vegas with his buddies over Christmas break, and Keely was glad. She didn't want to be his rebound lover. She didn't know what she wanted to be, except a novelist.

This Christmas, Keely was especially happy because the Lambrechts, a wealthy family from Texas, were spending the holiday in their picture-perfect brick house on Main Street. Keely was invited to be their housekeeper, hostess, and maid, bringing the exquisite heirloom platters loaded with turkey or ham or roast beef to the table and invisibly ensuring that the party of twelve never had an empty glass of wine. In the kitchen, Cindy Starbuck was in charge, stirring the gravy, telling her assistant it was time to take the rolls from the oven, not *that* oven, the other one. Cindy and the kitchen staff wore white shirts and white aprons, but Keely was expected to look appropriately festive because she was opening doors, serving the food, and generally moving quietly among the party.

She worked for the Lambrechts all day Christmas Eve and most of Christmas Day. She was paid a wage of sixty dollars an hour, and Dr. Lambrecht added an astonishing tip.

"Oh! Thank you, Dr. Lambrecht." Keely almost curtsied.

"Thank *you*," Dr. Lambrecht said.

Keely walked down to the main street of town. It was after nine and all the shops were closed. Her mother was working at the hospital—two women were in labor. Her friends were with their families. Keely wasn't really lonely. She liked being alone. She liked this stretch of time just before the calendar tipped them over into a pristine new year. In her tote she carried seven Tupperware containers filled with delicious food Cindy had given her.

Historically, Nantucket had been populated by strong women who kept the town's economy going while their husbands were off hunting whales. Keely strolled around the tic-tac-toe streets of town, nodding with affection at Stephanie's and Vis-A-Vis and Hepburn and Zero Main and Bookworks and the Hub and of course Murray's Toggery. Year-round women worked on this island, keeping it alive and vital. Keely was proud to be part of this group.

She was also glad that in the coming winter months she wouldn't have much work to do for Clean Sweep.

Which meant she could seriously concentrate on writing her novel.

On a blustery late December morning, Keely drove out to Surfside to walk on the beach. The wind tossed the waves about like a child splashing in a tub. Huge ruffles of white towered and collapsed on the shore, hissing as they were pulled back into the sea. Keely was dressed for the wind. She wore a down jacket and a wool knit hat that fit tight to her head so the wind couldn't blow it off.

She loved being here, and wished she had come more often. The ocean was so expansive, so full of relentless, reckless energy. She felt she was breathing in that energy with every step she took. She ambled along at the edge of the waves until she knew her face was almost frozen from the cold. She turned around and began to walk back.

In the distance, coming toward her, was a man. He was tall and broad-shouldered, and his figure was familiar. Keely's heart leapt in her throat before she had even said his name.

He came closer, his blond hair mashed beneath a wool cap, his hands shoved into his jacket pockets.

When they were face-to-face, he said, "Keely."

"Sebastian."

They smiled. And for a moment, they only gazed at each other, smiling, warming one another with the affection in their eyes.

"What are you doing here? I thought you'd be in Sweden or New York with your family."

"I came home to check on a few things."

Her love for this man bloomed all over her body. It was two years since she'd seen him. He was older, more adult, still the most gorgeous thing she'd ever seen.

She felt like a flower opening to the sun.

Don't be an idiot, Keely told herself, and asked, "How's Ebba?"

"She's good. How are you?"

"Fine, thanks. I'm working for Clean Sweep and doing odd jobs, and when I have time, I'm trying to write."

They had turned and were walking side by side now, with the wind buffeting them and the ocean roaring and tumbling next to them.

"You're still serious about writing."

"I am. Writing every spare moment I can find."

"You sound like Isabelle."

"Really."

"Yeah, she's just been accepted to some writers' group out in the Berkshires. She's going to live there for two or three years and do nothing but write."

Keely's heart stopped.

"She got accepted by the Berkshire Writers' Colony?"

"That's it. That's the name." He grinned. "You two girls were always writing when you were kids. Books or stories or newspapers."

"Yes," Keely said softly, "I remember when you drew a bee for me and didn't tell anyone you'd done it."

And as she spoke, she sank to her knees by the edge of the surging waves and buried her face in her hands.

"Keely. Are you okay?"

Her words were muffled by her gloves. "Fine. I'm fine. Just . . ."

memories." Let him think she was crying because of her child-hood friendship with Isabelle. She was crying, helplessly, because Isabelle had been accepted by the writers' colony, and Keely hadn't even heard from them.

Sebastian knelt next to Keely. He wrapped his arms around her and pulled her to him. "Did you apply to the colony, too?"

Keely couldn't answer.

He held her close. "The colony isn't everything, Keely. Writing isn't everything."

But to her, it was. As her sobbing ebbed, she realized she was in Sebastian's arms, where she had always longed to be. If she turned her head, she could kiss him.

But she was in his arms because he pitied her, and before ev-erything else, he was Isabelle's brother. *Have some dignity!* she admonished herself. Keely choked back her tears. She gently pushed away from Sebastian's embrace and stood up.

"Sorry. I get emotional when I'm tired."

Sebastian rose, too. He put his hands on her shoulders and held her tight, making her face him. "Listen, Keely," he began.

Something broke in her, something carried by the force of the waves made her brave. "No, *you* listen. All my life I've wanted everything you Maxwells have. I wanted to live in your wonderful house. I wanted Isabelle to be my real sister, and I wanted *you*—" She straightened her shoulders and held back her tears. "I wanted you," she finished. She turned and walked away on the edge of the beach where the waves had made the sand hard.

"Keely," Sebastian called.

She didn't turn around.

She ran up the sand dune toward the parking lot and her car.

A thread of words spun through her mind: Ebba was fine, Isa-belle had been accepted by the colony. Sebastian was with Ebba. Isabelle had been accepted by the colony.

She drove home, still choking back tears. The house was warm when she entered. Her mother was at work. She leaned against the door and let her tears flow.

Then she noticed the mail scattered on the floor, pushed in through the mail slot.

She spotted an envelope with the Berkshire Writers' Colony as the return address.

Her heart stopped in her throat. Her tears froze.

She snatched up the envelope and tore it open.

Two pages. One, a standard "we regret to inform you" letter.

The next was a private note, handwritten, from a woman novelist Keely idolized.

Hi, Keely Green,

I'm sorry we didn't have room for you in our new group, but I wanted to tell you how very much I like the writing that you sent us. If you finish this novel, you could write to Sally Hazlitt at the Hazlitt and Hopkins Literary Agency. Tell them that I recommended you. In fact, I'm dropping a note to Sally today.

Best wishes,
Liane Harington

Keely laughed again. "Tell me."

"There's a sexy little black dress at Hepburn. I tried it on. I told them to hold it. Because it costs exactly as much as a ticket to the New Year's Eve party. You can buy it for me."

"Janine, you should run the town."

"Hang on, Keely, that might happen one day."

The ballroom was packed. Colorful helium balloons floated above the crowd. Waiters bustled about removing dishes and glasses. Dinner was over. The band was setting up. Women hurried to refresh their makeup. Men—and some women—stepped out on the deck to enjoy a cigarette. Waiters skimmed through the room setting champagne flutes on the tables.

"I'm so glad you invited me," Keely yelled at Janine.

"Me, too!" Janine yelled back.

Their gang had a round table for eight, all girlfriends of Keely, all looking smashing in bright silks and extravagant jewelry, and all of them, including Keely, with rosy cheeks from the champagne they'd already enjoyed.

Keely wore a figure-hugging sleeveless velvet dress. Janine had come over earlier that day to put Keely's brown hair up in a curly mass at the back of her head, with slender red and gold ribbons wound through here and there. With Janine at her side to egg her on, Keely layered her eyes with smoky shadow and black liner. She wore scarlet lipstick—she'd never worn such a bright color before. She felt a bit like a 1950s doxy and when she told Janine that, Janine said, "You feel like a dachshund?"

"No, no, 'doxy' means a mistress, maybe for a gangster." For a moment, Keely was pierced with longing for Isabelle, who would know exactly what a doxy was, and what books and films it had been in.

But Isabelle was with Gordon Whitehead, skiing in Vermont.

The band started with "Love Shack" and slid into "Little Red Corvette." By the time they played "Girls Just Want to Have Fun,"

chapter
seven

Keely, wrapped in sweatpants and a flannel shirt, had settled on the sofa where she could enjoy the lights of their Christmas tree while she started one of the five books her mother had given her for Christmas.

Her cell buzzed. She considered letting it go to voicemail, but with Isabelle gone, Janine was her closest friend.

"Merry Christmas! Guess what, I got you a fabulous present!"

"Merry Christmas, Janine. When do I get my present?"

"On New Year's Eve. We're going to the Nantucket Hotel party. Champagne, dinner, and a live band!"

"Thanks, Janine, but I might babysit New Year's Eve."

"That is not allowed. I don't care how much money you'll make. If you keep working and hiding away in your house, you'll turn into one of those eccentric old women with facial hair who hoards cat food!"

Keely laughed. "I'm not that bad."

"Not yet. That's why you've got to come to the party with me."

"Who else is going?"

"Sarah B. and Sarah N. for sure. The usual suspects. Hey, think about it this way. You'll get more material for your books."

"Okay, I'll go. And thank you."

"You want to know what your present is to me?"

the dance floor was packed. Keely and Janine danced with each other at first. After only a moment, Janine's eyes went wide. Keely felt a tap on her shoulder.

Turning, she looked into Tommy's black eyes.

"You're back from Vegas!" Keely yelled.

He only smiled at her—no one could hear anything but the music. He pulled her into the center of the dance floor. The music continued, fast and loud and manic.

Tommy was an excellent dancer, catching the beat and making it belong to him, slowing the music down as he silkily moved his shoulders, his back, his hips. He sauntered through the music. Gradually, Keely changed her movements from frantic screaming hopping waving madness to catch Tommy's more languid style. It was amazing. She felt like her body was a dam, filled to bursting with desire, and the fast dancing splashed the desire all over the place but the slow dancing kept everything inside, so her yearning was contained and pressing against her skin.

Tommy knew how to make her want him. He brought his mouth closer to hers. Closer. She couldn't get her breath, but she had enough pride—or maybe it was an instinctive primitive understanding—that she didn't move her face toward him to kiss him. Another grin. He moved his mouth slowly and touched her lips. Her eyes were still open, but Tommy's eyes were closed, and she closed her eyes, and all the world existed right there, in the silk of his mouth, the sweetness of his breath, the wetness of his tongue.

He put both arms around her, pressing his hands against her buttocks, pulling her against him, pulling her to fit him, and she put her arms up around his neck and bravely ran her hands up into his thick black hair. She kissed him back. She pressed her breasts against his chest. She felt his erection against her pelvis and nearly melted into the floor.

For the rest of the night, whether the music was fast or slow, Keely and Tommy danced slowly, locked together, kissing or smiling at each other, and then kissing again. When the night ended, Tommy kept his arm around her waist and waved to his gang of

friends, and escorted Keely out of the hotel to his car. When they
got there, Tommy leaned her against the door and leaned himself
against her. He smiled down at her, and put a strand of hair behind her ear, and kissed that ear, and her cheek, and slowly, teas-
ingly, moved to her mouth. She knew what was happening now.
She knew she was caught in a current of sensation, like the current off the south shore of the island. You couldn't fight it. You
had to go with it, and sooner or later you'd be free and could swim
to shore. If you wanted to.

Right now all she wanted to do was to ride the current.

"Do you know what I'm going to do now?" Tommy asked.

Her lips were so swollen she could scarcely speak. "What?"

"I'm taking you to my house."

"What about your parents?"

Tommy laughed. "I've got my own entrance through the back
door right into my room on the first floor. My parents sleep upstairs at the front."

"Oh . . ." Should she stop to think about what she was going
to do?

Could she stop to think?

Tommy took her face in his hands and kissed her. It was a long,
slow, honey-sweet kiss, and when he was through, he smiled at
Keely, and she saw such emotion in his eyes that she trembled.

"Okay?" he asked.

"Okay."

She'd never been in Tommy's house before. A light burned at the
back porch. They stepped inside, into darkness. Tommy led her to
his room. He didn't turn on a light, but she could see him and his
room in shades of shadow. He tugged her coat off and laid it on a
chair. He took off his coat.

He kissed her mouth gently and trailed kisses down her neck
and onto her shoulders as he slowly tugged on her dress. She
pulled away from him to unzip her dress and undo her bra. He

touched her breasts, staring at them as if memorizing them, and then his breath came quicker, and he peeled off his clothes and kicked away his shoes. He moved her to his bed. She was frightened and excited and nervous about all of it, and then he raised himself above her. She wrapped her arms around him, she ran her hand down his back and touched the hollow of his spine. She marveled at such beauty, at the powerful muscles in his back, at the way his breath hitched and how he moaned, and she was so glad to make him happy, to give him pleasure. And for the first time, she enjoyed the experience herself.

"God, you're so beautiful," Tommy said afterward, panting next to her on the blanket.

Keely smiled and ran her hand over his chest. It was thick with dark hair and a silver chain lay in the tangled black.

"What is this?" she asked, picking up the small round medallion at the end of the chain.

"It's St. Peter. The patron saint of fishermen."

"Why are you wearing it?"

"I told you. That's what I want to do with my life. I was born next to the sea, and I want to be out on the sea as often as I can."

"I understand that. It's like I want to write novels for a living."

"You and Isabelle, what is it with you two? You live in a fantasy land."

Keely started to object, then paused. "I suppose we do live in a fantasy land when we're writing. But cleaning houses is the reality of my life."

"Yeah, like me working in Dad's office."

Keely laughed. "Maybe not exactly like that. I don't think you have to clean any toilets."

Tommy growled and roughly rolled Keely over to face him. "I refuse to discuss toilets when I've got you in my bed."

And he kissed her again and again, slowly, from head to toe.

part
two

chapter
eight

Hey, Isabelle, Happy New Year! I keep leaving voice-mail. What ARE you doing?

XO K

Happy New Year, BFF! What am I doing? Taking my final semester at Smith, getting ready to move to the Berkshires for two years where I'll write the great American novel, and spending every spare moment with Gorgeous Gordon! We'll talk soon!

XO I

Forgive me for doing it this way, Isabelle, but I haven't been able to get you on the phone . . . Isabelle, I'm, um, seeing Tommy. I mean sleeping with him, hanging out with him, the whole deal. I think it's fine because you're over Tommy and totally in love with Gorgeous Gordon. Right?

I know you're graduating in a month. Your mother told me they're going up for the big celebration. And then you go to the writers' colony immediately? No stop home?

XO K

Wow, you and Tommy. Really? You know he hit on you to get back at me, don't you? Tommy and I were together for a long time. He's having sex with you because he knows it would hurt me. You'd better get away from that guy before you get hurt.

Wow, Isabelle, that so wasn't what I was expecting you to say. I mean, you're "spending every spare moment with Gorgeous Gordon!" So you want Gordon but you still want Tommy?

Keely, don't do this. You know I've loved Tommy all my life. Just because I'm seeing someone else doesn't mean I don't care about him. And about you. I think you're both heading for a big crash. You know he's just using you.

Could we not talk about men for once? I want to know how you're doing at the colony. Are you writing like a mad thing? Learning some cool advice?

Are you coming to the island at all this summer? Let me know. I'm working every job I can get and I want to clear some time to be with you. Mom's doing great. She loves cooking. Can you plan to come over for dinner when you're on the island? Bring Gordon!

XO K

Hi, Keely, sorry I haven't been in touch for a while. I've been so crazy busy here at the writers' colony, and when I get a chance, I zip down to the city to spend some time with Gordon. He's been really patient about me being isolated here like some kind of nun. But I've met some cool people— and some odd ones—who are trying to write their first novel, too, and we get all our meals in the dining hall, so I don't have to cook and can focus on my work.

Are you still with Tommy? If you are, don't get your hopes up that it will last. Tommy doesn't know how to commit.

XO I

Isabelle! Aren't you coming home this summer at all?

XO K

Keely, don't you love this photo? It's me, standing in front of John Keats's house in London. Gordon and I flew over for a couple of weeks in August so I could take a break from the writing workshop. It gets so intense. Are you and Tommy still together? I hope not.

XO I

Hi, Isabelle, for someone in London with Gordon, you're awfully curious about Tommy. Yes, we are to-gether. And we don't talk about you at all. I mean, you're almost engaged to Gorgeous Gordon.

Are you coming home for Christmas and New Years?

XO K

Sorry, no, Gordon and I are going to Paris for Christmas. If you're with Tommy, don't buy him anything too senti-mental. It would be a waste of your money. And don't ex-pect anything like jewelry from him. He's clueless.

XO I

Hi Isabelle, are you coming to the island for a visit this summer? I miss you!

XO K

Oh, Keely, I'm sorry, I lost your last email, I mean I didn't really read it, I get so many. Something about spring makes

me want to write all the time, and I think I've got a bril-
liant novel going. Gordon is so patient and kind. Are you
getting any writing done or are you too busy trying to keep
Tommy happy? He can be moody. No one knows that more
than I do.

XO I

Hi, Isabelle, I got a lot of writing done over the winter
because I didn't have much work with Clean Sweep.
Now everyone's coming back so I'm working again.
It's fine, I think. It will give me time to let my novel
"cool."

Isabelle, you've got to stop with this Tommy business. You act like you own him, like you have him
fenced in. I just don't get it. What do you want?

XO K

Hi, Keely, I suppose we should talk on the phone sometime
but we'd both start yelling at each other. You're my best
friend, so I don't understand how you cannot get that
Tommy was my first love. We were precious to each other.
Feelings like that don't just evaporate. Why can't you date
someone else? Don't you see it wouldn't hurt me as much if
Tommy saw someone else?

So tired of trying to explain.

Hi, Isabelle, I can't believe you were here last week
with Gordon and you didn't even call me! I would have
loved to meet him. Your mother said you two came
for only a couple days, and Gordon asked your father
for permission to marry you. Your mother said you
have a ring the size of an ostrich egg.

Why didn't you call me? Didn't you want to see me?

K

Keely, I'm sorry sorry sorry, please don't be mad at me. I'm balancing so many balls in the air! Gordon's parents are very demanding. I haven't been able to write for weeks. He wants me to leave the BWC, but I want to finish out this year. I'm so close to finishing this novel, but I've shared some of it with Gordon and he got so upset about the sex scenes. His parents would probably never speak to me again if I published a book that had these sex scenes. But they're not perverted or weird, they're about love, and I don't know what to do. My advisor here tells me to leave them in, they're good, they're important, but I don't want to make Gordon's parents mad.

I'm so worried and unhappy! DON'T sign your emails without the XO! I need as many XOs from you as I can get. I know I've been a crap correspondent for the past two years, but everything has been so extreme. I'll phone you sometime. Will you talk to me?

XOXOXO I

Isabelle, of course I'll talk to you. You need to rethink this relationship with Gorgeous Gordon. He seems controlling. And puritanical. I do love you and worry about you. And I have missed you so much!

XO K

ISABELLE! I have a literary agent! I sent my novel to Sally Hazlitt at Hazlitt and Hopkins in NYC, and Sally called me! She loves my book! She's sending me a contract to sign! After her phone call I screamed so loud my mother thought I'd hurt myself! I hugged her so hard I picked her up off the floor! I'm so wired I could run to 'Sconset and back without stopping.

I've tried to call you but you never pick up so I'm sending this text.

I wish you were here, Izzy, we could pop a bottle of

champagne and drink it at Surfside and dance in the waves. No one but you really understands. I have an agent! Miracles do happen! My book probably won't get published—but I have an agent so maybe it will! Could you come home for a few days? Or maybe I should drive out to the Berkshires and take you out to dinner to celebrate. This is the best day of my life!

XOXOXO K

Sorry I couldn't answer sooner. It was Gordon's mother's birthday. (She makes Queen Elizabeth look like Lady Gaga.) How exciting that you have an agent. Congratulations. Did you tell Tommy? What does he think? I'll call soon.

XO I

Isabelle, no one understands the importance of getting an agent but you. I told Tommy. He's more excited about the size of the striped bass he caught last week.

I took Mom out to dinner to celebrate, but she doesn't really get it, either. I'm just cleaning houses and babysitting and keeping my fingers crossed.

XO K

part
three

chapter
nine

"Come on, Keely. Let's get married. It's time. It's *past* time."

They were seated on the beach in the late afternoon. The dune they leaned against was warm. The ocean was friendly, blue and white and lacework froth.

"Tommy," Keely said, trying to keep the strain from her voice. "We've talked about this so often . . . It's foolish to marry when we don't have the money to rent a house, let alone to buy one."

"*Keely—*"

"We're twenty-five years old. And we're still living with our parents."

"Maybe your mother would like us to move in with her. Keep her from being lonely. I could fix things around the house—"

"Sweetheart, you already help her when she needs something fixed. You're wonderful with her. You're wonderful, period. But *you* want to buy a deep-sea fishing boat, and *I* want to write a novel that gets published, and we've both worked a million hours a week for the past two years and we've saved and saved our money, and we don't have anything close to a down payment."

Keely pulled her knees up and rested her forehead on them, hugging her legs tightly, trying to keep from crying. She was so tired. She had tried so hard. Tommy was a wonderful man, sexier now than when he was in high school, and he was kind and hard-working and funny. He was the whole package.

But he wanted to start a family. *Now.* He wanted some little Tommy Fitzgeralds running around, playing Nerf ball with him.

He really wanted, although he hadn't yet come out to say it in words, for Keely to stop "messing around" with her "stories" and get a good full-time job, maybe something with the town, so they could have health benefits.

They'd argued about this for months. She could not get him to understand that writing was for her what deep-sea fishing was for him. She'd forced him to read a short story that was published in a literary magazine because she'd been sure that would help him understand her, her talents, her goals. Ha. He didn't even get the point of the story. Really, he didn't even get the point of fiction, unless it was science fiction, which Tommy said was actually kind of true because it was *science* fiction.

"Life isn't all about money, Keely. Remember what you and Isabelle used to call yourselves? Surfside Sisters? Because you would both leap into life instead of dawdling at the edge, waiting until it was safe."

Sometimes Tommy surprised her. "You remembered that? Oh, Tommy, I do love you." Leaning forward, she kissed him thoroughly.

How much should one person ask from life? Was she greedy? Selfish? Or simply self-deluded?

These things she knew: She was fortunate to live on this beautiful speck of land surrounded by the ocean. Fortunate to have a mother alive and well and a truly pleasant companion. She had a sexy, lusty lover who was good to her and did manly jobs around the house, but she didn't have to do his laundry or clean the sink after he shaved. She had several short stories published in literary reviews—smallish reviews, but respectable. She made a nice fat salary with Clean Sweep, and she helped her mother pay the mortgage every month. She had a best friend who was in her second year at the Berkshire Writers' Colony, who was halfway through writing a novel.

And Keely had an agent! She had finished a novel, and sent it to an agent, and Sally Hazlitt liked it!

But would it sell? Would it get published? The chances were one in a million.

Keely wished she could send the novel to Isabelle for her opinion, and yet she didn't want to, and she didn't actually understand why.

Tonight was Tommy's poker night with the guys. Keely would cook dinner for herself and her mother, do laundry, read one of the novels she'd taken from the library. A normal evening. She was fortunate. Anxious but fortunate.

She stepped out of the shower just as her cell rang. Wrapping a towel around her, she padded into her bedroom and answered.

"Keely? It's Sally Hazlitt. I have some very good news for you."

Keely's heart skipped a beat. "You do?"

"Keely. Listen. This doesn't happen very often. This is like a lightning bolt! Ransome & Hawkmore Publishing loves *Rich Girl*. They're making a low six-figure offer—I might be able to inch them up a little—and they want you to come in and meet with them. Keely? Are you there?"

"I'm . . . I'm here. Wow. This is . . ."

Sally changed to business mode. "So. How soon can you come in? We've got a lot to talk about. Can you fly in tomorrow? You'll want to stay for a few days."

"Well, my jobs . . . I guess, but I guess I can take some time off—"

"Keely, did you hear what I said? They're making a low six-figure, two-book contract—I might be able to inch them up a little."

Keely couldn't breathe.

"You're good for that, right? You've got another book or two in you?"

Deep breaths, deep breaths, Keely told herself. She choked out, "Absolutely."

"Okay, then, book a flight and let me know when you'll be here."

"Yes. Yes, I'll get back to you right away."

When the call ended, Keely didn't move. Couldn't. It was as if one twitch of her hand would disturb the universe around her, this universe so suddenly kind.

At last she took a deep breath. She stood up, and walked into the kitchen.

"Mom, I'm going to have a book published."

Eloise was slicing a lemon. "What?"

"I'm going to have a book published. *Rich Girl.* Sally Hazlitt, my agent, just called me. I have to go to New York."

Eloise gaped at Keely as if she were a puzzle. "I don't understand. You're going to have a book published?"

"Yes. A novel. I told you about it, you know I've been writing. I told you about Sally Hazlitt. She just called to say Ransome & Hawkmore are going to publish it."

"This is amazing."

"I know," Keely agreed.

Eloise dried her hands on a towel and wrapped her arms around Keely. "I'm so proud of you. I'm so glad for you."

"I wish Dad were here," Keely said quietly, hugging her mother close. "I wish he knew."

"Maybe he does," Eloise said.

"I'm taking you out to dinner!" Keely said. "We need to celebrate."

"Darling, could we order in? I've got to work tomorrow and I'm exhausted."

"Sure. Absolutely." Keely's mind was spinning. "But let's open a bottle of champagne, okay?"

"Will prosecco do?"

"Fine." She followed her mother into the kitchen and while Eloise got down the flutes, Keely dug around inside the refrigerator to find an unopened bottle of prosecco.

Keely opened the wine and poured.

"Here's to you, my novelist daughter!"

They clicked glasses and drank.

"I've got to make plane reservations for tomorrow," Keely said. "Where's my phone?"

"Have you told Tommy? Have you called Isabelle?"

Keely paused. "I'll call Tommy. I don't want to tell Isabelle yet. I don't know why. I guess it doesn't seem quite real."

"Ask Tommy over to celebrate," Eloise suggested.

"It's his poker night. Sacred. And I've got to let this sink in . . . I think I'm dreaming."

While Keely made the flight and hotel reservations, Eloise called Sophie T's for two Greek salads and one small anchovy and artichoke pizza. As always, they put the salads in bowls and the pizza on plates, but Keely discovered she had no appetite.

"I'm too excited to eat," she told her mother. "I'm nervous about what to wear in the city tomorrow. I've got to check on my clothes."

"In that case, I'll eat the entire pizza," her mother said, with a grin.

Keely whirled around in her room, pulling out three "good black dresses," trying them, finding her best heels, choosing a bag, digging out a small suitcase. She found her travel bag and filled it with toothpaste and brush, dental floss—where was her small jar of face cream? She couldn't find it! And her Jo Malone perfume that Tommy had given her for Christmas? It had disappeared, too! Her hands were shaking, her thoughts running on top of each other and falling into a void, like lemmings off a cliff.

Her cell rang. *Isabelle.*

Should she tell Isabelle? How could she not tell her? Isabelle was her best friend. And now the luck was tilting in Keely's favor, in a gigantic way. She was going to have a novel published!

"Isabelle, hi!"

"Keely, we broke up."

Isabelle's speech was shattered with sobs. She was hyperventilating, too. Keely could tell.

"Isabelle. Take a breath. It's okay. Whatever it is, it will be okay." She dropped onto her bed. This was going to be a long conversation.

"Gordon broke up with me," Isabelle wailed. "For good. He's going to marry someone else."

"Oh, Izzy, I'm so sorry. But he was kind of—"

"You don't have to insult him to make me feel better. I'll never feel better. He asked me to give him back his ring! God, I feel so *rejected*."

Keely watched the minutes on her watch tick by as she listened to Isabelle cry. She said the usual worthless platitudes, but nothing would help Isabelle, not now. She absolutely wouldn't tell her about her novel.

"I'm coming home tomorrow," Isabelle sniffed. "Will you meet me at the boat?"

"I can't, Isabelle. I have to go off to, um, Boston, dental appointment. But should you come home? You've still got a couple of months at the colony."

"I don't give two figs about the damned colony! It's all ridiculous, I haven't gotten anything published. I'm on my fifty-third draft of my hopeless novel. I want to come home and stay. I need my friends, my family, my life. I need to rethink everything."

"So how long will you be here?"

"Forever. I'm not going back to the colony."

"Isabelle, listen to yourself. The colony has nothing to do with the fact that Gordon broke up with you. The colony is about your writing."

"Well, *you've* been writing, haven't you?" Isabelle demanded.

"Um, yes."

"So I can do it, too. I can write at home. And be with all the people I love."

They talked for an hour. Isabelle calmed down. "I'm going to pack now."

"Okay. If you're sure. I still think you should talk to someone in charge at the colony. Someone wise."

"Wisdom isn't going to bring Gordon back. I don't need wisdom. I need comfort."

"I'll see you in a couple of days," Keely told her.

Keely texted Tommy and he came to her house at midnight. He smelled of beer and the cigars the guys smoked at their poker games and he was slightly tipsy. Keely met him outside on the porch so they wouldn't wake her mother.

Tommy ambled up toward her with a big grin on his face. "So why the urgent message?" He put his hands on her waist, pulling her toward him.

Keely put her hands on his chest, gently pushing him away. "I've got something enormous to tell you."

His eyes lit up. "You're pregnant?"

"Tommy, I sold a novel. I'm going to have my novel published and they're going to pay me and I'm flying into New York tomorrow to meet with Sally Hazlitt, my agent."

"How much money are you getting?"

Keely hedged that topic. "Money's not even the point—"

"We could make a down payment on a house."

"Maybe. Maybe we could. But, Tommy, listen, this is a very big deal! I'm going to have a novel published!"

"Yeah, I'm happy for you, babe. I get it. So how long will you be away?"

"I'm not sure. Two days, maybe three."

"When you get home, I'll take you to dinner at the Chanticleer to celebrate."

Tears sprang to Keely's eyes. "Oh, Tommy, thank you! You don't have to do that, but I'm so glad you want to do that."

"Crap, Keely, don't you know I want you to be happy? Just because I never read many books doesn't mean I can't understand about you writing one." He pulled her close again. "I'm proud of you, babe. I'm glad for you. I just wish you didn't have to go away."

"I won't be long," Keely said.

"Tell me when your flight is. I'll take you to the airport."

Keely wrapped her arms around his neck and kissed him thoroughly. She was grateful for his understanding, and she was high on her fabulous news, and right then at midnight with Tommy's arms holding her close, she thought she was the luckiest woman in the world.

The next morning, Keely wheeled her roller suitcase into the hall.

"You look lovely," her mother assured her.

"Thanks, but I don't want to look *lovely*, Mom. I want to look professional. I want to look sophisticated. I'm going to New York."

Tommy knocked on the door. "Your chariot, my queen." He did an extravagant bow and gestured toward his car.

Eloise came to the door. "Isn't it wonderful news, Tommy?"

"It is. I'm really proud of my girl."

On the way to the airport, Keely chattered as she double-checked everything in her purse. "I know I'm babbling," she said. "Sorry."

"Babble away," Tommy told her, laughing.

When they reached the airport, Keely grabbed her computer, purse, and suitcase.

"Don't come in," she told Tommy. "I'm sure the plane is boarding in only a few minutes."

"I've got to get to the office anyway," Tommy said. Leaning over, he kissed Keely passionately, but Keely only wanted to get out of the car and on the plane and into the city.

The JetBlue direct flights from Nantucket to LaGuardia were all booked. Keely had to fly to Boston and from there to New York. JetBlue was also booked at Boston Logan so Keely had to trek over to Delta's terminal, a hike she didn't even mind, because she was floating, really.

She had just passed an Au Bon Pain when she heard her name called.

"Keely! Keely Green!"

She looked. She stopped dead in her tracks. *"Sebastian."*

Sebastian came loping over on his long legs, lean and fit in jeans and a long-sleeved navy blue rugby shirt, a backpack fastened to his shoulders. He took hold of Keely and wrapped her in a tight embrace. He kissed her on the mouth—quickly, in a friendly way.

"What are you doing here?" Keely asked, almost angrily. Emotions battled inside her. She felt defensive, because the last time he saw her, on the Surfside Beach, Keely had been so pathetic, telling him how she envied his family, how she *wanted* him. Now she didn't want to seem *needy*—but she did want him.

Sebastian remained wonderfully relaxed. "I'm going home. I just arrived from Stockholm. I've got a long wait until I fly to Nantucket. What are *you* doing here?"

I'm standing here with every molecule in my body playing Ping-Pong at the sight of you, Keely thought. She said, "I'm going to New York. Sebastian, I sold a book!"

"Get out of town. Really?"

"Really." She couldn't hold back a perfectly silly grin of happiness.

"Wow, Keely. That's absolutely phenomenal! I knew you could do it! Look, I've got a long wait for my flight. Let me walk you to your gate."

"Oh, well, thanks." Keely felt like a child who'd been given both a bouncy house *and* a puppy for Christmas. So many dreams were hovering around her, she was surprised she remembered how to walk.

Sebastian took hold of her small rolling suitcase and pulled it along. "Who's your publisher? And don't you have to have an agent?"

"Yes. You need the agent first. And I have one, Sally Hazlitt at Hazlitt and Hopkins. My publisher will be—*is*—Ransome & Hawkmore. Very big deal. Sebastian, tell me about you. Are you coming home for a visit?"

"Right. Just a quick stop to see the family . . . and the island. I'll be sorry not to see you."

He has no idea what his words are doing to me, Keely thought. He was smiling down at her, warmly, even affectionately, and she swept her eyes to the floor, protecting herself from believing the tenderness in his eyes. She told herself: *Right now, I'm a cute little bit of the past to entertain him before his next flight.*

When she didn't respond, Sebastian said, "But you're on your way off the island, aren't you? You're on your way to fame and fortune and all your dreams coming true."

At that, Keely had to speak. "Maybe not *all* my dreams."

Sebastian stopped walking, the rolling case jerking to a stop next to him. "Keely, what do you mean by that?"

They were face-to-face now, and her heart was pounding so hard she felt herself shake with each beat. For a moment she allowed herself to study his face, memorizing each feature for the cold winter nights ahead. He was beautiful.

"Sebastian—"

He pulled her to him, one arm embracing her, and, with the other hand, cupped her head as he brought his lips down to hers. His kiss was warm, both gentle and intense. She sensed he was holding back his passion. "There. I've been wanting for you to grow up so I could kiss you like that."

It was too good to be true. "The way you kiss Ebba?"

A cloud passed over Sebastian's face. He relaxed his embrace. He grasped the suitcase again. Now his eyes were sad. "That's complicated."

"Yes, I thought so," Keely said, and she tried very hard to smile in a sophisticated, you-can't-hurt-me-kid kind of way, as if she were Madonna or anyone who kissed thousands of men. "Look, there's my gate. Thanks for walking me over, Sebastian. Have a great time *visiting* on Nantucket!" She took her suitcase from him, which involved her hand touching his, which sent the entire Fourth of July fireworks going off inside her, but she was too wary to be hopeful, and she was determined.

Sebastian said, "Goodbye, Keely."

She didn't look back. She didn't rush. Head high, she walked to her gate, to the plane that would take her to New York.

Isabelle had raved about the small, elegant hotel she and Gordon stayed in whenever they wanted to just "zip down" to the city to see a play or an art opening, so Keely had made a reservation there. The clerks at the Empire Hotel gave her the key to her room even though it was only one o'clock, two hours before check-in. Gratefully, Keely parked her luggage, freshened her face, and gave herself a pep talk before heading back to the street and hailing a taxi.

The Hazlitt and Hopkins Literary Agency offices were in one of the towering Lego block structures that kept the Wall Street area shady. After Keely signed in, she was directed to the bank of elevators on the left. She rode up to the fifteenth floor and stepped out into a great open space of glass and light.

For a moment, she stood there, looking around, taking a breath, reminding herself she wasn't dreaming.

"May I help you?" asked a harried-looking receptionist.

"I'm Keely Green. I have an appointment with Sally Hazlitt—"

"Keely!" A tall, buxom woman with masses of curly red hair arrived. "Barbara, this is our new star, Keely Green. Ransome & Hawkmore Publishing just made a two-book offer."

Before Keely could do more than smile hello, Sally whisked her off down the hall and into a glass-walled office.

"Sit." Sally pointed to a sofa.

Keely sat.

A tall, thin, frighteningly sophisticated woman with black lipstick entered the room.

"Keely, this is Fiona, my assistant. She'll be doing a lot of the work with you."

"Hi, Fiona," Keely said.

"Hi, Keely," Fiona replied, and smiled, and all at once she was enchantingly friendly.

Fiona asked, "Would you like water? Coffee? Scotch?"

"Nothing, thank you."

Fiona sank into a chair.

"Great," Sally said. "So, you lucky thing, I checked your Facebook page and you're more gorgeous than your posts. Great hair. You're not married, no kids, right?" While Keely nodded, Sally continued, "You're young, your book is good. We all want to see the spoiled rich girl get her comeuppance. We're going to meet Juan Polenski, he's your editor, for lunch, but first I want to go over some things with you. Standard boilerplate contractual blah blah blah. Here we go." She handed Keely a sheaf of documents.

For the next half hour, Sally walked Keely through the legalese, explaining terms like *sub-rights* and stressing the paragraph where Keely agreed the Hazlitt and Hopkins Literary Agency would receive fifteen percent of all money due the author.

"It's worth it to you, honey, believe me. You do the creative stuff, we work on these contracts and argue with the publishers. But you don't have much to argue about. You have landed in a big fat garden of roses. So. Tell me about your next book."

Keely stalled. "My next book?"

"Read the words. This is a two-book contract. They're investing a lot in *Rich Girl*. They want to ride on that, and so do I, and so do you."

Keely chewed her lip. "Does the next book have to have the same characters?"

"No. Not at all. But it should be set on Nantucket. That name is a powerful draw."

"Okay . . ."

"It should feel the same, though. Young people. Sex. Complications."

"I was thinking, something about rich summer people and the son falls in love with the maid . . . I'll title it *Poor Girl*."

"Love it! Oops, we've got to meet Juan. Let's go."

Sally led Keely between canyons of brick and steel to Cipriani, an Italian restaurant on Wall Street. They were seated, and a moment later a stunningly handsome man appeared at the table.

"Juan Polenski," the man said, kissing Keely's hand. "Keely Green. I am so happy to meet you. You and I are going to have a lot of fun together."

"Stop it, Juan," Sally said. "Keely, don't get your hopes up. He bats for the other side. Juan, don't I get a kiss?"

While Sally and Juan were bantering, a pretty young woman with gorgeous blue eyes leaned forward. "Keely, I'm Melissa Anderson, Juan's assistant. Anything you need, let me know. And congratulations on *Rich Girl*. I love this book!"

And they were off, talking more than eating, laughing at in-jokes, drinking red wine and eating amazingly delicious pasta. Keely could only swallow a few bites. She was in such a state of excitement she could barely sip her water, although the wine did help. Here it was, a dream come true, lunch with her agent and her editor because of a book she'd written! She had stepped into paradise.

"See that big fat guy over there?" Sally whispered, leaning close to Keely. "He's a literary giant, he's won the Pulitzer *and* the National Book Award. He's a famous womanizer, he tries to seduce every female he comes across."

"Yeah," Melissa added, "and if the woman refuses him, he'll say, 'Come on, honey, I won the Pulitzer.'"

Keely had scarcely finished laughing when Juan signaled for the check. Almost before she could believe she was talking to her editor, Keely was left standing on the sidewalk with Sally, Melissa, and Juan.

They took a cab to Ransome & Hawkmore Publishing. The offices were in a massive stone building shouldering up to a massive steel and chrome building. The foyer was impressive, and the re-

ception area on the thirty-second floor was elegant, and then, behind the scenes, a warren of cubicles and offices and mysterious
hallways spread in all directions.

They settled in a conference room, where they were quickly
joined by people from marketing, publicity, digital sales, and social media. Plans were unrolled, folders handed out, and Keely
tried not to smile too much.

"What's the title of your next book?" Juan asked.

Buoyed with red wine and happiness, Keely said, *"Poor Girl."*

"I like it," Juan said. "So we'll publish *Rich Girl* next June."

"Next June?" Keely asked.

Sally leaned forward. "Publication of a novel calls for lots of
production, Keely. They've got to create the cover, plan publicity
and distribution, send advanced readers' copies out for quotes."

"While you're waiting for next June," Juan said, "you can write
Poor Girl. We'll want to publish that the following summer."

"We need to have an author photo taken of you," Melissa said.
"Sally, I'll talk with you about that." Turning to Keely, she said,
"You can come back into the city in a month or so, right?"

"Right." Keely's head was whirling.

"Okay, we're set," Juan declared.

Everyone rose, shook hands or air-kissed, and Melissa escorted
Keely and Sally to the elevator. Moments later, they were back on
the street.

Sally grinned. "We talk fast in the city, don't we?"

Keely nodded. "Everything is so—exciting."

"Yes, there's nothing like the high of selling your first book.
Look, I've got meetings now. I suggest you walk back to your
hotel. It will be a long haul, but it's the best way to see the city.
You can stop for coffee somewhere. Take your time. Soak it in.
Keely Green, new author, strolls the big city. Enjoy it."

"I'll do that," Keely said.

"You fly back tomorrow?"

"I do."

"Safe travels. We'll be in touch." Sally kissed Keely's cheek and vanished.

Keely walked. Tentatively at first, unsure of her course, and then she found Broadway and headed north. She tried not to grin like a tourist as pedestrians, most of them yelling into phones, grimly strode past her, but she was too happy. She broke into a laugh, and thought, why not? She could talk out loud in this city. Everyone would think she was on Bluetooth.

She walked and walked, fascinated by the shop windows offering anything one could possibly dream of. She allowed herself to gaze upward at the sky-high buildings, because if she looked like a tourist, well, she *was* a tourist! But she also belonged to this city. She had an agency and a publisher and she was returning for an author photo. She had had lunch with her editor—*she had an editor!* There was something about New York that made her book more real, more exciting, more fabulous. Her mind was like a three-year-old child at a birthday party, wanting to eat more cake, open more presents, and run around the yard screaming. She kind of wanted to jump up and down, but only tossed her head and kept walking.

When she arrived at the hotel, she was trembling with exhaustion. She fell on the bed. She shouldn't have walked all that way in high heels. She was jazzed up. She wanted to share this miraculous day with someone. Her mother was working. Tommy would grumble if she called him.

Isabelle. She wanted to share her happiness with Isabelle, who would understand like no one else could what an enormous event this was.

But Isabelle had just been dumped by Gordon—maybe this was the wrong time for Keely to share her good news?

But Tommy had probably told some of his friends, which meant someone had heard the news and called Isabelle.

And Sebastian knew.

Keely called Isabelle.

Isabelle answered her phone with two words: "I know."

Keely took a deep breath. "You mean you know that I'm going to have a book published?"

"Sebastian called me."

"Are you on the island?"

"Not yet. I'm packing, but I'm so miserable, I don't have the energy to move."

"Well . . . I'm in New York right now. I've just met with *my agent*—"

"Don't, Keely. Just don't. Don't kick me when I'm down."

"Isabelle, come on. I'm not trying to hurt you. You're my best friend. I want to share my happiness with you. Like, okay, like if I have a delicious cake and I want to share a piece with you."

"No, Keely. You have the whole damned cake and it can't be divided. You're going to have a book published *and* you've got Tommy."

"Whoa, hang on. I've only *got* Tommy because you've been in love with Gordon."

"Rub it in. Add salt. Now I don't have anything and you have everything."

"Isabelle! Don't be this way. I want to share this with you. I mean, I didn't want to call you right away because you called me about Gordon, and I'm so sorry, he's an evil shit and you're a gorgeous woman. You'll have men around you the moment they know you're free. We've always had the same dream. I want you to celebrate with me."

"Your dream came true. Not mine."

"That doesn't mean your dream *won't* come true! You've been able to go to the writers' colony. I'm sure anything you write is better than mine—"

"Stop being so patronizing."

"Isabelle, I'm not—"

"I can't do this anymore. I can't be around you anymore, Keely. It hurts too much."

"Isabelle!"

Isabelle had disconnected.

chapter
ten

Keely sat on her bed in the lovely hotel watching the lights of the great city blink on. Even here with the window closed, she could hear the rumble of traffic, the massive convoy of cabs, Ubers, trucks, buses, and limos passing through the streets. She could go down to the lobby, find a nearby restaurant, enjoy the city at night. But her feet were killing her, and she was too sad and confused to enjoy anything much at all. She understood Isabelle's feelings. And how could Keely feel triumphant when Isabelle was so miserable?

She pushed back the crisp white sheets of the bed and lay watching television, because it was the only thing she could do to calm her mind. She was in New York! She was going to have a book published and she had to write another novel!

Isabelle was heartbroken about Gordon.

Keely forced herself to turn off the television, slide down beneath the silky covers, and try to sleep. She was sure she was too excited to sleep at all.

She fell asleep at once.

The next morning, Keely woke early, feeling energetic and rebellious. How could she allow herself to whine because two people she loved, Tommy and Isabelle, didn't go mad with happiness about her book deal? In the clear light of a new day, she was sure that Isabelle would come around. Why wouldn't she?

In the meantime, Keely all by herself would go mad with happiness, here and now, in New York City. She took a long shower, dressed and packed, tossing in the necklace she'd bought for her mother and the baseball cap for Tommy. She checked out and took a cab to the airport.

As she waited to board JetBlue to Nantucket, she called Tommy, but she went straight to voicemail. "Call me!" she said. "I'll be home on the JetBlue flight that gets in at three-twenty. Could you meet me? Let's celebrate tonight."

She waited, and waited, for Tommy to call or text. Finally she called her mother and left a message. "Tell the hospital you can't work tonight. I'm taking you out to dinner. I've got big news and big plans."

And then, so quickly, they boarded the small plane and in a roar and rush of prop jets and power, the plane shivered and shimmied and lifted up into the sky. Keely leaned her head against the window of the plane, for once not caring that she was separated from certain death by a small metal machine. She closed her eyes and remembered what had happened so quickly in the city. Was it all a crazy dream with firecrackers exploding, streaming confetti, balloons, and paper money down around her? It hardly seemed real.

But it was real. Her life had changed. Keely had to start work on the new book. She would have to tell Clean Sweep and the babysitting service she couldn't work for them anymore.

When the plane hit the tarmac an hour later, Keely rolled her suitcase out to the taxi stand.

She hoped Tommy would be there, waiting to take her home. No Tommy.

She took a taxi home. On the way, she tried to reach Tommy again, without success.

When she got to her house, she was too wired to unpack, so she pulled on running pants and a top. She was just tying her running shoes when her phone rang. It was Marianne Stanton, the editor of the local newspaper.

"Keely, we've just heard from the Hazlitt and Hopkins Literary Agency. You've sold a book to Ransome & Hawkmore Publishing! Congratulations! When can we come interview you?"

Maybe she wasn't crazy, Keely thought. Maybe her life had truly changed.

After she'd spoken with Marianne, the phone chimed again.

"Keely!" Janine was almost hyperventilating. "Raul who works at *The Inquirer and Mirror* just told me you're going to have a book published? Really?"

Her open laptop on the desk began to ding, notifying her of new messages. Keely forgot her running shoes, fell back on her pillows, and talked with Janine—*yes*. Yes, it was true. She had written a novel and it was being published.

It was late afternoon before Keely realized that Tommy hadn't phoned. She tried once more to reach him. She texted him: *Where are you?*

Immediately, *finally*, a text from Tommy blinked on her screen.

Off island. Isabelle called me. Needs help packing up. Don't know when I'll be back.

Her heart stuttered. Tommy was with Isabelle?

She texted Isabelle, who didn't respond.

She sat on her bed, staring at the wall, numb with confusion.

Her cellphone dinged. And dinged again. The news of her book was out.

Old friends, former teachers, friends of her mother, all called Keely to congratulate her.

As she'd promised, she took her mother out for a celebration dinner that night. Friends stopped by their table to congratulate her. The maître d' brought her a bottle of champagne, on the house. Keely smiled and smiled and smiled, but her mind replayed the same thought like an irritating song: *Tommy had gone to help Isabelle.*

Keely slept fitfully that night, torn between elation about her book and uneasiness about Tommy and Isabelle.

The next morning she took a cup of coffee with her to her desk. She sat down, opened her computer to a new document, and titled it: *Poor Girl*.

Writing had saved her sanity before. She hoped it would now. She typed sentences and deleted them. She typed more sentences and deleted them. She typed: *I'm going crazy.*

She didn't hear from Tommy or Isabelle for three days. The wonderful rush of congratulations from other island friends buoyed her up, kept her floating on happiness for hours at a time.

A large white envelope arrived in the mail on her second day home. Inside was a copy of her signed contract—and a big fat check. Keely's hands shook. She was being paid for writing a novel! No, *two* novels, because *Rich Girl* and *Poor Girl* were part of one contract, and she had a check for part of her two-book advance. She drove to the bank, deposited her check, and wrote a whopping big check of her own.

That night she handed her mother a beautifully gift-wrapped box with the letter terminating the mortgage inside. Her mother's face flushed rosy, and tears welled in her eyes.

"Keely! I never dreamed . . ." Eloise was too choked up to speak.

"I never stopped dreaming," Keely replied, pleased with herself. She'd never seen her mother look so happy.

Friends came over one evening, and they sat around drinking champagne, which was rapidly becoming Keely's favorite drink, and talked and laughed until midnight.

"Where's Tommy?" Janine asked.

"Oh, he's out in the Berkshires helping Isabelle pack," Keely said casually, as if she weren't nervous about this sudden helpfulness of Tommy.

She managed to fall asleep that night. She woke up ready to write.

Around noon, her phone buzzed and she saw Tommy's name pop up on her screen.

"Tommy! I'm so glad you called!"

Tommy's voice was somber. "I need to talk to you, Keely."

"You do? Are you all right? What's going on?"

"Keely—I'm with Isabelle."

"What?"

"Yesterday Isabelle and I talked. We, um, reconnected. I'm bringing her home. And we're getting engaged. We're going to choose the ring together."

Keely laughed in surprise and disbelief. "Come on."

"It's true, Keely." The next words came all in a rush. "I'm sorry."

Keely couldn't stop smiling. "You're joking."

"Not joking. Isabelle knew I was miserable because you wouldn't commit. She, well, I suppose she comforted me. And Isabelle was miserable because Gordon dumped her. We realized we love each other, always have, so . . ."

"Tommy. Promise me you're not kidding, not trying some kind of sick joke. Because I can't believe this."

"I'm sorry, Keely. We never wanted to hurt you. But it's done and it's . . . right."

"Why? I don't understand. Help me understand."

Tommy was silent for a while. "You know I'm not good with words like you. But, it's like you and I are on two completely different life paths. You want to write and rush off to New York. I want to live on the island and work for Dad and fish. Maybe even, someday, have my own charter fishing business."

"But what about Isabelle? What does she want?"

Tommy was silent for a long moment. But his voice was strong when he said, "Isabelle only wants me."

Keely knew, deep in her heart, that was true. Quietly, she said, "And now she has you."

"And now she has me."

Keely pushed back her chair and paced her room.

"What do Isabelle's parents think? When are you getting married? How are you two going to live, how are you going to afford ever to have a house on the island, what about Isabelle's *writing*?"

"She was afraid you'd get hysterical."

"I'm *not* hysterical!"

Tommy coughed, always a sign to Keely that he was about to admit something embarrassing. "We've already spoken with her parents. They gave us the apartment above the garage, until we can get financially solvent."

Keely nodded to herself. This one detail made it all true. "You won't have to pay rent."

Tommy was offended. "Not that it's any business of yours, but no, we won't be paying rent. Isabelle's going to work at her father's office. I'll work for my dad. We'll save."

"Very tidy."

"Be honest. You care about your writing way more than you care about me."

"That's absurd," Keely snapped, although secretly she knew he was right.

Tommy continued as if she hadn't spoken. "Isabelle has always loved me. You want to be a writer more than you want anything else. But Isabelle wants me more than anything."

Before Keely could reply, she heard a woman's voice in the background. "Let me speak to her."

"Isabelle is with you?" Why did this seem like even more of a treachery, an invasion? "Damn, am I on speakerphone?" Keely bristled at the intrusion—Isabelle overhearing Keely's words.

Isabelle began to speak. Her voice was shaking. "Listen, Keely. Remember how we used to call ourselves Surfside Sisters? We were the ones who leapt into the ocean. No matter how cold, how stormy. Remember? Well, Tommy wanted to marry you, and you didn't choose him. You didn't *leap*. Or rather, you ran. You *leapt* toward New York. But I leapt to Tommy. He is more important to me than any 'work' I might do."

"Wow. You sound—*smug*."

"I am smug, Keely." Her voice changed, became warmer, kinder. "Keely. *Keely*, come on. I know everything about you. We both know you're truly in love with Sebastian. Tommy was only ever second best."

"*Sebastian*," Keely said and his name in her mouth conjured his beautiful face and his humor and his kindness and his body, his body that his Swedish sweetheart was probably kissing right now. She would never have Sebastian. "Sebastian has always been just a dream." All at once Keely was dragged down with exhaustion, as if she'd been lifting bags of sand. That family, that fortunate Maxwell family! Isabelle wanted Tommy—and she got him. Anger and jealousy burned inside her, a toxic mixture that flamed so high it extinguished her rational thoughts. She wasn't angry about losing Tommy. She was angry—she was furious—that Isabelle had him.

And she was heartbroken that Tommy had Isabelle. That was the loss that struck most deeply.

Isabelle was still talking. "I hope you can forgive me someday, Keely. You know I thought deeply about this. You and I always meant to be brave and strong, choosing what we love, doing what is right for us, and the hell with what other people think. You always knew I would choose Tommy and I have. I know about you, too. I know you want to be a writer more than you want anything else, certainly more than you want to be with Tommy. So all I can say is that if we hurt you, I'm sorry." Isabelle's voice changed again, and Keely could clearly hear how Isabelle was grinning. "Sorry, not sorry, as they say."

Isabelle's smugness infuriated Keely. "Got it. Well, I'm done. Goodbye, Isabelle."

Keely collapsed on her bed and curled up in a fetal ball. *This must be what people feel like when they're shot*, she thought. It was like a hurricane, a lightning bolt. In a matter of minutes, everything in her life had changed.

She wanted to talk with her mother. Instead, she opened her laptop and went to Isabelle's page on Facebook. She had already added a post announcing triumphantly that she and Tommy were back together and as soon as they got back to the island, they'd look for an engagement ring. She'd posted a selfie, too. Tommy was there, shoulders straight, his smile bright enough to light a firecracker. Isabelle looked completely blissed out with her arms around him.

Keely's thoughts jangled. Her heart skipped a few beats. She tried to sort through her emotions.

To be completely true to herself, Keely had to admit that she wasn't absolutely heartbroken by Tommy's desertion. And she understood Isabelle's actions. But it *stung*. It felt wrong, *unfair*.

And it seemed like one more barrier between her and Isabelle. It was an error, a jagged break between them. As girls, she and Isabelle had dreamed of their weddings. They'd planned to be each other's maid of honor. As things were now, whenever Isabelle and Tommy got married, Keely wouldn't even be a bridesmaid. She might not even be invited!

Isabelle and Tommy got back to the island the same day the weekly issue of the town newspaper came out. Keely read it as she sat on the sofa in the late afternoon. Under the heading MARRIAGE INTENTIONS was a write-up of Isabelle and Tommy's engagement with another spectacular photo.

"Mom," Keely said, "I feel like I'm going mad."

"I don't blame you one bit," Eloise said. "This is a turbulent time for you." She sat on the sofa next to Keely and hugged her tightly. "You've been in spots like this before. When you had to quit college your junior year and come home to help me. When Isabelle got sent to that writers' colony . . . remember your distress? But you sucked it up and moved on and now look at you. You wrote a novel. You sold it! You paid off your ancient mother's mortgage. You have a wonderful life ahead of you."

Keely sniffed. "Thanks, Mom. You're right. I know that. I just don't know what to do. I wanted to throw a big party to celebrate my book contract. But Isabelle's parents are throwing a huge engagement announcement party at the White Elephant for Isabelle and Tommy. I can't compete with that, and I don't want to try."

"Why don't you do what you always do when you're upset?" Eloise asked.

"What's that?"

"Go in your room and work on a novel."

Keely burst out laughing. She dried her tears. She went into her room. She wrote.

Working on her second book, *Poor Girl*, kept her sane. She rearranged her room to make more space for her piles of paper and discarded pages and Post-it notes. She went for a long run every morning, wrote for most of the day, and collapsed with a book in the evening. Autumn arrived, with cooler, dryer air, and puffy clouds rolling across the sky. Keely took her mother with her for several days to New York when Keely had her author photo taken. Juan sent her the edited manuscript of *Rich Girl*, and as Keely read it, she was relieved and grateful for the opportunity to change and improve the book. *Write what you know*, everyone said. She had done that, using the emotions from her life to sharpen her writing.

She thought of Isabelle every day. She considered calling Isabelle, but decided Isabelle should call her. After all, Keely hadn't done anything wrong by having a book accepted for publication. Keely thought—hoped—they'd run into each other in the grocery store or the library, but that didn't happen.

Keely stalked her on Facebook, where Isabelle posted daily some adorable photo of her and Tommy. Apparently Isabelle was busy decorating their apartment, too busy to call Keely, or to text, or to send an email congratulating Keely on her book contract. Just as Keely was too busy to send an email congratulating Isabelle on her engagement.

But she missed Isabelle so much. Janine told her that she'd gotten an invitation card. Isabelle and Tommy would be married on December 2. Keely didn't get one.

Christmas came. Isabelle posted on Facebook a picture of a new Sea Hunt fishing boat tied up to the pier in Madaket. The caption read, "Thanks, Dad!" The boat had to cost over fifty thousand dollars. Tommy had christened it *Isabelle*. In the photo, Tommy was at the console of the boat, and Isabelle stood behind him, arms around him, head resting against his broad back, smiling like a child on Christmas.

"Well, well. Look at that," Keely said aloud in her room. "So Isabelle's father gave them a place to live *and* the boat of Tommy's dreams. Mr. Maxwell just about wrapped Tommy up in tissue, tied him with a big red bow, and presented him to Isabelle, a present for his darling daughter."

She thought she kind of hated Isabelle's father, how he could choose to buy his daughter the man she wanted, not caring or even noticing that Keely had been going with him for two years.

But her heart lifted to see Isabelle's smile. Really, she was glad Isabelle was happy. Her sorrow was how much she missed her friend. If she and Isabelle were together, they'd be jumping up and down and screaming with happiness about Keely's book, Isabelle's marriage.

New Year's Eve arrived. Eloise was working, as usual, so the younger nurses could have the time to be with their families. Keely didn't mind. The two of them didn't need to toast with champagne—they'd already been doing that. Keely was glad to spend New Year's Eve alone. She didn't want to attend any party where she might run into Isabelle and Tommy. She was a coward, she knew, but she was a coward with a book contract, and that made all the difference.

Most of the cold winter evenings she spent with her mother. On weekends, she went out to dinner with girlfriends or to a movie at the Dreamland or a lecture at the library. She didn't look for Tommy or Isabelle, and when she saw them in the distance driving down a street, she held her head high and acted as if she didn't know them. But she seldom saw them. The island was changing. Super wealthy people were snapping up land and houses. Islanders were selling their homes for fortunes and moving to the mainland. It was easy to avoid Isabelle and Tommy because the town, shops, and restaurants were packed with new people.

The flurry of activities surrounding her book's upcoming publication began to mount up. Excitement was building. The preorders were tumbling in. It was time for her to get involved in social media, so she worked with a website manager from New York. She took photos of the island to use on her website—a task that made her see the island with fresh eyes. She networked, connecting with other new writers in faraway states and book lovers and bookstore owners and fun bloggers. She put out a daily blog, counting down to her publication date, talking about what inspired the book, life on the island, the posh galas the girl in *Rich Girl* attended.

She could have this, Keely thought. She could have an island life. She could live here and take her runs through the charming streets of the town, swim in the ocean, have fun at parties and maybe even find a guy to flirt with. She didn't have to center her life on the loss of her best friend and her boyfriend. She was free. She was home.

In March, Keely drove out to Bartlett's Farm. She loved strolling through the farm store, feasting her eyes on the island-grown vegetables. She pushed her cart around a corner, heading for the arugula, when something flashed in the corner of her eye, as bright and restricting as a red traffic stop sign.

She pulled her cart back into her aisle. She craned her neck to see around the corner.

Isabelle and Tommy. Really, she thought, it was surprising that she hadn't run into them before now. She took a deep breath, her inner cheerleader telling her she had this, she could do it.

Isabelle and Tommy moved more into her view. They stood

before a pile of apples and pears. Tommy was smiling down at Isabelle with such tenderness Keely's eyes stung with tears. Isabelle turned toward Tommy, and tilted her head in that winsome way she had.

And Keely saw clearly the baby bump swelling from Isabelle's waist.

Isabelle was going to have a baby. She was at least six months pregnant.

"Oh, Isabelle," Keely whispered. Unconsciously, she put her hands over her heart, as if protecting it. All the moments of her life when she and Isabelle had discussed how many babies they would have, and what they would name them, and if they were going to have natural childbirth and how could they manage to get pregnant at the same time so they could have their babies grow up as friends—all of that flooded back around Keely, submerging her in such sweet memories that tears filled her eyes. How had it happened that they were so far apart, that their real grown-up lives were so different from their dreams?

As she watched the couple, another married pair, Rosaline and Warren, approached Isabelle and Tommy with hugs and kisses. Rosaline was pregnant, too, Keely saw, and the two women stood side by side, comparing bellies and laughing smugly.

Keely left her cart in the aisle and fled. As she wound her way through the aisles, keeping as far away from Isabelle and Tommy as possible, she dug her sunglasses out of her bag and put them on, so that no one would see her tears.

She made it out the door, across the parking lot, and into the safety of her car without seeing anyone she knew. She didn't pause to put on her seatbelt. She fired up the engine and drove away, down the narrow farm lane to the wider road. The seatbelt alert blinked rapidly and shrilly, keeping time, it seemed, to the pounding of her heart. At an intersection, she paused and clicked on the seatbelt to silence it.

She drove home with great care, afraid to get pulled over by a policeman—she knew so many of them personally—desperately wanting to avoid being seen as she was, with tears streaming down her face. She pulled into her driveway and rushed into the house, and while she caught her breath, she saw herself reflected in the mirror above the table that held their mail and keys.

She looked miserable. Well, she felt miserable. It was ridiculous to feel this way, but she did feel so betrayed by Isabelle, so very abandoned. After all the years of their friendship, Isabelle was out in the world, smiling, pregnant, and she should have told Keely the moment she realized she was pregnant, she should have asked Keely to be with her when she took the first pregnancy test. They would have screamed with joy, they would have hugged each other, they would have talked for hours about the baby that Isabelle was carrying.

Isabelle shared all that with Tommy. And with her family, and with her friends.

Keely sank onto the couch as another realization hit. Isabelle had of course shared the news with her friends—and not one of them had called to tell Keely.

Sometimes she feared she was going mad. She spent almost all her time alone, writing, or running, or doing chores for her mother, and her mother was her main source of conversation these days. What would it be like in a few months, when Isabelle would be strolling around town with a baby tucked up against her heart? Would Janine, or anyone, invite Keely to a baby shower for Isabelle? Not likely.

The next day, Sally Hazlitt phoned Keely. "Can you come into New York sometime soon? We've got several things to go over."

"Of course," Keely said. "Give me a date, and I'll be there."

Keely felt as if she were drowning in loneliness, and suddenly a life preserver was tossed to her. She would seize it and hold on to it and let herself be pulled up to the surface and into the glittering world of New York.

chapter
eleven

Keely and Fiona were having drinks at the Algonquin after a full day of work at the literary agency. Keely was learning about the publishing side of a book—the art department that was charged with creating a compelling cover, the publicist who worked to organize Keely's events at bookstores, libraries, and book festivals, the proofreading that made Keely's eyes cross. She was meeting people who were doing that work—artists, librarians, owners of bookstores, sales reps, editors. They were fascinating.

So Keely made the decision. "Fiona, I want to rent an apartment in the city."

When she spoke the words aloud, a shiver of fear went down her spine, and part of her wanted to crawl back under her bed in her mother's house, but she was a grown woman, a novelist! She wanted to live in New York.

Fiona helped Keely find a sublet for two years in a brownstone on the Upper West Side rented by a friend going off to Italy. Keely walked through the two small rooms, one with a view of the dumpsters in the alley, one with a view of the brownstones across the street, and liked it all. She signed a contract and wrote a check for security and first and last months' rent—and she had the keys to her home in the city.

For her first few months in New York, Keely's life was so full and rushed that she scarcely had time to sleep and no time at all to be lonely. Fiona was super sophisticated, very friendly, and at loose ends because she'd just broken up with her longtime beau. Melissa and Fiona took Keely to fabulous bars and introduced her to their friends, who welcomed Keely with rounds of tequila cocktails. Gradually, Keely felt at home there.

New York was brisk, exhilarating. Keely could feel the energy crackling around her. She walked constantly, everywhere, striding along the sidewalks with her hair tossing in the breeze, loving the sharp, cool surge of change that swept her up in its path. She visited museums, the important well-known ones and the lesser known small ones. She attended plays and concerts with friends. She entered bars by herself and sat alone, drinking a dry martini, people-watching, and sending selfies to her mother: *Look at me, alone in a bar!* The public library became her second home; taking her laptop, she left her tiny apartment for the generous warm glow of the library's spacious rooms. On rainy days, she wandered through the grand department stores—Saks Fifth Avenue, Bloomingdale's, Bergdorf Goodman, Barneys—pausing to study a coat or a dress, soaking in the look, learning how to upgrade her own wardrobe.

And then all at once it was the insanely marvelous month of June when *Rich Girl*, by Keely Green, hit the bookstands. Ransome & Hawkmore threw a party for her with lots of publishing people and a few minor celebrities and rivers of champagne. Keely signed books in the city and in surrounding suburbs, but she was most nervous about her return to the island in July.

She was invited by Mitchell's Book Corner, her favorite independent bookstore, to do a signing. Flushed with pride and almost dizzy with amazement that her writing had been transformed into an actual book, a beautiful object in the world, Keely had called her mother and made plans to come for a week's stay.

When Keely arrived at the airport, Eloise was there, waiting. She'd taken a day off work—an enormous concession for Eloise, given how busy the hospital was this time of year. Rosy-cheeked with excitement, Eloise treated Keely to lunch at Lola 41, where, she told her daughter, she felt like she was with a celebrity. People lunching at Lola spotted her and came over to say hello and congratulate her on her success. Keely drank champagne and dined on sushi. When lunch ended, she told her mother she wanted to walk home through town; she'd see her later.

Town was crowded with July visitors, the Atheneum garden was buzzing with children playing in the sun and shade, and the window boxes in town were vivid with color. Keely had sunglasses on, hoping not to run into anyone she knew. She wanted to have this walk through town all to herself. She wanted to soak in the atmosphere. She wanted to see her book in the window of Mitchell's Book Corner.

At the Atheneum garden, Keely perched on a bench, smiling at the library where her love of books had started.

Then she took out her cellphone. She was longing to talk with Isabelle. She hadn't spoken to her since Tommy and Isabelle had called Keely to tell her they were engaged. Now they were married and their baby had just been born. It was time. Keely was brave enough now. Isabelle had Tommy and his baby, but Keely had a book. True, the basic elements of the plot of *Rich Girl* came from Keely's envy of the beautiful rich girl who got the handsome man, but Keely had changed so many plot points and details that it wasn't really about Isabelle and Tommy at all.

"Hello, stranger," Keely said warmly.

"Keely. I heard you were in town. Congratulations on your book." Isabelle's voice wasn't warm, but neither was it cold.

"Isabelle, let's get together for coffee."

"Sorry. I don't have time."

"I'm leaving Nantucket tomorrow."

"I've got to go. Brittany's crying." Isabelle disconnected.

Keely sat in the small park for a long while, letting her emotions settle. The bad thing about having a best friend is that when you lose her, you have no one else close enough to turn to, no one who understands you like that best friend.

Yet Keely was certain that she couldn't have a *best friend* if she didn't admire and even envy that person, and in return, that person admired and envied her. She didn't mean the acidic, poisoning envy that was so powerful among stepmothers in Disney movies. She meant the kind of envy that made her feel complimented that such a person would be her best friend, the kind of envy that spurred her on to do her best.

She'd never talked with anyone about this. She wished she could talk to Isabelle about it now, about envy. Keely could imagine the two of them with a bottle of wine, talking deep into the night.

But Isabelle didn't have time for Keely. Maybe that was only a statement of fact. Isabelle had a daughter now. Or maybe Isabelle's envy of Keely's published book was still at the burning stage. Keely would need to wait until that envy had cooled. And if she could be honest enough to admit it, Keely was still hurt about Isabelle marrying Tommy, and the truth was Keely didn't miss Tommy half as much as she missed Isabelle.

People changed. Keely knew that. Keely had to adapt. She was a published author now. Her dream had come true. She gathered that triumph around her like a warm, invisible magic cloak to protect her heart.

Eventually Keely rose and walked home, taking little pleasure from the beauty around her. She stayed one more day, long enough to sign books at the wonderful event at Mitchell's Book Corner. *Rich Girl* was high on the bestseller lists. The publicists at Ransome & Hawkmore had arranged an extensive book tour for her. She flew to Boston, Chicago, Milwaukee, San Francisco, Dallas, Houston, Charleston, and Rehoboth Beach and Bethany Beach. She traveled for a month, living out of a suitcase, visiting bookstores and book clubs, signing autographs, and later eating room service salads on her bed as she remembered all the women she'd met. She missed their company.

She was glad to return to her tiny apartment in Manhattan in August. She stayed there during the rest of the hot humid summer with the air conditioner on full blast. She worked on her new novel while downing gallons of iced coffee, venturing out in the early evening when the heat was not quite so brutal to buy something for dinner.

Keely enjoyed the colorful autumn, walking through Central Park, kicking the flame-colored leaves. This was a pleasure she didn't have on Nantucket, where the gales and the salt air prevented maples from growing tall. In New York, the autumn air snapped with crispness, turning her cheeks red, filling her with expectation.

During the gorgeous fall, Keely spent hours proofreading the manuscript of *Poor Girl*, even though the publisher's proofreaders were carefully checking it. If one typographical error or misplaced question mark got through, Keely would get emails and comments on Facebook. She often met Fiona or one of that gang for drinks or a party or a concert or a reading at a bookstore. She still strolled the city streets like a kid in a candy shop.

But a strange kind of loneliness was seeping into her heart, like a tide finding a crack in a dam and slowly and inevitably breaking a barricade apart. She realized she'd been on a wild emotional high for a long time, exhilarated by her dream coming true. Now she was descending into reality. She couldn't understand what was going on with her. She was living the dream . . . and she was happy, but also sad.

Work was the antidote to too much navel-gazing.

With her second novel ready for the printer, and buoyed up by the wonderful reaction of readers to *Rich Girl*, Keely spent the dark November days focused on writing her third book, *Sun Music*. It was different from her first two books, more melancholy in a way, but she managed to have two women reconcile after a long embittered period of enmity, and that gave the book a rising finale. It might help her readers, and Keely as well, believe that forgiveness could happen, that jealousy could dissolve, that old friendships, old loves, could be rekindled.

She knew she was writing this book because she missed the island. She missed Isabelle's friendship. Her new friends were brilliant, screamingly funny, and amazingly ambitious. Outside of her apartment, Keely felt she lived her life at a different speed, but that might have been because so many sights, sounds, events, opportunities, and aromas seemed to zoom toward her with roller-coaster velocity. Would she change from island girl to city woman? Could she? Did she want to?

She enticed her mother to come for the week before Christmas. They took in the latest plays and ate at the most fashionable restaurants. Keely heard all the latest Nantucket news, especially about the doctors and nurses and hospital renovations.

"I have to retire in January," Eloise told Keely over steak frites in a chic new restaurant called La Boheme. "I'm sixty-five now."

"Wow, really?" Keely studied her mother. "How do you feel about that?"

Eloise shifted uncomfortably. "I'm not sure. I can't say I'm looking forward to it. What will I do with myself?"

"Mom, don't be silly. You have a thousand friends. You've been wanting to read about a hundred books. You'll be able to sleep late, have lunch with Brenda . . ."

"I suppose . . . I'm just not that kind of person."

"You can change. You can relax and enjoy life. Maybe spend more time with me here in the city."

"Maybe." Suddenly Eloise broke down, bringing her hands up to cover her face and her tears.

"You're so sweet to bring me here," she told Keely. "And I'm so very proud of you, darling. I can't imagine why you—why anyone—would want to spend time with me. I'm just a worthless old woman. You should just drag me out on an iceberg and let me float away to die in the ocean."

Keely burst out laughing. "Could you be any more dramatic? Come on, Mom. You're sixty-five, and lots of people retire at that age. You own your house clear and free, and that's amazing. You've got savings and your pension to pay your insurance and taxes and to buy a few luxuries if you'd ever think of yourself. You have friends, you can join a book club, a lunch group, a knitting group."

"I suppose you're right," her mother reluctantly agreed.

"I know you miss Dad. I know you miss me. But you've got so many talents of your own. I mean, have you thought about volunteering? There are only about three thousand nonprofits on the island that need help."

"How can I help? I've got a bad back. I know it doesn't show, Keely, and I wish it did, I wish it were some kind of rash breaking out all over my face, or a broken leg so I'd need a cane, something to show people I'm not just a lazy old lady."

"Mom! No one who knows you would ever think that!" She reached across the table to take her mother's hand. "I think you should try antidepressants."

"You know I don't like pills."

"You're a nurse. You are Pills R Us. You just think you're better than pills, and that's ridiculous. Everyone needs help at some point in their life. Mom, I really wish you'd see a doctor. At least a counselor."

Eloise sagged. "All right, darling. I'll try."

"Promise?"

"Promise."

When Eloise flew home to work on Christmas Day, Keely felt glad but guilty. Really, her mother had been hard work. Keely spent Christmas Day watching British mysteries and eating ice cream right from the Ben & Jerry's carton.

After Christmas, she forced herself to write. She felt as if she were trudging through molasses. When Juan texted her to remind her he was taking her to a New Year's Eve party, she almost cried with relief. She was so glad to think of something other than her plot and her own lonely inner world.

· · ·

When Juan had texted Keely about the party, he'd added: *I'm not merely inviting you. I'm ordering you. You will meet everyone there. So go out and buy something fabulous.*

At nine o'clock on New Year's Eve, Keely met Juan at the foyer of a penthouse on Park Avenue. She wore an expensive white T-shirt hanging almost to the hem of her ripped gold sequined short shorts, topped with a gauzy orange cardigan. And five-inch Manolo Blahnik stilettos that killed her feet. At Juan's insistence, Keely's glossy brown hair had been professionally piled high on her head with strands painstakingly teased to hang carelessly down. Her nails and lipstick were a deep burgundy and the eye shadow over her topaz eyes was noir. Her only jewelry was a heavy necklace of geometric metal links. Juan assured she looked rad, but secretly, Keely thought she looked like a bit of an idiot.

"Darling," Juan exclaimed. "Such a party!" Taking her arm, he escorted her up the elevator and into the room, already a crush of people and laughter.

"You must meet Keely Green," Juan said to a Botoxed woman weighted down with jewels. "She's a rising star in the bright young writers' scene. I'm sure you read *Rich Girl. Poor Girl* will be out this summer."

The other woman nodded to Keely, looking overwhelmed by Juan's rush of information.

Keely said, "Hello."

Juan said, "I'm off to get us champagne."

Keely knew by now that Juan was off to get *himself* a glass of champagne and then to find his friends. She made polite talk with the other woman, then excused herself and slid away through the crowd to the bar.

She wandered aimlessly here and there, holding her glass of Dom Perignon so it wouldn't spill, feeling desperately lonely. She talked with—yelled at—the few people she knew: another writer, a minor TV personality who had interviewed her, a reviewer for a popular blog.

Right now on Nantucket, there were parties and dances and dinners with friends, but at any moment of the evening, you could drive out to one of the beaches where the sea shushed and seethed into the sand and it seemed as if you were at the secret heart of the universe.

Here in this room, the laughter and chatter was getting to her. It was so loud it came at her like a solid thing, buffeting her and making hearing impossible. For sanity's sake, she gave herself a break from networking and wandered into another, quieter room. It was obviously a library, with walls of books on shelves and more books towering from coffee tables.

The silence was a relief. It would be nice if she were with a man right now, because it was twenty minutes until the stroke of midnight, and she had no one to kiss. She told herself that really, that was fine. She was a big girl now. She knew how to be alone. What was wrong with her? She wasn't happy at a fabulous party and she wasn't happy alone.

She stationed herself at the corner of the wide wall of windows in the quiet empty room, casually leaning against the adjoining wall. Regarding the world from this height always gave her vertigo, one of the prices she paid for growing up on an island with no buildings higher than three stories. The view here was spectacular. Far below, lights from the cars on the avenues glowed like rivers of gold. Stars of light shone from hundreds—thousands?—of buildings, so many lights, so many stars, it seemed as if she were in a separate sky. Well, she supposed she was.

A man entered the room. He almost ran into the room, glanced at Keely, and said, "I'm not here."

Then he threw himself behind one of the large burgundy sofas.

Keely glanced at the windows. They did not reach floor level, so they did not mirror the hiding man.

A few minutes later, a tall redhead stalked into the room. She was blazing with diamonds and her face was pinched.

"Did a man come in here?" she demanded. "Tall guy, brown hair, tux."

If the woman had been even a little less imperious, Keely might have sided with her. Instead, she looked the redhead right in the eyes. "No."

"What a shit," the woman said. "I thought he was going to propose to me tonight. But he just disappears? If you see him, do me a favor and kick him in the balls."

"Will do."

The redhead stormed from the room. Keely went to the door leading into the hall. She saw the redhead take her fur coat and slam out of the apartment. Keely returned to the library.

"She's gone. Left the party," Keely announced.

The man who rose from behind the sofa didn't look like the cowardly type. He was tall, dark-haired, and slender. His tux fit him perfectly, a slide of black elegance. His eyes were a pure green.

He was really handsome.

"Thank you," he said. "You just saved my life—and I know what I'm talking about because I'm a pediatric surgeon and save lives almost daily." He held out his hand. "Gray Anderpohl."

"Keely Green," Keely replied. In her mind she made gagging noises at the way he introduced himself. She threw his attitude right back at him. "I'm a novelist and I write books that make thousands of women happy almost daily."

Gray slapped himself on the forehead. "I've done it again, haven't I? I didn't mean to sound like a pompous ass. The sorry fact is that I'm socially challenged. Please let me start over."

Charmed, Keely laughed. "Of course. I'll start over, too."

From the other room, people began counting down. Ten . . . nine . . . eight . . .

"But first . . . It's almost midnight." Gray stepped toward Keely. He said, "This won't hurt a bit," and took her in his arms and kissed her soundly when they heard the crowd yelling "Four . . . three . . . two . . . ONE! Happy New Year!"

His breath smelled of mint, and his kiss was firm and knowing. She felt sheltered in his arms, and if that was simply because no one had held her for months, she didn't care. In the other room, someone was playing a piano and people were singing "Auld Lang Syne," not always in tune. The song touched Keely's heart and tears sprang to her eyes, which was ridiculous, because she was only twenty-seven. None of her days were *long* long ago.

Gray slowly released her, studying her face. "That was a good way to start a new year, don't you think?"

"An excellent way," Keely agreed.

"Let's not go back to the party," Gray suggested. "Let's begin this new year by making a new friend."

That was corny, Keely thought, and he was kind of formal, maybe pretentious, but he was an attractive, interesting man, and not someone she was likely to meet in her normal social circles.

Plus, she was curious.

"Sure, let's talk." Keely settled herself on a burgundy sofa. "You can start by telling me why the redhead wanted me to kick you in the balls."

Gray chuckled. He sat on the sofa, but not too close. "Candace." He shook his head. "We've been seeing each other for a while, but I swear I have no idea why she expected me to propose to her tonight." He sighed—rather theatrically, Keely thought. "I realize that I'm going to sound like a complete narcissist, but as a single, straight, well-to-do fellow in this city, I'm considered a catch. I'm divorced, no children. I have a housekeeper and a satisfying social life. I'm devoted to my work, which is enormously rewarding. So, frankly, it would take someone amazing to make me want to marry again."

Keely grinned. She understood the challenge implicit in his words—*see if you can be the special one to catch me*. And he *was* handsome. Even so, she felt no instantaneous rush of desire to be the amazing woman who would win his heart.

"You're safe with me," Keely told him. "I have no desire to marry." And those words threw the challenge back at him—could he make her want to be his wife?

Really, they were playing a kind of game. It was fun, and it woke up Keely's mind. Tucking her legs under her, she turned toward him on the sofa. "So tell me about the man who doesn't want to marry again."

As the noise level in the main room rose to a crescendo and the thump of music reverberated through the apartment, Gray spoke about himself: his training at Yale School of Medicine. The trips he'd taken with a group called Freedom Aid to countries that had few medical services. He'd just returned from Haiti, which was why he had such a good tan. And there was his position on the board of the Metropolitan Opera, and his art collection.

"Impressive," Keely said

Gray shrugged. "Fortunate, really. And you?"

The question threw her. "Fortunate? Oh, yes. Small-town girl gets novel published, makes the bestseller list, moves to the most exciting city on the planet." She tapped her lip, thinking. "I haven't been to Haiti or anywhere south of Florida, and I haven't attended an opera yet—I'm not sure I'd enjoy it."

"I'll have to take you to one," Gray said. "If you'd like to go . . ."

She knew the question was about more than one evening at Lincoln Center.

"I'd like to go," she answered.

At one-thirty, they left the party. Gray called an Uber and stayed with Keely until she was at her doorstep, which she thought was courteous. They made a date for the next night. And that led to another date, and another.

Gray was a serious man, always beautifully clad in Ermenegildo Zegna or Paul Stuart, his skillful hands clean and knowing, his mind quick and demanding. He was like no one else Keely had ever met, and she enjoyed his company. He was a surgical magician with rocket fuel energy, and he was also smart and charismatic and wealthy.

For their first date, he took her to the opera to see a thrilling production of *Carmen*. Afterward, they dined in a small, quiet restaurant that served them meltingly tender prime rib and rich red wine. They talked about easy things first. The opera reminded

Keely of one of her favorite movies, *Moonstruck*, with Cher. It was a favorite of Gray's, too, and for a long time they entertained themselves talking about movies.

Late at night, they walked along brightly lit avenues with laughing crowds going in and out of bars and restaurants. They talked. Keely told him about her childhood on Nantucket, about her dream of becoming a writer. Gray told her about his childhood in bucolic Connecticut, his dream of becoming a doctor. At some point, they stopped in an all-night diner to warm up, and over hot chocolate, they kept talking. It seemed to Keely that they were circling in increasingly smaller protective rings, sharing the easy stuff, saving the hard stuff, the inner core of their lives and loves, for the last. She didn't mind moving slowly this way. She liked talking about her life to a stranger. It gave her a new perspective. And Gray's green eyes were full of intelligence and understanding. If nothing else, he would give her material for a new character in one of her books—and she knew that thought was mostly a matter of self-protection.

As the new year unfolded, Keely saw Gray so often she believed, even though they didn't say the words, that they were becoming a couple. Certainly she had no other man in her life. Most of her time she spent in happy isolation, writing. She knew Gray's schedule. Most days he was busy at the hospital. Most nights he went right to his apartment to sleep. When he had a free evening, he took Keely to the opera, the newest plays, the best restaurants. On cold winter nights, he came to her apartment and they watched old movies.

Her writing was going along in fits and starts. She couldn't get settled in her own skin, and she thought it was all because of Gray. How did she feel about him? She didn't experience that instantaneous, breathtaking sense of yearning that had made her want to drop to her knees whenever she had set eyes on Sebastian. She didn't have the rush of warm affection and admiration and even a touch of maternal love she'd felt for Tommy. She never experienced any shock when she heard Gray's voice, her heart never leapt when she saw him. And yet, she liked him. She did like him.

Also, she was worried about her mother. Eloise turned sixty-five this month, and retired from the hospital. The doctors and nurses and staff gave Eloise a marvelous party, with cake and champagne and piles of gifts, both humorous and real. Keely called her mother often over the next few days, and Eloise sounded fine, maybe a little down, but normal.

"Why, yes, darling, I'm keeping busy," Eloise had assured Keely. "It's going to take me a century to clean out the basement and the guest room—all those things I've been promising myself I'd get to when I have time. And now I have time!"

"So are you seeing other people?"

"What do you mean?"

"I mean, like going to the movies with Brenda. Or joining a bridge club."

"Now, Keely," Eloise said, and her voice was as firm as it had been when she'd told Keely as a child to wash her hands before dinner. "You know I have never been the joiner type. I see my friends, of course. I promise you I am not isolated and babbling like some old hag."

"Mom, you could never be a hag!"

"I agree. And I'm not. So stop fussing."

Still, Keely called her mother almost every day. Still, she worried. The hospital had been her mother's life for over forty years. Her family and her work had been her world. Now she was on her own.

As the days grew longer, Keely and Gray had dinner several times a week, often at her apartment or his. They took turns making dinner and watching movies about writers and doctors. *MASH* one night, *Julie and Julia* the next week. *Night Nurse*, and a week later, *The Ghost Writer.* Maybe, Keely thought, this was the way Gray could spend time with her without having to talk about himself.

Or to make love.

Gray was such a puzzle to Keely! He was attentive and often affectionate. He phoned or texted her every day. He often treated her to restaurants she never knew existed, many of them in private clubs she'd never heard of. He took her to fabulous parties and he also took her to meet other couples for dinner. He began to say, "You remember Keely," as if it was understood that she was a permanent part of his life.

Keely had had sex with a guy in college, but she'd made love only with Tommy. So she didn't have a wide experience to judge from. But one April evening, she couldn't stand it any longer. They were at his apartment. He'd prepared a complicated beef Wellington, which involved fillets of beef and wild mushrooms and a flaky puff pastry.

"Beef Wellington! Gray, how fabulous. I've never had the courage to make one. It's magnificent. I almost don't want to eat it."

"And I have an excellent wine to go with it," Gray said.

He'd set his small table with a snowy white cloth, silver candlesticks, and sterling silver utensils. Side plates held green salads. Keely cut through the pastry into the tender beef and groaned with pleasure. They barely spoke during dinner, except for appreciative moans.

When they'd finished, they carried their dishes to the dishwasher. Gray liked things to be tidy.

Keely said, "If you weren't here, I'd lick this plate."

Gray smiled. "For dessert, we'll have fresh raspberries—the parents of a patient of mine brought me some they had specially flown in from Mexico. We'll have champagne with the berries."

Keely stood next to him, eyeing him with pretend suspicion. "I think you're trying to seduce me." She decided to be brazen and leaned in close, sliding her breasts against him.

He didn't look her in the eye, but a blush colored his cheeks. "And beef Wellington is the magic charm in seduction?"

She didn't hesitate. "Absolutely." She stepped closer.

Finally he turned and took her in his arms and kissed her. She wrapped her arms around him and kissed him back. He took her hand and led her into his bedroom, and they lay together for a long time, kissing, slowly removing their clothes, gently touching one another.

Afterward, they lay spooning in the dark bedroom.

"Now are you ready for raspberries?"

Keely was glad he couldn't see her face. It gave her the courage to say, "Not just yet, Gray. I'd like to talk . . . really talk."

Gray hesitated. "All right."

"Gray, I often feel that you're . . . isolated, even when you're with me."

After a long moment, Gray said, "I'm an only child."

"I'm an only child, too," she told him. "I know it can be lonely."

"Yes. Also . . ." Gray hesitated. "My family wasn't all that happy. I don't mean abusive. Nothing like that. My father was a physician. We had a nice house. I had friends. I did well in school. I took piano and played in recitals."

"Gray, I'm not trying to be mean, but it's almost as if you are filling out a form. I can get the surface stuff from you, but nothing . . . deep. Nothing important."

"You haven't told me anything deep," Gray responded.

"Maybe not. But I've always been myself. Open to you. And I'm willing to tell you about my childhood. But first, I want to hear you talk."

Gray took his arm from around Keely and turned on his back, arms behind his head, facing the ceiling.

"My mother had three miscarriages after I was born. Second-trimester miscarriages. Very painful physically and emotionally. Traumatic. Her heart was broken."

"Gray. I'm so sorry. How sad for her. For all of you."

"I felt like it was my fault. I know now it wasn't, but when I was little, three and five and seven . . . I wanted to make it right for her. She wanted another baby so much. She was happy when she was pregnant, and then so sad when she lost the baby. She grieved so much . . . she lay in her bed and wept all the time. She couldn't find the energy to cook or do laundry. My father helped her. And he cooked dinner for us, although if Mother came to the table, she couldn't really eat. He was a good dad. He told me Mother loved me, and Mother loved him, too, but she was going through a grieving process and it would take time. I heard his words, but I felt—unnecessary to my mother. My presence could not bring her joy. I worked hard to get good grades. I learned to play the piano. I was good, I could have entered competitions, but when I did perform at recitals . . . my mother never came. I wasn't . . . *relevant* to her life. I wasn't anything that could make her smile."

"Oh, Gray." Keely turned over so she could gently touch his shoulder. "That must have been so hard for you."

"She never really recovered. She and Dad live in Connecticut. He was a general practitioner, an M.D., and he couldn't fix her. So we both felt like we failed her. I felt guilty when I started dating, I mean guilty for being happy and having fun, when she was still so sad. She would seem normal to you. She cooks dinner for her and Dad now, and she belongs to a book club and she watches television and shops for clothes, and she smiles. I've seen her smile. She did see a therapist. She is trying to live her life in a positive way. But . . . losing those three babies changed her forever."

Keely waited, wanting to honor his sadness.

"What I'm trying to say is that I find it hard to be close to someone. I have been told by other women . . ." Gray stopped speaking. He cleared his throat. "I've been told by other women that I'm not spontaneous enough. That I'm guarded. Maybe they're right. Maybe I am guarded."

"I can understand that." Keely was touched by his confession. She wanted to kiss him, to heal him.

"Or maybe I just haven't met the right woman," Gray continued. "Maybe when I'm with the right woman, I'll be able to . . . open up."

Keely tensed. Here it was again, a kind of challenge, an invitation to some bizarre contest. Could she be the right woman, could she heal him, open him up? Was this a real question for Gray, or was this some kind of game?

"I'm glad you told me about your mother," Keely said. "It's all so sad. But she must be proud of you now. A pediatric surgeon—you've saved so many lives."

Gray sniffed. "I don't need a psychologist to tell me why I became a pediatric surgeon." After a moment, he said, "I wish so many things in my life were different."

"I suppose we all have things in our lives we wish we could change."

"Really?" Gray searched Keely's face. "What would you want to change? You have everything."

"Remember, we're talking about our pasts," Keely said.

"Then tell me about your past," Gray responded, and he sounded truly interested, and also maybe a little challenging—*can your past be worse than my past?*

"I think we have to drink the champagne if I'm going to tell you everything."

"Ah. I'll get the bottle and the glasses."

Keely talked about her life on the island. Her lovely, quiet parents. Her best friend, Isabelle, her first serious boyfriend, Tommy.

And somehow as she spoke, leaning back against the headboard with the sheets pulled up over her breasts, the old emotions perked up like flowers under sunshine.

"Isabelle and I were so close." Keely held up two fingers pressed together. "I was always jealous of her, and even though I told her, she didn't really *get* it. We were both going to be writers, novelists, when we grew up, but her family traveled all over the world in the summer, and I had to stay home and work. I knew she was going to have much more interesting subjects to write about."

"Yet you are the published author," Gray reminded her.

Keely smiled. "True."

She told him about Tommy, how she'd refused to go to homecoming with him in high school because she didn't want Isabelle to be sad. How Isabelle got accepted to a writers' colony and Keely didn't.

"I loved her and I envied her at the same time," Keely said. "Does that sound strange?"

"Research shows that people consider themselves rich if they have more money than their next-door neighbor," Gray said. "We compare ourselves to those we know."

Keely laughed. "How did you get to be so wise?" She snuggled against him, yawning. "Gosh, I'm so sleepy."

"Then we should go to sleep," Gray said.

"Wiser and wiser," Keely murmured, slipping down until her head was on the pillow.

Gray spooned himself against her. Keely felt warm and safe and content.

In the morning, Keely woke first. Gray's eyes were closed. He snored quietly, deeply sleeping. This was Gray's day off from the hospital, and she wanted to let him rest. She also wanted somehow to acknowledge how sweet he'd been during their talk last night.

But she really wanted to work on her book. It was her habit to make a cup of coffee and sit down at her computer. She needed to write, and her third manuscript needed to be resuscitated.

She decided that if Gray woke while she was dressing, she would stay. If he didn't, she'd let him sleep.

She dressed, found her purse, and brushed her hair. He didn't wake. She stood a moment in the bedroom, looking down at the sleeping man. He was so handsome, and in sleep he looked vulnerable and innocent. *Maybe we all look that way when we're asleep,* Keely thought. The blanket didn't cover his feet. Quietly, she adjusted the blanket. Gray didn't wake. She hurried down to catch a cab to take her home to her computer.

The early draft of her third novel, *Sun Music*, turned in this past October, had disappointed her editor. Somehow, the plot had gotten all tangled up on her, and the passion wasn't there. *Poor Girl* would come out this July. Her third novel was under contract and slated for next summer, so she had to get it to her editor by September.

Worried and frustrated, she let herself into her apartment. She stayed under a hot shower, letting her mind wander free, but once she was wrapped in a towel with another towel for a turban, inspiration wasn't there.

She glanced at her phone. A missed call from Gray. A voicemail from Fiona, reminding her they were meeting for lunch. Good. She needed to talk with someone, and Fiona had become a good friend as well as an agent, and she knew just how much to tell Keely about her editor's opinions.

Outside, the spring day was gray, with rain clouds darkening the sky. At home, she would wear a crimson sweater or a turquoise shirt, something to brighten her world. But here in New York most people, the chic and savvy, wore black, with shades of gray. Keely was used to fresh salty air sweeping over the island from all the way across the Atlantic or up from the Caribbean. But she was a New Yorker now, and she had no plans to return to Nantucket, no matter how much her heart yearned.

She pulled a dark tunic off her clothing rack, added black tights and knee-high black boots and brushed her long brown hair. Dangling silver earrings, mascara on her eyelashes to accentuate her topaz eyes, a touch of lipstick, and she was good to go. She looked sleek and slim and when she slipped on her sunglasses, she looked almost fabulous.

She slung her Hermès knockoff bag over her shoulder, checked her image in the mirror—she'd fit right in with the crowd—and headed out, being sure to lock the three thousand locks in her door before clattering down the four flights of stairs.

It took her a moment to break into the mass of pedestrians rushing up and down the street. She'd been certain that by now, after living in New York as long as she had, she'd be used to the pace and the noise and the crowds, but still, every time she walked, her mind flashed with memories of the brick sidewalks of Nantucket, humped and crooked from the roots of the grand shade trees, forcing people to slow down, pay attention, be there now. Now the window boxes would be spilling with flowers and the sidewalks crowded as friends met up after the long winter.

Keely missed her mother and her home and the golden beaches and the damn warped sidewalks of Nantucket, but she was *here* now, and why was she thinking about Nantucket so much this morning? She was a published author in the greatest city in the world on her way to meet her friend/agent!

She glanced in the storefront windows as she passed. Wow. She looked really good. She looked like she *belonged* in this amazing city. She even kind of looked like Kate Middleton if she cocked her head so that her long hair fell over her shoulder.

She admired herself so much she walked right into a man who was absorbed in his cellphone. They both muttered "excuse me" and Keely laughed out loud as she hurried along the sidewalk toward her lunch date.

It felt so good to laugh! She had to admit she was kind of worried, actually massively terrified, about her third novel. *Rich Girl* had made her a nice chunk of money. The pre-orders for *Poor Girl* were exciting. She hoped this glitch with *Sun Music* wouldn't put an end to her writing career.

Fiona was waiting in the foyer of Balthazar. They air-kissed hello and followed the maître d' to their booth. They both loved this place for its booths—they could talk in privacy.

"So," Fiona said. "Tell me everything."

Keely preened ostentatiously. "That might take a long time . . ."

Fiona squinted her eyes at Keely. After a moment she said, "You did not."

Keely laughed. "I did."

"You had sex with Gray Anderpohl?"

"I did," Keely repeated, grinning.

"Waiter," Fiona called, and the handsome dark man turned toward her. "Strike the order for wine. We want a bottle of champagne." She rested her arm on the table and tucked her chin into her hand. "Go."

"It was last night. At his house. He made beef Wellington—"

"I don't really want the details of your dinner. Get to the good stuff."

"Hang on, that's the way we got to the good stuff. I mean I was impressed that he made such a complicated dish, and I asked him if he was trying to seduce me . . . and he was. After dinner, we went to bed together."

"How was it? On a scale from one to ten."

"Don't be gross." Keely busied herself with her napkin, and the waiter arrived with their flutes and the bucket of ice. He made a small performance of popping the cork of the champagne bottle, and when he was done and had gone away, Keely said, "I stayed all night with him."

"Wow. He must be serious about you. I've heard stories about him. He's kind of an odd duck, Keely."

"So am I."

"From what I've heard from other women, he puts his work first, always, completely. Relationships come next."

"That's fine with me. I have my work, too. And I have fun with him, Fiona. I've seen so much of this fabulous city because of him. I've learned so much. I've been to operas and ballets at Lincoln Center. He's taken me to dinner at Buvette and Saint Ambroeus in the West Village. Jennifer Aniston goes there—"

"Do you have any idea how superficial you sound?"

Keely recoiled as if she'd been slapped. "What?"

"And it shows in your new book. The chapters you sent to Sally. I read them. The magic is gone, and now I know why."

"Oh," Keely said. "Wow." She took a sip of champagne. "I don't know where to start, Fiona. I mean, I welcome any suggestions about my book. You are one of my agents, after all. But somehow you've gotten Gray all mixed up with my novel."

"No, *you've* gotten Gray all mixed up with your novel. You've lost the magic in your novels."

"Okay. I get that. But I don't think it has anything to do with Gray."

"Really? I think that if Gray were the best man for you, you would be happy, and your writing would soar, instead of crashing."

"Crashing. That's a little harsh." Keely shook her head. "And I *am* happy."

"I think you miss your island."

Keely sat back, surprised.

"Look. Your first two novels were set on Nantucket. They emanated a kind of light and spaciousness and *pleasure* that made readers want to be in the book. What you've done with this new novel is missing that."

"Okay," Keely said slowly, thinking it through. "I can see that."

"So I think you need to go back to Nantucket."

Keely smiled at the thought. "Just like that?"

"Why not? It wouldn't be permanent. You could live with your mother. Walk on the beaches. Bike out to the Sankaty Head lighthouse. Watch the ferries arrive."

"But *Sun Music* is set in New York."

"Maybe it shouldn't be."

"It would mean major changes to set it in Nantucket."

"But you can do it."

Keely nodded. "I'll think about it."

The waiter arrived to take their order.

Fiona said, "Okay. Lecture over."

Keely smiled. "Good!" She was relieved to have the hard business talk done, and glad not to talk about Gray any more, because she was so totally confused about him.

After lunch, Keely walked out into the bright light of a spring afternoon and on a whim, headed for Central Park. Her mind was churning, and her heart . . . well, her heart *hurt*. She knew that Fiona's advice was spot on. She knew she'd lost the magic, but the difficulty was that she didn't think returning to Nantucket would restore the magic to her writing. Or to her life.

She didn't know *what* could restore the magic.

She found a bench across from the Bethesda Fountain, her favorite place in all of this brightly lit city. She loved the Angel of the Waters, and she could certainly use an angel in her life right now. She sat by the fountain, her thoughts tumbling, until the sunlight slanted in a different way. It was growing late. She rose and walked to the subway, got off at Fifty-ninth Street, and like an automaton, made her way to her building and up the four flights of stairs to her apartment.

She let herself into her apartment, locked the three thousand locks, and dropped her bag on the sofa. She'd had her phone turned off in the restaurant. She leaned against the kitchen sink, filling a glass with water. She curled up on her sofa and turned on her phone.

Gray had called twice, leaving a message both times, asking her to call.

She hit Call Back, and Gray answered at once. "I've had an idea."

"Really. I wish I had one."

"Seriously, this is a big deal idea."

Keely laughed, thinking he'd take her for a ride in a balloon, or fly her to Paris for the weekend. "Tell me."

"I want to take you to Connecticut this weekend. We'll stay with my parents. They want to meet you, and I want to show you where I grew up."

Keely was speechless.

"Good idea, right? I've got Friday off. We can drive up Friday morning and have the weekend to kick around in Mystic."

"*Mystic*," Keely said. How she loved that name. "That's on the water, right?"

"Right, and we've got a boat, but it's too cold to go for a sail.

Still, the town is historic, and they've got Mystic Pizza, and a museum . . ."

"It sounds wonderful, Gray. I'd love to go."

"Good. We'll go."

"What should I take for a weekend at your parents'?" Keely
asked.

"Casual clothes," Gray answered. "Jeans, sneakers, sweaters.
It's spring, but it will be cool up there. Maybe a nice shirt for the
evening."

"Tell me, Gray," Keely said, her voice teasing, "are *you* wearing
sneakers?"

She was rewarded with a low laugh. "What? You think I don't
wear sneakers?"

"Do you?"

"All right. You're right. I wear leather loafers. But I do have
boots up at the Connecticut house for riding."

"Of course you do," Keely said, her voice affectionate. "I'll see
you tomorrow morning."

Instead of packing, Keely sank down on the bed with her hands
folded at her lips, almost as if she were praying. This weekend was
a huge step for Gray, and for Keely. She felt the weight of responsibility on her shoulders—Gray was opening up to her. He was
taking her to meet his parents, the mother who had never recovered from her miscarriages, who couldn't show affection to Gray.
How would she react to Keely? What could Keely do to show his
parents how much Keely admired Gray?

And *admired* was the correct word. She was not yet ready to
say, even to herself, that she *loved* Gray. She wasn't a teenager
anymore, beguiled by her own adolescent passions. But was she
wrong to want just a touch of that magical, captivating, mesmer-
izing emotion that could make her feel helpless, limp, intoxicated
with love? She *wanted* to love Gray that way.

Her cell rang again. Absentmindedly, she answered.

"Oh, Keely, I'm so glad I got you." Brenda's warm, slightly

croaked voice summoned up her presence for Keely, her plump, bustling, rosy-cheeked, farmer's wife warmth.

"Of course, Brenda. What's up?"

"It's your mom."

"What happened?"

"Don't be scared, she's not in the hospital or anything. But, um, she's . . . she's *depressed*, that's what she is. You know she had to retire."

"Yes, I know. I've been worried about her. She seemed depressed in December. I've been calling her almost every day." Keely winced as she spoke. She hadn't been calling her mother almost every day. More like once a week.

"I know. You've been a good daughter, Keely. And I suppose we all thought Eloise would be okay, she's such a trouper. But she hasn't been going out very often, and I've been trying to call her and Marjorie told me Eloise wasn't returning her phone calls, so I went to see her."

"How is she?"

"Honey, she's, well, not good. I don't mean she's sick, although she's lost a lot of weight, well, she could stand to lose some, just like I could, at our age we seem to pack it on simply by breathing, but it's her, well, her appearance. And her, well, her hygiene, Keely. That's what worries me. Her hygiene, I guess, is the simplest way to say it."

"Her *hygiene*?"

"She wouldn't let me all the way in her house. And it was afternoon and she was wearing an old robe. And her hair was . . . Keely, you need to come home."

chapter
twelve

"I'll be there tomorrow."

"Call and tell me what plane and I'll meet you and drive you to her house."

"My old car is at home—"

"When you get there, you can use it. I'll pick you up. And prepare yourself, hon. The house is kind of a pit."

Keely thought of Brenda's house, where you entered into the back hall and tripped over several pairs of waterproof boots, dog toys, and gardening utensils. If Brenda thought Keely's mother's house was a pit . . .

"All right. I'll let you know when I know what flight I'll be on. And thanks, Brenda."

"Of course, sweetie."

Stunned, Keely walked to her small sofa and sat down, staring at the phone. Keely had always wished she wasn't an only child, and now she powerfully regretted not having siblings. A nice brother, for example, who could help their mother with handyman chores around the house. Who would be married and have children so their mother could fill her life with grandchildren. Who could jokingly urge their mother into seeing a doctor about her depression, although Eloise probably wouldn't be depressed if she had grandchildren.

But Keely was an only child, and she loved her mother. All her life she'd admired her mother and been proud of her. Once, during a play in elementary school, a boy had tripped on his costume and fallen on the side of a table, hitting his head. He sat up, crying, with blood running down his face, making the other actors and some of the audience scream. Keely's mother had quickly, calmly climbed the steps to the stage. Kneeling by the child, she'd assured him he was fine while she took an antibacterial wipe from her purse—because she always carried a pack. She ripped off part of his costume and turned it into a bandage for his wound by wrapping it around his head. By the time his worried mother reached the stage, the boy had stopped crying and actually looked quite pleased with himself.

How many times had Keely been told by islanders how grateful they were for Eloise's care when they were in the hospital? People adored Keely's mother, and so did Keely. She needed to figure out how she could help her, and she'd been longing to see the island again, so why was she stalling?

Well, Gray. He was planning to take her to the country to meet his parents. She might not be truly, deeply, madly in love with him, but she did enjoy being with him, and now that she was getting to know the real man, she did care about him.

"Snap out of it," Keely told herself. She booked a flight from New York to Nantucket for a staggering amount of money.

Next, she had to call Gray.

"Hi, babe," Gray said, and he sounded unusually happy.

"Gray, I have disappointing news. My mother's not doing well. Her friend phoned and told me I need to go back to the island. I'm flying out tomorrow."

For a long moment, Gray was silent. When he spoke, his voice was cool. "I'm sorry to hear that. Is she ill?"

"I don't know. She's depressed, and not leaving the house, not seeing people. I need to check on her. I don't know how long I'll be gone. I'm truly sorry I can't come to the country with you. I was looking forward to it so much."

"Well, the country will always be there."

"I know, but, Gray, listen. I mean it. I want to go to the country with you, and I'm sick that I can't, but it's my mother and I haven't seen her for almost four months."

"I understand. I hope she's okay. Let me know how she is. How you are."

"I will. And maybe you can send me some photos of the country."

"Sure. Well, good luck, Keely."

"Yes, thanks."

Her stomach felt hollow when she clicked off.

Then she looked at her laptop, standing ready and waiting on the table. She'd take it with her, and maybe a change of scenery would be just what she needed to kick-start her novel revisions.

As Keely's plane lifted off from LaGuardia, she looked down at the rows of skyscrapers separated by rivers of vehicles and linked to the mainland by bridges. In minutes, the plane was over Long Island Sound and the dark blue Atlantic, and forty-five minutes later, she saw Nantucket, low and green and surrounded by water, held to the mainland by nothing—no bridge could span thirty miles—with only a few roads linking the cluster of buildings at the harbor to the far points of the island.

The plane came in from the north onto the runway that ended at the ocean. It taxied up to a small gray shed. The pilot thanked his six passengers. Keely went down the ramp and walked across the tarmac to the terminal to wait for her luggage.

Brenda was there to greet her.

"Oh, honey, look at you, you're wasting away to nothing."

Brenda hugged Keely tightly, and Keely was surprised at how that affection warmed her and brought her emotions right to the surface. She blinked back tears.

"It's so good to see you, Brenda."

"I brought you a deep-dish apple pie and a hamburger casserole—they're in the back of the car. I'm not sure your mother has much food in the house."

"That's so nice. And you know how I love your pies." Keely lifted her rolling suitcase from the luggage bin and followed Brenda out of the small building. "I tried to phone Mom to let her know I was coming, but her landline doesn't work and she doesn't answer her cell."

"She lost her cellphone a few weeks ago. I helped her get a new one but she never uses it. See what I mean? She's let everything go. I am so relieved you're here. How long can you stay?"

"I'm not sure."

"It seems wrong to me that you're not living here, Keely. If you don't mind my speaking frankly. It's one thing that your mother misses you, but the *island* isn't the same without you."

Keely wanted to distract Brenda. "How are your chickens?"

"Oh, my, what drama we've had! A summer person's little dog got into our yard . . ." Brenda chatted away happily until they reached Eloise's house. "Okay, here we are." Brenda pulled into the driveway of the modest one-story ranch house on Kingfisher Drive. "I'll carry in the casserole and pie."

Keely hooked her laptop and bag over her shoulder and pulled her rolling suitcase up the walk. She stopped at the door of the house she'd grown up in. It had always been a glossy yellow, but now it looked faded and weathered. Her mother used to paint it first thing every spring, when the scouring winter winds had calmed and the daffodils were blooming. It was a plain house, but her mother had always kept some sort of greenery in the window boxes.

Keely knocked. No answer.

"Knock harder, hon. YOOHOO!"

Keely knocked again. At the front window, a curtain twitched.

The door opened. Her mother stood there in a shabby old chenille robe and grimy slippers.

"Keely!"

"Hi, Mom."

"My goodness, this is a surprise. Darling, I'm so happy to see you!"

Eloise hugged Keely. "Brenda," she said, "I'd ask you in, but the house is a mess. I've been sorting through old papers and clothes. Trying to declutter, you know."

Brenda leaned forward and set her two dishes on the floor. "Oh, that's fine, Eloise. I understand, of course. I'm just dropping off a casserole and an apple pie. You always loved my pies."

Keely turned to hug her mother's friend. "Brenda, thank you so much for everything. It was great of you to pick me up at the airport."

Brenda gave Keely a meaningful look. "Anything I can do, Keely, you just let me know." She bustled away down the walk to her car, turning to wave at Keely and Eloise when she reached her car door.

"Come in," Eloise said. "If I'd known you were coming . . ." She looked confused. "Did you tell me you were coming?"

"I tried to, Mom, but your landline doesn't work."

"Oh, maybe I left it off the hook again," Eloise said vaguely. "And my new cellphone is so confusing."

Her mother had loved technology when she worked at the hospital. Every year wonderful new diagnostic and therapeutic machines arrived on the island, making Eloise's work easier. It was a bad sign that her mother was having trouble with her new cell.

Keely hefted her suitcase inside and started to put her purse and computer bag on the table by the front door. But the table was so piled with mail and newspapers there was no room. She set them on the floor. There wasn't much room there, either.

Eloise picked up Brenda's dishes and carried them into the kitchen, but Keely remained by the front door, stunned.

The room was adrift in an ocean of papers. Piles and piles of papers.

"Mom."

Her mother came out of the kitchen and stood slumped, unable to meet Keely's eyes. "I know. I've let it get away from me. But I have a plan. I do. I'm sorting through all the papers and boxes from the bedrooms and basement. Have you heard of 'Death Cleaning'?"

"What? No!"

"It's Swedish. It's on all the television shows. It means decluttering your house so your children don't have to when you die."

"Yeah, well, this doesn't look like decluttering to me."

"I know, but they say you can take your time. It doesn't have to be done all at once and you can slow down and look at what you're getting rid of and appreciate the memories. I know this looks like a mess, but I've got a system. Come over here."

Keely obeyed her mother, wading through piles of paper to sit next to Eloise on the sofa.

"Now look." Eloise held up a construction paper collage of Christmas images Keely had made in first grade. "Isn't this pretty? How can I give it up? And you'll want to have it when you're settled in a house."

"Mom." Keely took the paper from her mother, set it aside, and took her mother's hand. "Stop a minute. Look at yourself. Look at this room. It's like—" *where a hoarder lives*, she almost said, but stopped herself. "Don't you wonder what I'm doing here? Why I just showed up like this?"

"Well, honey, you know I'm always glad to see you. This is your home. You don't need any special reason to come visit."

"But I *have* a special reason. Brenda called me. She's worried about you. When's the last time you got together with Brenda? Or with any of your friends? When have you gone to a movie, or to a concert, or to the library?"

Eloise yanked her hand away from Keely's. "I'm busy, that's all. I'm busy!"

"Too busy to wash your hair?" Keely leaned in closer, inhaling the unpleasant scents of body odor and hair that desperately needed washing. "Too busy to bathe? Or wash your clothes?"

"Why does it matter?" Eloise folded her arms over her chest in a classic defensive pose. "I never go anywhere, except to the grocery store. I've got too much to do here. So much stuff to throw out. All my life to throw out."

"Oh, Mom." Keely tried to put her arm around her mother, but Eloise pulled away, her mouth in a childish pout. Keely persisted. "We both know if you throw away these papers, you won't be actually throwing away your *life*. I mean, this Christmas collage, well, we can toss that, right? I certainly don't want it." Eloise bristled, but held her tongue. "So. I'm going to put my luggage in my room, and then I'll come out here and we can make a start."

"Keely—" Eloise struggled to say the words. "It might take more than a few days."

"Okay, well, that's fine. I can write every morning and help with the papers in the afternoon. I'll just get my stuff organized."

She walked out of the living room and down the hall between the three small bedrooms and bathroom.

The hall was filled with stuff. Clothes. Books. Clocks, lamps, pictures, mirrors, small boxes of God only knew what. And not piled neatly in a grouping, but all mixed together in a hodgepodge of odds and ends.

She looked in her mother's room. More stuff. Mostly clothing and shoes, much of it Keely's father's. A pang of guilt cramped Keely's heart. She should have helped her mother sort her father's things years ago.

She found her own room as chaotic as the rest of the house. Her parents had given her twin beds so she could have sleepovers with friends. Both beds were hidden beneath jumbles of fabric. Wading through old skirts, sweaters, and sneakers, Keely pulled her luggage to the closest bed. She picked up a wad of clothes and tossed them on the floor. She was determined to get down to her sheets and her mother's hand-embroidered lilac quilt and toss them in the wash before she tried to sleep in this room tonight.

"Keely? Darling?"

"I'm in my room, Mom. Gosh, I have a lot of books to take to the library for the book sale."

Eloise stepped into the room. "Oh, darling, don't do that. I might want to read some of them."

Keely started to argue, but held her tongue. It broke her heart to see her wonderful mother looking so—so lost. Unwashed and shabby and lost.

Lost in her own home.

"You're right," Keely said. "We'll do it together and you can decide which books can go and which can stay."

Her mother stubbornly faced forward, chin lifted defiantly.

Keely thought desperately and came up with the perfect solution. Islanders called their dump the Madaket Mall because so many summer people dropped off their cast-offs at the Take It or Leave It shed. A few minutes' search on the bookshelves and tables could provide new hardback mysteries from England, available a year before the American publication. The wealthy summer women had their help drop off clothes with the tags still on them—if they hadn't worn them that summer, they didn't want them; they wouldn't wear anything a year old. Antique chairs, slightly scratched, Italian majolica dinner sets that didn't work out for the summer house, wicker armchairs with one strand of wicker missing—the dump was like a mad hatter store. Many islanders stopped by there at least once a week, partly to cruise the shed, partly to visit with friends, because so many islanders were there. One of the great things was that when you met up with friends at the mall, you could be wearing old saggy clothes, crazy hair, and no lipstick and it didn't matter—everyone looked that way at the Madaket Mall.

"Listen, Mom. I'll stay a few days and help you sort all this stuff. We'll do it together. Then we'll take it to the dump and we can air out the house and I'll take you somewhere nice for dinner. Okay? Sound fun?"

"Okay. Just let me get my cheaters." Eloise brightened. "Isn't that a cute name? It's really readers, short for reading glasses."

"Very cute. But don't get them now. I want to help you take a nice long shower and wash your hair and get dressed. Then we can go for a drive around town and you can tell me about all the things that have changed."

"Oh, we don't have to go out. We can curl up and have a nice long catch-up."

Keely was silent. How was she going to handle this? Eloise was her mother, the one Keely turned to for advice. Eloise was only sixty-five. Had she become mentally incapable? Did she have Alzheimer's?

"No, Mom, I want to get out and see with my own eyes. I'm going to take you out to dinner, too."

Eloise shifted her gaze from Keely's. "Oh, I don't know about eating out . . ."

"So you have plenty of fresh food in the kitchen?"

Her mother's shoulders sagged, then she brightened. "Brenda brought us a casserole and a pie!"

"Do we have something for breakfast? Eggs? Bread? Coffee?"

"Um . . . I'm not sure . . ."

Keely stepped forward and took her mother gently by the shoulders. "Mom, are you okay? I mean, really?"

Eloise stared at the floor. "I suppose I've let things go," she whispered.

"Have you gone to the grocery store recently?"

Like a small child not wanting to admit guilt, Eloise shrugged her shoulders away from Keely. "It doesn't take a lot of food to keep one old useless person alive."

"Oh, Mom. You're not old and you're certainly not useless."

"You don't understand. Everyone else has someone. I'm all alone."

Keely was speechless. This attitude was a one-eighty from her mother's normal optimism. The question was, how could Keely help?

"If I had a grandchild, like Donna Maxwell has a grandchild, I could be useful then, plus I'd have"—she choked on the words—"someone to hold."

A flurry of emotions hit Keely. Pity. Irritation. Guilt. And—here it came—she thought she'd erased it from her life—*envy*.

"Oh, for heaven's sake," Keely said sternly. "What are we doing, standing here crying! Some people would give their back molars to be where we are in life. Now come on. Get in the bathroom and shower and wash your hair or I'll have to do it for you."

"I'm not sure—"

"I am. Let's compromise. You get cleaned up and we'll stay in tonight and eat Brenda's casserole, okay? Now go."

Her mother nodded and shuffled off to the bathroom. Keely leaned against the wall, listening carefully. When she heard the rush of water from the shower, she headed into the kitchen to see just how much of a disaster it had become.

Keely's second day back on the island dawned warm and sunny. She rose before her mother. She made coffee, opened the back door, and stepped out into the fresh day.

Ah. Now she was really home. And it was the first day of April. Spring.

Years ago, her father had built a small slate patio for his outdoor grill and her mother's wrought iron picnic table and chairs. Every spring, her mother bought new covers for the chair cushions and chose a small plant like a primrose or pansy to set in a porcelain pot in the middle of the table. Most summer evenings, the family ate outdoors.

Keely settled on a chair and raised her face to the sun. Her parents had planted flowering trees when they'd first bought the house, and now they were sturdy, their winged branches dappled with opening buds of pink and white. Birds flew back and forth between the trees, singing, and Keely leaned back into the chair and into the day and breathed it all in. She wanted to walk down South Beach Street to see the cherry trees in bloom. And maybe she'd bike over to the Wicked Island Bakery and get a morning bun, which wasn't a bun at all but a delectable swirl of sugary cinnamon pastry like nothing else in the world. And maybe she'd walk down to The Creeks at the end of the harbor and see how the water had shaped the inlets over the winter. And maybe . . .

First, she would concentrate on helping her mother with the house. Next, she would get her mother *out* of the house. This afternoon, she would set up her laptop and download the notes Juan had sent and start rewriting, again, her third novel. She went back inside, poured herself another cup of coffee, and rapped on her mother's door to waken her.

By late afternoon, she hadn't touched her laptop, but she had dropped her mother off at the hairdresser. She made a quick run to Stop & Shop, where she'd bumped into several friends and caught up on their news—births, weddings, divorces, feuds, and for some of her mother's friends, deaths.

Keely clapped her hands when her mother walked out of the salon.

"Mom, you look so pretty!"

"Thank you." Eloise blushed.

"Hey, Mom, guess what Janine told me at the grocery store. Kathleen Knight's art gallery has an opening tonight. I think we should go!"

"Darling, you go on without me. I'm not really up to it today."

"Oh, for heaven's sake. Come on, this will be fun. You know Kathleen always serves champagne and fabulous munchies."

Eloise waved her hand vaguely. "Too many people . . ."

"Yes, and they'll all point and snicker and whisper, 'There's that pitiful Eloise Green who retired from the hospital and now just sits around being uninterested in the world.'"

"Don't be mean."

"Don't be lazy." Keely bit her cheeks to keep in a smile. *Lazy* was, to her mother, a deplorable trait.

"I'm *not* lazy! I worked with you all morning sorting out the house. Now I'm tired."

"I'll take you to dinner at the Boarding House if you go with me."

"I'm not hungry. That sandwich you made was too filling."

"Mom, are you depressed?"

"Possibly. I certainly have the right to be depressed. My husband's dead and I no longer have the job that was my *life*."

"Okay, think about *me* for a minute. Obviously I don't rate very high on your scale of reasons to live—"

"That's not true! You're putting words in my mouth!"

Keely stifled a grin. She'd gotten a rise out of her mother. "Back to the subject of me. *I* want to go into town. *I* want to see old friends. But, Mom, what if I run into Isabelle or Tommy? They'll be together, the happy married couple and I'll be all alone, the pitiful and unattached."

"No one thinks you're pitiful!"

"No one thinks *you're* pitiful!" Keely fired back.

Eloise sighed and slumped. "You are a manipulative child."

Keely pulled into the drive. "Wait till I get some lipstick on you. Maybe some blush. You'll look gorgeous."

Early in the evening, Keely drove into town. Nightlife wasn't up to full speed yet, so not all the boutiques and galleries were open. Still, the winter was over, and the island was waking up. Lights shone from the stores, and the doors of some of the shops were open, allowing alluring fragrances to drift out.

She strolled side by side with her mother, window shopping.

"Do you remember, Mom, how Isabelle and I used to attend the gallery openings on Friday nights in the summer?"

Eloise smiled. "Lord, yes. You were fourteen, fifteen, and you draped yourselves in layers of black, wore mahogany nail polish and lipstick and kohl eyeliner, and such high heels I knew you'd break your ankles."

"But we didn't break our ankles. We were terribly grown-up and sophisticated, sauntering around with artists and the summer visitors who could afford to buy the paintings."

"Yes, and you also managed to snag a forbidden glass of wine."

"We did not!"

"Of course you did. I smelled it on you when you got home."

"Well, it was champagne. Or prosecco. Anyway, we didn't make fools of ourselves."

"I suppose not. You two were such beautiful girls. You both wore your hair down your back almost to your waist."

Keely laughed at the memory. Tonight she was wearing an apple green slip dress with an orange and gold shawl that brought out the flecks of gold in her eyes. Her mother wore slacks and a trendy geometric black and white top that Keely had given her for Christmas.

They turned onto India Street and in a few steps were at Kathleen Knight's gallery.

"We're here, Mom," Keely said. "Come on."

Reluctantly, Eloise followed Keely up the stairs. The gallery was a large, airy space with high walls displaying paintings and tables set here and there to hold sculptures. Dozens of people were studying the exhibits while sipping wine. Keely quickly scrutinized the crowd. She didn't see anyone she knew, and was oddly disappointed by that.

Suddenly, Daphne Hayes rushed up to Eloise. "Eloise! I'm so glad to see you! I've missed you at our lunches, and I have loads to tell you." Before Eloise could object, Daphne said, "Keely, if you don't mind, I'm going to steal your mother away for a minute."

"Of course." Keely was as happy as if her mother were a toddler greeted by a friend in a playgroup. She took a glass of prosecco and strolled around the gallery, studying the art.

In the corner, beneath glass, a display case showed pieces of scrimshaw, an art form from the days when sailors on the whaling ships passed the time finely engraving the bone and teeth of the whales with scenes from the ocean, the boat, and their memories of home.

Keely bent over the case, admiring the workmanship of the three minutely detailed square-rigged whaling ships. She'd always considered this work, requiring such concentration and skill, similar to writing a novel. She couldn't produce a novel all at once, with the broad sweeping strokes of a Pollock. She had to create her books carefully, a bit at a time. Just so with scrimshaw. Although, she admitted, she had the ability to erase and rewrite, to cut and paste, or toss out and begin again. With scrimshaw, the slightest slip could ruin a work.

"So you're interested in scrimshaw," a man said. "I never would have guessed."

Startled—she *knew* that voice—Keely looked up. Next to the display case stood Sebastian. He was tall and lean and his eyes were a startling blue against his tan. He seemed more grown-up than when she last saw him. His shoulders were so broad . . .

"Sebastian!" Flustered, knowing she was blushing, Keely babbled, "Yes, I do like scrimshaw, although I don't own any. Didn't I read somewhere that because whales are an endangered species, carving on whale teeth or bone is illegal? I certainly hope the artist, who I think is amazing, but anyway, I hope he or she is aware of the laws."

"I am," Sebastian said quietly, with a gentle smile.

"You are what?" Was she going mad? She was so attracted to Sebastian she wanted to lean up and kiss him, hard and long.

"I am aware of the laws. Because I'm the artist."

"What?"

"I'm a scrimshander. The whale teeth in the case are all over one hundred years old and legally documented." He rested a possessive hand on the back of the case. "They're expensive, which is why this case is locked."

"I had no idea," Keely said.

Sebastian shrugged. "I was working on resin when I was in high school. I was obsessed with this particular art."

"Doesn't it take forever to complete?"

"It does." Sebastian leaned close, smiling down at her. "But I like to do things slowly and surely. I like to take my time."

Keely went hot all over.

He grinned mischievously.

Keely went weak at the knees.

"I didn't know you were on the island," Sebastian said.

"I'm not here for long. I mean, I still have my apartment in New York. I flew home to"—she swiveled her head, checking to see that her mother wasn't near enough to overhear—"spend some time with my mother. She's retired and miserable. I hope I can cheer her up."

"I'm sure you will. And hey, I enjoyed your book."

"You did? Why?"

"Because you wrote it."

"Oh."

"It's a good book, Keely. Good writing. I enjoyed it, although I wasn't crazy about the descriptive passages of Hope and Adam having sex."

Keely blushed deeply. "That wasn't autobiographical."

"Yeah, it was."

He had read her book. He thought she wrote well. He'd read passages she'd written about sex. So much heat surged through her she was afraid she'd explode.

"You seem to know everything about me, Sebastian. I'm impressed. Maybe you can tell me how long I'm going to be on the island."

"I think you'll be here for the summer. I think I'll take you out to dinner like I've been waiting to do for a long time."

Stunned, Keely took a sip of wine to give herself a moment to process his words. *Sebastian wanted to take her to dinner.*

"Hello, Sebastian." Eloise approached the scrimshaw display. "I've read about your work. Congratulations."

Keely restrained a sigh of relief. Her mother was as friendly and relaxed as she had always been.

Sebastian leaned forward and kissed Eloise's cheek. "Mrs. Green, how great to see you. Thanks for coming."

"Oh, it's all thanks to Keely. Now that she's home, I find I'm much more cheerful."

"You know," Sebastian said, looking directly into Keely's eyes, "I feel that way, too."

"I think she should stay," Eloise said.

"I agree." Sebastian's mouth curled in a smile. "But maybe she's too much of a city gal now. We're too provincial for her."

"You're one to talk," Eloise teased. "You lived in Sweden for what, four years?"

Her mother's lighthearted interrogation of Sebastian gave Keely the courage to say, "And by the way, where is your Swedish girlfriend?"

"Ah, well, she's remained in Sweden. We're still friends."

"Are you really here for good?" Eloise asked.

"I hope so. I've bought the print shop out on Old South Road. We do invitations, posters, newsletters, brochures . . ."

Eloise brightened. "Why, yes, I know right where you are. So you've got the shop to support you financially, and I'll bet in the winter you have plenty of time for your art."

"Exactly."

"So tell me," Eloise asked, "how did you get interested in scrimshaw?"

Keely leaned against the wall, smiling. Her mother seemed to be sliding right back into her normal, friendly self. Maybe Keely could stop worrying.

"Hello, Eloise. Keely."

Donna Maxwell sailed up in an invisible whirl of perfume and confidence. Keely said hello and stood watching as the two mothers chatted.

And it all came rushing back. How charming Donna was, how charismatic, how blazingly beautiful. She was tall, with the powerful sleek body of a sailor and tennis player, and the sleeveless dress she wore displayed her taut muscular upper arms. Next to Donna, Keely's mother looked, well, dumpy. Eloise's months of reclusiveness had allowed her to become doughy and pale. The geometric top Keely had been so happy to see Eloise wear now looked sadly out of style and actually faded next to Donna's Lilly Pulitzer.

Keely had always admired Donna, and gotten on well enough with her, at the same time hiding a burning envy, almost an anger, that Isabelle's mother was so *all that* while her own mother was exhausted from nursing and seldom attractively and *never* glamorously dressed. Yet she had to admit that even though Donna was never affectionate to Keely, she had always allowed Keely to muddle in with her own children for meals or trips to the beach or late night thriller movie marathons.

Keely hadn't spoken with Donna for years. Here in the gallery, Donna was cool. Glancing sideways, she saw Sebastian watching her. When he caught her glance, he lifted an eyebrow and smiled, and something about his expression brightened her heart and made her remember all the times over the years when Keely and Isabelle or Sebastian—especially Sebastian—had done some stupid tween thing to try Donna's patience.

She tuned in to Donna's words.

"Yes, it's true," Donna Maxwell was saying, with the most tremendously smug smile, "having a grandchild is the most wonderful experience in the world."

"Thanks, Mom," Sebastian joked.

"Oh, don't be silly." Donna rapped her son's arm lightly. "You can't complain." She turned back to Eloise. "Somehow, a grandchild makes the universe magical. And, well, *right*. There seems to be a reason for things, and a rhythm. And the beauty, the sweetness, the pleasure . . . it's like falling in love for the first time."

"You're fortunate," Eloise told Donna. "To have your grandchild here on the island with you."

"That's true." Donna flicked a cold glance at Keely. "I suppose if Keely ever marries and has children, you'll have to travel to see them. Now that she lives in New York, or wherever."

Keely bristled, and before she could stop herself, she wrapped her arm around her mother's waist and said, "Nantucket is my hometown. I might move back someday."

"Really," Donna said. "Well, that *would* be interesting."

Eloise squeezed Keely's waist. "I would love that, darling."

Sebastian said, "I would, too."

Keely didn't dare look at his face for fear she'd break into an adolescent-in-braces wide-mouth grin. But his remark gave her the courage to say to Donna, "How is Isabelle? I'll bet she's loving motherhood."

Donna preened. "Isabelle is happier than she's ever been in all her life!" She looked at her watch. "I must dash. I'm meeting Al and some friends for dinner. It was nice to see you again, Eloise." She did not say it was nice seeing Keely.

With a twinkle of her fingers at Eloise and Sebastian, Donna surged away to the door. For just a moment too long, Keely, her mother, and Sebastian stood silent.

Eloise spoke first. "Your mother is so lovely, Sebastian."

Sebastian smiled. "I could say the same about you, Mrs. Green."

Flustered, Eloise waved her hand, as if shooing away the compliment.

Keely mouthed "thank you" to Sebastian, surprised at his kindness and sensitivity.

Sebastian asked, "What's your cell number?"

Keely's heart leapt. She told him.

"Keely, I'm rather tired. Would you mind if we went home?" Eloise asked.

Hmm, Keely thought and wondered if her mother felt she'd been overshadowed, shrunk merely by Donna's presence. She had never before considered how her mother might have felt, if she'd compared herself to the blazingly confident Donna. "Sure, Mom. I think I've had about all the excitement I can handle, myself."

"We can watch *Midsomer Murders* together," Eloise said, linking her arm with Keely's.

Keely looked over her shoulder as they walked away from Sebastian. She wanted to exchange one more heated glance with him. But another group of people surrounded him, asking about his work. Keely spent the rest of the evening sitting on the sofa in front of the television with her mother, but her mind was beavering away, thinking of ways she could get in touch with Isabelle . . . for so many reasons.

chapter
thirteen

K eely and her mother awoke energized. Coffee sweetened
with sugar and cream helped, too. Together, Keely and her
mother tore through the boxes and plastic bags in the basement,
uncovering old winter clothes, thick white linen tablecloths that
had been waiting for years to be ironed, stacks of Keely's father's
National Geographic magazines, clusters of children's birthday
party paraphernalia—plastic silver tiaras, not one but two broken
piñatas, Little Mermaid paper plates, cups, and napkins—and several shoeboxes of old photograph negatives. After they'd loaded
up the back of the Civic, Keely and her mother showered and
dressed, and Keely took them out to the Seagrille for dinner.

Keely kept checking her phone to see if she'd had a text from
Sebastian.

No, nothing from him. Two brief texts from Gray.

"Hey, Keely, Mrs. Green, good to see you!" The hostess, Mindy
Saffel, had worked with Keely for Clean Sweep years ago.

Keely hugged Mindy. "Good to see you, Mindy. We'd like a
table, not a booth." When she had been here before, years ago,
Keely had loved the privacy of a booth, but that had been when

she was with a friend, gossiping, or a guy, flirting. Now she was with her mother and she wanted her mother to see and be seen.

"You got it."

As they settled at their table and studied the menus, Keely knew she'd made the right choice. Several of the other diners were either women Eloise's age or nurses. By the time Keely had ordered prosecco for herself and her mother, some people had waved at Eloise, and Priscilla Hart was headed toward their table.

"Eloise! I haven't seen you in such a long time! Is it true you've retired?"

Eloise blinked several times, as if a spotlight were suddenly shining in her eyes. "Yes," she said softly. "I have."

"I'm so glad! You *have* to join our bridge club! We meet every Monday evening, and we take turns hosting it, and we always take a break in the middle of the evening for dessert and coffee. You'd love it."

Sadly, Eloise admitted, "I don't know how to play bridge."

Priscilla waved Eloise's objection away. "Don't worry about that! You'll pick it up in no time. Learn the basics on your computer. Come on Monday and observe. We'll be at Nancy Grossman's."

"Well," Eloise began.

Keely kicked her under the table.

"I'd like that," Eloise finished.

"Good! Six o'clock."

After Priscilla returned to her table, Eloise took a long sip of her prosecco.

"Good for you, Mom!" Keely said quietly. "You've always liked Priscilla. And Nancy Grossman."

Eloise took another sip of her drink. "I was Priscilla's nurse when she gave birth to Peter." She smiled. "Priscilla cursed like a sailor. And when Peter was finally in her arms, she said to Harold, 'Meet your only child.'"

Keely laughed with her mother. "Gosh, Mom, I never thought

about it this way, but there must be scads of people on this island you helped give birth."

"Not only that. Years ago, I wasn't just a labor-delivery room nurse. I did a bit of everything." She looked around the room. "I've probably seen the hind ends of half the people here." She giggled, her cheeks flushing.

Keely's spirits lifted. It was working. Her mother was out of the house and had plans to be with friends. "What was the craziest thing you ever saw when you were at the hospital?"

Eloise thought. "Once, long ago, I was taking the pulse of a woman who'd had a hysterectomy. A movement caught my eye. I looked down, and a snake was sliding out from under the bed. It probably came in with a pot of flowers from someone's garden."

"Eeek," Keely said. "What did you do?"

"I didn't blink an eye. I recorded the woman's pulse—it was one of the Stanley sisters—and slowly left the room. Then I ran to the nurses' station and told them to get a custodian up to the room right away." Eloise laughed. "But Jessie, she grew up on a farm here, you know, back when people actually had real farms. She went in, bent down, scooped it up, and put it in a pillowcase. 'For heaven's sake,' she said, 'it's only a harmless garter snake.' She took it outside and let it loose. We don't have any poisonous snakes on the island, so I wasn't really terrified, but I was glad when that thing was gone."

Keely laughed. The waiter came for their orders, and when he went off, Keely asked for another hospital memory. The food was delicious and her mother was brightening, at last almost her old self. They'd have to go out to dinner more often, Keely decided.

Sebastian walked into the restaurant, accompanied by a tall, curvy blond wearing Manolo Blahniks and a fabulous black dress.

"Oh, look, dear, there's Sebastian," Eloise said, starting to wave.

Keely caught her mother's hand, brought it to the table, and held it there. "Don't wave, Mom. He's on a date. He doesn't want to say hello to us."

"Why wouldn't he? We're friends . . ."

"Mom, stop staring. Look at me. Look at me *now*."

Eloise frowned. "I thought Sebastian and you . . ."

"It's fine, Mom. We're just friends. Enjoy your dinner. Isn't it delicious?"

Keely smiled, but her food had turned to chalk in her mouth.

The moment she got home that night, Keely called Gray.

"Hey," he said.

"Is this too late?"

Gray laughed. "Keely, it's only nine-thirty."

"Oops. Well, that tells you everything about my life with my mother. I just took her out to dinner at the Seagrille. Reservation time: six o'clock."

"It's good though, that you're getting her out to dinner."

"Yes. Yes, I think I am cheering her up." She fell back on her bed, stretching out as she told him about the excitement of sorting through her mother's treasures. "Tell me, how is your visit with your parents?"

Gray laughed. "Mother's cooking more food than I could eat in a month. Prime rib, twice-baked potatoes, carrots in brown sugar, apple pie with ice cream . . . I'm sure I'll split all my trousers when I get back to New York."

Keely laughed. "You could use a few pounds."

"Really? Would you like to elaborate?"

She laughed again. "I'll do it in person."

They continued to talk, their voices growing more and more affectionate. When Keely finally clicked off and got ready for bed, she felt a glow in her heart from Gray's humor and from the life she shared with him in the city, the city that never went dark. She clicked the Photos icon on her phone and scrolled through photos they'd taken or had taken of them together. Here she was at Lincoln Center, by the fountain, during the intermission of the ballet. She wore a floor-length, narrow rose silk gown with a spectacular silk wrap, rose on one side, white on the other. Her hair was piled high on her head, her lipstick was red, her eye makeup was dark and dramatic. She looked beautiful. Really, she looked amazing. She looked the way she had dreamed of looking when she was a little girl.

There was another photo taken in the grand foyer of the Metropolitan Museum of Art during a charity dinner. Here, Keely wore a little black dress with her dark hair sweeping down past her shoulders, accentuating her heavy pearl drop earrings, the only jewelry she wore that night. Gray was standing next to her in a tux, his lush dark hair and green eyes gleaming. They were holding hands, and both were smiling. Keely looked more than happy—she looked radiant. She remembered how she felt that evening, that at last she was living the life she'd always imagined.

All of her photos taken in the city seemed like glamour shots. The city behind them, the bronze statues, the Art Deco interiors, the gleaming shop windows, the avenues of cabs and Ubers and buses and pedestrians hurrying along the sidewalks, all of it looked like the sparkling center of the world. With Gray, she could have all that, and with Gray she knew she would be loved. After his confession that night as they lay together so close in bed, she knew he would be faithful to her, that he had entrusted her with his deepest secrets, and he believed she would keep those secrets safe. That was a gift of devotion.

She fell asleep, dreaming of the bright lights of New York.

"Keely?" It was Sarah B., one of her old high school friends. "Listen, I'm teaching tenth grade English, and I wonder . . . would you consider coming out sometime to talk to the class about writing? What it's like to be a writer, how you get published, that sort of thing?"

Keely brightened. "I'd love to!"

"Oh, my kids will be thrilled. Can we pick a day next week?"

"Absolutely."

After they said goodbye, Keely straightened her spine and focused on her writing. It always took a few minutes for her to write the first sentence, as if her mind was blocked and she had to patiently push it forward. After she got that first sentence out, her writing flowed.

She was almost finished with her day's work—it felt as if her work was finished with her. Her cellphone, set on silent, vibrated on her desk.

Impatiently, she checked who was calling: Sebastian Maxwell. She kept her voice cool. "Hi, Sebastian."

"Hi, Keely. Do you have some free time tomorrow afternoon?"

"Can't your blond friend join you?"

"What? Oh, the restaurant. Mae-Brit is an artist in Stockholm, a friend. Also, she's a lesbian. And she left the island today for New York. So no, she can't join me. Anyway, I want to take you to do one of my favorite things."

Keely tried not to sound too delighted about Mae-Brit. Calmly, she replied, "Well, that's intriguing. What's one of your favorite things?" She imagined sailing or walking on a beach.

"Let me pick you up tomorrow at two and you'll find out."

"Aren't you Mr. Mysterious. Okay, I'll be ready at two."

"Dress casually."

So it was going to be sailing, Keely decided. Fine. She'd be glad to swim with the sharks if it meant doing it with Sebastian.

Her cell buzzed again.

"Hey," Janine said, "listen, Keely, a bunch of us are going out to Surfside this afternoon to drink margaritas and eat chips and gossip. Want to come?"

Keely laughed. "What can I bring?"

It had been a long time since Keely had hung out with her high school friends, and she'd forgotten how much fun it was, especially after her first margarita. They set up beach chairs in the sand, or tossed down towels to lie on for a maximum effect tan in the late afternoon sun. They had bowls of chips and dips and young radishes with salt and bluefish pâté Norah had made from fish her husband had caught. Keely thought they'd want to know all about her life in the big city. Instead, they regaled her with all the gossip she'd missed since she'd been gone. Two married—and sexy even if they were thirty-eight—teachers ran off with two other married and not quite so sexy teachers and no one could understand why. Stanley Keene had embezzled ten million dollars from his boss's real estate business and was now serving time in jail. Cathy Higgins, a girl from their class, had married an older man with a house in Squam and a house in Boston and had gotten divorced a year later. Nothing was too terrible, and the fresh sea air and the sun glancing off the tips of the waves made it all seem material for laughter. When Sarah B. finally asked Keely about life in New York, she told them about Gray. Actually, she bragged about Gray, and brought out her phone to show them photos of the two of them together in their evening dress, and everyone screamed with admiration and jealousy.

"Marry him!" Norah ordered. "Marry him and make him buy a house on the island!"

Keely laughed. "I'll have to wait for him to ask me first."

Later that evening, as she showered off the sand and shampooed her hair and checked out the healthy glow on her cheeks . from the sun, Keely couldn't help laughing, and she didn't know why. She was, quite simply, happy.

Sebastian arrived the next day in his ancient, rattling, but beloved Jeep, the one he'd bought with his own money in high school. He wore board shorts and a T-shirt. Keely wore capris and a T-shirt, too, one of the three thousand tees she'd tried on that morning to find the most attractive one that also seemed less flirtatious. All of which was a lot to ask from a T-shirt.

He didn't just honk his horn, but came to the door and knocked. Keely was waiting. She called, "Goodbye, Mom!" and squeezed outside before Sebastian could get a look at her mother ensconced in her recliner in front of the TV.

"Hey," Sebastian said, and kissed Keely's cheek.

"Hey." As they walked to the Jeep, she said, "So now will you tell me what we're doing today?"

"Nope. But I guarantee you'll love it."

He drove from Keely's house, away from town and down the road to Madaket.

"Hmm," Keely said. "I don't think you have a boat moored out there."

"Nope."

"You're driving us to Take It or Leave It to treasure hunt."

"Uh-uh. That will be our next date."

After that remark, Keely didn't speak, because she couldn't get her breath. Sebastian thought there would be another date? She sneaked a sideways look at him. Yup, as gorgeous as always. Maybe even more so, now that an early tan set off his blue eyes and blond hair. Had his legs always been so long or was it simply that she hadn't seen him in board shorts for a while?

He turned off onto Crooked Lane, a short, winding street leading to Cliff Road.

"Curiouser and curiouser," Keely said.

He made a left turn and pulled into the parking lot of the animal hospital.

"You're going to have a chip put in my neck so you can find me whenever you want me," Keely joked.

Sebastian looked her right in the eye and grinned. "Nope, but that's not a bad idea."

Once again, she was breathless.

"I volunteer several days a week at Safe Harbor, the shelter for animals waiting for adoption. Remember Fido? He went to dog heaven a few years ago. I can't keep a dog in my apartment. But the shelter always has several animals waiting here. I come out to take the dogs for a walk, to spend some human time with them. It makes them happy, and it makes me happy. I thought you'd enjoy it, too."

"I do like dogs . . ."

"Come on," Sebastian said. "Wait till you meet the gang."

They went around the side of the building. There, in large, clean, wire pens were four dogs of various sizes and breeds.

Sebastian led Keely into the office, which was filled with smaller cages, each one home to a cat.

"Sebastian!" Nadine, the manager, jumped up and hugged Sebastian. "Hooray, you're here. The beasts are so ready."

"Nadine, I've brought a friend to help. You remember Keely Green from school."

"Sure do." Nadine folded Keely in her arms, then held her away, studying her. "Okay, you'll get Missy. She's the quietest of them all. Sebastian, you can take whoever you want. But remember, both of you, when you've got them outside on leashes, they have to obey you. You can't let them run off like they want to do."

"But we can run with them, right?" Sebastian asked.

"Right. And don't forget these." She handed them each a plastic bag. "For picking up doggie doo," Nadine told Keely.

So Keely spent most of her afternoon on one end of a green leash with a small mixed-breed female dog who preferred sitting in Keely's lap and being petted to running alongside Sebastian and his leaping, twisting, barking, hyperactive hound. Keely did get Missy to take a nice long walk, and at one point in the afternoon, she leaned against a tree with Missy licking her face and watched Sebastian on the ground, wrestling with a deliriously happy rottweiler/who-knew-what mix named Mike Tyson.

"Who's a pretty girl?" Keely asked the small furry creature as she scratched Missy's pink belly while Missy lay with her eyes closed in ecstasy. Missy really was pretty, with curly white hair and a black button nose. Keely envisioned buying her a pink collar with rhinestones and giving her to her mother. That would get Eloise out of the house!

In the distance, two other volunteers romped with two other dogs, a greyhound and a black Lab.

"They're not as pretty as you," Keely whispered in Missy's ear. Missy wagged her tail in agreement.

When the time came to return the dogs to their kennels, Missy turned in the doorway and shot Keely a beseeching look.

"She likes you," Nadine said. "She hasn't liked anyone the way she likes you."

"I can't," Keely said, backing away. "I'm not sure how long I'll be on the island, and I don't have room for a dog in my apartment in the city."

But when she turned away, she was surprised to find she was tearing up. She wiped her eyes before Sebastian could see her, but obviously he detected her mood because he put a strong, sustaining arm around her shoulders and pulled her against him. "Now it's time for a cool mojito and some nachos."

Keely swept her hand over her shirt. "I'm covered in dog hair."

"Brush it off," Sebastian said sensibly. "Anyway, half the people on the island are tracking sand in on their clothes. No big deal."

They went to Cru, a restaurant down on Straight Wharf, where they sat inside, looking out at small fishing boats gliding in to tie up at the dock. Once they'd ordered their drinks, Sebastian took out his phone and studied it.

"Something important?" Keely asked.

"Very important. I just double-checked. The new Star Wars movie is on at seven on the big screen. If we eat fast, we can make it."

Keely leaned back in her chair. "So this date we're having includes a movie, too?"

Sebastian gave her a sleepy-eye look. "This date we're having can go on all night if you want."

Keely laughed. "Still the same old Sebastian."

Reaching over, he took her hand. "Not the same old Sebastian at all. I think you'll find I'm the new, improved model."

He drew his thumb in a delicate swirl on her palm, such a soft touch to cause such an explosion of longing in Keely's body. She didn't pull away. She'd been waiting for this moment all her life. She didn't want to ruin it by being simply too afraid to go into the moment, to really be there. She was almost thirty, after all. She wasn't an ingénue.

She smiled back at him, slowly. "I always enjoy sampling what's new and improved."

"Excuse me," the waiter said.

They had to unlink their hands in order for the waiter to set the drinks on the table.

Was it the alcohol? She had only two drinks. Was it the afternoon of running and playing with Missy, enjoying the fresh air and sunshine, the sense of freedom, letting go of words, letting herself give in to a completely sensual part of herself? Maybe it was the delicious sweet mussels she ate, carefully picking the meat out of the iridescent shells, like a jeweler teasing out a pearl. The tangy taste of the sea. The thick soft bread she used to soak up the broth. The laughter of others around her. The slow fade of the bright blue sky to a dreamy lavender. The boats sliding so deftly into a slip.

Whatever it was, Keely and Sebastian lingered at the restaurant, talking about their pasts in New York and Sweden, their odd lives of writing and scrimshawing, the need for isolation and the need for fellowship.

"Do you still have feelings for Tommy?" Sebastian asked.

Keely smiled. "Honestly, no. The last time I even set eyes on him was over a year ago, at Bartlett's. He and Isabelle were such a couple, so happy together. I moved to New York, and so much in my life changed. I've changed. I love my work and I know I'm fortunate to be able to do what I love. Tommy, at least the Tommy I knew, would have been impatient with me spending so much time in isolation."

She hesitated, wondering how much Isabelle had told him. "You know Isabelle and I aren't speaking?"

Sebastian nodded.

"But you called me anyway."

"It doesn't matter what you and Isabelle do. I want to see you."

"Is that true?"

"Of course it's true."

"It's just that your family is so . . . entwined. Like I have to please everyone, Donna and your father and Isabelle, before I can"—she sought the perfect word—"please you."

"I can understand why it seems that way. When we were kids, it's true, our family was like bees in our own hive. But we're older now, and separate. I live above my print shop. Isabelle and Tommy and Brittany live in the apartment above the garage. It's true they see Mom every day, usually so she'll take care of Brittany while Isabelle goes off on errands."

"Sebastian, I miss Isabelle so much. I'd love to be friends with her again."

"You probably will be. Maybe it will just take time."

Keely bit her lower lip lightly, thinking. "I should tell you, Sebastian, I'm seeing someone in the city. Gray Anderpohl. He's . . . nice. I . . . like him."

"Are you committed to him?"

"No. And he'll always need to live in New York. While I . . . I thought I could be a New Yorker, but I'm afraid I'm crazy about this island." Keely looked at Sebastian. "And then there's you." Bravely, she asked, "What are we doing here, Sebastian? I mean . . ."

"I know what you mean. And I know what we're doing. What I hope we're doing. What I've been wanting to do for a very long time."

He paid the check and pulled out her chair. He took her hand as they walked out of the restaurant and up the wharf to his Jeep. He drove to the apartment above his print shop. They went inside and up the wooden stairs. They entered the apartment. He shut the door, and before she could speak, he had his arms around her and his mouth on hers. She put her arms around his neck and kissed him back with all the hunger and desire she'd been holding in all her life. Sebastian picked her up and carried her to his bed.

. . .

They didn't come out until the next morning.

When she opened her eyes, she saw Sebastian lying next to her.

"Oh my goodness," she said. "I can't believe it."

"Believe it," Sebastian told her. "Check out the covers."

The top sheet and light quilt had been twisted into a mountain of fabric.

"It's a work of art," Keely said.

"You're a work of art," Sebastian told her, and drew her close to him, so that her head was on his shoulder and his arm around her back.

"What time is it?"

His chin dug slightly into her head as he leaned over to check the clock. "Nine-thirty."

"I don't think I'm going to get much writing done today," she said.

"Maybe not, but I'm going to give you some good material." He lifted her hair and kissed the back of her neck, and turned her to face him, and kissed her throat, and then her collarbone.

I have morning breath, Keely thought in a panic. Then she forgot about everything except Sebastian's mouth.

Later, they sat on his sofa, drinking coffee. Keely was sitting propped with her legs stretched out and her feet in Sebastian's lap. They'd heard sounds from his shop—his employee entering and opening the doors, voices, a phone ringing. Sebastian was in no hurry to get to work.

"So," Sebastian said, "want to see that movie tonight?"

Keely smiled. "I'll see any movie you want to show me."

Sebastian ran his fingers over Keely's ankles. "Are you ready to take this public?"

"This?"

"You and me. As a couple. Together."

"Are we going from zero to sixty too fast?" Keely asked. Her heart was jumping rope and it wasn't from the caffeine.

"Are we? I don't think so. We're adults now. We've had some fun and we've been in and out of love. We've traveled. We can trust what our hearts tell us."

Keely dipped her head at his romantic words. They delighted her, and frightened her a little, too. "What about your Swedish stewardess—"

"She's not a stewardess and never has been. Ebba is an artist. And the Swedes were doing scrimshaw before we were. I learned a lot over there."

"Do you want to go back?"

"Do you want to go back to Tommy?"

Keely laughed. "No, Sebastian. First of all, he's married to Isabelle. They have a child. They're happy."

"But you were angry with Isabelle when she married Tommy."

"True. It happened so fast, sort of like the moment my back was turned. Isabelle didn't tell me what she was going to do. I felt—spurned. Scorned. By Tommy, yes, but also by Isabelle. Like she was playing a trick on me. But I'm over all that now."

"Okay, then, do you want to live in New York?"

Keely thought a moment. "Not anymore. I want to live here, on this island. But I want to go there often. You know my editor and agent are there, and I love the museums and plays and shops . . ."

"And the guy in New York? Gray?"

Keely stared down into her coffee mug, as if she could find the answer there.

Finally she said, "I admire Gray. I'm fond of him. He's a pediatric surgeon, and he's intense. I want to love him"—she glanced up at Sebastian with a smile—"but I can't . . . I don't know how to say it. I can't get *comfortable* with him."

"Can you get comfortable with me?" Sebastian asked.

Keely smiled at him. "More than comfortable, I'd say."

"But out of bed. Out in the world. Daily life."

She took a deep breath, marshaling her thoughts. Somehow she'd arrived at a crossroads, a place she never dreamed she would be. "I don't know, Sebastian," she answered honestly. "The thing is . . . well, your family." She held up her hand. "No, let me finish. It's not just about Isabelle. It's that all my life I envied your family so terribly it was like an open wound in my heart. Your mother is so lovely, and so *perfect*. She always took good care of you kids, and never missed a game or a meet. And your father is an important man in this town." She hesitated, wondering whether to mention Al Maxwell's coldness the day he read her father's will. *Let it go*, she decided. "And that wonderful house . . . and my mother is totally a good person, she's a nurse, she's helped so many people, but she is . . . quieter . . . than your mother. My father liked to do things with me—he taught me how to surf cast out at the Madaket Beach. Stuff like that. But often he was working, and too tired to do much else. I loved him. I miss him. But . . . it's terrible, and I feel guilty, but I just always wished I had your family."

"But if you'd had my family, you couldn't be with me. That would be incest. Our children would be cross-eyed."

Keely nearly fell off the sofa. *Our children?* Sebastian was thinking: *our children?*

"We did have a happy family," Sebastian admitted in a more serious tone. "We're fortunate. But God knows we're not perfect. My father's a lawyer, sure, but as the years have passed, his profession is wearing on him. He's getting short-tempered. Argumentative. Nothing lives up to his standards. Certainly not my work, which he sees as unworthy of a Maxwell. He wanted me to be a lawyer, too. He thinks scrimshaw is outdated and foolish. We argue about it a lot, which is one reason I don't go over for Sunday lunch anymore."

"I'm sorry," Keely said.

"As for Isabelle and Tommy—Dad disapproves of Tommy."

"But your father bought him that fishing boat . . ."

"Isabelle's always been Dad's favorite. He'd give her the stars from the sky if he could. So no guy could ever be worthy of her in Dad's eyes." Sebastian's voice softened. "But Brittany, now there's the one person who can do no wrong. No matter how much time Tommy spends out drinking beer with his buddies on his boat, Dad will always champion Tommy because of his granddaughter."

"Tommy spends a lot of time drinking beer on his boat?" Keely asked.

Sebastian shot her a look. "You want to talk about Tommy?"

Keely shook her head. "No. No, I want to talk about families. Your mother has two children and a granddaughter. I'm all my mother has. And she's become seriously depressed since she quit nursing. I'm doing my best to cheer her up, and I think she's gotten better, but it's sad to see her this way." Keely paused. "Sebastian, I don't know if Isabelle and I will ever be good friends again. I've reached out to her but she refuses to talk. I think she's kind of angry with me because I got a novel published first."

Sebastian turned toward Keely, lifting her feet off his lap so that she shifted positions and tucked her feet under her. "Keely, Isabelle is my sister, and I love her. I know how desperately she's wanted to publish a novel. I don't think she's angry at you. I think she's hurt, not by you, but by circumstances. I think the sight of you—the thought of you—wounds her."

Keely nodded. "I understand that. So maybe in time, she'll be my friend again."

"Right. Now look at me, Keely. I am not my sister. Nothing I do has anything to do with my sister." Impatiently, Sebastian stood up. "And at this particular moment, I'm hungry. I'll make us some eggs and bacon."

"All this and you cook, too," Keely joked.

She went with him into the kitchen and took on the job of microwaving the bacon. She thought this moment, with the smell of buttery eggs and salty bacon, with Sebastian, who loved her, sprinkling cheese over the eggs, with her body aching in the most delicious way from all they had done in the night—she thought this moment was the happiest in her life.

. . .

After breakfast, Sebastian kissed Keely for a long, sweet time. Then he drove her to her house.

He smiled as she opened the car door. "See you later."

"Yes. Later." She could hardly pull herself away.

When Keely entered, her mother was in her recliner again, watching television.

"That was a long date," Eloise remarked.

"It was wonderful." Keely didn't want to talk about it yet. "Have you eaten breakfast?"

"Don't worry about me, sweetheart. I don't want to interrupt your writing schedule."

"You mean you're addicted to your television shows," Keely said cheerfully. "I'm going to take a shower and get right to work."

Keely showered and dressed for the day and took her place at her desk with her laptop, and—she didn't have a thought in her head for her book. Her mind ricocheted back between flashes of her night with Sebastian—his gentle hands, his sweet mouth, his long legs—and anxiety for what might happen.

What if she got her heart broken? He had told her he loved her, but she knew it was too soon for them to promise to spend their lives together. Who knew what would happen when his family heard he was seeing her?

With sudden insight, Keely realized she had a family, too. Nervously, she called Sebastian. "Can you come to dinner here tonight?"

"Absolutely."

"Good. I'll call again about the time."

Keely hurried back to her mother. "We have to go. We'll get ice cream for energy, because after that, we're going to the grocery store. We're going to have Sebastian over for dinner tonight."

"Really? Oh, how lovely! Let's buy some nice juicy steaks!"

Eloise was up and out of her chair and dressed and ready to go in a matter of minutes.

. . .

That evening, Keely grilled steaks. Her mother made roasted potatoes with cheese and herbs, broiled broccoli coated with olive
oil and salt, and a salad. Sebastian brought over a bottle of wine
and they feasted out on the patio.

Sebastian was charming. He brought up names of islanders
who had been injured or ill over the years, and Eloise lit up. She
remembered each wound, each ailment, each recovery, and she
seemed to regain some of her positive spirit while talking about
them. As they ate, Keely ran her bare toes up Sebastian's leg and
was rewarded with a look that would have set off Roman candles.

After dessert—ice cream and cookies—Eloise rose from the
table. "If you'll excuse me, I'm going to tidy up the kitchen."

The moment Eloise was in the house, Sebastian said, "Want to
get in my car and make out?"

Keely laughed. "Yes, please. Oh, but what about our neigh-
bors?"

Sebastian kissed the tip of her nose. "I should be going. You
and I both have to work tomorrow." He stood.

Keely stood, too, and studied his face. "I don't want you to
leave."

"I know. Me, too. But your mother is right inside." Sebastian
pulled her to him in a warm, friendly embrace. When he spoke,
his breath ruffled through her hair. "We've got lots of issues to
deal with. And now that you're back here, we don't have to rush.
I don't want a fantasy, Keely. I want a real life, and that takes time.
And we've got time."

He kissed her mouth. And pulled away from her when the kiss
grew too intense.

"I've got to go."

Keely walked Sebastian to his car, kissed him lightly, and
waved at him as he drove away.

She returned to the house in a happy, dreamy mood. Her
mother was once again in a television trance, but Keely left her
alone. Eloise had been pleasant that evening, and she had tidied
the kitchen. *Great*, Keely thought. *I sound like I'm her mother.*

She returned to the patio, settled in a chair, and let her mind drift. The light was gone from the sky, but the moon was waning and the stars dotted the sky like freckles.

Her cell was on the table. When it buzzed, she jumped, startled out of her reverie.

"Hey," a man said.

"Gray!"

"You sound surprised."

"I think I am surprised. I'm just sitting out here, alone, stargazing." Why did she tell him she was alone? Why did she feel relieved that she was alone right now?

"I'm going to surprise you even more."

"My seatbelt is fastened."

"I'm coming to the island."

She sat up straight in her chair. "What? When?"

"The day after tomorrow. I've made my flight reservations, and don't worry, I wouldn't dream of imposing on you. I've got reservations at the White Elephant. A room with a view."

"Well . . . yes, that's one of the best hotels on the island."

"Keely, you don't sound happy about this."

"I'm just surprised, Gray. And my mother is still . . . depressed, and I'm working hard on my book, I'm right in the middle of it, and I've got so much going on . . ."

"I've scheduled leave from the hospital. I can't rearrange. I thought you'd be glad."

"I'm not *not* glad," Keely said weakly. "I'm just . . . I'm not sure how much time I'll be able to spend with you, Gray."

"Okay, how about this. I'll let you have the days to yourself if you'll be with me for dinner and the evening. And, if you like, part or all of the night."

Keely stood up and paced around the patio. She felt angry and touched by Gray's announcement. She was annoyed with herself, too. After all, *she* had phoned *him* just the other night after she saw Sebastian with the blonde. She had been affectionate and warm. She had talked as if she and Gray were a couple.

Still, why hadn't he called her first to find out if it was a good time for him to come to Nantucket? And would there ever be a good time for him to come to Nantucket? Should she tell him about Sebastian? Or would that be assuming too much too soon about her relationship with Sebastian? But even if things didn't work out with her and Sebastian, did she really want a future with Gray? Could she truly love him? Marry him? Live with him?

"Are you still there, Keely?"

"Yes, sorry. I'm trying to remember my schedule for the next few days. Also, I have to check with my mother about her plans . . . Gray, let me call you back tomorrow."

"Are you saying you don't want me to come to Nantucket?"

"No. Maybe. I don't know. It's such a busy time . . ."

"Are you involved with Tommy again?"

"God, no! I haven't set eyes on Tommy. I know I'll have to see him sometime, but I don't have feelings for him anymore, I promise." As she spoke, Keely felt like a creep for talking about Tommy and not saying a word about Sebastian.

"I know what's happened, Keely."

"You do?" She stopped her pacing, suddenly overcome with guilt.

"You've fallen in love with the island again. You've become an island girl and turned your back on the city."

"Maybe you're right," Keely said, grateful for his reasoning.

"That's why I definitely need to come out there and remind you of all you've got waiting for you in the city."

"Or, or, I could come in for a few days," Keely said desperately.

"How soon?" Gray asked. "I really miss you, Keely."

She nearly bent double with shame to hear such a reserved man speaking to her with honest emotion.

"I miss you, too, Gray." She had to say that. She couldn't not say that. If she were going to break it off with him, she couldn't do it over the phone.

"I'm glad. Then I'm coming."

Keely tried to sound normal. "Gray, tell me what you've done this week, at the hospital, I mean."

"It was a busy week. And a good one. I removed a tumor from a six-week-old boy. It was benign, thank God. I also repaired and rebuilt the face of a two-year-old who'd been in a car accident. And—" He sounded sure of himself, and yes, a bit smug, and he deserved his pride for changing the lives of such tiny human bodies.

As he spoke, it occurred to her that her mother would love to talk with Gray about his work. She would be able to understand the technical side of it. She could speak his language, and it would cheer her enormously to be able to be back in that world of the hospital again, her world.

"Gray," she said impulsively, "I'd love it if one night we could take my mother out to dinner. She's a nurse, you know, and she'd be fascinated by all this."

"I'd be very glad to meet your mother," Gray said solemnly.

Oh, rats, Keely thought. He completely misinterpreted her reason for wanting her mother to meet him. But it was too late now.

"Good," Keely replied.

"But not the first night I'm there. Let's have the first night to ourselves. We need some time alone together."

"I know." Keely injected warmth into her voice.

"All right, then. I'll email you my flight information. I've reserved a car at the airport. I'll call you once I've checked into the hotel."

"Great!" Keely said. She wanted to hit her head against the side of the house. "See you soon."

After their call ended, Keely had to move. She walked around her mother's garden. The flowers and shrubs were in shades of gray because of the lack of light, but their fragrances were strong.

She forced herself to think about Gray. About making love with him. He was a careful lover, as restrained in passion as he was in the rest of his life. He was diligent about pleasing her, but that very quality irritated Keely. She found him manipulative, as if he considered her similar to one of his patients. She did enjoy being with him, and he did take her places she'd never dreamed of going. But she didn't love him. And she had to tell him that.

Her heart ached. Her head ached. She was exhausted and a little bit terrified.

She went into the house and joined her mother as they watched Jimmy Fallon's late night show.

The next morning, she turned off her phone, made a pot of strong coffee, and sat down at her computer. Work had always been a helpful escape for her from hurt, anticipation, disappointment, and even hope. It was the blessing the gods had given to writers to make up for the curse of living a schizophrenic life, swerving between the isolation needed for work and the fellowship needed for life.

After three hours, she was drained, without another imaginative thought in her head. She dressed in running clothes, waved to her mother, who was once again watching two hyperactive women talk on television, and set off for her run. Her mother's house was not in the historic district of town. It was a kind of quiet suburb with no views of the sea or the moors. But as Keely ran, she noticed the dreamily purple-blue hydrangea, the New Dawn roses climbing up a lattice attached to a porch, the gleaming brass door knockers, the window boxes overflowing with flowers, the stone bird bath, the two old women sitting and laughing side by side in a garden, drinking tea from teacups, not mugs. The longhaired cat she often saw was sitting in his spot in the window. She waved at him. He was not impressed. It was quiet, except for the occasional sound of lawn mowers, and with the sound came the exceptionally sweet fragrance of newly mown grass.

She returned home dripping, waved at her mother, and headed

into the shower. Often when she ran, she returned home with a solution to a problem, but today she was as confused as when she started.

One day at a time, she told herself. One problem at a time.

Did that mean she considered Gray a problem? Well, yes, she did. Also, she had to tell Sebastian that Gray was coming, and what would that mean? How much would Keely like it if Ebba dropped by the island to visit Sebastian?

She would *hate* it. She'd be beside herself with jealousy. She'd do something irrational and completely idiotic, like going to a bar and picking up some old high school buddy and going to bed with him.

But she had to think seriously about whatever was going on with Sebastian. It felt like he was headed toward a lifetime commitment. Toward marriage? Her thoughts were racing.

If she was with Sebastian, Isabelle and Tommy, Keely's first love, would always be in her life. And so would perfect, smug, patronizing Donna Maxwell. Oooh, Donna would not be thrilled about Keely marrying her darling first child.

Plus, there was the unspoken issue of money. Sebastian made his living with his print shop. He couldn't make a fortune selling his scrimshaw. That was a small specialized market. While Keely made a very nice living from her writing. Amazing, yes, and something she couldn't count on because publishing was such an unstable business, and personal tastes were so unpredictable. Look at her now, writing like a mad thing revising her novel to satisfy Juan.

Fiona had told her that her new novel had no heart. She said Keely needed to be on Nantucket to regain the power of her emotions and creativity.

Fiona had been right. But could she stay here if she and Sebastian didn't somehow join their lives together?

Could she stay here if she had Dreadful Donna Maxwell as her mother-in-law?

Certainly she couldn't stay here if she married Gray, but she could visit here, and then she wouldn't need to see the Maxwells except accidentally. But on the other hand, she wanted to renew her friendship with Isabelle. That was important to Keely for so many reasons.

What should she do?

First of all, she had to get her mother up and moving. That was one goal she could achieve.

Next, she would talk to Sebastian about Gray tonight. She would tell Sebastian that Gray was coming to the island. That no matter what happened between Keely and Sebastian—Sebastian was not to feel obligated by this—Keely was going to end things with Gray.

As soon as the thought popped into her head, Keely was swept with a sense of relief so palpable it seemed she'd drunk an elixir. It would be difficult talking to Gray, and it wouldn't be that much fun telling Sebastian tonight, but she was determined to do it.

Clouds rolled in overhead that afternoon. The sky was dark, and a wind came up, tossing the trees, tearing petals from plants. Keely worked with her mother in the basement. They were almost finished there, and they didn't want to go out in the unsettled weather. They could tell that any minute a fury of rain would plunge down, driving summer people and day-trippers and islanders alike into the safety of shelter.

Of course Eloise was ready to settle in front of the TV again, but Keely had a brainstorm.

"Mom, I've set my computer up on the kitchen table. Get your laptop and sit next to me and we'll go shopping. You could use some new clothes."

"Keely, I don't have the money for new clothes. Or any reason to wear them, for that matter."

"Well, I have the money to buy you a few things, and as long as I'm here, you'll have lots of places to wear them. Art openings, theater, movies, galas . . . Come on. Join me. We'll have fun."

Keely made a pot of Earl Grey tea and poured them each a cup, set on a saucer, to elevate her mother's mood. Eloise's clothes were practical and comfortable. She wore clogs. She wore shapeless tops in neutral colors, as if she were trying hard not to be seen. She wore no jewelry except her wedding ring. Keely showed Eloise some clothing sites and suggested, gently, new possibilities.

"Oh, those are far too young for me," her mother protested.

So Keely dragged her reluctant mother into her bedroom, took out the few dresses she'd brought from New York, and insisted Eloise try them on. Eloise carried more weight than Keely, and her weeks of inactivity had made her plump and baggy, so she insisted nothing of Keely's would fit her.

Keely persisted. She managed to pull one of her looser sundresses over her mother, and all at once her mother smiled.

"This is a pretty dress," Eloise admitted.

"Okay, wait." Keely searched through her jewelry box and brought out a pair of small multicolored earrings. "Like? Or maybe this necklace?"

"I wouldn't feel comfortable in too much jewelry," Eloise said.

"Yeah, but look at this." Keely slipped a necklace over Eloise's head. "It's so casual, and playful, all those little silver hearts and flowers. It's so summery." Keely laughed. "I have a genius idea. Let's order this dress for you and we can have mother-daughter dresses."

"Oh, silly," Eloise chided, but she continued to preen in front of the full-length mirror, getting accustomed to the sight of herself in a pretty dress.

They spent the afternoon playing dress-up. Keely ordered several things online for her mother, including a luxuriously flowered silk robe. It would be one giant step to sanity to get her mother out of her hideous stained relic.

The rain continued to sheet down. It was one of those days that seemed like twilight all day long. Before Keely knew it, it was after five. Eloise collapsed in front of the television. Keely went into the privacy of her room to call Sebastian.

He didn't answer.

Probably with a customer, Keely thought. She hoped that while she'd been shopping with her mother her own little brain would have worked out exactly how to deal with Gray without hurting him. But she knew she had to break it off with him in person, face-to-face. Which meant she had to talk with Sebastian about where they were headed as a couple. As much as she loved Sebastian, had always loved him, she was older and wiser now, and much had happened between her and Isabelle. What did Keely want? Could she live with Sebastian in an apartment above his shop? Could she bear to spend Sunday lunches with the family, with Donna Maxwell subtly insulting her?

Right now she had to focus on telling Sebastian that Gray was coming to the island. She would promise that she wasn't in love with Gray, and wouldn't sleep with him but would have a serious breakup conversation with him. Still, it would be awkward, talking to Sebastian about this.

Her phone buzzed. *Sebastian!*

"Sorry I didn't answer right away. Listen, Keely, I'm sort of in a zone right now. I'm working on my scrimshaw piece, the one with the tall ships in a storm. I'd like to keep at it. Could I take a rain check on tonight?"

"Rain check sounds appropriate," Keely joked. She was both disappointed and relieved. "Of course, Sebastian. I know how it feels to be in the zone. I'll spend the evening with my mom. She'll like that."

"Good. I'll call you later."

Keely made a delicious mac and cheese and crispy green beans and a salad for dinner. She ate in front of the television so her mother could watch *Jeopardy!* Later, she persuaded her mother to play gin rummy with her at the kitchen table. When her mother drifted back to an old black-and-white movie, Keely decided she'd been a good enough daughter for the day and curled up in her room with a mystery.

The next morning, her phone woke her at six. *Sebastian. Ha,* Keely thought, *he misses me.*

"Hi, Sebastian," she said, her voice hoarse with sleep. She hoped she sounded sexy.

"Keely, I'm sorry to wake you, but my father had a stroke last night."

chapter
fourteen

"Oh, no! How is he?"

"They medevaced him to Mass General. I'm here at the hospital right now. I brought Mom up. I don't know when I'll be home."

"Sebastian, that's terrible! I'm so sorry." She sat up in bed. "Can you . . ." Was this too intimate to ask, when they were only just beginning a close relationship? "Is there . . . any way to tell how serious it is? I mean, I know from my mother that strokes are all different."

Sebastian was eager to talk, in the way that talking helped to make sense of a catastrophe. "We don't know for sure, but I don't think it's life-threatening. Mom said he woke in the middle of the night and got up to go to the bathroom. He staggered and didn't know which way to go. She went to him, and he was awake, but he was confused. He couldn't talk right. He couldn't understand Mom. She called 911. The ambulance came right away. She called me and I got there just after the ambulance. Mom was so upset because Dad peed himself and she couldn't change his wet pajamas before the EMTs arrived."

"Oh, poor Donna."

"But he didn't lose consciousness. The doctors told us he had an ischemic stroke. That means a blood clot in the brain. The ER doctor administered an IV of something unpronounceable, alteplase something or other, that breaks up the clot and restores blood to the brain. Keely, I don't even know what I'm talking about, really."

"How is your mother taking this?"

"She's freaked out. She's been sobbing a lot. The hospital scares her. She can't deal with seeing Dad with tubes in his nose and arm. I mean, of course, she was in there, talking to him and so was I, but they wanted him to rest, so now Mom's down the hall, calling Isabelle."

"Is there anything I can do?"

"I can't think of anything now, but I'll keep in touch. We're really just waiting for the doctors to tell us something. Waiting to see how Dad is."

"I'm so sorry, Sebastian. This is frightening."

"Yes, and at this point we can only go from minute to minute. I've got to phone Eric and tell him to run the shop today. And Mom wants me to call some of Dad's friends. And the office. Someone will have to take over his cases. I don't know how long I'll be up here. I don't have a change of clothes . . ."

"I can help you. I can express mail you some clothes or shaving stuff, whatever you need. I could call some of your parents' friends."

"Thanks, Keely. If I stay, I think Isabelle will come up, and she can bring me what I need." He cleared his throat, sounding on the verge of tears. "Keely, I'm almost more worried about my mother than about Dad. She was hysterical when we got into the helicopter."

"Flying in a huge noisy machine like that must be scary."

"No, no, it was because Dad was so helpless and . . . not himself. He was . . . making sounds. Sometimes he could get some words out, but they were slurred. We're supposed to hold his hand, talk to him, and I do, and Mom does try, but it's difficult for her."

"I can understand that. Would you like me to have my mother call you? This is exactly the sort of thing she knows about."

"Maybe. Let me think about it. Let me ask Mom. The doctors will tell us what to do."

"Let me know if I can do anything. I'm so sorry, Sebastian. I'm praying for you all."

"Thanks, Keely. I should go."

Keely rose, pulled a light robe around her, and padded quietly into the kitchen. She made coffee. She took it out onto the patio and sat for a while listening to the morning begin.

Her first thoughts were for Al Maxwell and his family. She still resented the man for the way he'd treated her when her father died. How he had callously told her to leave college. But when she was younger, he'd been nice. Poor Sebastian and Isabelle . . . it didn't sound as if Sebastian's father's life was in danger, but certainly that his life would change. Should she call Isabelle? But no. Keely wasn't part of their family. It wasn't the Maxwells she should be thinking about. She should be thinking about what to do with Gray when he arrived on the island.

Gray. Sebastian.

She had planned to tell Sebastian about Gray, that he was coming for a brief visit to see the island. She had planned to stress that he would be staying in a hotel, not with her. But she couldn't tell Sebastian now. Compared to what the Maxwell family was going through, Gray's visit wasn't even on the radar of importance.

Still, she wished she could let Sebastian know Gray was coming. She didn't want to seem to keep it a secret from him. She felt unsettled and irrationally guilty.

The day became one of those stop-and-start, restless days, when Keely couldn't force herself to write and instead compulsively checked her phone to see if Sebastian had called. When Eloise drifted from her bedroom at eight, Keely nearly jumped on her, needing to talk with her about Al Maxwell. After that, they were both nervous, wanting to help the Maxwells, resigned to waiting for the phone to ring. The two women agreed it was the perfect time to use their nervous energy, so they gathered all the items they'd set aside for the Seconds Shop and delivered them, then filled the trunk once again with treasures for the Madaket Mall. Eloise kept up a running commentary, recounting all the people she'd seen over the years who'd had strokes and how they recovered and how necessary physical rehab was for the entire mind-body return to health.

Sebastian didn't phone. Was that a good or bad sign?

In the afternoon, Keely checked her calendar on her phone and discovered there was a fund-raising event for the Maria Mitchell Natural Science Museum that night. She nearly wept with relief. This would be the perfect occasion for her to entertain Gray.

Gray called a little after three to tell her he was on the island and at the hotel.

She told him about the event that evening, cocktails, a full dinner, champagne.

Gray said he'd be delighted to attend with her. He'd pick her up at six-thirty. Keely's stomach went all funny when he said that. Her mother's house was so humble. During her visit, Keely and her mother had groomed the yard and planted blooming daffodils in the window boxes, so the place had a kind of cozy charm about it. But compared to Gray's apartment, the house Keely had grown up in was, at best, modest outside, and as for the inside—well, Gray wasn't going to set foot in her house!

This gala was the first big charity event for the island. Keely had guessed that some of the stylish summer people would already be on the island, so she'd packed a few evening dresses. Because the night was unusually warm and humid, she chose a chartreuse silk slip dress with a pale lavender silk shawl and her highest heels—wisely, the gala committee did not force their patrons to stand on a lawn. She put her hair up, wore eye shadow for the first time in days, and fastened dangling silver earrings in her ears.

"Goodness!" her mother said when Keely entered the living room. "I can hardly recognize you. My, you look stunning, Keely."

"Thanks, Mom. Listen, call me if there's any news about Mr. Maxwell."

"Do you want me to answer it if Sebastian or Isabelle calls?"

"Yes. Please. Tell them I'm at a benefit. I'll try to be home by eleven."

"And Gray is picking you up here?"

"He is. But, Mom, let's wait for you to meet him tomorrow, okay? I don't know exactly what my relationship with Gray is right now. I mean, well, you know I'm seeing Sebastian."

"An embarrassment of riches."

"Well, certainly an embarrassment. I've got to tell Sebastian about Gray, and tonight I need to tell Gray about Sebastian."

Eloise smiled. "Such problems you have."

Keely waited outside for Gray to arrive. He'd rented a Mercedes. Of course he had. When he stepped out of his car, she hurried down the walk to meet him. He wore a lightweight navy blazer and white trousers. White bucks, a red tie, an all-American look. She pecked a kiss on his cheek and stepped back.

"You look absolutely ravishing tonight," Gray said. "Maybe we should forget the benefit and go straight to my room."

Keely laughed, as if he couldn't mean what he was saying. "You look rather gorgeous yourself."

"I'm glad you think so, Keely. I want to do everything I can to please you."

Keely shook her head, stunned. This was an extraordinary event, this expression of his emotions, the depth of his feelings for her. She was overwhelmed. She didn't want to thank him—she didn't want to own the reason for his action.

"I'm speechless," she said, and that was true.

As they drove out to 'Sconset, they talked of insignificant things. This was no time for Keely to bring up Sebastian, and no time for Gray to get serious with Keely. Once they were at the private club, its spacious rooms leading to remarkable views of the southwest part of the island, they were engulfed by other benefit guests. Waiters came by with trays of drinks. Gray chose a martini, but Keely stuck with prosecco, her old reliable bubbly pal that never got her drunk.

She was only slightly surprised that so many people at the party recognized Gray. Many people were from New York, and the luscious women, flashing with diamonds worth more than Keely's mother's house, came fluttering up to Gray to kiss his cheek. Their husbands shook Gray's hand and patted him on the shoulder. They talked about the Yankees, about a benefit at the Metropolitan Museum of Art in New York that coming summer, about the stock market.

Keely studied Gray as he talked. No doubt about it, if he were cast in a movie, he'd definitely be chosen as the lead. It wasn't just that he was broad-shouldered and handsome. He carried himself with a natural authority, almost a nobleness. And he deserved it.

The New York women eyed Keely cautiously until she told them she had a pied-à-terre in the city (it amused her to think of her tiny apartment in such terms) and that she was a novelist. Some of the women had read her book and loved it.

At the end of the evening, the valet brought the car up to the club entrance. Keely slipped inside and immediately removed her high heels.

"I'm in pain," she told Gray, laughing. "No, seriously. I haven't worn such high heels for weeks. I'd forgotten that it's complete torture."

"Wear comfortable flats," Gray suggested as he turned out of the long private drive and on to Polpis Road.

Keely laughed. "No, thanks. I can deal with the occasional high heels when I'm here. Mostly I wear sandals. After all, it's spring, it's Nantucket."

"But what about when you return to New York? I have a fond memory of you in short skirts and high heels." Reaching over, he took Keely's hand. "You have amazing legs."

They were on the curve of road that took them past Sesachacha Pond. The pond was often breached by the ocean storming over the small sand barrier between them. On the other side of the water, several summer houses stood, their lights twinkling like lightships, and every few seconds the beam of the 'Sconset lighthouse would flash.

"Gray," Keely said impulsively, "pull over here. At that small overlook."

"It's a nice spot," Gray said, turning off the engine and reaching to put his arm around Keely.

She pulled away. He had misunderstood her intentions, and it was her fault.

"Gray, wait," she said quickly. "I need to tell you something."

Gray drew back. Immediately, his guard was up, an invisible shield Keely could almost see.

"Gray, I've been . . . seeing someone since I've been home. His name is Sebastian Maxwell. He's Isabelle's brother. I know I've spoken about her. I would have told you about Sebastian before, but I didn't know that he'd be here, I didn't know that he . . . he loves me. I don't know what's going to happen, especially because his father had a stroke last night. I can't expect to talk about the future with Sebastian now, and I don't want to mislead you."

Gray stared out at the water, his face impassive. "What you're saying is that if you have the chance to be with this . . . Sebastian . . . you will take it. Between me and him, you choose him."

Keely looked down at her hands. "Yes, I suppose that's what I'm saying. I'm sorry."

Gray was quiet for a long time. Then he said, "You told me about Isabelle. Once, for most of your childhood, your best friend. Then she stole your boyfriend."

"Yes, that's right. I was angry with her when she married Tommy. She suddenly just snatched him back, without even telling me. And to be honest, Isabelle was upset with me when *Rich Girl* came out. Mostly because I sort of *won*, because I had a book published. Also because she probably thought a lot of the rich girl was based on her, and it wasn't really, although I did use bits and pieces of her life, her clueless sense of entitlement. But I really hope we'll be friends again."

"That family means a lot to you," Gray observed. "Maybe too much? Keely, I want to marry you. I want to spend my life with you. I don't say that lightly. I'm not going to run away. I can be patient. I can wait while your friend's father recovers from his stroke, until you have time to speak with Sebastian about your future."

"Gray . . ."

"It's okay, Keely. I'm okay. We're all right." He reached for the ignition button and started up the car. He pulled back onto the narrow, winding road.

After a moment, Gray continued, "And let's say you marry this Sebastian. Will you live on the island? Permanently?"

"Probably, well, definitely. But it's not definite that I'm going to marry Sebastian. It's all very complicated. His father—"

"Listen to yourself. If you marry Sebastian and live on this island, you'll be constantly in touch with his family. You've told me that islanders are close. You told me once that the best thing about living here is that everyone knows you and what you're doing, and the worst thing about living here is that everyone knows you and what you're doing."

"I remember saying that, yes," Keely said quietly.

"Maybe you should give some serious consideration to what it would be like to live your entire life here, instead of in New York."

"I do love the city—"

"I could always buy a house here, Keely. A summer house. We could come here for Christmas, Thanksgiving. You wouldn't lose your island completely."

In a very small voice, Keely said, "It isn't only the island I love."

As if he hadn't heard her, Gray said, "And *that* house. The Maxwell house. I could buy it. I could offer enough money so they'd sell it in a minute. Then you could have that house for your own."

"That house?" Was Gray trying to bribe her with his money?

"You've told me how much you love that house. How you longed to live there when you were a child."

"But I'm not a child anymore, Gray. I'm a grown woman, and I love Sebastian, for better or worse. Gray, I do care for you. I admire you, I enjoy being with you, and I'm so—"

"If you say you're so *fond* of me, Keely, I'm going to stop the car right here and make you get out and walk home in those wretched high heels."

Keely was surprised at the lightness in his voice. He didn't sound hurt or angry. He sounded almost amused.

"Gray, please . . . I do care about you."

"And I *love* you, Keely. I think I love the *real* you. I know you as you are now, an adult, a brilliant, capable, well-read, knowledgeable woman. You're not the child you once were."

"You think that being on the island makes me feel like a child again. Funny, because Fiona wanted me to come here to write because she thought it would make my work better, that being here is magical for me."

"We all have our magic spaces and places," Gray said. "But real life can't be magic all the time. Sometimes it's damned hard work."

Keely nodded.

"You said that Mr. Maxwell had a stroke?"

"Yes," Keely said.

"This will change the family dynamics. Some will show their mettle. Some will be unable to deal with it. A health crisis is always unsettling."

"I understand. I won't expect Sebastian to make any kind of significant decision in the next few months." *Good Lord*, Keely thought. *I'm beginning to talk like Gray.*

They had arrived at Keely's house. Gray turned into her driveway, parked, and faced Keely.

"I won't push you, Keely. I'm willing to step back. I can wait. I'm willing to give you all the time you need. No conditions added."

"You seem so cool about this, Gray."

He smiled. "I have learned to be cool when necessary. Would you like me to walk you to the door?"

Keely blinked. So he was not going to try to kiss her? It felt very intimate inside the car, the two of them turned to face each other, the night outside dark, offering privacy.

"No, no, you don't need to walk me to the door, Gray. But I would like it if you and I and my mother could have dinner together tomorrow night. I've told her all about you. She'd love to meet you."

"I'd love to meet her. I'll make a reservation at Topper's. I'll text you the time and I'll be glad to drive us there."

"Lovely. Thank you." Keely tilted her head, gazing at the handsome, formal man seated so near. "You've surprised me tonight, Gray."

"I hope it's been a good surprise."

"I think it has." In one quick move, she leaned forward and kissed his cheek, then opened her car door and hurried to her house.

From her chair in the living room, Eloise asked, "Did you have a nice time?"

"It was great," Keely answered, her mind on other things. Keely picked up her phone, collapsed on the sofa, and scrolled through the messages.

From Sebastian: *Dad's doing well. They're keeping him here one more night. Home tomorrow, we hope. Maybe to rehab clinic on Cape for him. Isabelle's here. I'm taking care of Mom. We'll be at the nearest Marriott tonight. I'll call tomorrow.*

From Sally: *Hello, ma cherie, how's it coming with the new book? Want to send me and Juan a few chapters?*

From Janine: *I loved meeting your Gray at the gala tonight. Your dress was smashing and he is hot! We were totally buzzing about him. Do tell all!*

• • •

In her bedroom, as she slid out of her high heels and silk dress, her mind spun like a roulette wheel, binary, black or red, two different worlds. New York, Sally and Juan, her new book, Gray. Nantucket, Sebastian and Isabelle, Mr. Maxwell, her mother. She was unsettled and confused. What Gray had said about the Maxwell family and her obsession with them was perceptive and true. Wasn't it? But her love for Sebastian was separate from her infatuation with the Maxwell family. Wasn't it?

She had admired Gray tonight. He was unexpectedly cool, not at all unsettled to hear her say she loved Sebastian. Why didn't he say goodbye and fly back to the city?

Why was she thinking about Gray at all?

She needed to drink lots of water and take a good long sleep.

"So," Keely said, returning to the living room and plopping down on the sofa with her legs stretched out on a pillow. "Tonight was fabulous. An open bar, scallops wrapped in bacon, caviar, boned chicken drumsticks in honey and—"

"Oh, for heaven's sake, Keely. I don't want to hear about the menu. At least not yet. Who else was there and what were they wearing? How did you get on with Gray? Did you have a good time?"

Eloise had actually clicked off the television, giving Keely her full attention.

"I had a nice time with Gray. He is a true old-fashioned gentleman. *And* he's going to take you and me to dinner tomorrow night at Topper's."

"Really? That's extravagant." For a moment, Eloise seemed to shrivel up again, back into her depression. "Are you sure you want me to go? I don't know what I'll wear and I certainly don't know what I'll have to contribute to the conversation."

"Oh, get over yourself, Mom! We're hardly going to discuss the latest UN resolution. Gray is a very nice person. He's a doctor.

He'll have a lot in common with you. I promise, you'll like him and he'll like you." Keely stood up. "I'm going to bed now. I've got to write tomorrow."

All that day, Keely stayed in her bedroom, in her T-shirt and boxer shorts, writing and tossing back cup after cup of coffee. She was wound tight, and once she got started, her focus was entirely on her new book. She reread and rewrote the first three chapters, wanting them to be perfect, knowing they couldn't be perfect until the entire book was finished.

It was a relief when evening came and she could shower and dress and coax her mother into preparing for their dinner out. Sebastian phoned once, to say that the hospital was keeping their father for another night, but not to worry, and that he was staying with his mother while Isabelle flew home to her own family.

Eloise allowed Keely to put a slight bit of makeup on her face. Lipstick, light eyeliner, blush. The style the hairdresser had given Eloise was becoming, slightly longer and bouncier than when she was working. Keely's mother seemed pleasantly surprised.

Gray arrived, completely swoon-worthy in his navy blazer and white ducks. As he helped the women into the car, Eloise quickly mouthed "wow" to Keely.

The chat was light and easy on the drive out. When they were seated at a table at Topper's with drinks and orders taken, Gray said to Eloise, "Keely tells me you're a nurse at the local hospital."

Eloise looked down. "Well, I was. I've retired now."

"Did you happen to know David Vanbrack?"

Eloise lit up. "Of course I did. He was our only surgeon here for about thirty years. How did you know him?"

"He was a guest lecturer in med school one year. He was a great advocate for pediatric surgical instruments. He used to make rough sketches of the Ballenger sponge forceps and the Metzenbaum dissecting scissors, before they were actually designed and utilized. He would get so worked up talking about them that he'd storm out of the lecture hall down to his office and phone one of the many hospital directors he tormented in those days."

"Yes, he was an emotional man," Eloise agreed, nodding. "I worked with him often on difficult births. He really hated C-sections. He had all the latest statistics on the tip of his tongue. Too many unnecessary C-sections were given in the United States. He would roar that while he was getting ready to help a child being born with forceps. He had the most remarkable forearms."

"I remember that. Large. Sturdy."

"Like Popeye." Eloise laughed.

Keely watched, amused and delighted, as her mother blossomed in the light of Gray's attention. Clearly Gray was charming her mother, and Keely felt her heart softening toward him. Gray was nicer than he seemed in New York. Maybe that was Nantucket magic at work.

Gray said, "In his last years, he was obese. But many of us who work at the hospital eat for comfort."

"Especially in a small, isolated hospital like ours," Eloise agreed. "In the winter, the harbor often freezes over, or we have gale force storms that prevent the freight boat from coming, so fresh vegetables and fruits become rare or nonexistent. We have such long dark winters here, it's easy to seek pleasure by baking dozens of chocolate chip cookies and eating them while reading by the fire."

"Well, Eloise, you clearly have found a way to stay in shape," Gray said. "Excuse me for being too personal, but I can tell from whom Keely gets her good looks."

"Hey, are you hitting on my mother?" Keely asked playfully.

Her mother blushed, and with diplomatic skill Keely didn't know she possessed, Eloise said, "So, Gray, tell me about your parents."

Keely leaned back in her chair, letting the conversation between her mother and Gray flow past her like a spring breeze. Here, tonight, she was witnessing sides of both Gray and her mother that she'd never seen before. Was everyone this way, a kind of benign Jekyll and Hyde? Was she?

"Keely? Earth to Keely," her mother said.

"Sorry," Keely said. "I was lost in thought."

"About your next book?" Gray asked.

"No. No, to be honest, I was wondering if we, especially Gray, you and I, are composed of two different people, and the city brings out one part and the island brings out the other."

"Go on," Gray urged.

"Well . . . you seem different here. Less formal, easier to talk with."

Gray nodded. "I see what you mean. You're different here, too, Keely. And maybe it is the difference in location. Maybe it is that here we feel on vacation, less pressured, but in the city we're on red alert all the time. And maybe," he added, smiling at Eloise, "it also has to do with our companions. Eloise is especially easy to talk with, not simply because she knows about the medical field. She's like chocolate, tranquilizing and stimulating at the same time."

"Goodness!" Eloise laughed, blushing. "I've never been compared to chocolate before!"

It was almost midnight when they gathered themselves and left the restaurant for the winding drive back to Eloise's house. Gray walked both women to the door and told Keely he'd phone her tomorrow.

"Are you leaving tomorrow?" Keely asked.

His face was partly in shadow, and his tone was gentle but also distant. "We'll see."

Gray leaned over to kiss Keely's cheek, and then, to Keely's surprise, and to Eloise's, he kissed Keely's mother's cheek.

"My goodness!" Eloise said when the two women were alone in the house. "He's wonderful, Keely! He's so intelligent and charming and handsome!"

"Mom, I think you're in love," Keely teased.

Eloise burst into embarrassed laughter. "Don't worry, darling. I won't try to steal him from you." In the kitchen, she ran cold water into a glass and drank it straight down. Turning, she put her hands on Keely's shoulders. "My sweet girl, thank you for tonight. I don't know when I've had so much fun." She hugged Keely. "I only hope I don't have a hangover tomorrow."

"I don't think it's the wine that made you high," Keely said.

Eloise smiled with a twinkle in her eyes. "I don't, either."

As Keely went through her evening routine, she realized she wasn't tired. She felt like a child after a birthday party, all wound up and clueless about how to calm down. She knew what she wanted to do, and after tossing and turning in bed, she allowed herself to do it. She called Gray.

"Are you still awake?" she asked.

He laughed. "Are you?"

"Thank you for such a brilliant evening. You made my mother very happy."

"You seemed happy, too," Gray said.

"I am. I was." Keely hesitated. "Listen, I don't want to make any rash decisions tonight, but could you come over here for dinner tomorrow evening?"

"I wish I could. I'm flying back to New York tomorrow afternoon."

"Oh." Keely was surprised at her disappointment. "I thought you were going to be here for three days."

"Yes, so did I. But things change."

"Gray—"

"Besides, I've been called in to consult about a new patient. It's urgent. I need to be there."

"I see. Yes, of course. Maybe some other time."

"Maybe."

"Gray, I'm sorry—"

"We had a great evening together, Keely. I thank you for that. I'm off to bed. Good night, Keely."

"Good night, Gray."

Keely turned on the small fan on her dresser to allow the white noise of the spinning blades to lull her to sleep. She snuggled down in bed and closed her eyes. But it was a long time before she slept.

She woke with the morning sun beaming into her room. The rest of the house was quiet. So her mother wasn't up yet, and it was after eight. Keely realized that she was unconsciously hoping that the dinner last night had changed her mother, at least a little. Eloise had been so happy and talkative. Clearly she had enjoyed herself. Keely prayed Eloise wasn't retreating back into her solitary state.

Maybe her mother was simply sleeping late.

She brought her laptop out to the patio and began to work. First, she answered emails and checked on Instagram posts, but before long, as it often happened, scenes and dialog for her new book began to intrude into her mind. She opened the document file and wrote.

At some point in the morning, Eloise rose, poured a cup of coffee, and settled into her chair facing the television. Around noon, Sebastian phoned.

"I can't talk long. I just wanted to touch base. I'll be up here another day."

"How's your father?"

"The doctors say he's recovering, but it's not that obvious to us," Sebastian said. "Poor Mom is beside herself. He needs physical and speech rehabilitation, but when we talk about taking him to the facility on the Cape, he roars and pounds his bed. He wants to go home."

"I can understand that."

"Yes, but it makes it harder for the rest of us. Well, for Mom. She's overwhelmed. I'm afraid *she's* going to have a stroke or a

heart attack. Dad is a frightening sight. His right side isn't working well, and the right side of his face sags."

"Your poor father."

"I know, but he's not in pain. He's going to recover. It will take
time, and it will take a lot of work, but he can do it. Every stroke
is different, they said, and we don't know how well he's comprehending what's going on, or the future, or even the present." Sebastian's voice hitched. "We've been told to be gentle with him.
Not to rush him. So we're trying our best, but it's as if an alien has
taken over our father. You know what he was like. So strong, so
powerful. Suddenly, he's a little old man."

"Oh, Sebastian. I'm sorry."

"It's going to change everything, Keely. Everything for him.
Everything for us."

Later, Keely wished she'd asked exactly who was included in that
"us," but in the moment she sensed that Sebastian was focused
entirely on his father. Their own relationship was on hold; that
was obvious. It wasn't what Keely had dreamed of happening, but
then it surely wasn't what Al Maxwell had reckoned for.

Did Keely think for even one brief moment that Karma had
given Al Maxwell what he deserved for the way he had treated
Keely so long ago? She allowed herself to consider that thought. It
was shabby of her to think that way. Quickly, she let the thought
dissolve, disappear. She was truly sorry for Mr. Maxwell. She
wished him well.

Which was a good thing, since she wanted to marry his son.

For the rest of the week, Keely kept to a strict writing routine.
An odd sort of dynamism operated inside her, so that she could
use the pressures of the real world to fuel her fiction writing. By
the end of the week, she sent three chapters to Sally and to Juan.
She was anxious about what Sally would say. Would this be the
book that Juan hoped for?

Her mother continued to come out of her shell. She had lunch with friends. She volunteered at the Seconds Shop. She tried on the new clothes Keely had ordered and was quite pleased with how she looked. She was happier, and Keely went with her to a movie, and a lecture at the library, and out to the Seagrille again.

It was working, Keely thought. Keely's presence on the island was cheering her mother, reviving her. She hoped the same was happening for her manuscript.

By Saturday, Mr. Maxwell had been moved from the hospital back to his house, where he insisted, in his own loud but clear way, he wanted to be.

When Sebastian called, he was distracted, clearly stressed out.

"Dad's home, but they've put a bed in the dining room and moved all the dining room furniture into the den until we can have it stored. He has a portable toilet next to his bed! A portable toilet in the dining room! Poor Mom is nearly insane. We're supposed to spend as much time with him as possible, helping him to speak clearly or remember stuff, and I'm doing that, but I can't tell if it's helping him or not."

"What can I do?" Keely asked.

"Come to my house tonight."

Keely smiled. "Do you want me to bring some dinner?"

"Sure. Anything. I just want to see you. Well, I don't want to just *see* you—"

"I know what you want." Keely laughed.

During the day, she barbequed spare ribs, coating them heavily in her special sauce. She took over some cold Whale's Tale Pale Ale and bowls of guacamole and salsa and a giant bag of chips. They ate in front of the television, watching the Red Sox battle the Yankees.

Afterward, Sebastian said, "Man, it's good to relax."

"Do you want to talk about it? I mean, about your father?"

"No. Not tonight. He and Mom are in my mind enough. I want to be purely selfish. I want to focus on my own needs."

"I think I can help you do that," Keely said.

Later, as they lay in bed together, watching through the bedroom window as the light faded from the sky, they talked.

"Isn't it odd?" Keely said. "I came home to help my mother, and now you're helping your father."

Sebastian groaned. "That's the easy part for me. I don't mind spending time with Dad or helping him into his wheelchair, eventually helping him do easy exercises so he doesn't lose muscle. I'm glad to do that, and the doctors and nurses have been brilliant, telling us what to do."

"What's the hard part, then?" Keely asked, and she knew she was being vain when she thought, silently, that Sebastian would say the hard part was being away from her.

"Mom," Sebastian said. "She's not tolerating all this change very well. She's angry—I think anger is often a kind of recycled fear. She . . . sometimes she's not as patient with Dad as she should be."

"Is there any way I can help?" Keely asked.

"I don't know. Let me think about it. He's known you since you were a kid, so he would probably feel comfortable with you. On the other hand, Isabelle might feel funny about you being there."

"She knows you and I are seeing each other, right?"

"Yeah. She just needs more time to adjust to having you on the island again."

"Well," Keely said softly, struggling to keep any bitterness from her voice, "it's not exactly *her* island, is it?"

Sebastian turned and burrowed his head into his pillow. "God, Keely, let's not fight. I wish you and Izzy were friends again. It doesn't feel right having you estranged. You don't hate her because of Tommy, right?"

"Of course not. I don't hate her at all."

"I don't think she hates you, either, Keely. I think she's jealous of you, because you're a novelist now. She hasn't gotten anything published yet. I think she's given up trying. I know she's happy with Tommy and she's crazy mad in love with Brittany. But I don't think her life is complete without you."

Keely ran her hand over his back, his beautiful, long, broad-shouldered, muscular back. "Okay," Keely said softly. "Okay. I'll think about what I can do . . ." She lay there quietly a moment, gathering her courage. "Sebastian?" She kept her hand on his back, keeping a physical connection between them. "We've all been so worried about your father, so I didn't tell you, because really, it's not worth bothering about, but Gray Anderpohl came here for a few days. I didn't invite him. He came on his own. He had some leave from the hospital. He didn't stay with me, he stayed at the White Elephant. I took him to a Maria Mitchell gala one night, and he took me and my mother to dinner at Topper's one night."

She felt Sebastian's muscles tense as she spoke, but he didn't say anything.

"I told him I didn't want to see him anymore. I told him it couldn't happen between us. He went back to New York the next day."

Sebastian didn't speak. He lay so still that Keely was afraid he'd fallen asleep. Could he really be so indifferent to her?

"Sebastian . . . say something."

Sebastian turned toward Keely, pulling her against him so that her face nestled against his shoulder. He held her tightly, as a man would who was about to jump from a burning building. "I know you needed to tell me. But no more talk of Gray, okay? I can't get through this summer without you. I can't get through my life without you, Keely. I love you."

Keely smiled and hugged him tightly. "I have been waiting all my life to hear you say that."

"And what about you?"

"What? Oh, Sebastian, you know I love you."

"Still, it's nice to hear." He took her face in his hands. He kissed her slowly, firmly, for a long time.

"Okay," Keely whispered. She felt in Sebastian's body how he was struggling to control his breathing. She sensed his alarm, and she recognized how he calmed himself as he held on to her, not speaking, preserving his pride, not moving but lying pressed against her, making her his, making the two of them one. She held back her own tears. Oh, how she loved this man, and she respected his confession and his need. She would never betray him.

chapter
fifteen

Keely returned home early in the morning. By noon, she'd written so much and so quickly her back ached and she had a twinge in her neck.

She stood up and stretched. At that moment, her phone buzzed.

Juan Polenski. Her editor.

"Keely, how are you?" he asked.

"I'm good. Well, pretty good. Life has gotten complicated here—"

"Sorry to hear that, but I don't have much time. Listen, I've read your first three chapters, and I love them. How soon will you have the revised book finished?"

Keely laughed. "Wait, Juan, give me a moment. Wow, I'm so glad you like the book!"

"So how close are you to the end?"

"Um, I've still got a long way to go, Juan. I mean, I only started revising this spring. I'm working on it, but I can't see finishing it before January."

"How about November?"

"What?"

"If you get it in by November first, we can rush production through and have it ready for next summer."

"I don't know. I'm not sure I can do that."

"I know you can do it, Keely. *Poor Girl* comes out in July. We need *Sun Music* for next summer. Readers want more of your books."

"Good to know! It makes me want to get back to work."

"Great! Let me know if there's anything I can do."

The moment they disconnected, Keely plunged back into her book.

She was lost in her fictional world when Sebastian called.

"Keely, could you come over now? And help me with Dad? Maybe sit and talk to him?" The urgency in his voice was compelling.

"Of course. I'll come now."

Keely found her bag, dropped the car keys in her pocket, told her mother where she was going, and hurried out to the car. She parked in front of the Maxwells' house, not blocking any of the cars in the drive, and hurried up the slate walk. Sebastian opened the door before Keely could knock.

"Keely." Sebastian pulled Keely into the house and hugged her tight. "Thank you."

"I'm glad to help, Sebastian," Keely said. And thought: *Also, I hope I don't meet your mother or your sister while I'm here.*

He took Keely by the hand and led her along down the hall to the dining room. "All you have to do is sit by Dad's bed and talk. Not fast. Be slow and not too loud. He's not deaf. It's like his brain is asleep and we have to wake it up but we can't do it all at once."

"Sebastian," Keely said, stopping still before the door to the dining room. "Where are you going to be?"

"I'll be around. Probably in the kitchen. I've got to talk to Mom. If you need me, just yell."

Sebastian quietly escorted Keely into the dining room. A hospital bed sat majestically where the long dining room table had been. In the middle of the bed, Al Maxwell sat supported by a number of pillows, wearing striped pajamas, covered to the waist by a light blanket. Near the bed was a table littered with medicine bottles, tissues, a water pitcher, and a glass. Al Maxwell's eyes were open, but unseeing.

"It's so dark in here," Keely said.

"Dad can't tolerate bright light yet. We've got the shades down and the curtains drawn. Things need to be muted for him."

"Got it."

"Dad, look who's come to see you!" Sebastian spoke cheerfully, moving Keely in front of him. "It's Keely. You remember her. She's come to say hello." Still with a light, cheerful tone, he continued. "Keely, why don't you sit here in this chair. This is where we sit when we want to talk with Dad. Dad, I'm going to do some house-hold chores, but I'll be around. Keely wanted to have special time with you."

"Hello, Mr. Maxwell," Keely said.

Sebastian squeezed Keely's hand and whispered, "I'll be in my room."

It took a moment for Keely to gather herself. It was bizarre to see the powerful Al Maxwell reduced to this silent, still, discon-nected invalid.

She flashed on a day years ago when Mr. Maxwell, so strong and powerful, told Keely she should drop out of college to help her mother. He'd had no compassion for Keely then. And her heart burned with old anger . . . but it was tempered now, with sympathy.

She spoke quietly, as if everything were normal. "You might be surprised to see me, Mr. Maxwell. Usually I'm in New York. But this summer I'm living with my mother on the island while I write my new novel."

Al's eyes slowly moved to fasten on Keely's face, but he showed no signs of recognition. Keely wasn't certain that he even under-stood what she said.

"I'm so sorry about your stroke, but Sebastian assures me that you will be better soon. I guess we all need to let you rest, and I won't sit here blabbing on and on like I used to." She sat silently for a while, but his eyes remained on her, and she began again. "Do you remember the time you drove me and Isabelle to the Justin Timberlake concert in Connecticut and we were so excited we chattered away like a pair of monkeys and you told us we were driving you mad? You said you would *pay* us to be quiet for just five minutes. And you did!"

Keely laughed at the memory. Al Maxwell didn't react.

What could she say that would interest him? She didn't know what she was doing. Should she ask him questions? Or simply sit droning on and on?

"I'm having such a good time being back on the island. Spring is so wonderful here. I never knew Sebastian did scrimshaw. I was at a gallery opening with my mother a few weeks ago, and I was astonished by a display of the most gorgeous scrimshaw, and—"

Nothing Keely said elicited any response, not so much as a blink, from Mr. Maxwell. In the corner of his mouth, on the side that drooped, a bead of saliva shimmered.

"I hope I'm not irritating you, blabbing on and on like this. Maybe you want to sleep? Are you comfortable? It must be odd to wake up in the morning and find yourself in the dining room. You look good, so that's positive, right?"

She stole a glance at her watch. Not even ten minutes had passed. As she talked, Keely thought maybe he didn't like being stared at constantly, so she let her gaze circle the room, spotting the familiar fireplace with the Victorian mantel and the marble clock. When she looked back at Mr. Maxwell, his eyes were closed.

She'd bored him right into sleep. Should she keep talking? Or let the poor man rest? Should she sit here with him? Was it necessary for someone to be with him at all times? Her throat was dry from talking. Rising, she tiptoed from the room, down the hall, and into the kitchen to get a glass of water. She was at the sink drinking when she heard Sebastian and his mother in the living room.

". . . can't go on like this!" Donna Maxwell was saying. "We had booked a cruise down the Danube! We were going to see Austria and Hungary! Now—*now* what do I have to look forward to? Taking care of an invalid all my life?"

Keely froze. She shouldn't be hearing this conversation. But she couldn't tear herself away.

"Mom, it won't be for the rest of your life. And we'll all help you."

"All my life—*all my life!*—I have done nothing but take care of other people. Feed people, and with only the healthiest ingredients! I've always been the mother who helped on school trips. I baked probably three million birthday cupcakes! I'm fifty-eight years old! Do you think I wanted *this* when I was your age? When do I get to have something for myself?"

"Mom—"

"How can you possibly understand? You're young. You're beginning your life. *I'm* facing old age and white hair and wrinkled skin and arthritis. I want to have fun while I still can move without a fucking cane!"

Keely's hands flew to her mouth to cover her yelp of shock. Mrs. Maxwell said *fucking!* For one weird moment, she thought: *I can't wait to tell Isabelle!*

"Mom, let's work something out. I mean, you should go on that cruise. We can hold down the fort."

"Go on a cruise *alone?*"

"Well, take a friend. That would be fun, wouldn't it? Take Mary Ellen."

"I can't go on a cruise when your father is ill, Sebastian. Don't be ridiculous."

Donna Maxwell began to sob, great wrenching, hiccupping sobs so heartbreaking that Keely felt guilty overhearing them. Quietly she left the room, carrying her glass of water with her.

Al Maxwell was still sleeping. At least his eyes were closed. Keely sat in her chair. Should she continue talking? She'd heard that people should talk when someone was in a coma, that they could hear even if they couldn't react. But Isabelle's father wasn't in a coma. Maybe he needed to sleep. Maybe she should hum very quietly, so he knew he wasn't alone. Sebastian hadn't given her sufficient instructions. Probably he didn't know the perfect thing to do, either.

As Al Maxwell slept, saliva began to dribble out of the drooping side of his mouth, down his chin, and onto his pajama top.

"Oh, man," Keely said under her breath. *Now* what was she supposed to do? The dribble continued. His pajama top darkened with moisture.

Should she dab at his chin? Even as a sleeping invalid, Al Maxwell intimidated Keely. Touching his face while he slept seemed too intimate an action for her. She quietly pulled some tissues from the box, patted them into a tidy square, and very carefully laid them on the pajama top to absorb the saliva. Her hands shook as she performed her small task. She was afraid she'd accidentally jar his chin and wake him. If he opened his eyes and glared at her, or worse, displayed shock at her leaning so close to him, she'd have a heart attack!

She settled back in her chair. For a few minutes, she watched Mr. Maxwell sleep. She wished she'd brought a book to read. If she had her laptop with her, would she be able to write? Would that seem offensive to Sebastian's father or to Sebastian? And what about Donna Maxwell? It made perfect sense to Keely that after a lifetime of tending to others' needs, Donna Maxwell craved some special time for herself. Still, Mrs. Maxwell had sounded so spoiled, so *indignant* that her husband had had a stroke that might prevent her from going on a cruise.

Maybe all her life Donna Maxwell had wanted to go on a cruise. Maybe she had been only acting the part of perfect mother, and she couldn't keep up the pretense any longer. Maybe Donna Maxwell was a big fat phony!

Or maybe Donna Maxwell was like everyone else, her selfish desires restricted by duty and the need to be who she seemed.

Another thought followed: All her life Keely had envied the Maxwell family. Now she realized how fortunate she'd been to have the mother and father who'd raised her.

Tears came to her eyes. She missed her father. But while she sat there near Mr. Maxwell, she allowed herself to be with her father again, in memory. Her father had not been wealthy in terms of money, but his life—his wife, his daughter, his friends, this island—had been a fortune to him.

After an eternity, Sebastian came to relieve Keely.

"Did he sleep the entire time?" he asked in a whisper. "You don't have to stay with him when he's sleeping. I'm sorry I didn't explain it to you, but we're only figuring it out ourselves. Keely, thanks so much for being here today. This isn't how I wanted to spend time with you—"

"I was glad to help." Keely hugged Sebastian. She wanted to tell him how liberated she felt. The powerful Mr. Maxwell could be weakened like everyone else. But she couldn't say that to Sebastian; it would sound vengeful. "Take care."

"How was Al?" Eloise asked when Keely walked in the front door.

Keely flopped down on the sofa across from her mother. "Oh, Mom, I'm such a terrible human being. Mr. Maxwell wasn't like himself at all. He was like a zombie."

"Well, he would be, wouldn't he? The poor man has had a stroke."

"I know, I know. He looks fine, except one side of his face droops. But he has an expression in his eyes like no one's home. I tried to be entertaining, I tried to talk about stuff from my childhood, but nothing interested him. I felt guilty and bored and useless. And wait till I tell you what I overheard Mrs. Maxwell say!" She gave her mother the full, dramatic account.

Eloise frowned and nodded to a private thought. "She should go on that cruise. She's got a long and difficult time ahead of her."

"Because recovering from a stroke can take, like, months?"

"Of course. And while it's necessary to help stimulate the brain cells as soon as possible, before the brain loses its functions, *sleep* is the great healer."

"Mom, maybe you could talk to the Maxwells about this. You know so much, and they seem overwhelmed."

Her mother smiled. "Keely, I'm sure they have plenty of professional help and all the medical advice they need." Raising the remote, she changed channels on the television. "Look, a rerun of *Monk*. I do love this show."

Keely glared at her mother, mentally challenging her to look away from the television and pay attention to her. But Eloise was locked in.

"I'm going for a run," Keely said. It was late in the afternoon and she was too cranky to sit still.

She returned home sweaty, exhausted, and still cranky. To her surprise, her mother wasn't in the living room. Keely followed the sound of her mother's voice to the kitchen.

"Absolutely not," Eloise was saying, her voice firm but friendly. "If you insist on paying me, I won't come." Seeing Keely, Eloise smiled brightly and held up a finger: *one moment.* "All right, then. I'll see you in the morning."

"What's going on?" Keely asked when her mother put down the phone.

"That was Donna Maxwell. She asked me to come help Al. She said they've hired a couple of licensed practical nurses, big strong men, to help Al bathe and dress in the morning. She likes the people working with Al to heal his mind, but she thinks that since Al has known me for so long, he might feel more comfortable with me."

"Donna called you?"

"Yes. Why are you surprised?"

"Because Donna is so . . . snobbish."

Eloise said, "Illness makes us all equal."

"Are you going to do it?"

"Oh, yes, and I know I'll be able to help Al." Eloise moved around the kitchen with light steps. "Go shower. I'm making spaghetti and a big salad for us for dinner."

"Okay, then," Keely agreed. She left the room with her heart full.

So Aloysius Maxwell, who had been uncharitable and condescending to Keely and her mother when Keely's father died, Aloysius Maxwell, who coldly refused to help George Green's widow and daughter, that same Aloysius Maxwell was now in need of the most basic help, would be aided and carefully tended to—for with her patients, Eloise was always careful and tender—by George Green's widow.

And Eloise Green would regain her sense of value in the world and the priceless and ordinary day-by-day pleasure in her work.

Real life was like a plot by Dickens, Keely decided.

Late in the afternoon, Keely and her mother sat in the backyard, sipping lemonade and enjoying the shadows that cooled the patio. Keely had bought a birdbath, and for long minutes at a time, both women laughed softly together, watching the lovely birds splash.

"Mom, I don't know what to do," Keely said.

"What's your problem?"

"Sebastian. Well, not Sebastian. I'm in love with him and I think we're serious, very serious. But Isabelle is like a shadow looming over us."

"You should call Isabelle," Eloise said.

"She should be the one calling me. She's the one who married Tommy the moment I stepped off this island. And I did call her last year. She was too busy to talk."

"I'm sorry to hear that. You and Isabelle were so close. So alike. Passionate, intense children. I've never known how to make things perfect for you, Keely. Now, I guess, you have to decide things for yourself. Can you be with Sebastian if you are estranged from Isabelle?"

"I don't know," Keely said. She was close to tears. "But Sebastian or no Sebastian, I hate being without Isabelle!"

"Isabelle is a good girl—

"She's hardly a girl."

"You two will always be girls to me. But okay, Isabelle has a good heart. She'll come around in time. I suppose all you can do is wait."

"You're right. So. Let's talk about you." Keely twisted in her chair. "Look what I found in the paper." She folded the town newspaper so that a certain article showed and handed it to her mother. NANTUCKET VOLUNTEER OPPORTUNITIES.

"Over two dozen organizations need help. Why not choose one or two that interest you the most? You could be really helpful, with all your experience as a nurse."

Eloise nodded. "You're right. I'd like to volunteer. I'll check these out. Oh, and Keely, look! Here's something you might like." She handed the newspaper back to Keely.

Are you a writer? Come join the Nantucket Writers' Club at the Nantucket Atheneum Wednesday nights at seven to talk about your fiction and non-fiction work. No age limit.

"It doesn't say who's involved," Keely murmured. "Or where they've published or if they've published."

"Does it matter?" Eloise reached over to take Keely's hand. "When you were a child, you loved talking with people about words. How 'set' can be a subject and a verb, the difference between 'gloomy' and 'grim.' You might have fun being around people who love words."

"Mmm. Maybe."

"My point is," Eloise said, pointing at the newspaper, "the people in this group are *writers*. My life has changed, Keely, and I'll admit I'm having trouble adjusting to it. It helps to have you here. And I'm glad you're seeing Sebastian. But you spend so much time isolated in your room, working . . . I think you should try this group. I think it would be good for you."

Keely laughed. "Okay, you know what? I'll make a deal with you. I'll go to the writers' group if you'll volunteer."

"Deal." Eloise extended her hand and Keely shook it.

chapter
sixteen

Wednesday evening Keely entered the town library, just as she'd promised her mother she would. Nantucket had become a celebrity and intellectual paradise. Writers of all genres and levels of success came for the summer or a year to soak up the atmosphere. Some of the writers were well-known and enjoyed their celebrity, drinking at the island bars, picking up a man or a woman for the night and often making some kind of scene that the island would feast on for days. Other writers preferred their privacy. Maybe Keely's high school English teacher would be there; Mrs. Atwater had always talked about a book she was going to write.

The young woman at the circulation desk directed Keely to a small conference room on the handsome ground floor. Keely went down the stairs, through the hall, pulled open the door, and entered.

First, Keely spotted Grace Atwater, her former teacher. It had been only a few years since Keely had seen her, but Grace had stopped dyeing her hair. Now she'd taken on the appearance of someone who wrote by candlelight with incense curling up around her halo of frizz.

"Hi, Mrs. Atwater!" Keely said happily. She entered the room and glanced to see who else was in the group.

Isabelle.

Isabelle was seated at the table, across from Grace Atwater.

She was more beautiful than ever, with her thick blond hair sheared short, accentuating her blue eyes. Keely's heart was like Niagara Falls, *thundering* as emotions cascaded through her. Keely wanted to race toward Isabelle and embrace her. But of course she couldn't. Sharing one's writing was a brave and intimate deed, done only when the writer felt some degree of safety, some sense that no one would laugh or sneer at the work. Isabelle might feel anxious with Keely in the group. Keely would definitely feel anxious with Isabelle here. Keely felt Isabelle studying her, and wanted to run from the room. She had spoken to audiences of four hundred people and felt less nervous than she did now.

"Keely." Isabelle's voice was cool, but she looked strained, almost fearful. "I didn't know you were coming."

"I only decided today." Keely gripped her notebook tightly, hoping to conceal how her hands were trembling. "How is your father?"

"He's getting better, thank you," Isabelle replied, her voice formal.

"What are *you* doing here?" a man asked, his tone belligerent. He looked to be in his sixties, with thick white hair. He wore horn-rimmed glasses over his bright blue eyes. His face was flushed almost burgundy. "You're a published author," he continued. "Why would someone successful like you deign to hang out with a bunch of amateurs like us?"

Keely hesitated. She could leave. Maybe she *should* leave. But she answered honestly. "My mother suggested I come. She reminded me that when I was a young girl, I had a best friend. My best friend and I dreamed of being authors. Novelists. We read the same books and discussed them. We were passionate about words. We couldn't get enough of words, the way they sound, the way they look, what they can do when they're arranged one way or the other. We were like a very intense, determined fan club of two. We sat in our bedrooms or on a porch, and shared the stories we wrote with our words." Her chin trembled when she admitted, "I've never been happier in my life."

Isabelle ducked her head, took a tissue from her bag, and blew her nose.

The man growled, "I see."

A confident, almost aggressive voice spoke up. "Hi, Keely. Cool that you're here," a young woman said.

"Thank you." Keely's legs were shaking.

"Yes, welcome, Keely," Mrs. Atwater said. "Why don't you take the chair over there?"

Keely obediently sat. Five people stared at Keely appraisingly.

"Let's go around the room and introduce ourselves," Mrs. Atwater directed. "Also, say something about what you're working on."

Keely's champion spoke up. "I'm Violet Lefebre. I'm writing a novel about Dorothy Wordsworth, you know, the poet's sister?"

Keely nodded. Violet looked to be about twenty-three years old, with long, glossy black hair, blue eyes framed by thick black glasses, black fingernail polish, a black tank showing off her tattoos, and a short black skirt. If Dorothy Wordsworth knew that this young woman was writing a novel about her, she would faint.

Keely peered closely at Violet. "You grew up here, Violet, right? Did you play Annie one year for the Theatre Workshop school production?"

A beautiful smile spread over Violet's face and she looked prettier and much less terrifying.

"I did!" Violet agreed.

"I saw you. You were amazing. Are you still acting?"

"No, but I'm singing. And . . . writing."

A plump, pretty woman in her fifties, with curly hair and pink cheeks and a shirt embroidered with flowers introduced herself as Bonnie Watts. "I'm writing a mystery about a woman who cooks for a rich summer family. It's going to have lots of recipes in it."

"Bonnie. I remember you, too. You did a lot of baking for the Wicked Island Bakery."

Bonnie laughed. "It's a good place to get material," she said. "Everyone talks about everything when they're waiting for a morning bun."

"The Wicked Island Bakery is a good title for a book," Keely said.

"Why thank you. That's what I'm calling it."

Someone cleared his throat, gruffly. The angry man was the fourth member of the group. "Mike Reynolds. I'm writing a thriller about an unfaithful wife."

Well, that explains a lot, Keely thought. "Hello," she said, smiling at him.

"Isabelle?" Mrs. Atwater prompted.

Isabelle's face went red. "I'm writing a comic novel about motherhood. At least I hope it's comic."

Mrs. Atwater announced, "Okay. Here's how we arrange our time. First hour, we take turns reading aloud from something we're working on. It helps to take notes. We break after an hour, and when we return, we take turns giving feedback. We talk about a general topic, something that might have come up during our reading, for example, how important setting is, or how to pace a scene."

"Okay," Keely said. She was aware that when she smiled, her mouth quivered nervously. Her heart was tossing out bombshells of adrenaline and her body was in full fight-or-flight state, but she would not run from this room where Isabelle sat, head high, cheeks flushed.

"Violet, let's start with you," said Mrs. Atwater.

The young woman was happy to oblige. Her selection raced along as Dorothy Wordsworth and the poet Coleridge and the writer De Quincey indulged in drugs. Violet obviously had done research on the effects.

"We'll keep notes on our thoughts," Mrs. Atwater reminded the group. "We'll discuss after we've all read."

Mike was next. In a low, gruff voice, he read a section about his hero's reaction to finding his wife in bed with his best friend. His writing was terse, acidic, fast, and as he read, Keely became sure that he was writing from experience. Her heart swelled with pity, but her mind was making notes about what he could improve and how.

Isabelle read next. She was nervous, but her voice grew stronger as she read. She had them all laughing by the end of her reading. Keely felt oddly proud.

Bonnie's few pages of mystery were more about how to prepare pan-roasted lobster than the people who would eat it. Keely made a few notes on her pad.

"Now, Keely," Grace Atwater asked, "what do you have for us?"

Keely took a deep breath. It was one thing to read from a published book, quite another to read from new, raw material. "Listen," she said with quiet honesty. "I'm stuck on the book I'm writing. I did really well with my first book, but I missed the island, so I came home. I could really use this group."

"Good to know," Bonnie said.

"I'm revising a book set on Nantucket," Keely continued slowly. She was superstitious and wary of telling anyone here her real title, *Sun Music*. She improvised. "The working title is *Learning to Tack—*"

Mike interrupted. "That's a terrible title! People will think it's about laying carpet."

"Mike," Grace admonished calmly, "remember we're going to save our reactions to discuss later. Please write your thoughts on your pad."

"Mike's right," Keely said. "It's a terrible title, that's why it's a working title. I'll, um, read a scene I've been working on . . ." She felt her face grow hot as she read aloud. This new book, *Learning to Tack* or *Sun Music* or whatever it would be titled, was not about her or her and Isabelle, but parts of it came directly from Keely's childhood. Could it seem to the others that everything she wrote was based on her life? And was that right?

When she finished reading, she forced herself to smile briefly and sat back in her chair with relief.

"And finally, I'll read from my magnum opus." With a nod to Keely, Grace said, "I'm writing a novel set in the Roman Empire during the days before Caesar was emperor."

Keely almost laughed aloud as she listened to her beloved but slightly daffy former teacher read about gladiators, swords, togas, and green grapes. Her work was romantic and certainly not true to facts, but much more fun than what she'd have expected from her.

"All right," Grace said when she'd finished her reading. "Time for a ten-minute break. Use the restrooms, stretch your legs, drink some water." She rose and left the room.

"I'm going outside for a smoke," Mike announced. "Want to join me, Keely?"

"No, thanks. I don't smoke."

Bonnie rose. "I'll join you, Mike. I don't smoke, but I could use some fresh air."

Keely glanced at Bonnie and quickly lowered her eyes. Was Bonnie hoping to link up with Mike romantically? *Passion in the Writers' Workshop*, Keely thought, smiling to herself. She rose and stretched her arms, trying to decide what to do. She wanted to speak with Isabelle, but she was afraid of being rebuffed. How strange life was, how strange people were, how strange Keely was, that as a child she could throw herself into the cold, uncaring ocean, yet now was timid about walking six feet across a room to speak to an old friend.

She gathered her courage and pushed her chair back from the table. At that moment, Isabelle walked up to Violet, murmured something obviously humorous, and the two women walked out of the room, grinning like a pair of mean girls from high school.

"Let's walk," Grace said.

"Oh, what?" Keely's thoughts were so tangled, she almost jumped when Grace spoke to her.

"Walk. Up and down the hall. It's good for the body, good for the brain." Grace held the door open and Keely joined her as they left the room.

"I never had the chance to congratulate you," Grace said, comfortably linking her arm through Keely's. "A novel published and a new one coming out this summer? Phenomenal. How do you like living in New York?"

"I like it a lot," Keely said. "It's . . . stimulating. Electric with energy."

"Mmm. I go in once a year to see theater. I always find myself dazed and exhausted."

"Oh, me, too. But when I lived here, the Cape Cod Mall dazed and exhausted me."

They laughed together.

"Are you retired from teaching?" Keely asked Grace.

"I am. I took early retirement. I do miss it. But I want to do so many other things while I'm still reasonably young, and my husband died last year, you know—"

"I didn't know. I'm sorry."

"Yes. Well. He was a good deal older than I am, so it wasn't an enormous surprise, but it was a breathtaking loss. I'm glad I live in this small town where I have so many friends to help me keep from falling into despair. I don't know that I would be sane without them. Certainly I wouldn't be happy."

"My mother retired about six months ago," Keely confided. "She's finding it difficult. She doesn't really know what to do with herself."

"I've been there. You think, when you're working, that you can't wait to retire so you can do all the projects you're longing to do. Knitting that sweater. Learning to play piano. Writing a book. But woman is a social animal. We're not meant to cower in our caves, painting the walls. Studies have shown that people live longer if they have an active social life." Before Keely could respond, Grace said, "Don't tell your mother I said that. She'll figure it out for herself. She's a smart cookie."

They'd reached the end of the hall and did an about-face.

"So," Grace said. "I remember when you and Isabelle were best friends in high school. You were inseparable."

Keely smiled. "Well, things change."

"People change," Grace said. "And they can keep changing."

"Her life is so different from mine." Keely wasn't thinking about Tommy and their daughter as much as she was thinking about Isabelle's large, loving, close-knit family. The Maxwells' wonderful spacious house, their sprawling yard. The garage was a three-car unit, so the apartment above was large and airy, and in the backyard was a playground set complete with turrets, slides, and swings the Maxwells had built for Sebastian and his friends, and then Isabelle and her friends, and now Brittany.

"True." Grace's voice broke into Keely's thoughts. "And yet here you both are, writing, just as you did when you were young."

With that, Grace clapped her hands, summoning her group back to the room. When they were all seated, she said, "All right. Time for discussion. And may I remind you that even though we've got a published writer in the room, I'm the boss here. Okay, let's talk about Violet's scene."

Violet started the discussion and remarks looped back and forth like a Frisbee. People laughed, people scribbled notes. People were kind to each other. When it was Mike's turn to be discussed, he groaned and covered his head playfully, as if waiting for an assault of rotten tomatoes.

When Isabelle's scenes came up for discussion, Keely felt her mind click on to super vigilance.

"I adored your scene," Bonnie crowed. "So sweet and funny!"

"Yeah, but she doesn't have a plot," Mike said. "We've talked about this before. Just lots of vignettes, no plot."

"It is kind of more like a memoir than a novel," Violet agreed. "I mean, I suppose if you have children, you'd find this appealing, but I don't have kids, so this is kind of useless to me."

"Well, I don't have kids," Keely said, speaking before she realized she was going to speak. "And I find it fascinating . . . maybe because I've *been* a kid. We've all been kids." She couldn't look at Isabelle as she spoke, and she didn't know why she so quickly sprang to her former friend's defense. How odd it was, to feel protective of someone who'd hurt her. But then, she'd heard other people talk about how they disliked their brother or sister and did all manner of torture to them, but aggressively defended that same sibling from any possible insults or injuries from others.

And that was something else Isabelle had, Keely thought, her heart plummeting. Isabelle had Sebastian. Could Keely become Sebastian's partner if she and Isabelle were estranged? Christmas dinners would sure be fun.

"Bonnie," Grace said. "Let's talk about your work."

Violet pounced. "Too much action too fast!"

"Bonnie and Isabelle should critique each other," Mike suggested.

"Keely? Earth to Keely."

She glanced over at Grace. "Oh, yes?"

"Mike thinks the action is overwhelmed by descriptions of food. What do you think?"

"I *love* descriptions of food," Keely said earnestly.

The discussion continued, heated but brightened with laughter. No one had anything insightful to say about Keely's scene but promised they would when they'd heard more.

In what seemed like minutes, the workshop was over. They gathered up their pages, folders, pens, and notebooks and wandered from the room, some of them talking, others rushing off. Keely hoped she might have a chance to speak with Isabelle, but she didn't chase after her, and Isabelle ascended the stairs quickly, almost running, as if she were afraid to speak with Keely.

But when Keely stepped out of the library into the warm, bright summer evening, she found Isabelle waiting by the sidewalk. She held her notebook to her chest like a shield.

"Hi, Isabelle," Keely said. Behind her notebook, her heart thudded fast. She knew more than anyone else in the world how much Isabelle wanted to write books. She knew more than anyone else in the world how painful it was for Isabelle that Keely had become a successful author. Why someone wanted to write books was a mystery. It was a lonely, crazy-making profession in which a human being could spend hours deciding on the arrangement of ten words in one single sentence. It was mystical, because where did those fictional people come from, so individual and resolutely themselves? Why one book was chosen to be published over hundreds of other equally fine books was a mystery, too. It was a kind of literary roulette. To the author, it often felt like a literary Russian roulette.

Keely had spent time hating Isabelle for marrying Tommy—but not much time. She was more hurt that Isabelle didn't call Keely right away with the news. Isabelle had *conspired* with Tommy. He was Isabelle's special person now. Isabelle had cut the cord to Keely like a line from an anchor, letting Keely drift away into the world on her own. But she didn't hate Isabelle any longer. She couldn't even feel angry. More than anything, she missed Isabelle's friendship.

Isabelle cleared her throat. "Could we talk about writing, Keely?" Her cheeks were flaming. "Just writing, not personal stuff?"

Keely studied her friend carefully. "I think we can. Certainly we can try."

"I mean, it sounds like what you're writing isn't personal. And doesn't seem based on anyone I know."

"Yes, well, that may be a problem," Keely admitted. "When I write about anything here—I don't mean you and me or Tommy—I mean the town, and the experiences I've had here, well, then it flows. What I'm trying to do now keeps hitting speed bumps."

Isabelle laughed. "Speed bumps? I just keep driving off cliffs into the ocean."

"But you're writing," Keely said.

"Sort of. It's hard, because of your success. I mean, what are the odds that I could have a book published, too?"

"What are the odds that I'll marry someone I love and have

children?" Keely countered. She remembered Grace Atwater's advice. "Come on. Let's walk down to the harbor."

After a long silence, Isabelle said, "You didn't really ever love Tommy. Not like I did. Do."

"How can you say that? I was with Tommy for two years. I had sex with Tommy. We were talking about marriage when my book sold."

"*Tommy* was talking about marriage, right? He told me you weren't so keen. I don't think you wanted to marry him."

Keely chewed her lip and didn't reply.

Isabelle continued, "I'm not saying you didn't feel affection or even love for Tommy, but never like I did. I think he was a distraction for you because you always loved Sebastian and he was so out of your league."

Keely's breath caught in her throat. "Out of my league? Thanks a lot."

"Stop it. I mean he's two years older, and in your teens that means a lot. Then he went to college, and then off to Sweden. He was a lost cause."

"When I was in fifth grade," Keely said softly, with laughter in her voice, "I made a vow by drinking cooking sherry and placing my hands on seashells, that I'd never tell you that I was in love with Sebastian."

Isabelle chuckled. "The thing is, Keely, you never had to tell me. It was obvious."

They passed the Dreamland and came to Easy Street, with benches on the brick sidewalk facing the harbor where the Steamship Authority boats docked. Mallards swam in the water. It was low tide, so gulls were striding up and down the exposed bit of beach as if patrolling. The women sat side by side on a bench, facing out. It was easier, Keely thought, to talk this way.

"I suppose you're right," Keely admitted. "I thought I'd never be with Sebastian. But I did care for Tommy. And you did grab Tommy the moment I went to New York."

"I'd do it again in a heartbeat," Isabelle said defiantly. "Keely, Tommy and I are right together. I know you think my dad kind of bought Tommy with the apartment and the boat, but Tommy and I fell in love before that. Tommy came when I called him. I was broken, devastated. He rescued me."

Keely sniffed. "How romantic."

"We never meant to hurt you."

"*You* could have *told* me, though. *You* could have emailed me, or phoned, but instead you kept it all secret and then *boom*, just dropped it on me."

"I know. That was wrong, probably. But you were in New York. Seeing your *editor*! You were miles ahead of me. You won!"

"What? Come on! You've always had so much more than I have, Isabelle! Your big house, your wealthy family, your brother, your fabulous mother who is never tired or stressed, your adorable dog and cats, your fabulous travels, and then the writers' colony? And then Tommy? You had to have Tommy, too?"

In a small voice, Isabelle said, "I didn't know you were jealous of my family. I thought you liked my family. Loved us."

"Of course I did. But you can love someone and envy them, too. Damn, Isabelle, I didn't even have a pet, because my parents were allergic!"

"Okay, I get all that. But, Keely, look at you now. You're the one who has everything now."

"Right. I have a husband who adores me and a darling little daughter and parents who dote on me and have all the money in the world."

"Okay, no. You don't have that. But you do have one published novel and one to come out this summer! You have a life in New York, a publisher, an editor, an agent, and I've seen your website and Facebook page, I know you have lots of readers. I'll bet you get picked up in limos when you tour. I'll bet you have plenty of money." Isabelle paused. "I'll bet you have a New York boyfriend you're not telling me about."

Keely hesitated. "You said you wanted to talk about writing."

"Yeah. Okay, then." Isabelle took a deep breath. "Keely, would you read my manuscript? But, not poking along like we do in the workshop—I mean, sit down and read it straight through, and then tell me exactly what you think." When Keely didn't answer right away, Isabelle continued in a rush, "I think it might be really good. And frankly, the workshop is good in many ways, but it's going so slow. And you've been published, you're out in that world, you would be by far the best judge of what I've written. And maybe, just maybe, if you liked it enough, you could show it to your agent?"

Staring straight ahead at the harbor, Keely said, "But what if I didn't like it that much? It seems like you're willing to be my friend, with the condition that I take your novel to my agent."

"I didn't mean it that way."

"Isabelle, writing isn't this dream profession where they take our precious words and worship every comma. They rip a novel apart and ask you to rewrite the whole thing and change the ending . . . it's not like we thought it was when we were kids."

"I'm not an idiot, Keely. I know that."

"So if I read it, does that mean we're friends again? Even if my agent doesn't take it?"

"Keely, when you walked into the room tonight, my heart actually leapt. Before any conscious thought, I was glad, I was *delighted* to see you. I know our lives are so different now, so I guess we can't be friends like we used to be . . . I mean, I don't see you wandering into my parents' house and throwing yourself on the sofa and talking with Mom or Dad the way you used to do, and I really don't think we're ready for you to come up to the apartment I share with Tommy and Brittany. We broke something. Well, okay, I broke something when I married Tommy and nothing can ever be the same again. But it can be new. We can go carefully. We can start over."

Keely nodded. "I'd like that, Isabelle."

"Good!"

Isabelle made a quick rustling move. For a moment Keely hoped and feared that Isabelle was going to hug her. But Isabelle stood up, adjusting her books and bag.

"I've got to get home to put Brittany to bed. I'll drop my manuscript off to you tomorrow, okay?"

Keely rose. "Okay. Where are you parked? I'll walk you to your car."

They strolled for a while, occupied with their thoughts.

"Sebastian told me you two are together now."

Keely couldn't help smiling. "He said we're together? Those exact words?"

"Those exact words. And I'm happy for him, and for you, Keely."

Keely wanted to say so many things, how now they'd see more of each other, be in each other's lives, talk about clothes and movies and books like they used to . . . but she held back. Their renewed friendship felt fragile and this was a difficult time for Isabelle.

"I'm happy, too," Keely said.

They turned down Oak Street and crossed Federal to Isabelle's waiting car.

"You still have the Jeep," Keely said, reaching out to caress the curved door, remembering all the times she'd ridden with Isabelle to parties and games and the beach.

"I want to keep it forever." Isabelle dumped her books in the passenger seat. "But I have to admit, it's different now." She gestured to the child's car seat in the back.

"How do you like being a mom?" Keely asked.

Isabelle clasped her hands together and smiled like an angel. "Brittany is the sun in my universe."

"I'd like to meet her sometime."

"Sure. Come over—wait. Scratch that. Don't come over. Let's make a date to meet somewhere for lunch or on the beach."

"Fine. And you'll bring me your book tomorrow."

Isabelle squealed, "Fingers crossed!"

Keely looked up just then to see Janine walking down the street, looking at her and Isabelle with wide eyes. By tomorrow, everyone Keely had gone to high school with would know that she and Isabelle were friends again.

chapter
seventeen

Keely woke to the smell of coffee and bacon. She padded into the kitchen in her boxer shorts and T-shirt.

"Mom! What are you doing up so early?"

Eloise smiled. She was already dressed in a loose sundress, and she had put on lipstick and blush. "I'm going over to the Maxwells' today." She checked her watch. "I said I'd be there at eight-thirty. I don't know how long I'll be, but I thought you might enjoy a nice breakfast for a change."

Keely munched on a piece of bacon while she poured herself a mug of coffee.

"Also," Eloise continued, "I'd be grateful if I could run these pages off on your printer."

"Good grief, Mom, have you taken up writing, too?"

"Not novel-writing, no. I've made a list of helpful hints for the Maxwells. I know the hospital gave them literature, but that can be overwhelming, and they've probably already misplaced half."

"Let me see the list," Keely asked.

"It's on the table. Next to your plate."

Keely munched bacon and eggs as she read the list.

Stick to a schedule. Routine is comforting.
Encourage Al to respond. Be gentle and patient.

Don't expect Al's responses to be what you want.
Smile. Speak softly. Hold his hand.
If he falls asleep when you're speaking to him, don't
take it as an insult. Sleep is a great healer.
Believe that Al will recover completely. Let Al know
you believe that.
Don't be afraid to repeat what you say. We don't
know what Al's brain is capable of comprehending.
We're only at step one. We have a long way to go.
Don't despair.

Keely looked at her mother. "I don't think the Maxwells have a schedule."

"They don't," Eloise said. "We'll make one this morning. Al needs as much routine and gentle stimulation as he can get. The first few weeks after a stroke are a time of significant improvement."

"Put me down for an hour or two in the afternoon."

"Mmm, no, sweetie, I'm not adding you to the list."

"Why not? Al knows me."

"You need to write, and when you're not writing, you need to have a normal life. Al has a family and plenty of friends, his staff at his office, for example, who are closer to him than you are. Don't be insulted. I'm trying to protect you. The Maxwell family is going to suck up everyone's energy for quite a while." Eloise smiled. "You can help the most by keeping Sebastian happy."

"Mom, how can you do this? How can you be so kind to Mr. Maxwell when he was so mean to you? When he sat behind his rich man desk and refused to help us find money for my college tuition? And the way he acted? As if he didn't know you and me. As if we were nothing at all!"

Eloise sank down onto a kitchen chair. Reaching over, she took Keely's hand. "I'm a nurse, Keely. What Al Maxwell said or did or was or is doesn't matter. He's ill. I know how to help him. It's that simple."

"So you'd help a criminal?"

Eloise laughed. "There you go, being dramatic again. Yes, I probably would help a criminal, but Al Maxwell is hardly a criminal. He's an ordinary human being, with more money than most, but I'm sure right now he's as confused and frightened as anyone who's had a stroke. Anyway, Keely, it's not about who he is. It's about who I am."

Eloise kissed Keely's cheek and rose. "Must go. Good luck writing."

Keely dove into her own routine. A long, exhilarating run. Quick shower. Yoga pants, T-shirt, and flip-flops on, and with a fresh cup of coffee, she closed herself in her room, opened her computer, and wrote.

As always when she wrote, time disappeared. When she heard a knock on the front door, it took her a moment to remember where she was.

She checked her watch. Almost noon. Jumping up, she flew from her room down the hall to the front door.

"Isabelle! Hi. Sorry to be so long answering. I was working. Come in."

"I can't stay long, I left Brittany with Mom."

Isabelle held out the cardboard box. "Here it is. It's a copy, so you can write all over it. If you want to, I mean. I mean, I'd love any and all comments."

Keely took the box. "I can't promise anything, Isabelle. I can't promise I'll like it, but more than that, I can't promise that my agent will take it or even read it." She grinned. "I feel like I've got a ticking bomb in my hands."

Isabelle grinned back. "Then you'd better like it."

"Look, I want to establish something. I'm in the middle of my own novel now. I want you to know I will not use anything from this." She patted the lid of the box. "Except maybe 'the' and 'and.'"

Isabelle made a sweeping motion with her hand. "Keely, I'm not worried about that. What I've written is so different from what you would write." With a flick of her wrist, Isabelle checked her watch. "I've got to go. I'm taking Brittany to play time at the library. So, um . . . how long do you think it will take you to read this?"

"Probably weeks and weeks and weeks," Keely teased.

"Keely!"

Keely broke into a smile. "I'll read it as fast as I can," she promised. And that was true. Keely couldn't wait to read Isabelle's book.

For the first time since she'd returned to the island, Keely didn't focus on her mother. She didn't coax her into getting dressed or prepare a healthy salad for lunch or even take the time to make a hair appointment for Eloise.

She sat on the patio, with the umbrella slanted to keep her in the shade, and read. She got up once to make iced coffee and another time to take a banana from the fruit bowl, but other than that, she read.

By early afternoon, she'd finished three-fourths of the book, and she'd had to force herself to go that far. Mike Reynolds had been right. What Isabelle had written wasn't a book but a series of scenes. Some of the scenes were vivid and engaging, but many fell flat, and some were absolutely embarrassing. Several times Keely blushed at the obviously autobiographical content, especially when Annette—Isabelle's fictional persona—interacted with Archie—Tommy's fictional persona.

What was Keely going to say to Isabelle? Their newly mended friendship was so delicate, so fragile. Anything negative, even couched in the most constructive terms, could endanger their truce.

The next day, Keely phoned her agent.

"My book is coming along nicely," Keely told Sally. "You and Fiona were right. I needed to be here on the island to write it. Although I do have a problem."

"And?"

"It's Isabelle. My old best friend. She's written a novel and she wants me to read it and tell her what I think, and what I think is that it's not very good."

"Okay, have her send it to me. I'll give it a quick read. I'll call her and be the bad guy. I've done that enough times, heaven knows."

"Maybe you'll like it. Maybe I can't get into it because of all the history Isabelle and I have together."

"We'll see. The point is, I'll deal with it. You work on your own book."

"Will do."

Keely knew the special torture of waiting to hear a reaction to a manuscript. Each minute waiting was a stab to the heart. So she picked up her phone and pressed Isabelle's number.

"Hi, Keely!"

"Hi, Isabelle. Listen, I read your novel—"

"You did? What do you think? Do you like it?"

Oh, man, Keely thought, *this will be like telling a child there is no Santa Claus.*

"I did like it. I think—"

"What about the scene on the ferry? And the breastfeeding in public scene, do you think that was too much?"

"I liked it all," Keely said firmly. "I think you should send it to my agent."

"You do? Keely, this is so exciting! Oh, my God! I'm over the moon!"

"Wait, Isabelle, that doesn't mean she'll take it. Or that she'll take it without wanting changes."

"I know, but—"

"Isabelle, you have to be prepared for disappointment."

"I thought you said you liked my novel."

"Yes, I did. I do. But Sally's opinion is the one that counts."

Isabelle went quiet. Keely envisioned Isabelle's lower lip sticking out in a childish pout.

"Do you want Sally's email?" Keely asked. "I've already told her you were sending her something."

"Yes, please. And thank you, Keely, for reading the book. It's just that . . . I suppose I was counting on you being wild about my novel. I thought you'd want to get together with me and go over every scene and tell me which ones were so great and which needed work, like we did when we were kids."

Keely rubbed her forehead. If she spoke the truth, she'd say that no rewrites could turn this gushy memoir into a novel. But she was beginning a renewal of her friendship with Isabelle. She didn't want to derail that.

"We could do that, Isabelle, but it wouldn't matter. Sally's the one who matters. If she makes suggestions, you should take them. She's the pro. Now get a pen. I want to give you her email address."

Isabelle took the address. "Keely. I'm scared. What if she doesn't like it?"

"You've got to prepare yourself for that. Not everyone will like your novel. You should be checking out other agents. I know writers who've sent their books to dozens of agents before getting signed. You've got to grow a thick skin."

"I suppose," Isabelle said.

"Let me know what happens."

"I will. And thanks."

Keely pushed back her desk chair and walked to the window, staring out at the perfect summer day. Years ago, she and Isabelle would be in the Maxwells' back garden, constructing a fort out of old blankets and cardboard boxes, and now that Keely remembered it, Isabelle also had a playhouse in the backyard, a real playhouse, made to resemble a Victorian mansion, with a door that opened and window boxes with flowers and inside, two child-size chairs, a rug, and a table set with a toy tea set. Often they would pretend to run away from home to live in the fort they built. Or they would pretend they were poor waifs living in their hovel, eating dandelion leaves and suddenly they were discovered by their real parents and taken to live in the Victorian mansion, where they had tea and cupcakes, real cupcakes baked and frosted by Mrs. Maxwell.

Isabelle and the other Maxwells had no idea how much Keely longed to have a big house just like theirs, a wonderful Victorian full of children. In those long ago days, Keely had been full of envy. Pangs of remorse stung her at the thought of how much of her life she had lived in envy.

And now? Now she still loved the *house*. It would always be the house of her dreams. But she was grown up. And there were many houses in the world.

Her phone buzzed.

"Keely! I emailed her! Sally Hazlitt! Your agent! She emailed right back, said she'd heard about me from you, and I should email her the novel! Listen, I want you to come over right now and be with me when I send it. I've put some champagne in the freezer and we can open it and celebrate!"

"Wait wait wait!" Keely warned. "This is not the time to celebrate, Isabelle. Sally might reject it. Or she might sign you but no publisher will buy it. Don't be rash."

"So you don't want to drink champagne with me?"

"Isabelle, it's not even noon."

"Fine. Come over anyway and be with me when I hit the Send button. Then we'll have tea. Plus, I want you to meet Brittany and see our little home."

Keely took a deep breath.

"Tommy won't be here, if that's what you're worried about. He never gets home until after five."

"Well . . ." Keely checked her watch. Her morning of writing time was gone, anyway, and all she could think about was Sebastian. "Okay. I'll be over in about fifteen minutes."

She quickly showered and pulled on a loose sundress, slipped her feet into flip-flops, and—just in case Sebastian came by—put on mascara and lipstick and blush.

As she drove from her house to Isabelle's, she thought the car was like a living creature moving by instinct and memory to its lair. She could have biked to Isabelle's house with her eyes closed. But she was nervous, too, not just because she hadn't really liked Isabelle's novel, but because it was going to be weird to be in the home Isabelle shared with Tommy.

She parked on the street and walked up the driveway to the garage. The steps to the apartment were at the back of the house, and Keely headed that way. She climbed the stairs. She knocked on the door.

"Keely!" Isabelle threw the door open and hugged Keely. "Come in."

The last time Keely had seen the garage apartment, it had been a kind of hideout for Sebastian and his college buddies to crash in during the summer. Futons, sleeping bags, and men's underwear and socks had covered the floor. The bathroom had been disgusting.

Now the large open space was clean and bright and shining. The walls were a pearl gray with marshmallow white trim, the floor carpeted wall to wall in a slightly darker gray. Beautifully framed mirrors hung in strategic spots to reflect the light and make the place appear larger. Doors led off to two bedrooms bright with light from the windows, and Brittany's room was cheerful with pastel colors. At the back of the living room was a state-of-the-art kitchen and a table with four chairs and a high chair, and in the high chair sat Brittany. Almost a year old, Brittany was obviously Tommy Fitzgerald's child. She had glossy black hair and huge dark eyes and a natural, unaffected charm.

"The place is lovely," Keely said. "And Isabelle—*Brittany.*"

Isabelle was so pleased she did what she did as a girl, squeezing her shoulders practically up to her ears. "I know."

"Hello, Brittany," Keely said. "I'm Keely." She wished she'd brought a present for the little girl.

Brittany's stubby fingers mashed a banana into her tray. Lifting her hand, she offered a glob of banana to Keely.

Keely's gaze flew to meet Isabelle's eyes, and they shared a smile of mutual delight. Tears came to Keely's eyes.

"She's lovely, Isabelle."

"I know. We're so lucky."

Isabelle's computer was open on the kitchen table. Isabelle slid into the facing chair. "Stand next to me, Keely. Put your hands on my shoulders. That will strengthen the luck."

"When did you get so superstitious? I promise you, it's not luck that will decide the future of your book."

"Please."

Keely took a moment to wonder whether she should tell Isabelle what she really thought about the book. She held her tongue. Whatever she did, it seemed she was once again betraying Isabelle.

She put her hands on Isabelle's shoulders.

"Wish Mommy good luck!" Isabelle told her daughter.

Brittany blew a raspberry at her mother.

Isabelle took an operatically deep breath and hit Send.

"There. It's done." Isabelle stood up. "You won't drink champagne, so will you have some tea?"

"Please."

Isabelle set about boiling the water and filling the tea egg with leaves of white tea.

While Isabelle was fixing the tea, Keely spotted a sheaf of papers on the table. It was a story about teenagers on the island who'd been told by strangers in a yacht to search the Polpis Harbor beaches for a suitcase. If they found it, the strangers would give them each five hundred dollars' reward.

"Okay," Isabelle said. "Now. Let's talk." She pulled out a chair at the table, removed a stray piece of macaroni, and sat down.

"Isabelle," Keely said. "What's this?"

"It's only something I'm playing around with when I'm not in the mood to work on my novel. I guess you'd call it a YA, young adult. It's probably stupid, but I like writing it."

"Isabelle, from what I've read, it's marvelous. You have a completely different voice here, and the action comes fast. You should bring it to class."

Isabelle glanced sideways at Keely. "So do you know any young adult agents?"

"Actually, no. I don't. But I could probably find out."

"Well, maybe wait? I want to see if my adult book gets published first."

Isabelle's computer dinged.

"Oh!" Isabelle jumped up. "Maybe that's from Sally Hazlitt!" She hurriedly clicked. "Listen to this! 'Dear Isabelle Fitzgerald, thank you for sending me your manuscript. I'll read it within the next two weeks and get back to you. Sally Hazlitt.'" She clapped her hands together. "Oh, Keely, how am I going to survive the next two weeks?"

Brittany waved her arms and wriggled in her high chair.

"We should go outside," Isabelle told her daughter. "Time to head to the swings!" Wiping banana from Brittany's hands, she lifted her onto her hip.

Keely followed Isabelle and her daughter outside and down the stairs.

"Thanks for coming over," Isabelle said. Reaching out, she enclosed Keely in a warm hug. "You've been really great about this." Standing back, she looked Keely in the eye and said, "And I want to see you a lot, even if Sally doesn't take my book."

Maybe, Keely thought as she drove home, just maybe Sally

would like the novel. Maybe that would make Isabelle's parents like Keely again. Maybe the day would come when she would sit at their dining room table again, next to Sebastian.

Over the next few days, Eloise told Keely that Al was improving slowly but steadily. Sebastian and Isabelle were optimistic now that Eloise was in charge and could point out the small signs of recovery or discomfort. Donna Maxwell regretfully postponed her cruise until the next fall.

Keely stayed with a schedule as comforting for her as she hoped Mr. Maxwell's was for him. She went for a run early in the morning when it was still cool. Returning home, her mind was so amped up with ideas, she didn't bother to shower but wrote furiously for hours. Then she showered, ate a late lunch, enjoyed good phone chats with Isabelle and Sebastian, and went back to work in the afternoon. She bought groceries and cooked meals for herself and her mother.

And she spent the evenings and nights with Sebastian.

Keely and Sebastian lay side by side on his bed, propped up on pillows, watching the Red Sox. They'd just had a deliriously long session of lovemaking, and they were drinking Whale's Tale Pale Ale and eating sandwiches they'd hurriedly slapped together before the game started.

We're like an old married couple, eating in bed, Keely thought.

"We must look like an old married couple," Sebastian said.

Keely laughed. "Exactly what I was thinking."

To her surprise, Sebastian hit the remote and the television went blank.

"So we should be an old married couple. The sooner the better."

Keely was speechless.

"I know this isn't very romantic. I know I should get down on my knee and propose . . ."

Keely grinned. "Yeah, you should. Right now. While you're naked."

Sebastian threw the covers back, walked around to Keely's side of the bed, kneeled and held out his hand.

"Keely Green, will you marry me?"

Keely tried not to laugh at the sight of Sebastian kneeling naked before her. "I'd love to marry you, Sebastian Maxwell."

Sebastian stood up. He opened the drawer of the bedside table and took out a black velvet box. Inside was an antique ring, a ruby surrounded by diamonds.

"Oh, Sebastian. It's beautiful."

"It was my grandmother's. My mother gave it to me last night."

"Your mother gave it to you? She knows you want to marry me?"

"Why are you so surprised?"

"Because your mother hates me, or at least resents me, for getting a novel published when Isabelle hasn't."

Sebastian nodded. "Mom might resent you for Isabelle, but she loves you for me. Here. Try it on."

Sebastian slid it onto Keely's ring finger. The ruby glowed deeply. The diamonds sparkled.

"It fits," Keely whispered, thrilled.

"We fit," Sebastian said.

Keely patted the space next to her. "Come sit next to me. Let's look at it together."

Sebastian crawled back under the covers next to Keely. They looked at the ring. They kissed. They kissed again, and embraced, and Keely cried a bit, and Sebastian comforted her, and when they finally turned on the television two hours later, the baseball game was over.

The Red Sox had won.

In the morning, Keely went to her house to shower and dress and work on her book. She knew she'd get no work done really. She'd stare at her ring and cry with joy.

Her mother was at the Maxwells' house, helping Al. Keely wanted to tell her mother about their engagement but not over the phone.

As she came out of the shower, Sebastian called.

"Hi, almost Mrs. Maxwell," he said. "Could you meet me at my dad's house? I think everyone is here, including your mother. We could tell them all together."

"I'll be right there," Keely said.

She tried on five dresses before deciding on a simple sundress. She slipped into her sandals and put on lipstick and wiped it off so it wouldn't get all over Sebastian's face. She jumped in her car and drove very carefully, staying exactly at the speed limit until she got to the Maxwell house.

She found Sebastian inside, sitting with his father. Her mother was next to Mr. Maxwell, carefully brushing his hair. Mr. Maxwell looked better today. He was propped up in a sitting position and his eyes were open and focusing.

"Hi, Mr. Maxwell," Keely said cheerfully.

Her mother said, "You just missed Tommy and Brittany. Tommy's taking her home for a diaper change."

"Your granddaughter's so adorable," Keely told Mr. Maxwell. He blinked. A good sign?

Keely walked around the bed to stand next to Sebastian. "Good morning." She kissed his cheek. "How are you today?"

"Me? I'm fabulous." Sebastian leaned over toward his father. "Dad, Keely and I have something to tell you."

Keely flashed her ring to her mother, who mouthed, "Wow!"

"Dad," Sebastian said. "We want everyone to be here when we make our announcement." To Keely, he said, "I'll get the others."

As Sebastian left the room, Keely's nerves made her shiver. Isabelle would be glad about their engagement, but what about Mrs. Maxwell? What about Mr. Maxwell? She remembered Sebastian telling her how his father had roared when they wanted to take him to a rehab instead of his own home. What if Mr. Maxwell roared in protest? She looked to her mother. Eloise gave her two thumbs-up. That was reassuring, but Keely still felt jittery. She busily smoothed the sheets and blanket over Mr. Maxwell.

"You look really well today, Mr. Maxwell," Keely said. "Did you see the Red Sox game last night? It was very exciting."

Sebastian came into the room, with his sister and mother at his side. He went to stand next to Keely.

"Mrs. Green, Mom, Dad, Isabelle, Keely and I have something to tell you."

Isabelle's eyes went as wide as saucers. "Oh, hurry, tell us!"

"I've asked Keely to marry me, and she said yes."

Sebastian took Keely's hand and held it tight.

"I'm so glad!" Isabelle cried, and burst into tears. "Now you really will be my sister."

"Congratulations," Donna Maxwell said formally. "I'm happy for you both."

"Yes," Keely's mother said. "It's wonderful."

"Thank you." Keely was on the verge of tears.

Something touched her hand. Something bony and warm.

Keely looked down. Mr. Maxwell had taken Keely's hand in his.

"Look," Keely told Sebastian, tears falling from her eyes. "Your father . . ."

"Did he move?" Mrs. Maxwell asked.

"Daddy?" Isabelle squeezed next to Keely and Sebastian.

Everyone gathered close to the bed, staring at Mr. Maxwell's hand enclosing Keely's.

Sebastian's voice was hoarse when he spoke. "I think Dad approves."

chapter
eighteen

Even though they weren't married, Keely spent that night in the Maxwell house.

In Sebastian's room. Donna had asked them to stay. She wanted lots of people in the house during the night in case her husband had a problem.

Donna slept in her husband's room—the dining room—on a futon carried in from the family room. So she was downstairs and on the other side of the house from Sebastian's room.

Even though Keely knew her presence was expected and approved, she had to stuff a pillow in her mouth to stifle her giggles. "I can't believe I'm here! In the inner sanctum! Look at all your trophies. And posters of JLo!"

Sebastian pulled her close to him. "In a show of respect, I took down my poster of Gisele Bündchen in her Victoria's Secret Fantasy Bra."

"If I'd only known I'd be in this narrow little twin bed with you someday, I would have been much happier as a kid!"

"Be happy now," Sebastian said, and kissed her mouth.

How she loved being in that house at night. Memories like moths fluttered through her senses as she recalled all the nights she and Isabelle had whispered secrets to each other, or lay side by side reading the same book for school and sharing their thoughts, or fell into helpless fits of giggling over something as normal as the school principal's name, Mr. Cross.

Yet it wasn't only because of the people who lived in the house. Keely loved the house itself, for its expansive graciousness, its combination of authentic and historic wide board floors and its old, almost threadbare, carpets. For its high ceilings and two stair-cases, one broad and elegant with art hanging from the wall, and the other narrow and uncarpeted, the one the housemaids used back in the 1800s when the house was built. For its modest but sparkling chandeliers in the front hall and the upstairs hall and the master bedroom. For its many cupboards and crannies, its floors that sometimes bulged or slanted like the floors of a whaling ship, its six over six paned windows, so much more interesting, Keely thought, than the large windows of her parents' ranch house.

She adored being in the kitchen. During her life, she'd spent hundreds of hours sitting at the oval walnut table. Now in the mornings, when she made breakfast for herself, Sebastian, Donna, and Al, she fantasized that this was *her* house, and she was mak-ing breakfast for herself and her family. She imagined children racing into the room, yelling for food, kicking each other under the table, while she reminded them to use their napkins instead of wiping their fingers on their pajamas.

One morning, as Keely was cutting up fruit for breakfast, a tap came on the sliding screen door. She reached into the refrigerator for eggs and when she shut the door, Tommy was coming up the back steps of the wide porch with Brittany in his arms.

Tommy had put on weight—beer weight, it looked like. He had quite a beer belly and his face had gotten round. His beautiful black hair was cut short, almost military style; Keely would bet that his father made that a stipulation of being employed at the accounting agency. He wore suit pants and a button-down shirt and wing-tipped shoes. *You, my old friend, have been tamed,* Keely thought, and the thought made a sorrow sweep through her, a sense of something ineffable lost, as if a wild bird had been caged.

Yet he looked happy. And he had Brittany and Isabelle. She was glad for him, and glad for herself, that she felt only an enormous fondness for this man.

"Tommy." She pulled him and his daughter to her in a warm hug, then held them away from her so she could scan him up and down. "Look at you, all grown up."

"You look grown up yourself," Tommy said.

"Sit down. I'll have breakfast ready in a minute."

"How's Al?" Tommy asked, as he fastened Brittany into her high chair.

"Still sleeping. Joe Garcia, the LPN and a big strong man, comes over every morning to help Al get washed up and dressed. He'll be here at eight. And my mother arrives at nine."

"Isabelle said that Eloise is making a big difference."

"Maybe only a small difference," Keely said, "but it all adds up."

She set a plate before Tommy and put Cheerios on the high chair tray. Sebastian entered the room then, and Keely, delighted with life, gave him a big smooch on the lips.

"What was that for?" Sebastian asked.

"Think about it," Keely replied flirtatiously, because he'd wakened her this morning by gathering her in his arms and making love to her. "Sit down. I've got bacon and eggs ready for you."

It was a pleasure to have so many people in the room, talking and laughing. Or maybe it was simply that she was over-caffeinated by her fourth cup of coffee, but this sunny morning seemed especially fine. When they all went off to work, Keely sang as she did the dishes.

Joe Garcia came and left. Her mother arrived, kissed Keely's cheek, and went in to see Al.

As Keely dried her hands, her mind was already framing the next scene in her new novel. She wanted to get back to her mother's house where her laptop lay waiting. This was the way her mind worked, ambushing her with important new information when she wasn't near her computer. She took out her phone and dictated some sentences and emailed them to herself. They'd be waiting on her computer at home.

"I'm off now, Mom," she said, peeking into the dining room where her mother and Al seemed to be in some kind of conversation.

Eloise waved goodbye.

Keely stepped out into the bright hot day, and as she walked to her car, her phone rang.

"Keely, can you come over here a minute?" It sounded as if Isabelle was crying.

"Um, can it wait? I've got—"

"Please."

"Sure. I'll be right there."

She ran up the stairs to Isabelle's apartment and found Isabelle siting on the sofa, tears streaming down her face.

"Honey, what's wrong?"

Isabelle waved her hand at her computer. Keely went to the table, woke the computer, and read the email there. It was a pleasant but definite rejection of Isabelle's novel by Sally Hazlitt.

"Oh, sweetie." Keely sank down on the sofa and put her arm around Isabelle. "I'm sorry. But remember, that's only one agent, and there are dozens out there."

"But she took *your* book!"

"Yes, and she's *one* agent. One. You need to buck up and send off multiple submissions to other possibilities. I'll look through the list with you. And in the meantime, did you google a list of young adult agents?"

Isabelle lifted her head, sniffed, and pushed her hair back from her face. "No. I didn't. Because a young adult book doesn't seem as important as an adult novel."

Keely removed her arm and gawked at her friend. "Isabelle

Maxwell Fitzgerald. You don't even know what you're saying. If anything, young adult books are much more important than adult books."

Isabelle directed a suspicious glare at Keely. "Do you mean that?"

"Of course!"

"Then why don't *you* write young adult books?"

"Because I wouldn't be any good at it. Isabelle, you should go where your talent is leading you."

Isabelle sighed. "Okay. Maybe you're right."

"Come on. Let's google YA agents and select a few."

An hour later than intended, Keely entered her own house. It was quiet and shadowy, all curtains and blinds closed to keep out the sun. She poured herself a glass of iced tea, turned on her room air conditioner, whose steady hum insulated Keely from other noises, and curled up on her bed to read Isabelle's YA novel.

At some point, she heard her mother come in, rustle around in the kitchen, and go out again. Keely didn't even call hello; she was entranced with the book.

She finished the book at five. Sally was probably still in the office. Keely punched the Sally button on her keypad.

"Hi, there," Sally answered. "What's up?"

Sally was all about not wasting a minute of time.

"Isabelle has written a dynamite young adult novel. She's sending it around to YA agents. I'd love it if you could recommend it to a few good agents."

"Oh, good grief, Keely, I don't have time for this."

"Sally, this book is extremely good. Amazing. I could hardly put it down."

"Fine. I'll see what I can do. But I'm not promising anything."

"Thank you, Sally. Really. This means the world to me."

"Then hurry up and finish *your* book."

"I'm on it." They disconnected. Keely took a moment to think how far she'd come, how much her life had changed, that she had an agent and was working on her third book. A kind of courage swept through her. She picked up her phone and called Gray.

"Hi, Keely." His voice was deep and calm.

"Hi, Gray. I'm calling to tell you that—" She took a moment, not wanting to blurt it out. "I'm going to marry Sebastian. It's official. I have his ring. My mother knows and his family knows. So I thought, well, that I should tell you, too."

"I see. Well, Keely, I appreciate your calling. I wish you well."

Keely almost laughed. He was always so formal. Yet she was grateful for his kind response and she guessed his formality acted as a shield for his emotions.

"Thank you, Gray. I wish you well, too."

She clicked off, slipped her phone into her pocket, and realized suddenly that she was very hungry. She'd read Isabelle's book all day without stopping. And her brief conversation with Gray had somehow lifted a burden from her. She felt light. She felt like her true self. She went into the kitchen and opened a can of pickled beets—one of her favorite foods—and stood eating them over the sink, so she wouldn't stain anything. Now and then, she burst out laughing.

In June, the days flipped past like a flock of butterflies—vibrant with color but too fast. Families with children returned for the summer. College kids worked as waiters alongside year-round employees. The super wealthy attended galas but otherwise stayed secluded in their compounds with their many staff venturing out on errands. Ferries brought over countless vacationers while private jets streaked to the airport.

The summer days were hot and fine for swimming, and the sky blazed with stars at night. The Maxwells and Eloise bustled around taking care of Al. Keely got to hide away with her computer and write. If she kept up this pace, and she knew she could, she would finish the new novel before Thanksgiving. Keely and

Sebastian were waiting until spring to be married. They wanted a proper ceremony, but most of all, they wanted Mr. Maxwell to be in better health.

Keely was so happy she was terrified. Writing during the day, being with Sebastian at night—could this happiness last?

One afternoon she finished early. She showered, dressed, jumped in her car, and drove to Fast Forward to pick up two iced lattes. She'd surprise Sebastian at his shop with coffee and a kiss. The day was cloudy, almost cool, and brisk. Families in bike lanes struggled to pedal against the wind.

She turned into the parking lot and squeezed her car between two pick-up trucks. Keely thought she saw Isabelle's red Jeep parked at the far end, so she wasn't surprised when she entered the print shop and found Isabelle sitting near one of the desks with Sebastian.

Donna sat across from them.

The three glanced up when the silver bell over the door tinkled.

Keely paused. "It looks like I'm interrupting something serious. I'll go."

Sebastian stood up. "No, Keely, stay. This concerns you."

"Oh, dear," Keely said under her breath.

He crossed the room, kissed Keely on the cheek, and ushered her to the desk. He pulled a chair over for Keely.

Keely set the coffees on the desk and sat down.

"We're talking about the house," Donna announced, looking Keely square in the eye.

Isabelle continued. "And the future. Mom and Dad need to move into a smaller house. Everything on one floor. No stairs. Mom wants to simplify their lives."

"Okay . . ." Keely nodded.

"So we're discussing options," Sebastian said. "They could sell the house and they'd have plenty of money to buy a smaller house on the island. And maybe they'd have enough left over, especially considering the IRAs and savings they have, to split the profit between me and Isabelle."

Isabelle took over. "But I don't think they should sell the house. I think you and Sebastian should buy it from them for a dollar or something and live there. I'd hate for our wonderful old house to go to anyone who's not part of the family. Plus," she added with an embarrassed grin, "it needs a lot of TLC. I don't think many people would want to restore it. They would just knock it down and start over."

Keely blinked and shook her head. "You've skipped way ahead of me here. Don't you and Tommy and Brittany want to take the big house? I mean, there are already three of you. You might have another child, even two or three."

"Not for a while," Isabelle said. "Besides . . . this is a secret, but Tommy is working on a deal to become partners in a marina out at Madaket. We'd want our own home, our real home, to be out there. Anyway, Keely, think about it. Does Tommy want to deal with keeping an old house in shape or does he want to spend any free time out on his boat?"

Before Keely could speak, Donna waved her hand dismissively. "I told you Keely wouldn't like the idea. She's far too busy with her work to want to take on that house."

"Wait," Keely gasped. "This concerns Sebastian, not me."

Donna leaned forward, putting herself between Sebastian and Keely. "You're going to marry Sebastian. You have a say in this matter. I can understand why you wouldn't want our shabby old house. You probably have the money to buy a showplace."

"Mrs. Maxwell—"

"Donna."

"Donna, I love your house. I've always loved it. But I would do whatever Sebastian wants to do. If he wants your house, I'd be delighted to make our home there."

"You'd have to pay market value," Donna said. "But I suppose you make enough money to do that."

Keely exchanged glances with Sebastian, who said, "I suppose you and Dad would be good enough to be the mortgage-holders."

Isabelle added, "And, Mom, since you and Dad gave us the money for Tommy's boat when we got married, you'd have to give Sebastian and Keely an equal amount when they marry, and you could just *not* give them the money but deduct it from the down payment."

Donna held out her hands in surrender. "Fine. Whatever. Sebastian, you really must take the house. It exhausts me. The thought of sorting through all the years of accumulated stuff . . . never in a million years would we be able to get the house ready to show."

"Mom," Isabelle said. "Even if Sebastian and Keely take the house, you still have to clear out years of junk . . ."

"Yes, of course. I know that. But if we don't have to put it on the market, I can take my time."

Isabelle said, "And of course we'd help you."

Keely added, "I've gotten very efficient at clearing out old . . . possessions."

Donna nodded. "I know, Keely. Your mother says you've been invaluable." Her face changed, softening. "It's daunting, you know, changing one's life so completely. This is not where I thought I'd be at this age."

"I'm sure it's not where Dad thought he'd be at this age, too," Isabelle added delicately.

"Please," Donna said softly, "could you all give me a break?"

Sebastian leaned over to put his hand on his mother's. "We'll do anything you want, Mom. Just ask."

Donna's face flushed. "I don't know what I should ask for, not now."

"A cruise," Keely said. "You want to go on a cruise."

"But I can't. Not with Al so incapacitated."

"Mom, we can take care of Dad," Isabelle assured her.

Donna nodded. "I'll think about it." She sniffed, and surprised them all with a smile. "Actually, I can't *stop* thinking about it."

The silver bell tinkled and a man entered with a portfolio under his arm. "I'm sorry. Are you closed?"

"No, no." Sebastian stood up. "We're just finishing a business meeting. How may I help you?"

Keely, Isabelle, and Donna rose, too. Waving goodbye to one another, they went out to their cars. Donna drove away, but Isabelle came to talk with Keely.

"Are you okay with this?" Isabelle asked.

"I think so. It's overwhelming, what we all talked about. You know how I've always admired your house and your family. I grew up wanting a house and a family like yours—actually no, I wanted *your house*. And now . . ."

"Now," Isabelle said, "like it or not, you've got us all."

chapter
nineteen

Together, Keely and Isabelle took Donna Maxwell's immaculately white tablecloth from the cupboard and flew it up between them and brought it down on the dining room table, which had extra leaves put into it because so many people would be sitting at it for this Thanksgiving dinner. They smoothed it out with their hands, tugging it this way and that so the cloth would hang equally on each side of the table.

Isabelle set a long, low, lush arrangement of orange lilies and dark green moss and ferns in the center of the table. Keely set the Maxwells' heirloom Haviland china in place.

"Let's see," she said, counting on her fingers. "We've got your father at the head of the table in his wheelchair. You and Tommy are next to him on either side. Brittany sits next to Tommy and your mother sits across from her. My mother sits next to your mother, I sit next to Brittany, and Sebastian sits at the other head of the table."

"Often called the foot of the table," Isabelle chided playfully.

"Oh, I think Sebastian has earned his place at the head of the table." She took a handful of sterling silver flatware from the felt-lined mahogany box and began to lay it out. "After all, he's the oldest child. *And* he's about to be married."

"Sebastian is hardly the king of the United States."

"But he's kind of the king of the family," Keely said, looking at Isabelle with an arched eyebrow.

"All right. Point made."

Keely grinned. She knew Isabelle had to back down now and then because the doctors had said that Al Maxwell would do best if he remained in his own house while he fully recovered his health and faculties. No one could predict how long that would take, but Donna, Keely, and Sebastian would be the ones to check on Al in the night.

Donna had announced that after Thanksgiving, she was taking a cruise with her friend Joann. It was a "Winter Wonderland" cruise, going down the Danube, stopping to visit all the cities and towns lit up like fairy tales for the Christmas season. Donna would buy them all Christmas presents from the winter markets. Sebastian and Keely would take over the Maxwell house, and part of their responsibility was to tend to Al, who was speaking more clearly now and attempting to walk, wobbly, just a few steps, helped by a cane.

Eloise would come over every day to help Sebastian with physical and speech therapy.

Brittany would start to toddle. She'd scream with glee when she saw her grandfather tottering into the room, as if recognizing someone from her very own tribe.

Tommy would shop for a larger fishing boat and begin the paperwork and website for the deep-sea fishing business that he would commence next May.

Keely had turned in her third novel, and Juan had loved it. Soon she'd start another book in her contract.

Donna spent hours sorting through the trunks and boxes and bags in the attic. Sebastian and Keely took the discards to the dump.

Donna had invited Eloise to come on the cruise with her, but Eloise declined. She was much happier on the island, helping with Al. She had also taken on a few private nursing assignments, which added money to her wallet and a spring to her step.

Keely had privately debated whether or not to take Sebastian's last name. Should she remain Keely Green? That was her professional name. But she liked the idea of being a Maxwell. Legal arrangements had already been made to put ownership of the wonderful old house in Keely's and Sebastian's names. It was, in a way, a protective measure, in case something happened to Donna on her travels or Al never quite recovered all his faculties. Already Keely had made changes to the house. She'd redone Donna and Al's master bedroom first thing—it would be bizarre to make love with Sebastian in his parents' bed. She rented a humidity- and temperature-controlled storage locker and filled it with much of Donna and Al's furniture to go into their new home when they'd found it. She'd bought new, sleeker furniture to replace the dark Empire furniture that Donna and Al had favored.

Now Isabelle and Keely returned to the kitchen to double-check on the turkey. The windows were steamed over, and the aroma of onion and chestnut stuffing was irresistible.

"It needs another hour," Isabelle said.

"Let's drive out to Surfside for a quick walk," Keely suggested. "Everything's set here. I need a walk."

"Good idea." Isabelle untied her apron and lifted it off. "Let's see if anyone else wants to go."

Tommy, Sebastian, Al, and Brittany were in the family room, watching a football game. Brittany was asleep on Tommy's lap.

"We're going for a quick walk at Surfside," Keely announced.

"Have fun," Sebastian called without taking his eyes off the screen.

Keely and Isabelle pulled on sweaters and wool caps. The wind was picking up. The temperature was falling. They climbed into Isabelle's old Jeep. The town was quiet—everyone else was probably watching the Patriots, too. Most of the trees had lost their leaves, but bushes everywhere blazed with scarlet and orange leaves. Isabelle parked in the empty lot at the top of the bluff.

"Nobody else is here," she said.

"I'm not surprised. It feels like it's going to rain any moment." Keely eyed the sky doubtfully.

Isabelle lightly slugged Keely's arm. "Don't be a wuss. Come on, let's have a quick stroll. That way we'll be really hungry for dinner."

Keely ran behind Isabelle down the hardened sand path to the beach and the water. Today the ocean was a great rumbling indigo creature, flinging its waves up on the shore.

With the instinct gained from years of walking on the beach, Keely and Isabelle started their stroll facing into the wind, so it would be behind them on the return.

"So!" Isabelle said. Reaching out, she took Keely's hand.

"So?" Something was up, Keely could tell.

"So New Frontiers Press has bought *The Island*. And they want a young adult series."

Keely slammed to a halt in the sand. "Get out of town! Really? Isabelle, that's fabulous!"

"I'm going to sign a contract with an agent, and I'm going up to Boston—New Frontiers is in Boston—to meet my editor." Isabelle's face lit up like the sun. *"My editor!"*

"Isabelle, I just *knew* you'd get that wonderful book published!" Keely said.

"Keely." Isabelle was glowing. "We're both writers, just like we'd hoped."

"I know! Wait till we tell the writers' group!"

"I'll tell them, thank you very much!"

"Mrs. Atwater will explode!"

"They don't even know I've been working on a young adult novel."

"You're good at keeping secrets."

"We both are."

"That's true." Keely grinned. "Because I've got news, too."

Isabelle took Keely by the shoulders and stared into her eyes. "You're not!"

Keely nodded, smiling and tearful at the same time. "I am!"

"Does Sebastian know?"

"I haven't told him yet. I haven't told anyone but you."

"This is wonderful!" Isabelle pulled Keely into a hug.

"I know." Keely's skin was covered with goose bumps—from the wind? From pure amazing life. "We are *so* creative!"

"In more ways than one!"

"The sand's blowing into my teeth!"

"Mine, too. Let's go back."

They spun around.

"Have you started throwing up yet?"

"Only once. I wake up feeling kind of green."

"Keep saltines on your bedside table."

"I will—after I tell Sebastian."

"I have lots of pregnancy books and maternity clothes you can use."

"Fab! Hey, I'm hungry! I want turkey and stuffing and sweet potatoes and . . ."

"Pumpkin pie with whipped cream!"

They dug their feet into the sand as they climbed the long rise from the beach. Keely reached out to take Isabelle's hand. "I just had an idea! Let's write a book for children!"

"Yes!" Isabelle cried. "No! Let's write a *series* of books for children!"

"What should we call it?"

"*The Young and the Hungry,*" Isabelle joked, and they laughed all the way to the car.

about the author

NANCY THAYER is the *New York Times* bestselling author of *Surfside Sisters, A Nantucket Wedding, Secrets in Summer, The Island House, The Guest Cottage, An Island Christmas, Nantucket Sisters, A Nantucket Christmas, Island Girls, Summer Breeze, Heat Wave, Beachcombers, Summer House, Moon Shell Beach,* and *The Hot Flash Club.* She lives on Nantucket.

nancythayer.com
Facebook.com/NancyThayerBooks

about the type

This book was set in Berling. Designed in 1951 by Karl-Erik Forsberg (1914–95) for the type foundry Berling-ska Stilgjuteri AB in Lund, Sweden, it was released the same year in foundry type by H. Berthold AG. A classic old-face design, its generous proportions and inclined serifs make it highly legible.